SKYHUNTER

SKYHUNTER

MARIE LU

ROARING BROOK PRESS
NEW YORK

Text copyright © 2020 by Xiwei Lu
Map copyright © 2020 by Rodica Prato
Published by Roaring Brook Press
Roaring Brook Press is a division of Holtzbrinck Publishing
Holdings Limited Partnership
120 Broadway, New York, NY 10271
fiercereads.com

Library of Congress Control Number: 2020908739

Our books may be purchased in bulk for promotional, educational,
or business use. Please contact your local bookseller or the Macmillan Corporate
and Premium Sales Department at (800) 221-7945 ext. 5442 or by email at
MacmillanSpecialMarkets@macmillan.com.

First edition, 2020
Book design by Michelle Gengaro-Kokmen
Printed in the United States of America

ISBN 978-1-250-22168-1 (hardcover)
1 3 5 7 9 10 8 6 4 2

ISBN 978-1-250-78541-1 (international edition)
1 3 5 7 9 10 8 6 4 2

ISBN 978-1-250-80153-1 (signed special edition)
1 3 5 7 9 10 8 6 4 2

For my mom, survivor and superwoman,
the inspiration behind Talin's mother
and everything I do.

N

W · E

MARA

★

NEWAGE

BASEA

SUR
KAMA
·

LARC

KENTE

MARA

HOUNDSFANG

NEWAGE
★

MORNINGMAN
·

TRADE
BRIDGES

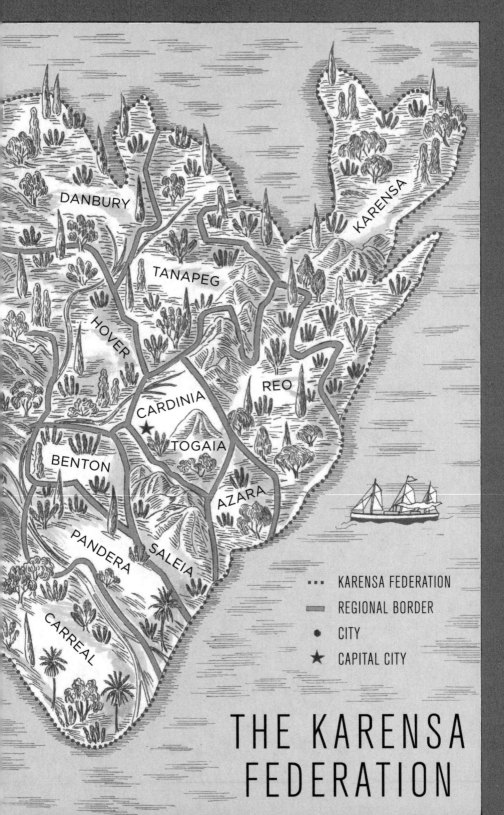

DANBURY

TANAPEG

HOVER

CARDINIA

★

TOGAIA

BENTON

REO

KARENSA

AZARA

PANDERA

SALEIA

CARREAL

···· KARENSA FEDERATION
— REGIONAL BORDER
• CITY
★ CAPITAL CITY

THE KARENSA
FEDERATION

SKYHUNTER

GHOSTS TRAVEL IN PACKS.

This is the first lesson you're taught when you become a Striker.

You learn that Ghosts used to be human, before the Karensa Federation strapped them down and poured dark poison down their throats, twisting them into monstrous war beasts.

Now you'll see them hunting in the forests at the foothills of the mountains in groups of six or more, a grotesque contrast to the serene, snow-dusted landscape.

Their faces are white as ash, their skin split with deep cracks that expose scarlet, rancid flesh underneath. They are taller and stronger than any human who has ever lived, their limbs grown out all wrong, spindly like a spider's. They smell like blood and earth.

Though their eyesight is poor, they can detect movement well. Their hearing is superb, their ears stretched long and tapering to points. They can make out human voices a mile away. In their territory, to speak is to be found, so we remain silent, invisible to the eye and ear.

Their teeth, too, grow longer and sharper than ours. The discomfort of it makes them gnash their fangs constantly, slicing new tears into their already ripped and rotting mouths.

That's how you know they're coming. The grinding sound.

But the most important thing to remember is this: To kill a Ghost, you must starve its eternally regenerating body. To do this, you must bleed a Ghost out, cutting it at its neck, the only place with a vulnerable vein.

It's what I have trained my whole life to do. My name is Talin. I am a Striker for Mara, the last free nation on this side of the sea. We are legendary bringers of death, assassins of monsters.

And the only thing standing between our home and annihilation.

THE
WARFRONT

THE NATION OF MARA

1

THE MORNING DAWNS WITH BOTH SUN AND RAIN.
Drizzle drifts in the sunbeams, dewing everything with a shimmer of
light.

A storm is moving in. We need to finish our sweep early.

Cool wind streams my coat behind me as I head toward our defense
compound's main gates. We are at the warfront fifty miles from the
steel walls of Newage, Mara's capital, out where our southern mountain
ranges give way to dense forests and valleys.

The other sides of Mara are protected by sheer cliffs rising a thousand feet above the ocean, natural formations supposedly caused hundreds of years ago by a cataclysmic earthquake—but here in the south,
we are vulnerable to attacks from the Karensa Federation, whose vast
territory now extends up to the other side of the pass. They send their
Ghosts to wander this in-between land, trying to find a weak spot in
our border. So we do a silent sweep every morning, killing any Ghosts
we encounter.

It has been a month since the Federation launched a full-scale attack
against us, which we barely survived with a temporary cease-fire. But
compromise is difficult when what they want is our nation itself. So the

next siege could come today. Tomorrow. A month from now. There is no telling.

When you're fighting a losing war, you are always on edge.

Morning light has turned the sky a bruised pink by the time I arrive at the edge of our compound. As I walk, I notice the metalworkers bustling around their stations, the seasilk trim of their hats trembling in the wind.

"It's the Basean," one of them says with a sneer.

Another lifts an eyebrow at me. "Still alive, huh, little rat? Well, if you die before Tuesday, I'll still win my bet."

Words like these used to stick in my chest until it hurt to breathe. I'd turn my head down in shame and scurry past. But my mother always told me to keep my chin up. *Look proud*, she would say to me as she patted my cheek, *until you feel it*.

So now I wink back and smile a secret smile.

The metalworker looks away, annoyed that his barb didn't hook me. I stand straighter and continue down the path without a word.

I haven't spoken out loud since the night my mother and I first fled to Mara's borders, when a Federation shell of poison gas permanently scarred the flaps of my vocal cords. I was eight years old at the time. My memories of that night are inconsistent—some clear as crystal, others nothing more than a blur of soldiers and the light of fires engulfing homes. I can't remember what happened to my father. I don't know where our neighbors went.

I think my mind has buried most of those memories, shrouded them in haze to protect me. That night left my mother with a head full of snow-white hair. I came out of it with no more voice and scar tissue twisting the inner lining of my throat. To this day, I'm not sure if I can't speak because of those scars or because of the trauma of our escape, of what I witnessed the Federation doing to our people. Perhaps it's both. All I know is that when I open my mouth, what's left is silence.

I suppose I now make use of that silence. In my line of work, at least, it is essential for survival.

That was what first drew me to the Strikers. When I was small, I would join the crowds to watch the famed patrols head out past Newage's walls, ready to face the Federation's monsters. They are Mara's most elite branch of soldiers, revered by everyone, notorious even in other nations. My eyes would shine at the elaborate harnesses looped around their shoulders and waist, their guns and knives and black steel armguards, the masks covering their mouths, the circular emblem embroidered on their sapphire seasilk coats that draped down to their boots.

I loved their silence. I loved that it meant survival to them. They moved like shadows, with no sound except the hush of boots against the ground. I would linger there, balanced on the branch of a tree, transfixed by their lethal grace until they had disappeared from view.

Now I'm one of them.

It is less glamorous when you are the one riding toward death. Still, it's a job that means I can afford to put food on my mother's table and a roof over her head.

Other Strikers are at the gate now, ready for our sweep. Corian Wen Barra, my Shield, is already here, his back turned to me. Dew shines in the high knot of his hair, and a breeze pushes against his coat's hem.

I'd heard him leave his room this morning when I was still under my furs. He moves so lightly that no one else would have noticed the hush of his door closing.

As always, the sight of him settles my nerves. I'm safe here. I tap his shoulder as I reach him, then give him a mock frown and sign to him, "You left without me."

Corian looks sidelong at me. He clutches his heart, as if I've wounded him. "What—and leave little Talin to fend for herself? I would never," he signs, his gestures teasing and light.

"But?" I sign back.

"But they were serving fresh fishcakes this morning."

"Did you at least save me one?"

"I did, but then I had to eat it because you took so long."

I roll my eyes. He just laughs before he reaches into the pouch at his belt and tosses me a cake, still hot, wrapped in cloth. I catch it easily in one hand. My belly growls on cue.

Corian laughs again. "Look at you, nimble as a deer this morning."

I shrug at him before biting down on the cake's tender meat. Savory juices flood my mouth, along with the grit of minnow egg in the center. When I finish, I let out an exaggerated breath and grin. "Nimble and starving," I answer him.

"'Thank you for saving me breakfast, Corian'?" he suggests.

I gesture to him with greasy fingers. "You're welcome for my company, Corian."

All Strikers work in pairs. We are bonded until death from the moment we take our oath. Corian and I have trained together, have fought side by side, have been able to guess each other's thoughts since we were twelve. I'm more a sister to him than his blood sisters. When I move, he watches my back. When I lead, he follows. I do the same for him in return. Our lives are intertwined, one indivisible from the other.

He is my Shield, what we call our Striker partner. I am his.

We're a strange pairing. Corian and I have always been opposites in everything. He is the thirdborn—*wen*—son of the Barra family, one of the wealthiest in Newage. His appearance is golden in every way. When he laughs, he leans into it with his entire body, a constantly shifting mosaic of strong lines. It's the kind of aura that you can't help but be drawn toward. People buzz around him at holiday banquets, all eager to be seen chatting with him.

My full name is Talin Kanami. I'm a refugee from Basea, a nation south of Mara that fell to the Federation ten years ago. My skin is light brown, my eyes green and slender and long lashed, my hair so black that it shines blue, like a slick of oil in the light.

I'm proud of my Basean features, but many in Mara call refugees like me rats. The Maran Senate has banned us from serving in the Striker patrols. I'm here only because Corian asked the Firstblade to make an exception for me.

Now that we've eaten, Corian and I do our routine weapons check, making sure our blades are fresh and bullet chambers are loaded.

"Daggers," he calls out.

I run my fingers against the hilts of mine, then tug once on the harnesses looped securely around my shoulders. We each carry a dozen daggers: six strapped across our chests in a bandolier; two against the harnesses around each thigh; and one tucked along each boot.

"Good," I sign to him. "Blades."

We simultaneously touch our hands to our two swords hung at the hips, then pull them out in unison and sheath them again with a flourish. Like the daggers, these are made of a near-indestructible metal, capable of slicing through almost anything.

I nod at his left blade. "Could use an extra polish, Corian," I sign. "That edge is looking a little dull."

"It'll still cut a throat," he replies. "I'll sharpen it tonight."

"Guns," I move on.

We have two sniper pistols each, equipped with mufflers to silence them when they fire. A cloth bandolier running around my belt is full of bullets. Corian tosses me a few extra ones from his stash. I catch them and drop them into their slots.

"Bow," he finishes. "Arrows."

One crossbow each, strung across our backs, plus a light quiver of arrows, each cushioned with a fabric wrap to keep them from clanking against one another.

Finally, we check our armguards and gloves, then our black half masks, which will cover our mouths and muffle the rasp of our human coughs.

As we finish, Firstblade Aramin Wen Calla comes striding down our ranks for a final check. Our leader is young; some grumble that he's too young for his position. Not long ago, he'd trained alongside the rest of us as a recruit. But even a few short years as the Firstblade has prematurely streaked silver into Aramin's thick knot of hair tied atop his head. His eyes are as gray and hard as a thunderstorm, rimmed with ferocious dark powder. His lips are twisted down in a permanent scowl. Black fragments of jawbone stud his ears like multiple earrings. Following the tradition of other Strikers who have lost their Shields in the past, the Firstblade had cut those bones straight out of the Ghosts that had killed his own partners years ago.

It's hard to grow old in this profession. You promote who you can.

He progresses along our line, stopping occasionally in front of the newer recruits to check a harness, tilt a chin up, offer a few words of courage.

"Talin," he says when he reaches me.

I place my fist against my chest in a salute to him. He does the same before moving on.

Finally, when he finishes, he stands before us one last time. There are no speeches of glory, no rousing battle cries.

No one needs to tell us that we are the last defense Mara has against the Federation.

Down the line, a hush falls over all the Striker ranks. We pull on our masks at the same time, covering the bottom half of our faces in black. Corian looks straight ahead, his features flattened in concentration.

My heart hardens into stone. My mind pushes away everything except a single goal:

Protect my country.

The Firstblade gives the order. We step forward as one out into the silent world.

If not for the Federation on the other side of this mountainous warfront, if not for their Ghosts stalking the narrow passes, the land is achingly beautiful. The air is cold and crisp, half the sky clear and half a darkening gray. The moon hangs powder white above the tree line, craters visibly speckling its body. A cloud of birds glides through bands of fog drifting through the valley's basin. The water of a nearby stream glows bright blue from the light of tiny river minnows, what our breakfast of fishcakes had been formed from, although now they teem only in the thousands where there used to be millions. Farther down the plains, I glimpse a herd of rare shaggy cows grazing in the mist. Even now, close to winter, they are searching for the sweet, yellow wildflowers carpeting the foothills, gemstones gleaming in the snow.

But what really makes this landscape breathtaking are the ruins of an ancient, long-gone civilization. The structures, scattered everywhere across all nations, are strange and lovely—bones of crimson steel bridges that rise hundreds of feet in the air, crumbling white and dark pillars cut into huge, impossibly perfect cubes. Now the steel and stone are overgrown with blankets of dripping green vegetation.

No one knows exactly how long ago this civilization existed. As old as five thousand years, some say. Whoever the Early Ones were, they were far more advanced than us. They left behind entire cities. Machines with wings. Ships made of metal. Sheets of engineered rock. A few suggest that some of the species we see now, like the wild cows roaming the plains, evolved from animals domesticated during their time. From the fallen skeletons of their steel structures, we broke down the parts and used them to fortify our halls and towers and bridges. From their abandoned weapons, we created our guns and bullets and blades.

From their books, the Federation learned how to twist humans into Ghosts.

I wonder where they went. One theory says they died out, killed by a sickness, and that we descended from the few survivors. Another claims they abandoned this earth to live elsewhere among the stars, and we are the stragglers left behind. Or maybe they too had demons to face, had destroyed one another with their hatred. I wonder if they would approve of how we have scavenged their leftovers.

We have all spread out by now, cutting a trail through the grasslands toward the woods nestled in the Cornerwell Pass. Occasionally we stop to listen, wondering whether the wind whispering through the pines will also carry the sound of teeth.

But the forest is still today.

We reach the edge of the woods. Here, the light dims, filtered through the thick canopy into rays dotting the floor. Dense layers of fallen logs pile in a green blanket of moss and ferns. The scent of cool, damp earth surrounds us, and from somewhere far away comes the faint trickling of a stream.

As time goes on, I start to notice the finer sounds. The drip of water on a leaf, the thud of a frog leaping onto soft soil. Corian walks several yards away, but our bodies always turn in sync with each other, used to years of our rhythm.

Then I notice a snapped twig against a branch. I pause and lean close for a better look.

Corian senses the shift in my movement without even looking at me. A moment later, he's at my side, warmth radiating off him, his stare focused up on the twig too.

I sign to him with my gloved hands. "See the angle of the break?"

Corian signs back. "It's down," he replies. "Not sideways. Broken by something taller than this branch." He points into the wood. "Came from that way."

"Stag?" I ask.

"Would be more snapped branches here, if it was."

"A scout, maybe? A spy?"

"Could be," he responds. "I heard the southern patrols caught a prisoner of war fleeing through the valley this morning. There might be others."

A glint of something wet on the forest floor catches my eye. I crouch. "Blood," I tell him as I stare down at the single, fresh dot of crimson, the color a shade noticeably darker than human.

Corian nods in agreement, his lips pulled into a tight line. It's not a stag or a scout. We have tracked hundreds of Ghosts. By now, the smallest hint is enough to let us know they're nearby.

I point up once at the trees. "Take top watch. I'll wait for your sign."

Corian taps a fist quietly against his chest at the same time I do. Then he heads for the trees. In two steps, he pulls himself up into a nook. There he crouches, nearly invisible against the dark wood.

I shift toward the thick undergrowth near a pile of mossy logs. During training, I would glide across floors littered with stacks of coins, careful not to disturb any with my boots. Now I pass between the logs without a sound until I settle into the crevice of a hollow trunk.

Long minutes drag by.

A bird's trill catches my attention. Corian's call. I turn my eyes up to him. He's still hunched in the shadow of the tree nook. He signs to me again, pointing three fingers to my right. Then three fingers toward me.

"Three Ghosts east of you. Three Ghosts north. A hundred feet away."

They're here.

My hands rest against the hilts of my swords. I always choose them first. They are the quietest, they have the range I need, and above all, they let me move quickly. In the trees, Corian pulls a gun from its holster and rests his finger on the trigger.

Another pause, followed by an abbreviated sign from Corian: "Warning. Close by."

The forest's silence gives way. The crack of twigs against rotting feet. The crumble of sodden leaves.

Then, finally, I hear it.

The gnashing of fangs wet with blood.

To my right comes the first trio. They move on all fours in a jolty skitter, their arms stretched longer than their legs. An iron cuff circles each of their necks to protect their vulnerable vein. The closest of them turns its milky eyes skyward, searching the treetops before continuing on. New blood drips down its humanlike chin.

I have seen countless Ghosts on the warfront. And yet, to this day, that four-limbed skitter still makes the hairs on the back of my neck rise.

They edge closer. As they do, the second trio comes into view. They reach up on two legs, stretching themselves tall as they peer between the trees.

My gaze focuses on the leader of the group. It is bigger than the others, its cracked muscles more prominent. Like alligators in the southern lands, Ghosts continue to grow in size and strength until something kills them. If nothing does, they will live forever. Some, I hear, tower higher than elephants.

When this one stretches itself up to its full height, it looks like a hulking beast, its skin cracked and bleeding.

Up in the trees, Corian rises into a predator's crouch and lifts his gun. I tense, willing him to be safe. My hands close on the hilts of my swords. The stillness of the forest settles heavily on my senses, and all my strength coils tight in my muscles.

You only get one chance to move. After that, there is no room for hesitation, no time to rest or regroup or change your mind. Everything— *everything*—depends on your speed. You take them down fast, or they will take you down.

Corian aims his gun at the leader.

He shoots.

The bullet strikes the Ghost hard in its neck cuff, cracking the iron. It lets out a deafening shriek and whirls in Corian's direction with a speed that defies its size. It throws itself at the tree and begins clawing furiously for him.

The others instantly turn in his direction too.

I dart from my hiding place at the same time I yank my blades out. The familiar hush of metal sliding against sheath hums in my ears. My swords catch the light. I race along a fallen log. The closest Ghost to me doesn't even see me coming before I launch into the air and swing my blade at its neck.

It slices clean into the cuff, splitting it. My second blade cuts its vein. The Ghost collapses to the ground, twitching violently as blood stains the green forest floor crimson.

I don't stop moving. The Ghosts are now in a frenzy of rage, their movements like the strikes of an adder.

One swipes at me. I slide to my knees and arch so far back that my head scrapes against the ground. Its claws miss me. I pop back up and slash a fatal wound in its neck, then whirl in the same move and cut through the cuff of the Ghost beside it. My other blade stabs it in the throat.

From his vantage point, Corian fires a second bullet down at the leader, hitting its neck again. It flinches away, then lunges at him. My heart lurches. From the other side of the tree, another Ghost digs its clawed hands into the trunk and tries in vain to pull itself up toward him.

I whip out my gun and fire at it. The bullet strikes true. The Ghost screams, halting its attack against Corian for an instant.

Corian points his gun down at the wounded Ghost and fires three times. The bullets shatter its neck cuff. He fires a fourth shot at the exposed vein. It stumbles to its knees.

The fifth Ghost screams at me. My boot snags against a branch on the forest floor. It costs me just a fraction of a second—but in that moment, the Ghost manages to grip my leg. It hurls me off my feet. I go crashing into the underbrush.

As I scramble back up, it's already lunging for me again. I'm about to lift my blade when an arrow suddenly blooms right underneath its jaw, keeping it from opening its mouth. It lets out a snarl of fury. Behind it, Corian nods at me from his tree. I lash out at its cuffed neck with both blades. One, two, three slashes, and the cuff finally breaks. I yank out a dagger and stab hard into the vulnerable vein.

Only the leader remains now. Stuck with arrows, it whirls and races toward me. I pull out another dagger, tighten my grip on my blade, and brace myself for its attack. Behind it, Corian leaps down. In the blink of an eye, swords appear in his hands.

He rushes toward the Ghost. At the last second, he darts to one side. I twist to follow him. Corian slides into a crouch right as I reach him. I jump. My boot kicks off against his shoulder and I launch into the air.

I slice down hard, cutting through the cuff. It falls to the forest floor. Without missing a beat, Corian darts up from his crouch and cuts its throat.

A shudder courses through it. As I land lightly on my feet beside Corian, the Ghost falls onto all fours, then collapses to its side.

Corian looks at the bodies littered around us. My hair is tangled and mussed from the fight, and dark strands cling to my damp forehead. My senses still tingle with unease, and my body stays turned protectively toward Corian.

I push my hair back and sign to him. "Are you okay?"

He nods. We exchange a brief smile. Then he breaks his stare with me and goes to check each Ghost's body, making sure their veins are cut clean through. I do the same, pausing to watch as he stops before the dying leader.

Corian has told me before that Ghosts remind him of humans the most when they are in their last throes. Their movements slow, their breaths curl in the air, and their shrieks, weakened, turn into the sound of something anguished and pitiful. Their eyes water with pink, blood-tinted tears. It is said that they cry because their rotting, eternally grow-ing bodies are in excruciating pain all the time. Their dying whines are a plea for mercy.

I always warn him that they do not have the heart he has. He always reminds me that they once did, that before the Federation filled them with poison, they had smiled and laughed and been in love, that real hearts used to beat in their chests.

Even though Corian stands over the leader as its executioner, he reaches down to pick one of the blue flowers dotting the forest floor. Then he bends a knee in the middle of the glade, his long coat pooling in a circle around him, and places the flower carefully beside the body. He pulls down his mask and bows his head. His fingers sweep across the floor in a single arc. His lips move without a sound. He always does this, and it is why I respect him.

He is saying: *May you find rest.*

I see the seventh Ghost too late.

It is smaller than the others. Maybe it had been a child when it turned. Ghosts travel in packs—but this one had been lagging behind.

It materializes in the shadows of the woods behind Corian's kneeling figure. Its eyes, milk-white with hatred, turn on my Shield, and its jaws open. It lunges.

My blood turns to ice. I grip my blades and rush forward.

But it is far too late. The Ghost sinks its teeth into Corian's shoulder before he can whirl around in time. It throws him off his feet and onto his back in a single move, then dives onto his chest.

Daggers are already in Corian's hands. He stabs at the Ghost again and again, seeking its vein. I throw myself at the beast with all my strength. It's enough to force the Ghost's attention onto me instead of my Shield. I cut its throat with one swing.

I slide to a halt beside Corian and press down on the wound in his shoulder. He shoves me away with a snarl. His body is already trembling, and his lips are tinted blue as if from the cold. He is signing the same words to me again and again.

"Do it. Do it."

And I know it is over.

If your Shield is bitten by a Ghost, you must cut his throat before he turns. This is the last thing we are taught. It is taught last because none of us want to think about what it means. Because sometimes the things that cut closest to your heart deserve the weight of being last.

Corian looks straight at me. His eyes are bright with unshed tears.

I tighten my grip on my blade and stand over him. The world takes on the blur of a dream. We never break our stare. For a moment, I think I won't be able to do it.

But my body remembers the motions, even when my mind cannot.

My blade slices through the air. There is a sickening sound, then a sigh.

The forest is still again, and I am the only one left to hear it.

I turn my face up because I cannot bear to look down. Rain beads against the forest canopy. Light rims the leaves in icy gold. It takes me a moment to realize that I am trembling.

As always, I don't utter a sound. But a heart can grieve in silence, so I sink to my knees beside Corian's body and allow the tears to come.

NEWAGE
INNER CITY

THE NATION OF MARA

2

WHEN YOUR SHIELD IS KILLED IN BATTLE, IT IS your duty as a Striker to deliver his uniform to his family.

This is the display of shame we offer for failing to protect each other, and we give it to the family in the hopes that they accept our apology. So on this morning, one week after Corian died, I find myself heading into the heart of Newage's Inner City, Corian's sapphire uniform folded into a neat square and tucked safely under my coat.

The drizzle that had fallen during our sweep has now turned into a steady storm soaking the entire nation. Rain undulates in glittering waves across the pavement as I walk, and I pull my collar higher against the wetness. The hat I wear offers scant protection. My hair hangs in dripping black strings against my face, but I don't bother brushing them aside, as if perhaps I should appear as miserable as I feel. Corian, resembling the sun as he did, had always hated the first heavy rain of winter. It is a cruel irony to deliver his uniform to his family on this day.

The Barra family estate is located at the top of a hill. From the bottom, you can't even see it—built over the bones of a crumbling temple by the Early Ones, the mansion is fully hedged in by cypress so that onlookers can only catch glimpses of the white stone of its walls through thickets of green.

From this vantage point, I can see the gentle slope of the rest of Newage, the sprawl of estates and apartments and pillared halls protected inside two enormous circles of steel walls. Beyond that radiates the miles of dense shantytowns of the capital's Outer City, where my mother and all other refugees live. Along the horizon rise the shapes of the Early Ones' ruins, silhouetted against the stormy sky.

There are twenty large ruins scattered throughout Mara, and most of the other small cities that dot this country are erected upon or around them. Each of them has a name. There is Houndsfang, the ruin of a jagged steel needle jutting up toward the sky at the edge of our cliffs, upon which is set a small city of the same name. There is Morningman, a city built around a conelike structure of metal and concrete covered in rose vines. And so on.

Newage, the capital of Mara, was constructed right on top of the remains of an entire city from the Early Ones. It's why our streets look cobbled together from two different eras—shards of ancient black steel form the backbone for apartments made of white stone and wood, while cylinders of strange metal act as the buttresses supporting National Hall. The ground of Newage's Inner City is made of a mysterious dark stone that exists only in other Early ruins. It absorbs heat in the winter, keeping the city warmer than it otherwise would be. And as for the huge steel walls encircling the city . . . they existed long before Mara did. On top of the walls' front gates is a mantra engraved by the Early Ones:

We sow the seeds of Infinite Destiny for our children
so that they may rule from this earth to the stars.

Infinite Destiny. It is a phrase that the Karensa Federation believes the Early Ones had meant for them, that they are the children who are destined to inherit their ancient empire. I just stare out at the city and wonder why the Early Ones left it all behind. They must have built the walls thousands of years ago to protect their city from something—but whatever that was, the walls must not have worked.

I don't know why we think they will save us from the Federation's Ghosts, just like how I don't know why I thought I could protect my Shield. I don't even know if I can protect my mother now. My position as a Striker pays me enough to bring her money in the Outer City every couple of weeks. What now, without Corian to stand up for me? Will the Firstblade even allow a Basean like me to stay?

The Barra family knows the instant I arrive at the estate's front gate why I'm here—they had received the Firstblade's handwritten letter of condolence days ago. The two guards standing at the entrance don't even bother to ask my name or purpose. I just stand there, silent and soaked, swaying on grief-exhausted legs, Corian's folded uniform tucked under my arm, until the guards disappear behind the side doors and open the gate for me.

The storm mutes all the sounds in the Barra courtyard. My mother's entire neighborhood in the Outer City could fit in this space alone. I listen to the faint squelch of wet stone under my boots as the guards lead me toward the glowing windows of the estate's front hall. The dripping trees, the fog of my breath in the damp air, the front gate carved with the Early phrase DEO OPTIMO MAXIMO . . . all of it feels like a dream.

I've been here only once, the summer when Corian first chose me as his Shield. He and I had shaken hands solemnly, then lazed under the green canopy of these same trees, stripped down to our short sleeves, our mouths sticky with sweet grapes plucked from the vines.

"If you could go anywhere in the world," he asked me then, his face turned toward the horizon, "where would you go?"

"Basea," I signed without hesitation.

"It's probably different now, you know," he signed gently in return. "After the Federation took over." There was no malice or pity in his expression, just a grave truth. "It's not the home you remember."

"I know. I'm just curious." I looked back at him. "Why does it matter to you?"

"Why does what matter?"

"How I feel about Basea?"

"I don't know. Shouldn't it matter to everyone?" He shoved a grape in his mouth and offered me another cluster of the fruit. "It might be how I feel someday about Mara," he signed. "If we lose."

He was sympathetic, but also afraid. I'd never heard a highborn Maran put himself on equal footing with a Basean before. I stared at him, surprised, and then took the cluster of grapes he offered.

"To our home." I lifted the grapes to his.

"To our home," he repeated.

Those same grapevines now wind brown and lifeless along the walls. This place flanks the beginning and end of our bond.

The guards stop at the front door and motion for me to enter. "Master Barra is already expecting you," one of them tells me.

I nod at him and step inside.

A rush of warm, dry air hits me. The faint smell of wood burning in a marble fireplace permeates the space. My boots echo against the floors. When I turn my head up, I see the soaring atrium of the estate's main hall, a space that stretches up at least three stories, the arched ceiling painted into rainbows from the multicolored glass windows through which shines the weak winter light. Original architecture salvaged from the Early Ones. Beyond the main atrium, the Barra family had installed their own embellishments—a second floor lined with balconies, a spiraling staircase, and a main floor dotted with soft, cushioned seats and speckled cow pelts. The white engraving around the marble fireplace is embellished with gold. Arched windows reach from the floor to the ceiling, divided by thin black lines of metal, and the light stretches long against white-and-gray wooden floors. Stark beauty, everywhere, of a family centuries old.

Here, I feel myself clash against the pale floors and white walls like a stain. My mother and I had survived our first few years in this nation by running odd errands in the Outer City's shantytowns. I'd deliver messages crumpled in my fists, shovel horse manure for the people who ran stalls rimming the walls, steal and sell metal from the scrapyards dotting the muddy, crowded landscape. I'd collect what little money I could for my mother. I'd huddle on the side of the narrow paths, surrounded by the stench of grease, fried fish, and sewage. No one spared me a glance. There were too many kids like me fighting to survive in the shanties. I was just another face lost in the crowd.

Now I'm here, standing inside the home of a family with obscene wealth, and all I can do is imagine myself as a child, dirty and startled, lost here. How did Corian come out of a house like this? He must have looked like the sun running through these halls, golden hair and skin and laughter against these white surroundings. And I feel the pit of my grief all over again, its pain the same as the hollow bite of a hungry stomach, tipping the world around me until I can no longer see.

No one is in here. I wait for a moment, wondering if maybe I'd come to the wrong room, except that the guards ushered me to this spot.

Finally, I hear the faint echo of footsteps coming from down the corridor. They are the solid, sure steps of an aristocrat.

I don't wait to kneel. Before the figure emerges into the hall, I lower myself onto both knees so that I can feel the cold floor through the fabric of my trousers. I hold Corian's folded uniform out, presenting it flat before me with both hands. Then I bow my head deeply. There is still a faint scent of Corian from his Striker coat. I catch it now in my bent state, the smell of smoke and sugar, still lingering there from the candies he always kept tucked in his pockets.

The footsteps enter the hall. From the corner of my eyes, I catch sight of a pair of black boots, polished to perfection, and the sweep of a pale coat against pant legs.

I remember the color of that coat. Corian's father has come to greet me.

I swallow hard. I don't know how to apologize for the death of his son. Cannot tell him my deep shame at being unable to protect his favorite child. I can do nothing except remain in this position, holding out Corian's uniform. So that is exactly what I do. I remain perfectly still, waiting for the man to say something.

The boots stop right in front of me. I can feel the heaviness in the air of his father's looming presence.

Tradition usually dictates that, when a Striker delivers his fallen Shield's uniform to his family, the family responds by accepting the uniform with both hands. As Shields are bonded to each other like siblings, the family should then embrace the Shield as if he or she were also their kin.

But long moments pass. I wait. Corian's uniform stays heavy in my hands, untouched, and his father's boots remain leaden before me.

Then his voice echoes above me in a low, rumbling growl. "Do you know why my son chose you as his Shield?" Master Barra says.

I don't dare look up. I can barely manage a shake of my head.

"Because Corian had a bleeding heart," his father continues. "He felt sorry for you, little Basean girl, always crouched like an animal outside the arena. I told him not to choose you. You weren't good enough. He did anyway." His voice turns grating, harsh and cold with grief. "That's why my boy is dead. Because he selected a rat to protect him."

calling for his execution today. Still, he looks relieved, so serene in the face of death that he seems almost bored.

Adena frowns and leans over to Jeran and me. "Does he not understand what the translator's saying?" she asks.

"I think the translator made a few mistakes," Jeran says above everyone's shouts. "The Firstblade's words were 'We will let you live.' The translator repeated it as 'We will *make* you live.'"

"So? What does that mean, other than that our tutors are terrible at teaching languages?"

Jeran gives her a wounded look. "*I* used to be a language tutor," he protests, and she pats him twice on his cheek. "I'm serious! Actions translate poorly between Maran and Karenese. It might be making the prisoner react differently."

"That isn't a big enough difference to make the guy stay quiet. Why doesn't he just talk and save himself some torture?"

"Because he wants to die," I sign.

Both of them look at me. "What makes you say that?" Adena signs after a pause. "You think he's actually faithful enough to the Federation to throw away his life?"

I don't want to explain that his expression is how I've felt for the past few weeks. Instead, I nod down at the scene. "I've witnessed this before. He has the same look the Baseans who were executed in my village had," I explain. "He has already accepted his fate. If they told him that they'd make him live if he talks, and he has no interest in living, then of course he'll stay quiet."

Adena whistles. Under her casual question is an undertone of bitterness. "Who knew the Federation treated anyone well enough to earn that kind of loyalty?"

"Perhaps he doesn't believe we'll execute him today?" Jeran suggests.

I see the man's boots turn away and point in the direction he'd come. His voice snarls above me with disgust.

"Keep his uniform," he says. "It's already been dirtied by the hands that allowed him to die. This House does not accept trash as an offering."

Then the voice stops, and the boots walk away, leaving me kneeling on the floor. He did not bother dismissing me. Without his permission, I am obligated to stay here.

Families simply do not refuse the uniforms of their fallen children. I hesitate, confused, unsure in the moment what to do. My arms shake from the effort of staying still. My eyes point down at the floor. The wood pattern breaks at the edge of each plank. All I can do is repeat his words, which are spinning through my mind.

He felt sorry for you. This House does not accept trash.

I stare down at my hands and arms and think of Corian's last moments. I see his bright blue eyes pleading for me to end his life before it is too late. *Trash.* I know, logically, that I am not. But it doesn't matter.

I had let Corian die. I'd killed him because I never belonged in the Strikers. My Shield's blood will forever taint my fingers.

I have no idea how long I kneel here. No one else comes to greet me. No one takes Corian's uniform from my outstretched hands. No one wants to accept the apology I have come bearing. The House of Barra will make sure I alone carry the weight of Corian's death.

The light disappears from the room and is replaced by evening. I will myself to stay trembling in place. Waiting. Hoping.

I don't know whether I make it to dawn or not. All I remember is waking up with my cheek pressed against the cold floor. A servant is quietly shaking my shoulders.

"You need to leave, now," he whispers to me. I look up into the grave eyes of a young servant boy nervously wringing his hands. His eyes dart to the hall behind us as he holds a hand out toward the door. "The guards will show you out if you don't go yourself."

In desperate shame, I hold the uniform out to him, as if even a lowly servant of the House of Barra accepting my offering would be better than nothing. But the boy shrinks away, not daring to touch it. He gives me an apologetic stare, then straightens and leaves me.

I wait a moment longer before I slowly pick myself off the floor. Corian's uniform stays clutched in my hands. My breaths come in slow, shallow gasps as I think about what comes next.

I have lost my Shield, my closest friend. But there is more to lose. If Corian's House refuses to accept my apology, then my standing as a Striker is threatened. They will appeal to the Firstblade to release me from the forces, say I'm unfit to be entrusted with the life of another, unfit to protect this nation. Corian was the only reason I'd been allowed to become a Striker. Without him, I'm left unprotected. And without my aid, so is my mother.

If the House of Barra does not accept me, then I may have just seen my last days as a Striker.

3

I'M DREAMING AGAIN. IN THE DREAM, I'M TWELVE,
and Corian is there.

I'm crouched in the shadows of the back gate leading into the Strikers' training arena, a vast amphitheater in the heart of Newage's Inner City. From here, I can see the apprentices practicing their attack formations, their sapphire coats spinning in lethal unison. It is always like watching a dance, and I'm hypnotized.

I'm not the only one in Mara who loves to watch the Strikers train.

I look down at my own clothes. They're ragged. Even my patched elbows are worn so thin that the cloth seems translucent. Hunger claws at the base of my ribs. Sometimes, I think I longed to become a Striker only because I knew their apprentices got living quarters, three meals a day, and a healthy weekly pay. So I'd fantasize about having all of that, giving my mother the safety of a home of her own. I'd sneak into the Inner City to watch them train at the arena. Now my gaze stays fixed on the youngest recruits as they face off against one another. They're all around my age, some a little older. Soon, each will be paired with someone who best complements their personality and fighting ability.

When you can't speak, you spend a lot of time watching. Parsing. Listening. This, at least, I do well, so I analyze the forms of the students and take mental notes on how they keep their footing. From the scrapyards dotting the Outer City, I'd learned how to shift my weight in my favor. I knew how to climb up haphazardly stacked metal ruins discarded in the yards, leftovers from the Early Ones dug up by farmers and builders. I could weasel my way inside some ancient engine to strip it of parts, then leap from one stack to another if it teetered. I could dance on unstable sheets of steel, using a blowtorch my mother had bought to sever the valuable pieces to sell. I knew how to twist between the wreckage to hide from bigger kids that vied for the yards with the best metals.

As I watch the apprentices, I mimic their steps, and my movements rise and fall in near-perfect sync with them. A grin lingers on my lips as the exercise warms my limbs. I lose myself in the concentration, until I can believe that the rags streaming behind my limbs are no different from their sapphire coats.

I don't remember how long I stay there in the darkness, going through the motions. All I know is that I'm in midair when a young voice calls out to me from above the back gate's entrance.

"You're really good, you know that?"

The voice throws me off balance. I land awkwardly and fall with a thud, sending up a cloud of dirt. My head jerks up.

There, leaning idly over the top of the gate, is a boy with bright golden hair and a thoughtful tilt to his head. Even in a dream, his features are so clearly defined that it's as if I were looking at him through a magnifying glass. His clothes are finely spun, and rings glitter on his fingers. He's confident, his shoulders straight and chin raised. A highborn Maran.

My grin vanishes. My mother had warned me about rich boys.

"You've been out here every day for months," he tells me. It is a voice that has never hesitated before.

Panic lodges in my throat. I scramble to my feet and immediately start running.

"Hey!" he shouts at me, but I don't dare turn back. Refugees aren't allowed inside the Inner City without a permit. If they catch me, what will they do? I've witnessed a woman shot in the head for trying to sneak past the wall guards. I've seen a refugee whipped to death for attempting to sell bushels of seaweed without a license at the Inner City's night exchange.

I don't stop to dwell on it. I just keep going.

Suddenly a force tackles me from behind. Before I know it, I'm facedown on the ground, and the boy's voice is hovering over my head. I flip instinctively. He goes flying off me as I scramble into a crouch, my fists up.

He laughs, shaking dust out of his hair. All I can think about is how little he cares that he's dirtied his fine clothes. I try to still my trembling hands. What kind of punishment will this mean for me?

"You've obviously never fought anyone in your life," he says with a smile. "But I've been watching you. Your reaction time is incredible."

When I flush, he offers to help me up. I stare at his outstretched hand, trying to figure out whether he's serious or about to play a prank on me. Then, tentatively, I put my hand in his. He yanks me to my feet in a single motion, as if he's been waiting to pull me up all his life. "I'm Corian," he adds.

I don't answer.

He frowns at me. "Well?" he asks. "And your name is?"

I pat my throat twice and sign to him. "I'm Talin. I can't speak."

I don't expect him to understand what I said. But his eyes widen—and then he smiles and signs back. "Good. All Striker apprentices must learn how to sign," he answers. "You know that, right?"

I remember everything about that moment—the movement of his

hands through the air, the easy way he took in my soundless words, the kind smile on his face. I knew that Ghosts on the warfront had powerful hearing, but I didn't know that Strikers used sign language to communicate out there. My lips twitch with a grin. He'd understood me. He *understands* me.

"They use the same signs that I do?"

"Very close. You'll pick it up in no time." I notice some of the differences now, like how some gestures are simplified, while others are more elaborate.

"So you want to be a Striker?" he asks.

I shrug, unsure what I'm allowed to say. "Doesn't everyone?"

"I'm surprised a Basean would want to defend us," he says, and now his face is grave. "Mara doesn't treat your kind that well."

I pause in surprise—a highborn Maran has never even laid eyes on me, much less paid such close attention to me. Much less sounded sympathetic to Baseans.

"We still all have the same enemy," I reply. "Mara isn't the Federation."

He considers me seriously. "Why don't you try out for the apprenticeship, then?" he asks.

"Baseans aren't allowed to."

"So? You move as fast as anyone inside that arena." He nods over his shoulder. "You should at least come to the exams. I'll put in a word for you with the Firstblade, if you're interested."

When I just stand there, stunned, he puts his hands in his pockets and turns away. I envy the straightness of his back, the wild confidence in every line of his figure. He really believes his words can carry that kind of power. It makes me think he must be right.

In that moment, I make a vow to be like him. I'm going to find a way to walk through life with courage seared into my bones.

"No pressure, of course," he calls over his shoulder as he turns in the direction of the arena. "I just thought I'd suggest it."

The sun is warm, the sky a cloudless blue. My heart beats rapidly against my ribs. I wait a breath longer. Then my legs finally loosen, and I find myself doing what I would do for the next six years—I follow him. I run and run and run.

But in my dream, I never catch up.

● ● ●

A knock against my door jerks me awake. My face is still streaked with tears.

I swing my legs over the side of my bed. Weak morning light bands across my arms. My head throbs in a rhythm, aching from nightmares I can't remember. It takes me a second to register that I'm back in my Striker apartment in Newage, and another to remind myself that I now live here alone. My hand goes instinctively to the black bits of Ghost bone studding my ears. The piercings are still fresh enough to hurt when I touch them.

It's been two weeks since I tried to deliver Corian's uniform. I wonder if I will ever stop dreaming about him. The shadows are haunted by echoes of where he used to be. Across the hall is his room, the door closed. I haven't looked in there since I hung his uniform back in his closet. There's no need to see his bed, tidy and unused. His dressers empty and weapons cabinet hollow. I can feel his emptiness in the air around me, and the reminder every morning sends such a sharp pain through my chest that I want to curl back into my bed and drift off into oblivion, to lie here and never wake, to stay and stay until death comes to claim me too.

Corian would scoff at me if he saw me like this. He'd roll me right out of bed and toss my coat at my head. The thought of his exasperated glare is almost enough to make me laugh through my grief.

Corian, I think. *When you first met me, did you see someone with potential? Or is your father right? Did you really just feel sorry for me?*

What does it matter, anyway? No new Striker wishes to pair with me. The Firstblade is debating what to do. Soon, I have no doubt, he'll kick me off the patrols. Then I'll be forced to stand by, as helpless as the day my mother and I fled our home, as the Federation comes marching through the gates of Newage.

The pounding against my door starts up again.

Walk with courage, I remind myself, thinking of the vow I'd once made to be more like Corian. I sigh, force myself to push up from the bed, and reach for my shirt.

When I finally answer the door, I see Adena Min Ghanna from my patrol standing there in her uniform, her smile so big that it looks like it hurts. Her frizzy hair is tied up into a neat bun, and the morning sun gives her dark skin a warm highlight. She adjusts a pair of goggles on her forehead and wrinkles her nose at me.

"You look like hell," Adena scolds. She reaches down to brush a few strands of hair away from my eyes, then tugs once on the bottom of my shirt, which I'd left carelessly loose. "Tuck it in, you heathen."

"I thought Marans didn't have an official religion," I sign, my mood turning me sarcastic.

"It's a saying, Talin," she signs back.

"Why do you look like you swallowed a frog?"

"All Strikers are to gather in the arena this morning."

I squint up at the sky, my gaze settling on the bands of distant clouds. "For what? Is the cease-fire over already?"

Adena shakes her head. "No. We caught a deserter from the Federation." She leans forward eagerly. "He's to be interrogated today, before an audience."

A prisoner of war. Now I remember Corian mentioning someone being seized during the same sweep when he'd died. This must be the soldier.

My heart hardens. By tradition, the Firstblade of the Strikers is the one responsible for interrogating enemy soldiers we capture. He questions them in public at the arena, often by stone or by whip, until they tell us what they know about the Federation. If they don't cooperate, they are executed before an audience.

It sounds cruel, torturing a prisoner to death. But sometimes cruelty is catharsis. I've witnessed firsthand what Federation soldiers can do to the people they conquer. To women. To families. To children. This public death is a kindness in comparison, a pitiful fragment of justice for all of us who have lost loved ones in the most horrific ways.

"You made me get out of bed just because we're executing some Federation coward today?"

"Is arguing with me your new habit?" Adena responds.

I hold my hands up innocently before replying, "Just asking questions."

"Firstblade's orders. Strikers to the arena. So stop playing around and go put on your full gear."

Adena had been close with Corian too, but the way she copes with his death is to drown herself behind her meticulous habits, nitpicking everything as if she could organize the grief out of her system. She's stopped by my apartment every day for the past two weeks, bringing me savory pancakes and meat pies wrapped in cloth from the cafeteria, checking to see if I'm sleeping and putting on clean clothes.

I hate myself a little for forgetting that others are also learning how to move on from Corian's death, that Adena is the more considerate one of us, that she knows to think of me even as she struggles.

I haven't lost my Striker uniform just yet. And watching the execution of a Federation soldier might at least distract me from my haze of grief. I bow my head to Adena and start to turn away. "I'll be quick," I promise her.

Adena waits in the open doorway while I wash my face and strap on my harnesses and weapons. A few minutes later, I emerge in my full uniform, and together we head out of the Striker quarters in the direction of the training arena.

Everywhere, there are signs of strain from years of war. The streets are cracked and in desperate need of repair. People buying food in the exchange market clutch ration cards for seaflour, while auctions run high for cuts of beef from the limited numbers of wild cows we're allowed to cull for the month. When a string of children run past us, I notice their bony arms, the too-sharp jut of their chins.

The conditions are even worse beyond the walls, in the Outer City's shanties. Every time we head to the warfront, we ride through their narrow mud paths, lined on either side by shacks made of rusting tin sheets and threadbare cloth. Hollow-eyed refugees from Kente, who brought their famed metalworking skills here to help us build our walls and weapons. Merchants from Larc, whose reams of fabric and bags of colorful spices are popular with Marans. Baseans, whose agricultural skills and hardy crop seeds have helped in harvesting the land more efficiently.

Basean refugees are the most difficult for me to see. Their eyes always light up at me, as if the fact that I'm one of them means that I can somehow save their families.

But I can't remember the last time we didn't have a food shortage.

38

Mara's ruin-dotted cliffs and mountain ranges have served as a natural advantage for us in the war—but in the end, they may be what kills us. The only crop that Mara harvests is camifera, a leathery, nutrient-rich plant that thrives on the wet cliffs fed by salty waves. Originally an invasive species that leached the damp soils of nutrients, camifera could be pounded into a flour for breads and noodles or woven into a coarse fabric called seasilk, we learned.

But without trade, this harvest isn't enough to feed everyone. The few herds of wild cows left in Mara are strictly regulated by the Senate to ensure their populations can remain steady enough to feed us. The meat distributed is reserved for Senate leaders and those who live in the Inner City, while people in the Outer City have to resort to eating the rabbits and mice that run rampant in the shantytowns. People risk imprisonment and death to poach the remaining animals, but even then they will all be gone in a few years. If the Federation's Ghosts don't find us first, starvation will.

The worst part is knowing that this is still nowhere near what life would be like under the Federation's rule. I've seen the destruction first-hand in the territories they conquer. It is the fire of an empire that believes so strongly in their superiority, is so certain they are destined to inherit this land from the Early Ones, that they are determined to prove it.

In the silence, Adena glances over at me. Her gaze settles on the dark circles under my eyes. "Jeran told me you've been at the arena before dawn every day," she finally says. "That you've been training past midnight."

"I thought you'd be impressed with how busy I've been keeping."

"I'd be more impressed if you were efficient about it," she replies. "But you're just exhausting yourself. You collapsed twice during training this week. No one has seen you at the mess hall in days."

"Who needs a mess hall when they have you delivering them meat pies?"

"I wouldn't need to deliver you meat pies if you'd just go to the mess hall," she replies witheringly.

"Forgive me for enjoying your daily company."

"Look, if you want to practice in the arena until you're unconscious, at least use your time right. Come by my shop. I can replace your swords' hilts with a design that locks together. It'll let you use both blades at once and free up your other hand for a third weapon."

I nudge her. "New gadgets you've been tinkering with?"

Adena grins and pulls out her own double blades. I can see that she has fitted both ends with an interlocking piece. She slides the two hilts together and twists until there's a satisfying click. Then she twirls the connected swords with one hand. They've been transformed into a single weapon with a blade at either end.

"See?" she says aloud as she twists the hilts again. They separate back into two swords.

I smile. All of Adena's weapons are altered like this—daggers with serrated blades; bullets that explode on contact with a target; arrows tipped with poison. She's the only Striker who was given a shop in the metalworkers' Grid.

"Anyway," she adds as she sheaths her swords, "take it easy on your training. Come sit with the others once in a while. You can't hide away forever."

"I'll be fine," I sign. "Really."

"Convincing argument," she signs back.

"I just . . . Give me time."

Adena's eyes soften at me, and she touches my arm. "Losing your first Shield is always the hardest." Her gestures pause, turning uncertain. "I know it's only been a couple of weeks."

Adena's first Shield had been her brother, her only family. She'd lost him three years ago to a hostage trade gone wrong between us and the

Federation. I had been the one delivering food to her door then, forcing her out of bed and away from her grief. Ever since, she has looked forward to the executions of enemy soldiers.

"But you know a Striker must have a Shield, right?" she continues now. "The Firstblade's not going to let you stay unpaired for much longer."

You can't stay a Striker without a Shield. If a lone Striker is bitten by a Ghost, there is no one nearby to kill them before they turn. Corian would have twisted into the gnarled, cracked body of a Ghost and come for the rest of us at the encampment. They don't trust us to have the strength to kill ourselves first.

I look away from her as we approach the arena's front gates. "I knew my Striker days were over the instant Corian's father turned me away," I sign. "Who else would want to pair with a Basean?"

"Plenty would. Don't lose hope. Aramin hasn't dismissed you yet."

"Yet." I raise an eyebrow at her. "I appreciate your faith in me, but you don't have to lie."

"I'm not lying!" she blurts out.

"I know what the other Strikers think of me being on a patrol."

"Well, they're fools," Adena finally adds. She loops her arm through mine and presses herself closer to me. "You're one of the most talented Strikers ever recruited. Even the Firstblade has admitted that. If he lets you go, we might as well open our gates and wave the Federation in."

"Well, that makes you the fool," I sign. Then I smile and lean back against her. "But thank you, all the same."

Adena shrugs, nudging me affectionately. "Figured you could use the moral support."

We reach the arena's front gates and walk through. Inside, Strikers are scattered throughout the space. Some are already waiting up in the seats, while the most dedicated are running through a few quick drills down in the arena's center. Ema Wen Danna, expected to join Mara's Senate next year, is sharpening her sword as she lectures her sullen brother, Sano, on proper weapon etiquette. They exchange nods with me as I pass by. Others, like Tomm and Pira, both offspring of old money families, sneer and whisper under their breath. I keep my chin up and ignore them.

I see a cluster of onlookers gathered around one Striker in particular. It's Jeran Min Terra, Adena's Shield, sparring with random opponents.

At first glance, Jeran looks like nothing more than a slender boy, his hair tied up in a knot of red gold and his eyes the blue of glacier water, his face too shy for a Striker. It's not the appearance of someone who has racked up more kills than anyone else in the patrols. Deathdancer. It's the nickname he's earned by the fluid way he moves around a Ghost, slicing a thousand cuts with his daggers while dodging every claw the creature might slash in his direction. He always reminds me of water carving through a canyon.

Today he has blindfolded himself, relying solely on his hearing to determine where his opponent is. His leg sweeps in an arc across the ground. His back arches like a bow. As we look on, he disarms one challenger, then smoothly sends another falling backward into the dirt. His movements are lithe and precise, a hypnotizing dance of daggers flashing, blades glinting.

To anyone unfamiliar with Jeran's techniques, it'd seem as if he doesn't even need to think. He just acts. But Adena and I both know how much work he puts into his moves. The onlookers let out a cheer now as Jeran disarms a third opponent, then slides off his blindfold.

Now I notice the Firstblade among those watching Jeran practice. In the midst of applause, Aramin steps toward Jeran and points out some small weakness in the Striker's moves. Jeran listens closely, then copies Aramin's motion. The two move in sync, Aramin explaining as they go.

And in this moment, I remember how young Aramin is, how he used to do these same exercises with Jeran in the arena before our last Firstblade was killed and Aramin was promoted. It still surprises me that Aramin never asked Jeran to be his Shield.

Finally, the Firstblade nods his approval and leaves the circle. Jeran watches him go, distracted, as the other Strikers begin to mill around.

I keep my head down as we enter the space, but it doesn't stop the ripple of attention that hits me. I can feel the stares from the recruits and the soldiers, can hear their whispers and mutters to one another.

"That's the Basean Striker," one recruit says to another. "I guess rats can sneak into the tightest kitchens."

"No wonder her Shield died. Pity."

"Well, I hear she won't be a Striker for much longer. Firstblade's to make a decision this week."

"My mother says Baseans get their black hair from sleeping in the mud."

"I heard it was from sleeping with the scrapyard pickers."

Muffled laughter.

My posture stiffens at that. Last year, I'd had a fling with a young Larcean refugee, a sweet, pretty boy with an easy smile, who worked to sort valuable steel from trash in the Outer City's scrapyards. We only fooled around for a few weeks, sneaking time together in hollowed-out carriage husks in the yards, but it lasted long enough for word to get out to the other Strikers. I haven't been in another relationship since.

The precariousness of my position hangs over me like a storm cloud. *Corian felt sorry for you.* The words buzz again in my mind.

Adena's grip tightens on my arm as she glares at the others. "So eager to insult a fellow Striker when you could probably rip all their guts out," she says to me, raising her voice loud enough for them to hear.

Jeran sees us approach. His face softens with a smile that turns his eyes into crescents as he hurries toward us, tripping in his rush. I can't help smiling back. Jeran is ruthlessly graceful when practicing the art of death. When he's not, he can't find his balance.

"It's good to see you out of your quarters," he signs.

"You can do a blind run better than anyone," I sign back, smiling at the cloth still looped around his neck.

"I was studying your techniques, you know," he tells me, his expression bashful. "That last move was one I saw you do at the warfront at midnight."

"Me?" I make a mock gesture of fluffing my hair. "What a flatterer, Jeran."

He laughs a little. "Only when deserved. Aramin says I still can't do it quite as well as you."

The thought of the Firstblade's indirect praise lifts my spirits somewhat.

"Why can't you appreciate *my* techniques?" Adena says to him. "You still haven't tried out the ax I designed for you."

"It's too heavy," he insists. "Have you tried lifting that thing during battle?"

"It's the same weight as your sword! I designed it specifically for you."

"It's hard to carry."

"Be honest. You don't like it because it doesn't look good."

Jeran gives me an embarrassed glance before looking back at his Shield. "The hilt doesn't match the rest of my ensemble," he finally signs.

Adena throws her hands up. "I quit. I'm going home. Call me when the warfront no longer requires a sense of fashion."

I walk behind them as they bicker, watching how their steps sync up as if they could read each other's minds. It is the way of Shields, and how I used to walk with Corian. The pang in my heart is all too familiar now. I clamp down on it before it overwhelms me.

We settle in our seats right as a horn sounds from the far side of the arena. I look toward it to see two guards pulling with all their weight on a chain that keeps one of the central arena's gates weighed down. The door groans as it inches open.

"So, what do we know about this prisoner?" Adena asks Jeran.

"He was captured at the warfront two weeks ago," he replies, fiddling restlessly with his hands like he always does. "The rumor is that he's a soldier who defected from the Federation."

"A soldier? Because he was in uniform?"

"No uniform. He has a brand, though." At that, Jeran brushes a hand idly along the thin trim of black silk on his coat's neckline to indicate where it is. "Some kind of military insignia. They said he was running across the warfront as if being chased, and not with the deliberate movements of a scout."

"Apparently he won't talk," Adena says, then tugs at her gloves. "Not even to save his life. But we'll see if that changes in the arena. By the time they've whipped his back to a pulp, he'll be spilling out the Federation's secrets like a broken water line."

"Maybe he'll want to cooperate now," Jeran offers hopefully, "and we won't have to. Whip him, that is."

I just listen as they go on. Why would a Federation defector not want to tell us what he knows? If this soldier was unhappy enough to risk life and limb to escape to Mara, wouldn't he want to help us defeat a common enemy?

"I think they're about to bring him out," Jeran muses, nodding toward the far end of the space, and my thoughts churn to a halt as I crane my neck in the same direction.

A shout goes up from somewhere in the arena.

"Firstblade!"

The call has barely echoed through the space before every Striker rises in a uniform clatter. I follow suit.

It's the Firstblade, and his expression now is a mask of grave calm. As he walks to the center of the arena, we all tap a fist in unison to our chests. Jeran's eyes linger on him longer than the rest of ours do; from the corner of my eye, I can see him leaning forward as if to get a better glimpse. Aramin flicks a hand at us, and only then do all the Strikers sit down again.

I hear the clank of metal. My attention shifts back to the gate at the arena's end.

A team of guards emerges, dragging a young man between them.

He's tall, built strong like a soldier. Shadows obscure his eyes. Heavy chains hang from his neck, wrists, and legs, clanking with every move he makes.

At first glance, he seems unremarkable. But there's something about him that keeps my gaze locked, makes me afraid to look away.

"This is the prisoner of war?" I sign to Adena beside me.

Adena frowns too. "He doesn't seem like a soldier. Where's his Federation haircut?"

I shake my head. Most Karensan soldiers I've seen have their hair clipped short on the sides in a distinct look. This man's locks look naturally grown out.

"He seems weak," Jeran adds as he nods toward the prisoner. There's real pity in his voice.

Adena lets out a disappointed sigh. "They've starved him too long. This won't be much of a spectacle."

I take a better look at him.

One thing that separates apprentices from seasoned Strikers is a well-honed instinct. You develop a sense for everything around you—the shift of eyes and feet, the people not seen in the shadows, the small gestures that others don't notice. The feeling that something is about to go wrong. It is why we practice exercises like what Jeran did with his blindfold, isolating our senses one by one in order to enhance them. Survival out on the warfront depends on cataloging every tiny detail around you.

Over the years, I've honed my instinct into a blade. But when I look at this man, I don't see anything I can grasp. Nothing in his eyes feels familiar—not a glint of hate, fear, or uncertainty. I feel only like I'm staring into an abyss. Like I don't know where I am.

Now that instinct in me flares like a fire. I don't know what it is about him—an unnatural grace in his movements, an emptiness in his eyes—but something else lies beneath the weakened exterior of his figure, some undercurrent of power. It makes him seem less like a soldier and more like a weapon. I have the unsettling suspicion that, if he wanted to, if he didn't look so lifeless, he could kill every guard around him.

Lifeless.

And then I realize, all of a sudden, that the only reason he's a captive at all is because he wants to be. Because he *wants* to die.

4

IT'S CLEAR THAT NO ONE ELSE IN THE ARENA
suspects this. Only I sit and watch him, my heart suddenly in my throat,
as I recognize the lack of fire in his eyes. They reflect the way I feel in
the early mornings, when I remember that Corian isn't here anymore.
They are the eyes of someone who just wants to waste away the minutes
until he no longer has to be here.

The prisoner stands, swaying, as the Firstblade now approaches him.
"You have been brought before us to answer for your actions," Aramin
says, his voice ringing out across the arena. Beside him, a young translator struggles to keep up, her tongue tripping over the Federation's
clipped language. "Because you chose to fight for an enemy of our nation, because of the atrocities you have committed, the Senate has sentenced you to be judged before the Strikers of Mara. If you choose to
help us by answering our questions about the Federation, we will let you
live. But if you continue to stay silent, you will be executed here in this
arena. Do you understand?"

As the translator repeats in Karenese what the Firstblade said, the
young man gazes out at the arena. I observe him closely. He may not
speak Maran, but even he must know from their voices that they are

"That all this is a prank to try to keep him alive to extract more from him later."

Adena snorts. "Well. He's about to learn that Strikers aren't great with jokes."

The Firstblade shakes his head in disgust at the prisoner's silence. "Why did you cross the warfront into our territory? Were you fleeing the Federation, or have you been sent here on a mission?"

The prisoner doesn't answer. Instead, his eyes swivel to the audience, and for a beat, his gaze locks on mine.

I don't flinch, but his look makes every muscle in me tense. There is a strange kind of desperation there, a pit of hopelessness that must have been hollowed into him long ago. Has life been so traumatic for him that he thinks of death as a release?

My gaze wanders to the sharp cut of his clavicle, where part of his brand peeks out from under his prison suit. There is something familiar about it that tickles the edges of my mind, but vanishes the instant I try to concentrate on it.

Aramin sighs and takes a step back. One of the guards approaches the prisoner from behind, lifts a bucket of icy water, and pours it over his head.

He lets out a sharp gasp and falls to his knees. Before he can get to his feet, a second guard kicks him viciously in the stomach.

The cheers around us grow deafening. Jeran doesn't join in, but Adena stands up, craning her neck to see over the Strikers in the stands right in front of us, shouting herself hoarse. In Adena's voice, I hear the raw anger that remains from her brother's death. So neither Jeran nor I intervene as she calls for death in the arena.

The Firstblade now strides over to where the prisoner sways limply against the arms holding him up. He asks him a question in a voice too low for anyone else to hear. The prisoner doesn't even try to meet his gaze. He continues to stare listlessly out at the chanting arena.

The guard swings a bladed whip down on the prisoner's back with all the force he can muster. His eyes widen as he lets out a wrenching gasp. Still, he doesn't try to avoid the whip's strikes. Around us, the audience boos in disappointment at his lethargic reactions.

Adena scowls and throws her hands up. "This isn't worth the wait. Let's leave early. We can make it back to the mess hall before everyone else."

Jeran gives her a disapproving glance. "Adena. Please be a little respectful."

"Of who? Him?" Adena shoots back.

"Of the process. We may see a man die today."

I've witnessed plenty of executions. There have been dozens of other Federation prisoners who have died in this same spot. But somehow, when I watch this prisoner, I find myself looking away. If Corian were here, he'd say there is no satisfaction in punishing someone so unresponsive. They are never going to get him to talk at this rate, not if he has no interest in living.

The snap of the whip echoes throughout the arena every time it hits true, and with each lash, he takes longer to get up. His hands clench and unclench. His boots shift against the ground as if in a fighter's stance. But he doesn't do anything else. He waits until they hit him again, and he goes down in another shower of blood and dust.

Something isn't right.

The thought swells in me until I can't ignore it. Something isn't right about this execution—or this young man. There's a difference in his gaze, his stance, the way he bears his punishment without a sound. Who was he in the Federation? Why the brand? No man can endure this kind of torture for this long. How can he bear it? Everything about this moment feels like a mistake, and the sharpness of this instinct rises in me like a tide.

"We should be reaching the end now," Jeran says quietly beside me. "I'm shocked he's still alive."

"A shame," Adena says through clenched teeth. She folds her arms across her chest in satisfaction at the sight. "Those serrated whips could be more efficient, you know, if they'd just place the blades closer together."

"Why did he desert?" Jeran asks.

"Who cares?" Adena says. "They said he refused to cooperate when interrogated. Won't say anything about where he came from or what he does for the Federation. Won't even say his name."

The whip strikes the prisoner one more time. He collapses in the dirt to an arena full of cheers. It takes him long minutes to rise again. Jeran is right—we're reaching the end. It won't be long before the guards drag his body away and send in Striker apprentices to clear the blood-soaked dirt.

I don't know why I do it.

Maybe it's because I'm Basean, and I know what it's like to be alone. Maybe it's because of how I woke this morning, struggling to find the will to live. Maybe it's because I'm about to be stripped of my Striker uniform, so none of it matters anyway.

Or maybe it's because this all reminds me too much of the day Corian had died, and the sight of blood staining the ground fills me with memories of him.

Corian. Perhaps that is what feels so familiar about this. As the prisoner lies against the ground, he makes a small, sweeping motion repeatedly against the dirt, as if to comfort himself. It's an uncanny reminder of the way Corian would wave his hand beside fallen Ghosts. *May you find rest.*

If he were here, Corian would get up from his seat and walk down into the center of the arena. He would take advantage of his good standing with the Firstblade and speak for this prisoner, not caring about any punishment the Firstblade would give him. And later, he would sit beside me at the mess hall, his head propped casually against his hand, smiling cheekily at me as I scolded him for his reckless behavior.

I picture Corian and rise from my seat. Jeran shoots me an alarmed look and signs for me to sit back down. Adena just blinks at me in confusion.

"Talin," she hisses at me, then switches to signing, "*Talin*, what are you doing? Sit down—the Firstblade's staring at you."

Still, I don't stop. My long coat drapes behind me as I take the steps down toward the center of the arena. Now other Strikers around me are murmuring. One of them shouts, "Down, little rat." Laughter.

I keep going. The Firstblade watches me as I make my way to the arena floor and head toward them. He shakes his head once at me, the only warning I'll get. And yet, I still don't back down.

Before me, the prisoner lies in a fetal position on the ground, not attempting to protect himself from the guard's endless blows.

The stadium echoes with boos now as I walk up to the guard. He gives me a startled look—my steps are so silent that he hadn't even noticed me approach him. I meet his gaze and see the bloodlust hot in his eyes.

When he reaches back to whip the prisoner again, I step between them. I unsheathe one of my long swords. In one move, I catch his whip on my blade and yank it out of his grip. The whip goes flying to land a short distance away.

The other guards all draw their weapons at me in unison. Roars ripple through the audience.

I stand my ground as if in a dream. My heart beats shallow and rapid in my chest. *What the hell am I doing?* I had not come here today with the intention of defying the Firstblade in front of his entire Striker force. He could strip me of my uniform right here and have me removed from the patrols. Perhaps this is what's making me so reckless. Just do it, do it and get it over with.

One of the guards points a gun at me. "Get back up in the stands," he snaps.

Another comes with him. I eye them both carefully.

When I don't move, the first guard curls his lip at me. "Rats are always such poor listeners," he snarls. The second guard hefts his sword and lunges at me.

When you've trained your entire life to fight Ghosts, facing humans becomes the work of a moment. I sidestep, whirling, and slash out at them both with one swing of my sword.

My blade catches both of theirs so hard that they clatter to the arena floor instantly. The first guard tries to fire his gun at me, but I'm already darting toward him. My sword's hilt knocks the gun from his hands as the bullet fires, hitting the ground and sending up a plume of dust.

The stadium's roars have turned excited again. They're getting the show they came to see. The prisoner stays crumpled in the dirt, covered in welts—but for the first time, his expression changes. Through the blood on his face, he looks at me with vague surprise. A ray of life.

"Talin." The Firstblade approaches me. He draws his sword. Stillness ripples across the arena like a stone in water. "Step away." In his voice churns an undercurrent of anger.

I turn to face him. My head lowers in respect, and I kneel—but I don't sheathe my sword.

"That wasn't a request, Striker."

I tap my fist to my chest, then lay my weapon beside me. "First-blade," I sign. "Don't do this."

"Are you giving me an order?"

"Please," I answer. "He isn't fighting back." I look over at the prisoner. "Even though he can."

At that, Aramin raises an incredulous eyebrow. "It is only out of respect for your late Shield that I'm going to let you explain yourself."

My fingers move rapidly. "The way he stands. The brand on his chest. The shift of his posture and the movement of his arms. They are not the movements of an ordinary soldier."

The Firstblade's eyes look up to search mine when I pause in my explanation.

"I don't know what it is about him," I continue. "All I can tell you is that killing him will be a mistake."

Aramin's gaze returns to the prisoner lying on the ground, covered in blood and grime. For a moment, I myself am not sure of what I saw in him. He certainly doesn't look like much now.

Then, through his tangle of hair, I see his eyes locked steadily on me.

His glance sends a shiver rippling up my spine. I didn't intervene expecting gratefulness from him—but I'm still surprised by the look of sheer rage that he directs at me. There is a glint about his eyes that seems inhuman, a powerful darkness in him that I can't see. The Federation has done something to him, and even though I don't know what it is, I feel as if I'd just witnessed a Ghost emerge from the shadows of the woods.

At least his eyes now have the glint of life in them.

"You're telling me not to execute this soldier because of a *feeling* you have," Aramin signs to me.

His words are designed to make me feel like a fool. Maybe I am one. My resolve wavers under the prisoner's furious stare. I can hear the laughter and unrest in the stands. The crowd shifts in their seats, mumbling.

I take a deep breath and lift my chin. "Didn't he flee the Federation?"

"He's still the enemy."

"He's not their loyal soldier. He left them willingly. His movements are far too precise to belong to a common soldier. If we kill him now, we could lose a well of information that he might be willing to give us."

"We've already questioned him to exhaustion. It's useless."

"Give him more time. He may know something invaluable."

"Step aside, Talin," Aramin answers coldly.

"Corian wouldn't."

Aramin sighs at that. This is Corian's spirit haunting me, giving me the stubbornness to take a stand here. I grit my teeth, not knowing how else to answer him. Not caring. "Haven't you said before," I sign, "we could use any help we can get? What if he can give us what we desperately need?"

He grunts in irritation as I use his words against him. "Help?" he says with disgust. "We need a miracle."

"And yet things clearly aren't desperate enough, are they?" I'm angry now, and my signs turn cutting. "After all, we still haven't opened up Striker recruitment to the refugees in the Outer City."

"I'm not having this argument with you today."

"When, then? When the Federation's banners fly over our nation?"

The tension between us grows thicker. I've challenged him, dared him to remove me. "What do you want to do, Striker?" he finally asks. "Or are you so noble as to take his place?"

I cast my eyes down at the ground. "With all due respect, sir. If you want to waste a prisoner like this during a losing war, then so be it. But if we execute him now, we might be digging our own graves."

It's a reckless, stupid answer—here I am, facing my superior before an audience of our entire Striker force, banking on nothing but the fact that we were once equals, two soldiers fighting a losing war.

He faces me in silence, and for a moment, I think he will raise his blade and cut me down.

Then, finally, he takes a deep breath and nods once at the guards. "Leave him," he says.

Murmurs ripple through the audience. Disbelief. Even I stare up in surprise. The Firstblade does not take orders from a Basean rat.

He casts one last, disgusted look at the bloodied form of the prisoner, then points his sword at me. "He lives," he says, loud enough for the audience to hear.

The surprised murmurs turn into a disgruntled chorus. People had come out today for the catharsis of an execution, and now I was the reason they would be robbed of it. Up in the stands, I can see Adena's stormy expression.

Aramin lowers his sword. The blade's tip buries into the ground with a heavy thud. "But since you seem so fond of him, I assign him to you."

I look sharply at him. "Sir?"

"You're in charge of him now." Aramin's gaze pierces through me with an edge of vengeance. "Every Striker needs a Shield, don't they? And it seems to me that you need a new one. Well, here's your wish. You get to stay. You get your Shield. Your prisoner gets to live. Are we all satisfied now?"

The insult of his words sinks into me. Heat rises on my cheeks. I had made the mistake of embarrassing him before the entire Striker force and the Maran public—so this is my punishment. Of course a prisoner of war couldn't join the Striker forces. So instead of dismissing me from the Strikers, instead of taking my challenge, the Firstblade has instead turned me into a joke. I picture myself having to lead a chained prisoner around during training sessions. Forced to sit with him beside me in the mess hall. Would the Firstblade go as far as making me share living quarters with him too? The stares from the arena weigh against my shoulders. Snickers echo around me, their laughter cutting.

Aramin reads my expression with a look of grim satisfaction. "I'll hold you responsible for anything he does," he says. "Look out for him. He's your Shield now. Maybe you'll be able to get the information that you so firmly believe he holds."

"And how long might that be, sir?" I ask him.

His eyes stay cool and calm. "As long as any Striker stays with her Shield."

This is worse than a dismissal. It's a death sentence.

The laughter continues. The words that Corian's father had spoken to me echo in my thoughts. *You weren't good enough.* On the ground, the prisoner slowly pushes himself up to a seated position and meets my eyes with an accusing glare. I stare back, loathing myself for being sympathetic, hating him for forcing me to be kind.

A rat and a prisoner of war. Perhaps we're not so different after all.

5

EVENING FALLS. I CAN'T GET HIM OUT OF MY
head.

The sound of clashing blades in the arena still rings in my ears as I head out through the Inner City's walls and into the streets of the Outer City, toward my mother's home. Roads of mud cut through columns of haphazard shacks leaning this way and that. Everything is cobbled together out of scrap wood, threadbare cloths, and sheets of thin, rusted metal useless for anything else, leftovers from the worlds where we all came from. That no longer exist.

I pass all of it in a daze. My mind lingers on the prisoner—my new Shield, I have to keep telling myself.

The reminder sends a fresh wave of revulsion through me.

I haven't yet changed out of my Striker gear. I can hardly believe I still get to wear it. Basean refugees call out to me from their stalls, holding out reams of bright fabrics or gesturing to their burlap bags filled with red and gold and purple spices, hoping I have money to spend. Servants sent by their noble Maran masters point at the hanging trails of crimson peppers and black garlic, haggling for the lowest price. Though Marans won't let us live inside the walls, they have certainly developed a taste for our food.

I pause to buy a bag of spices, then continue until I reach another shanty neighborhood, my mother's. Difficult as it is to be apart from her, here she is surrounded by a community of other Baseans. A small comfort that I hold dear. You can always tell the Basean streets apart because of the green they somehow manage to coax up from the dirt: tangles of squash vines snaking along the ground, mint and rosemary shrubs cutting through the scent of grease and perfumed rice and spiced fish. Fires burn low, dangerously close to doors, and in front of them crouch an assortment of people, cooking in iron kettles and on home-made metal grills laid over their fires.

They are my people and I am theirs, but they still stare at me as I pass by, eyeing my Striker uniform with a mixture of fascination and dislike. A familiar murmur from them buzzes in my ears. There are such things as spies who patrol the Outer City. They're sent by the Senate to listen for rumbles of unrest from these people who have been stripped of everything. Pushed to their limit, some lash out, inciting attacks against Maran guards and riots in the streets. I've seen the occasional Outer City resident dragged from their leaning shack, locked away after some spy or other has reported their plotting. I always feel confused afterward, a mix of pity and anger and grief.

There are enough people in my mother's neighborhood who think I'm one of these spies, dressed up in the fine uniform of a Striker and sent to watch over everyone's affairs here. That I'm the eyes and ears of the elite, reporting who to punish. In this way, they see me the same way that the Marans do: undeserving of the Striker uniform. It keeps me suspended between the Inner City and the Outer—where I'm neither accepted nor entirely cast out by either side.

Even so, I can't help feeling a bit at home as I walk these streets. Here, to me, is the part of Mara I understand, the people that Mara had allowed into its borders even as the Federation pushes in from all sides. We're still here and alive. It's enough of a reason to defend this place.

Now I slow my walk as I reach our quarters. From the end of this muddy path, I can see the humble little home I grew up in, its door open to let in fresh air.

If I could have, I would've moved my mother into the Striker apartments with me years ago. But even my position isn't enough for the Senate to let her into the Inner City. It would set *a dangerous precedent*, said the Speaker. Instead, my friends each gave their offerings, the limits of what they could do to make her life in the Outer City more bearable, without inviting punishment on her or me. Corian made sure her house was built better than many in the shanties. The walls are now made of solid terrywood, and our slanted metal roofs are sturdy and don't leak. Corian helped us install a proper chimney that Adena hammered into shape in her shop, so that my mother could cook indoors, and dug a tunnel underneath the house so that she had something like a toilet instead of the public outhouses at the end of each makeshift street, places so filthy that my childhood nightmares were filled with visions of falling into their dugout troughs. Knowing my mother's skill with plants, Jeran had brought her seeds from his family's garden—lettuce and carrot and radish—and even climbing roses, which now hang their beautiful blooms along the walls, and pink feather grass, which sways in a ring around the house.

She's feeding a log into the stove when I step up to the open door. I just stand there for a moment, watching her sturdy shoulders at work, unaware of my silent arrival.

The house is small but warm, the single room barely big enough to walk a few steps from one end to the other. Potted plants crowd the damp corners and leaning ledges. Lush green vines, still dewy from being watered, drape down from her rusted windowsill. A little tree with long spring-colored leaves sits by the doorway, its scent as clean and sharp as lemon.

It's not our home. But you try your best to take your home with you, even if it's a shack in the middle of a desperate place.

She pours a spoonful of water onto the stove's hot surface. Steam sizzles, humidifying the space. When she finally steps away from the flames, I knock twice against the doorframe.

She turns at the sound. Her eyes widen with joy at my smile.

Every corner of my heart fills as she steps toward me and reaches up to cup my face in her calloused hands. "There's my girl," she signs, then runs a hand through my hair. "She doesn't visit often enough." She pats my cheeks and adds aloud, in Basean, "Or eat enough."

Like my Striker companions, with whom I flip back and forth regularly between our sign language and Maran, my mother communicates with me in a mix of Maran sign language and, when she can't quite figure out what signs to use, in Basean. I lean into the familiar rhythm of my homeland's tongue on her lips and the coarse movements of her fingers, then hand her the bag of spice from the market. "You said you missed woodruff."

She sighs at the dried leaves and flowers, taking a moment to inhale their aroma. "Oh, it's perfect." She nods toward the table. "Sit down. I'll fix something for you."

"Ma, I'm not hungry."

She clicks her tongue disapprovingly at me. "Never hungry, never learned how to cook. What a daughter. Tea, then."

I follow her to the makeshift table in the corner of the room. It's only large enough for two people to crowd around. As I take a seat, my mother puts the dried woodruff into two tin mugs. Then she takes a pot off the fire and pours me a steaming cup of water.

"Will you stay for dinner?" she asks me.

I close my eyes and inhale the scent of tea. "Can't. I have to be back at the mess hall."

She smiles a little. "How are your friends?"

"Fine." I hesitate, not sure how to begin my story of what had happened in the arena.

"Tell Adena that I appreciate her bringing over that box of ginseng for me."

"She said you helped her prepare some samples of camifera so she could experiment with its strength as catapult rope." I smile briefly. "She always tells me no one has steadier hands than you."

My mother shrugs and winks at me. "Well, she's not wrong."

Then I reach toward my belt and unhook a pouch of coins. Half of my weekly pay. I put it on the table between us.

She smiles sadly at me. During a normal visit, she would scold me more, telling me to keep a higher portion of my wages, buy myself something nice. But she knows I'm here because I always visit before we head back to the warfront. She knows this time is harder, given Corian's death. So she spares us her usual argument and just leans her head against her hand. "I heard the Firstblade paired you with an unconventional Shield," she says.

The rattle of her breathing is strong tonight. I'm lucky that the Federation's poison gas that had destroyed my vocal cords did not permanently injure my lungs. My mother wasn't so fortunate. Her lungs have never fully healed from that attack, and Mara's cool, damp winters haven't helped. Every year around this time, liquid rasps in her chest, and the shack will fill with the scent of lemongrass and mint.

"Less a Shield," I answer, "and more a punishment for me. He was a prisoner. They said he surrendered willingly at the warfront."

"What happened?"

I sigh. The smell of dust and sweat from the arena still lingers on me. "He was due to be executed, but I got in the way."

"You mean you saved someone's life," my mother signs gently. "That's not something to be ashamed of, Talin."

Not something to be ashamed of. A sudden memory comes to me of the night when Federation soldiers first arrived in our Basean town of Sur Kama. I'd awoken to the sound of breaking glass, the din of voices outside. Then someone, a soldier, was dragging me out of my bed and across the floor of our home. His grip around the skin of my arm burned. I yelped, my heart startled out of slow slumber into a desperate beat, my voice shouting for my mother. And my father, where was my father? What had happened to him?

The soldier forced me to stand outside my home. When I looked up, sobbing, searching for any familiar face, I'd found myself staring up into the frightened eyes of another soldier. He'd been so young, perhaps no older than twelve or thirteen—but he was pointing a gun at me, the insignia on his red sleeves shining. My memory has blurred away the details—in my mind, the emblem is now nothing but a smear of silver.

The first soldier had snapped at the second, at the boy, in Karenese. Probably telling him to hurry up and shoot me. But the boy just stared at me, his hand trembling under the weight of the gun.

Then he said something in protest, voice small and trembling. The first soldier cursed at him, and when the boy stayed frozen, he shoved me again so that I lost my balance on my hands and knees and fell to the ground, my cheek scraping the dirt.

My eyes tilted up enough to see the cut of branches over me, the sinews of the ancient tree that twisted in front of our house. And there, I saw my mother, moving along the branch like a cat, soundless. Her dark gaze met mine, and she shook her head once. I stayed silent. The boy continued to hesitate.

The first soldier lost his patience with the boy and yanked out his own gun. Then my mother moved. She leaped down from the tree, directly onto the first soldier, and snapped his neck with such a clean break that I heard the crack ring through the air. In almost the same movement, she seized the gun from him and pointed it straight at the boy.

The boy stared at her in terror. My mother kept her gun steady, daring him to hurt her daughter. When he hesitated a moment longer, my mother pulled me to my feet. Already, flames were devouring the roof of our house, lit by the embers from a neighbor's. I didn't look back at the boy before we ran. Even now, I don't know whether or not he would have pulled the trigger, if given enough time. He hadn't fired, but his hand hadn't dropped either.

Was that saving someone's life? Or hesitating because you lost your nerve?

Did my mother ever have nightmares about the soldier she'd killed? Or did she thank the skies every day, knowing I could have died instead?

I leave the memory behind and shake my head, irritated at how much it can still shake me. "It was a fool's act," I tell my mother now, and I know it. "I shouldn't have."

"Why not?"

"He's a prisoner of war from the Federation, Ma."

"And?"

I look up at her. I'd half-expected my mother to flinch at the thought that I'd endanger my position because of an enemy soldier. To my surprise, though, she just looks intently at me. "Why did you choose to save him, then?" she asks.

"He's someone important to the Federation." I offer her the reasons

I've been listing in my head. "There's more to him that he's not letting on, and he might be our best chance to learn more about what the Federation's war scientists are doing."

"And is that really why you saved him, Talin?" my mother asks.

She thinks I did it out of pity too, just like the Firstblade. I scowl at her and lean back in my chair. Why did I? Looking back, it all seems so stupid. He had run out of reasons to live, an emotion I knew all too well, and his gesture had reminded me of Corian. Corian, who said blessings over the bodies of monsters, who I wanted so much to be like, who would have stepped into the arena to confront the Firstblade had he been there.

But this prisoner wasn't Corian. He wasn't me. Had I really bet my entire career on a moment of desperate grief?

"Does it really matter?" I sign instead. "The Firstblade paired him with me as punishment. I wonder if he really means to let a prisoner of war into the Striker forces or if this is his way of executing the prisoner anyway, forcing him out to the warfront with us."

My mother takes one of my hands in hers. She turns my palm up, massaging it by pressing her thumbs gently into my skin. I think back to when Nana Yagerri, the old woman who lives at the end of my mother's street, first taught me how to sign in Maran. She had fled to Newage from a small village near the border between Mara and Basea. "Come here," she'd said to me one day as she watched me try and fail to sell herbs I'd picked on the street to the houses around us. She had patted my hand and led me to her shack to share oatcakes and tea. "We've all forgotten how to take pity on one another," she'd told me. "But you can talk to old Nana. She'll teach you how."

My mother had then learned it from me so that she could understand her daughter once again.

"There was one summer when the rains came early," my mother says in Basean, rubbing the base of my thumb. "You were only five years old.

Do you remember that? You went out to the garden when the sky was already black with clouds, and came back cradling a thin branch with a butterfly's chrysalis hanging on it. You were so determined to save it from the storm."

It had been a beautiful turquoise-colored chrysalis dotted with flecks of gold, and inside it I could see the first fragile outlines of a wing. The rains would rip it from its branch, I'd known without a doubt.

"You spent the entire week guarding that chrysalis until the butterfly emerged," my mother continues. "And when the storm passed, you were so proud to release it." Her eyes soften, and this time, she signs to me. "My Talin. You're just like your father."

My father had been the one to help me cut the small branch it hung from, had sat beside me as we balanced that branch carefully between two rocks on the table. *It's a fragile thing, Talin,* he'd told me as I sat there, legs swinging impatiently, waiting for the chrysalis to break open. *So be gentle to it.* He mussed my hair, and I leaned my head against his side. *You'll see, it will come out when it's ready.*

I remember every detail of this moment, but not my father's face. I can't even recall where he went. I've asked my mother many times what had happened to him that horrible night, whether we'd lost him at the house or during our flight from the Federation. My mother deflects the question each time. All she will tell me, over and over again, is that I have his easy smile, his compassionate eyes. And I'd go to bed each night haunted by dreams of that smile and those eyes, of his soft laughter filling the house on warm, rainy days.

I don't know how much of his kindness I inherited, though. I have killed men and monsters in ways I will never share with my mother.

"I was just a child then," I sign.

"You haven't changed, my little love." She leans closer. "We aren't trusted here—not because of who we are, but where we come from. Is that so different from this prisoner you decided to save? Go talk to him. Find out why you were drawn to him."

I give her an annoyed frown. "He doesn't understand my signing. He doesn't even speak Maran."

"Aren't we all always searching for someone to understand us? Find a translator. Your sweet friend Jeran. He speaks Karenese, doesn't he? You saved the prisoner for a reason, even though you might not yet know what it is. Try to find out what made him flee the Federation."

I roll my eyes. "Now you sound like the soft one."

She shrugs. "Everyone has a different story."

I stare at my mother's long, graceful hands. They bear new scars since I last saw her: burn marks from the stove and pale cuts and calluses from skinning mice and rabbits—the reliable protein that runs rampant out here—but they don't make her fingers any less deft. She drums them against the table in an idle dance. My memory of her during our life in Basea comes to me in snatches. Her dark, lush hair, her tall figure. She used those skilled hands to serve as our village doctor and as a huntress who'd come striding home with a young boar slung over her shoulders. The same hands that gutted and skinned an animal could also sew the most careful stitch against a wound or tend to delicate medicinal herbs in our garden. At night, those hands would stroke my hair until I fell asleep. My father had been drawn to that contrast in her, the huntress and healer.

"I'll go see him," I sign.

My mother squeezes my hands before pulling away and looking out her window. Despite her strong shoulders, she looks small and alone. "Visit me when you return from the warfront. You will tell me all your stories."

It's her way of making me promise to return home alive and safe, a promise we both know I can never be sure to keep. But I bow my head anyway. The truth is, for the past few weeks, when I've struggled to find a reason to get up every morning, I think of my mother. I think of this tiny home. And I always push myself out of bed.

"I will, Ma," I reply.

6

THE ROAD LEADING TO THE PRISON IS QUIET
tonight. No one notices Jeran and me as we make our way down the
path, nothing more than a pair of shadows in the darkness.

The buildings that make up the National Plaza include one of the
most spectacular ruins in Mara—twelve buttresses lining a structure
with three arched entrances. This building was once a grand library of
the Early Ones, with rows and rows of shelves uncovered when Newage first began cleaning up the ruin, but many of its books had long
ago rotted away. By some miracle, a few remained, and from those, we
learned what little we know about the Early Ones. Inside the building, the space is cool and dark, with towering stone pillars. Once upon
a time, the sides were lined with narrow glass windows that rose up
along the building's walls. Now, this ancient library has been modified
into our National Hall. We've fortified its crumbling sides with steel
and added hallways that radiate from where the windows used to be.
Down each hall is a fine apartment where a Senator lives, paired with
a team of soldiers to safeguard them and their family.

Below the National Plaza, we discovered an enormous, cylindrical pit
five levels deep. Originally, this pit had been dug out by the Early Ones,
the walls made of smooth metal, like a silo for storing grain. Adena thinks

they may have once used it to launch weapons more massive than any-thing we've ever seen. She's always sniffing the air when she's down here, murmuring about the lingering scent of something sharp and chemical.

I suppose it doesn't really matter what it used to be. We now use it as our underground prison.

Guards standing drowsily at the prison entrance snap awake at the sight of my approach, then relax at the Striker emblem on my coat. Jeran gives them a polite smile and bows. They part and let us through toward the damp steps that wind into the darkness.

As we go, the familiar smell of water and blood and mold hits me, the filth of people kept here for decades, of interrogation chambers built into the metal walls. Shafts of dim blue light illuminate the steps from the gratings above. We move down the stairs at an even pace, spiraling and spiraling, passing one level of archways after another. Every floor is lit sparsely with torchlight, and against their flickering circles, the steel prison doors reflect a shiny black.

Beside me, Jeran moves without a sound, his steps sure and steady tonight as if he were out on a sweep. Light and shadow band across his face in a silent rhythm.

"They still aren't feeding him?" he asks me as we go, his eyes flicker-ing to my hands for my response.

I shake my head and raise my hands so he can see me sign in the near-darkness. "They are. He won't eat. No one can make him."

"I guess he's determined to die, isn't he?"

"Maybe this was all part of the Firstblade's plan to get rid of me."

"Aramin thinks you're a valuable Striker, Talin."

"Oh, is that what he told you?"

"It's just the truth. You did defy him in front of the entire arena."

"You're always defending him, Jeran."

Jeran looks embarrassed. "Not always," he mutters under his breath.

"If this prisoner dies of hunger," I sign gloomily, "at least my punishment will be brief."

"Is that why you brought him a bag of bread and fish from the mess hall?"

"Stop wringing decency out of me."

"It's an honest question."

"I need something as bait if I'm going to try coaxing answers out of him, don't I?"

"Well," he says, "don't tell Adena that you're trying to feed the prisoner."

"Is she still upset with me?"

Jeran hesitates long enough for me to wonder if he couldn't see my signs in the dark. "She'll get over it," he finally replies. "But you have to understand how hard it was for her to watch you defend the life of a Federation soldier."

"We don't know if he was a soldier."

"She doesn't care about that."

I don't respond for a while. A part of me rears up in my own defense—I had tried to save a life and a friend I've known since childhood is holding it against me. But then I think of Adena's meat pie deliveries, the way she'd looped her arm into mine as we walked to the arena. I think of years ago, how she had screamed when Federation troops shot her brother dead as he tried to run across the warfront to us. It's the only time I've ever seen her break the Striker oath of silence out in the field. Aramin had refused her plea to send Strikers into enemy territory to retrieve his body, but even he hadn't had the heart to punish her for the outburst.

I picture the memories coming back into her life, crowding her head. She must be in her workshop now, furiously sharpening her tools.

"I'll visit her tomorrow," I tell Jeran. "I'll apologize in person."

72

We finally reach the lowest floor. There are only a handful of cells down here, all arranged in a circle around the central spiral of steps. So little light reaches this floor that the walls around us seem to extend into blackness beyond the glow of torches. Guards stand at attention before each steel door.

Prisoners from the Federation are kept down here. One of the cells holds a Ghost that had been captured alive months ago. I used to hear its shrieks echoing beyond the gratings five floors above, the rhythmic clang of it throwing its body against the steel doors. Now it is quiet, stirring into a rage only when people enter its cell. I've never seen its face, although I know the Speaker has authorized us to experiment on it to understand how the Federation could possibly have mutilated a human into such a creature.

There are Federation soldiers down here too—or, at least, there used to be. Their screams would fill the air for weeks as they were tortured for information, for any desperate lead we could get in order to help us fend off the Federation for another month.

But now, as we make our way to the last cell, I hear nothing. Guards nod at us in silence, wary of disturbing the captive Ghost. We give them our silent salute as we stride by.

There are four guards standing at attention before the prisoner's—my Shield's—cell. Jeran approaches one of them so quietly that he jumps, drawing his blade before he sees the cut of our coats.

"Striker Jeran," he mutters in greeting. "Hells, you blue coats sneak up like a rogue wind."

"Hello," Jeran says politely, blinking. "I'm sorry for startling you."

The second guard snorts at the sight of me. "A nice display you put on in the arena yesterday. I'm surprised the Firstblade didn't cut your throat right then and there."

Common soldiers are also trained to sign, so I could respond if I wanted to, but I choose just to glare instead. We wait for them to slide a metal disc along the edge of the cell door. A series of clicks echo through the space. Then the door creaks open, and we walk past the guards and into the prisoner's room. They shut the door behind us.

The cell reeks of mold and death, torchlight from outside coming in through the door's grating and weakly illuminating the back wall, where the prisoner sits.

He's wearing the same shackles I'd seen him in yesterday, thick bands of metal clapped around his neck and wrists and ankles and waist, the chains nailed to the wall behind him. The strange, metallic texture of his hair is noticeable even in this low light. His head is down against his chest, as if he's asleep.

Perhaps he didn't hear the door open, or us step in.

Then he lifts his head. Beneath his dirty, mussed hair glitters a pair of near-black eyes. Now that I see him alone, without the distraction of the arena, I can tell he has the physique of a fighter—tall and well-muscled, built solidly underneath his prison suit.

Jeran hesitates beside me, reluctant to come closer.

The prisoner says something to us that I can't understand. I find myself taken aback by his voice—deep, gritty as the scrape of stone on stone, but with a tone so refined that I wonder for a second if he's a trained singer.

When I just stare, he turns to Jeran and gestures impatiently at him, then repeats what he said.

Jeran clears his throat, eyes darting uneasily away from the prisoner. "He's wondering why we didn't bring any weapons with us."

I watch the prisoner, careful not to let my hands stray to where the hilts of my weapons should be. He doesn't need to see that he makes me wary, or that I hate being without my blades. I take a few steps closer to him, listening to the rhythm of my boots against the stone floor.

"I didn't think we needed them," I answer. My hands move in slow, measured movements, so that the prisoner doesn't think I'm about to attack him.

He watches me as Jeran translates into Karenese. There's a challenge in his eyes, but he doesn't move a muscle. My gaze goes to the chains still wrapped tightly around his chest.

He mutters something.

"He can tell that you regret stopping his execution," Jeran says for him.

I shrug. The light filtering in is so weak that it barely outlines the silhouettes of my hands in orange. "And you hate that I did," I answer, looking directly at the prisoner.

His eyes flash at that, dark and angry. "You had no right," Jeran says, adding a softness to the prisoner's words.

"Or you could say 'thank you.' Some gratitude for saving your life would be nice, you know."

I watch Jeran as he translates my reply. "Did you actually repeat what I said?" I ask him when he finishes.

Jeran is embarrassed enough to trip over his feet as we edge closer to the prisoner. "I said, 'My duty is my duty,' instead," he replies.

I give him an exasperated look. "Being polite for me now?"

"Sorry, Talin. I don't know how to say *gratitude* in Karenese and I'm trying not to upset him."

The prisoner watches me, curious. I want to ask him if he ever fought for the Federation. If he's ever slaughtered my people, if his swords ever ran red with Basean blood.

We're close enough now that I can smell the stench of his breath, the stale, unpleasant smell of someone who hasn't eaten in weeks. I reach into my coat and pull out the bag of food I brought for him, some breads and dried fish I'd saved from my own rations. At my movement, the prisoner stiffens, stirring uneasily, and for a second I assume it's because he thinks I'm pulling out a weapon. But even when he clearly sees the food in the bag, he doesn't change his posture.

"I know you don't want to eat," I sign as Jeran translates, then slide the bag next to his feet. "But this is just in case you change your mind."

He doesn't bother picking up the bag. Instead, he peeks inside it before turning his head away in apparent disgust. From this angle, I can see the hollow pits of his cheeks, the shadows under his eyes.

"Eat," I sign, now frustrated. But he doesn't bother moving, and only after another long silence does he finally say something in reply.

Now Jeran looks genuinely awkward. "Er, he says he doesn't like fish."

I shoot Jeran a withering glance. "He doesn't like fish?" I sign flatly.

"Maybe best not to belabor it," Jeran says.

"The bread, then?" I sign to the prisoner, annoyed.

His lip curls in distaste, but this time he grabs the bag and takes out a hunk of bread. That's when I see a slight movement wriggle from his shirt pocket. A small, furry head peeks out from it, its nose sniffing the air, beady eyes locked on the food. It's a fat mouse with a missing tail. To my surprise, the man lifts his hand so the mouse can climb into his palm, then lowers the creature to the bread, where it puts its tiny foot-paws on the crust and starts nibbling away.

Beside me, Jeran makes a face and shudders. "I feel like it's on me," he whispers, his eyes locked on the mouse.

"Glad to know I brought food for your pet instead," I sign at the prisoner.

He just shrugs, one thumb idly rubbing the mouse's head. "It was here first," Jeran translates with a queasy expression. "And it keeps me company."

Something about the prisoner's gentle movements around the mouse makes my dislike of him waver. I think of my father leaning beside me as we watched the butterfly's chrysalis.

I sigh. "Tomorrow, you fall under my charge," I sign instead, changing the subject. "So I thought we should get to know each other a little better before we spend more time together. Don't you think?"

Still, he doesn't answer.

"Were you born in the Federation?" I ask.

The first serious light comes into his eyes. His lips go flat, but he shakes his head. "I lived there for as long as I could remember," Jeran says for him. The prisoner's hands move unconsciously, like they will somehow help him explain, and I find myself searching for words and meaning in the gestures. After a while, he looks at me again. "You?"

"My mother and I fled here when your Federation conquered Basea."

I can't keep the bitterness out of my gestures, and he notices it. This time, Jeran hesitates.

"What did he say?" I ask him.

"At least your mother still lives," Jeran replies quietly.

Anger flares white hot in me. Maybe it'd been a mistake to save this prisoner's life. My mother has lived to bear the permanent scars of what the Federation had done to her, and I do not have the patience to listen to a former Karensan soldier shrug that off.

"What happened to yours?" I sign. If I had a voice, the words would have come out ice cold.

He looks away, refusing to contribute to our conversation. The mouse finishes nibbling and darts back into his shirt pocket.

"And your father?"

Still nothing.

"Why don't you want to live anymore?" I ask him, my signs gentler now.

He pauses for a long time before he gives me a steady look. I watch his lips move as he speaks to Jeran.

Jeran glances apologetically at me. "He wants to know why this matters to you."

"Why what matters?"

"This. Him. His past."

The conversation I'd once had with Corian comes back to me in a torrent of emotion, and for an instant, I'm twelve again, lounging by the grapevines beside my Shield. *Why does it matter to you, how I feel about Basea?* I'd signed, and I can hear his answer in my memory. *Shouldn't it matter to everyone?*

The similarity of this moment, here and now, takes me aback. For a moment, I feel as if I were Corian, the one reaching his hand out to this foreigner.

I bend down to balance on the balls of my feet and rest my elbows against my legs. Our eyes are level. If I really do have to lead him around in shackles for the unforeseeable future, I'd at least like to be able to trust him enough to be near him.

"My mother and I lost everything," I tell him, "when we fled into Mara—everything except for each other. Our pasts matter because they created us, helped mold us into who we are."

He gives me a suspicious frown. "You want to dig into my life by holding out pieces of your own."

Well, he's not as generous as Corian was. Now I think he's mocking me with the tilt of his head, as if it were easy for me to talk about the broken pieces of my childhood. I nod at the brand peeking out from under his shirt. "Your brand. What did the Federation do to you?"

Again, no answer. I realize that he's studying me now, his gaze focused on the fresh black studs of bone in my ears. He likely doesn't

Sometimes I wonder whether Jeran feels relieved after his father's punishments, as if it resets the clock on when his father will lash out again. I remind myself to ask my mother to make a poultice for his bruises when we return.

Red responds, and after a moment, Jeran nods at me and points up at the structure. "Back in the Federation's capital, there are ruins of old ships, with walls made of some kind of mystery metal. It's where they used to find artifacts of the Early Ones' books."

I lean forward instinctively in my saddle. Is he finally trying to tell us something useful? "A library?" I ask, nodding at Jeran to translate.

Jeran shrugs as Red answers. "No idea," he says. "Maybe. All the steel towers here around Newage make me think this was once a city."

"It was," I tell him. I look back at the remnants of their civilization and try to imagine what it was like. "I heard the Federation used those books to learn how to create Ghosts," I go on, nodding at him. "Did they use that on you?"

His expression shutters in an instant. He nudges his horse hard enough to make it skip a step.

"He's asking if it really matters," Jeran tells me, his voice more hushed. "Doesn't Mara use the Early Ones' technology without understanding it?"

I turn my frown on Red. "*You* brought up the ruins in the Federation," I sign at him.

Jeran looks more uncomfortable in his translations. "Now he's asking what happened to you on the night you fled into Mara," he murmurs at me.

I look away from Red. "Forget it," I tell him, my signs cutting and angry.

We fall back into a tense silence. Whatever small bond we might know what it means, but somehow I feel he can sense the weight of sorrow on my chest. He's quiet for so long that Jeran looks questioningly at me before the prisoner finally replies in a softer voice.

"My little sister used to have a mouse for a pet," Jeran translates.

It's the most genuine thing the prisoner has said so far. I can hear the loss in his words, the grief lacing his voice.

"I'm sorry," I sign, and I mean it.

"Do you remember your life before they came?" he asks me.

It takes me a moment to realize he means before the conquest of Basea—and yet another to notice that he refers to the Federation as *they*, not *we*. Corian had once asked me if I had any other relatives, but when I shook my head, he'd let the matter drop and never brought it up again. At first, some part of me flares in defense at the prisoner's words. It is easier not to talk about the painful places of your past, better sometimes to let it go. But his question conjures an old memory of a sunlit garden, a hot, humid breeze, and broad green leaves hanging wet in front of our windows.

"Fragments," I reply. "Nothing significant."

The prisoner says nothing as he reaches into his shirt pocket to pet his mouse's head again. The creature leans up into his touch, its eyes closed. When he speaks again, he doesn't mention my past. "I've never met a Basean before. This is my first time venturing out beyond the Federation's borders."

He hadn't answered me when I asked him what the Federation had done to him, so instead, I sign, "Do you remember your name?"

"They called me the Skyhunter."

The mystery of the word sends shivers down my spine. Jeran and I exchange a look.

A long pause follows. I'm about to tell him that it's not a question he has to answer, but then he lifts his head to give me a strange expression. I realize that he had been taking so long to respond because he was trying to recall his name. How long has it been since he last used it?

"Redlen," Jeran translates at last. "Some call him Red."

I watch him rub incessantly at the spot of grime. Then I frown and look closer. He notices my gesture, and as if to acknowledge it, he holds his arm in the light so that it's bathed in light blue. Now I can see the faintest hint of an artificial groove underneath the skin, running from his wrist up to his shoulder.

Had the Firstblade noticed this on him? It appears as if something had been grafted to him underneath his skin, something that turns his skin into this strange, unnatural surface. I remove one glove, then hold my hand out questioningly at him.

He nods, moving his arm closer to me, indicating that it's okay for me to touch it.

"Careful," Jeran signs, casting me a sideways glance.

"I am," I reply, then let my fingers brush against the prisoner's skin. It feels as natural and alive as anyone's, although noticeably warmer. I push down slightly against his arm, then jerk away. There is the figurative saying of muscle hard as stone, but this truly feels like it, as if his skin had been stretched over something as firm and unmoving as steel.

When I don't try to touch his arm again, he leans back against the wall with a clatter of chains. "The Federation's work."

Jeran casts me a quick glance as he translates the sentence. He's not surprised that the prisoner—Skyhunter—Red—had been altered by the Federation, but that he told us.

The instinct I'd had in the arena flares again. "Something is wrong with him," I sign, unable to shake the feeling. But I still can't tell why the Federation would do this to him, what benefit it is to them to deform his body. Was he just an experiment, not meant to be used?

What can he do?

I go back to his eyes. He still has his scowl on, and his expression is defiant, his lips on the edge of baring his teeth.

But I'm silent. I think of what it must be like to have something artificial embedded into your body like this, what he must have experienced, what the Federation's plans for him had been. What unspoken things lie in his past. Here, in this cell, he looks less like a threat and more like just a prisoner in a strange place, among strange people.

My thoughts make me shake my head, irritated with myself. "I don't know what might have happened to you," I sign to him, "and I don't expect you to tell it to me. We all have pain from our past. But at the warfront, none of that matters. I've been handed the responsibility of your care, and that means you will accompany me as I go about my duties. And if you help us, we might even be able to help you."

He turns distant again and glances away. "I don't need your help," Jeran says, his soft voice a mismatch to the acid in Red's.

"Maybe you'll be surprised," I retort.

"I don't like surprises."

"Apparently you don't like anything." My gestures are so annoyed that Jeran backs slightly away, his eyes going to the prisoner and his hand to his belt before he remembers he doesn't have his weapons with him.

Red meets my eyes again. We hold each other's stare, and for a moment, I think I see something vulnerable in him. It is the part of him that has not yet been touched by the Federation.

Then the moment ends. He looks away from me and tilts his head up to the light beaming down from the ceiling grate. The mouse stirs in his pocket, its whiskers peeking out. A sigh rumbles in the prisoner's chest as he pats the creature absently. I wait a moment, wondering if he's gathering his thoughts, but when he doesn't speak again, I finally stand up and turn my back on him. Jeran walks with me. I can feel the questions stirring in him, and his hesitant eyes on me, but I don't answer and I don't look back. I can't. If I see the prisoner's face again, I might want to throw a fist at his stubborn jaw. The reasons why I saved him are beginning to wane in my mind.

"Any luck, little rat?" one of the guards says, sneering at me as he opens the cell door to let us through.

The look I shoot him is so dark that it sends him scurrying back to his position.

7

THE GUARDS TELL ME THE NEXT MORNING, AS the Firstblade sends me to retrieve my new Shield, that Red ate the rest of the bread out of the bag I'd brought him. In truly irritating fashion, he'd left the fish untouched.

They've also cleaned him up. How they got him to cooperate, I don't know, but when they deliver him to me at the front gate of the prison, his hair is washed, trimmed, and tied up into a typical Maran knot, and his body has been scrubbed so hard that his skin looks pink. Even his pet mouse looks puffed up in a ball as if it'd been caught under a deluge of water and soap, its fuzz sticking out from the sides of the shirt pocket. My eyes water at the peppery smell of prison soap wafting off him. He gazes warily around the National Plaza, as if barely able to believe that he's out of his prison cell.

I have nothing to communicate to him that he can understand, so I don't try. I just tug on his chains, making sure they're still locked tight around his wrists and waist, then secure a length of it around my arm. Now that I'm able to walk beside him, I get a sense for how tall he really is—more than a full head above me, and even after weeks of starvation, still solid in his shoulders and chest and arms. They've shaved his beard too, and underneath the grizzled scruff, his face is lean and smooth, younger than I originally thought. His breath is pleasant now, the sign of having eaten and gotten his teeth scrubbed. He doesn't smile. My hands hover persistently near the daggers against my thighs, ready to move if he turns on me. Maybe he no longer wants to die, at least not right away, but that doesn't mean he might not want to take someone else's life.

The Firstblade wasn't willing to offer him clothing beyond his prison suit. Who knows if Red might try to make an escape, maybe attempt to deliver news of what he's seen in Mara to the Federation? So he wears a clean set of the white tunic and pants instead, which he's already spoiled with mud at the hems. In case he breaks free, he'll at least have to shed his prison clothing to avoid being a moving mark.

I'm a moving mark. The thought makes my shoulders tight as I head from the Plaza toward the Striker arena, where the others had long ago begun their exercises. As I walk, others turn their heads in our direction, first at me, the Basean Striker, and then at the white-clad prisoner beside me. People move aside as if we're poisonous to touch.

Red's chains drag too long before him. His legs tangle around them, forcing him to lurch to a halt. He takes me with him—I'm pulled off balance and stumble backward, shoving into his chest like an unsteady drunk.

Snickers around us. A gaggle of children cover their mouths and whisper something to one another, their eyes on Red, before dashing off again into the morning crowd.

I shove away from Red, annoyed, keenly aware of the unnatural warmth of his body. It's not his fault the chain's too long—but he had been the one who refused to answer in the arena, who hadn't wanted to defend himself, who had forced me to step in—

He scowls at me as I tangle in his chains again. His hand closes around my arm to keep me from falling.

I yank out of his grasp. "Don't touch me," I sign, my teeth bared.

He understands my expression well enough to take a step back, lifting his hands in a seemingly universal gesture of surrender. Then he gestures widely again, exaggerating with his arms as he attempts to explain that he'd been trying to help me. It only irritates me more.

The laughter around us goes on. I turn away from him and stalk toward the arena again, yanking him with me, knowing how ridiculous we must look, hating that the Firstblade chose to punish me this way.

"I'm sorry," I sign as I go, refusing to look him in the eye, not caring whether he understands. Then I gesture at the chains dragging in front of him. "Let's do something about those."

He casts me a hostile side glance and tightens his lips. Fine. I guess we won't be defending each other's lives anytime soon.

I swallow my impatience. Maybe it would be helpful to teach him a few words, after all. So I hold my hands up at him and sign the letters of my name slowly. "Talin." I point at myself and use the established sign I use with others for my name. "Talin." Then I spell out the letters of his name. "Red."

His eyes follow my gestures, and then he lifts his own hands, attempting the signs. I stare as he moves, mildly surprised by the grace of his fingers. He has a good memory and manages to be accurate enough for me to understand both our names. I try more words.

"Yes." I hold my middle and index fingers together, then wave them toward myself. He imitates me.

"No." I make my hand into a fist and twist my wrist.

"Friend." I hold my middle and index fingers up and make a cutting V motion straight toward him.

He does the same.

Well, it's a start. Now I point in the direction we're walking, then again at his chains. I make a breaking motion at the chain itself by sliding my palms against each other, then tap my chest twice with my right hand. "We're going to fix it," I sign.

I haven't yet moved away from him when his mouse suddenly jumps out of his pocket and onto my arm. It scurries up to my shoulder before perching there.

Years on the warfront, ready for any Ghost's attack—and yet I still suck my breath in sharply and jump back, shaking my arm wildly. The mouse lets out an undignified squeak as it goes flying and lands on the ground. It scampers up Red's body and shoves itself firmly back in the pocket, its tailless bottom poking out from the top.

Red laughs—a rich, guttural sound—and I hate that I immediately want to hear it again. He only smiles enough to lift the edges of his lips a bit, but it brightens his entire face. "Talin," he signs at me. "Red," he signs the letters and points at himself. "Friend," he signs down at the mouse before petting its head.

He has a sense of humor. Wonderful. My skin is still crawling from the feeling of tiny feet running up my arm, and I shudder, glaring daggers at the creature's little head that now pokes out to stare at me.

"Next time," I sign at Red angrily, then drag a finger across my throat.

Red just shrugs and pats the mouse's head again. "No," he signs back, amusement lingering on his lips. Then he says something to me in Karenese, knowing full well that I can't understand him, and walks on, forcing me to follow him instead of the other way around.

My annoyance flips into outright anger. I wonder how much trouble I'd rile up if I simply killed him now, just stuck a dagger in his back and let myself be done with him, or even just stabbed his foot so that he has to hobble the rest of the way. I fantasize about it until we've passed by the arena's entrance, where I finally abandon the thought in the presence of so many others.

86

Without a cloud in the sky, the stadium looks blindingly bright, and I have to shield my eyes from the light. I don't go into the arena. No need to put my punishment on full display to my fellow Strikers if I can delay it a little longer. Instead, I head toward the rows of workshops located next to the arena, where Adena's shop sits.

I don't know what this area used to be. A park, maybe. The workshops were built from the ground up without any foundation from the Early Ones, and they came up haphazardly, so that each workshop crowds tightly beside the next, all of them forming a snake of buildings folded over and over into a rectangular area we all call the Grid. Every shop is a different size. One shop showcases three enormous, unfinished catapults built from wood and steel looming several stories high. On top of them sit metalworkers fitting giant hinges onto the shoulders. Other shops specialize in our armor, a lattice of chains so finely made that they look like a silver shirt underneath our vests. These stores are narrow and brightly lit with dozens of torches, the metallic shirts stretched out flat against weaving looms. Still others are workshops crafting the blades we use or melting down steel from broken weapons to recycle into bullets. Some are even used as research areas, where various combinations of herbs, woods, and metals are tested and retested against vials of Ghost blood to see if any of them can be used as a deterrent against the creatures.

During the day, as it is now, the area is usually filled with bustling workers in goggles and heavy gloves and vests to protect them at their stations. But as the war has worn on and our supplies have dwindled, some workers shutter their stations and use the space to drink instead. It has caught on—and now, at night, the Grid turns into a place where Strikers and metalworkers alike, dejected from a losing war and dead friends, come to horse around, drinking and playing with the stoves, daring one another to mad antics out in the test yard.

Adena's workshop sits on the last row, looking out across the acres of yellowing land they use to test everything designed in the workshops. I don't expect to see her when I reach the shop—I'd been hoping that she would have a tool on her wall that I can use to shorten Red's chains.

But when I arrive, she's here, goggles and mask on, hair strapped back, her dark skin illuminated by the sparks coming off a small steel cylinder she's welding. In her hand is a metal rod connected to a furnace, and at the end of the rod is a concentrated spout of fire so hot it looks blue.

As always, my eyes wander around the rest of the shop. One entire wall is dedicated to tools of every shape and size, knives and hammers and tongs, needles so thin I can barely see them, curling lengths of metal that I wouldn't begin to know how to use. Against another wall are four stoves, all lined up in a row. Every spare inch of the other walls is covered in carefully sketched schematics and scribbled notes, as well as shelves of glass jars containing her collection of anything she's found interesting—which is everything. Unusual feathers. Bird bones. Colorful stones. A perfect spiral of shell. Chips of wood. Dried grasses and flowers. This would almost be a problem, Adena's obsessive collecting, if she didn't organize it all so neatly. Instead, everything just looks like an extension of her eternally curious mind.

Standing not far from Adena now is Jeran, his arms folded, as he watches her. At the sound of our approach, he looks up at us. His eyes jump to Red. "Oh!" he says, then glances nervously at Adena. "I thought you'd both be in the arena."

"Same with you two," I sign back.

Adena pulls her mask back and goggles up, stares at me, and then looks down again as if she'd never noticed us.

We all stand there for an awkward moment, Jeran glancing uncertainly between Red and me, Red looking around the workshop with a wary expression, me staring at Adena and trying to figure out what to tell her. Adena, pointedly ignoring us.

Finally, I reach out and tap her gently on her shoulder.

Adena's face jerks up, her white-hot-flame rod still in her hand. We all startle back from its heat. Even Red blinks.

"What do you want?" she says to me in a clipped voice.

I give her an apologetic look and nod at Red's chains. "Something to shorten this," I reply. "I can't function if he's stumbling on this all day. I was wondering if you could help."

Adena glares at me, gesturing haphazardly with the burner. "You didn't know I'd be here. You came over hoping I'd be gone, so that you could take one of my tools and do it yourself."

I give her a guilty look. "Maybe?"

Adena points the flame at Red, who blinks at her. "Sneaking around my shop. For him. *My* tools."

"Talin just wanted to make his life easier," Jeran tells her, an attempt to defend me.

"Would've been easiest if she'd just let this one die," Adena says to Red without flinching. When he narrows his eyes at her, she sticks her chin up at him, daring him to react. "You would've done him a favor, Talin. At least he wouldn't have to be paraded around like this, trying to understand what everyone's saying about him."

She goes back to her work, leaving me standing there without knowing what else to do.

Jeran steps closer to me and puts a gentle hand on my arm. "Why don't I ask Red if he wants to eat anything at the mess hall before practice starts?" As a hint, he glances pointedly in Adena's direction before looking back at me. My chance to patch things up.

I give Jeran a grateful nod, then unclip Red's shackle from my wrist and look on as Jeran tries to make casual conversation with the prisoner.

Red stares ominously at him, enough to make Jeran fidget, but at least his posture softens, knowing this boy is his only link to his surroundings.

As Jeran starts asking him about his favorite foods, I approach Adena. She still doesn't look at me, but at least she doesn't move away. I look on, watching her shape the soft metal into a small cylinder before turning off the flame and refining its edges.

"He reminded me of Corian," I tell her after a beat. "It was the way he swept his hands across the arena floor."

Adena is silent for a while, forcing all her concentration onto her work. The clink of metal against metal rings in the room. There's a furrow between her thick brows that always appears when she's going between two emotions—like when the Firstblade handed her the gold threaded cord that graduated her to Striker but didn't give one to her friend, and when she chose Jeran as her Shield after her brother's death.

"I didn't mean it, you know," I add, hesitating, and then, "I didn't think about how it would affect you. I should have."

Adena stops hammering at the steel cylinder long enough to glance up at me. "You're as bad as Corian," she mutters at me, shaking her head. "Your mother agrees."

"You talk to my mother about me?"

"Of course I do, every time I stop by her place."

I think of the housewares that Adena has begun making lately out of scrap metal and the collection of them growing in my mother's kitchen. It's not until now that I realize how frequent her visits must be.

"Like when you gave water to that recruit who got in a fight with a Striker in the arena," Adena continues. "What was his name again? Anyway, it doesn't matter. He was supposed to be punished and withheld food and drink, and there you were at midnight, sneaking him a flask."

"What about you?" I remind her. "Remember when you spent all night wrapping bits of copper around every weapon you could find?"

After a few coincidences at the warfront, Adena had been convinced for a while that copper was a deterrent against Ghosts, that the metal repulsed them and kept them away. In her eagerness to protect us, she'd spent a sleepless, feverish night tinkering with every single one of our weapons, stringing copper wiring around their handles. It ended up not working, of course. But I've never forgotten that night— the hope in her eyes that she might have something to save us.

She shrugs grumpily and ignores my reference. "You're lucky the Firstblade went easy on you." As usual, though, the anger is already seeping from her gaze. "I thought he was going to cut you down right there in front of us all."

"Don't worry. I won't make saving Federation soldiers a habit."

Adena glances skeptically at me, then takes a pair of pincers and sinks the steel cylinder into a bucket of cold water. It hisses, steam obscuring the air between us. Adena takes out the cylinder and hands it to me.

"For your blades," she says.

I take the cooled cylinder curiously. "Why?"

Adena reaches over and yanks out both of my swords. She twirls one expertly, then attaches the cylinder to the end of one hilt. It fits so neatly that I wonder if she'd stolen my blades in my sleep just to measure them properly. Then she takes the second sword's hilt and fits it into the cylinder's other side. It snaps neatly into place, transforming my swords into a double-ended weapon.

Adena hefts it twice and gives me a confident nod, her eyes shining. "Twist once to take it apart," she says, doing it. The swords separate again.

"You were doing this for me?" I ask her as I take back my weapons. "I thought you were angry."

"I can be both. I told you I'd make you one, didn't I?"

She doesn't mention her brother once. Maybe it's for the best, not to acknowledge the memory of his death right now. But I understand all the same, and I bow my head once. "Thank you."

Adena glares at where Jeran and Red have stepped right outside her workshop to talk. "Don't thank me yet. I still don't know about your new companion."

Suddenly, we both hear the Firstblade's voice outside, addressing Jeran.

Adena shoots me a startled look. "I didn't think today was an inspection day in the Grid." Then she steps away from me and darts outside. I follow her.

We come face-to-face with Aramin, standing with his hands tucked behind his back. Beside him is Jeran's father, Senator Barrow Wen Terra, and older brother, Senator Gabrien An Terra.

I look quickly at Jeran. The easy attitude he'd had moments earlier has vanished, and his face is drained of blood. He looks down, away from these two Senators who are his family, pretending to be fascinated by the samples of glass that a metalworker across the path is laying out across a table. Everything about his posture has stiffened. His father, Senator Barrow, looks at him without much of an expression, but even then, I can feel the tension between them crackling in the air like a living thing. Jeran speaks so rarely about him that I sometimes forget his position.

But I never forget that this man exists. The bruises on Jeran's arms always remind me.

"Training to be a metalworker now, Jeran?" he says to his son.

Jeran doesn't dare look up. "No, sir," he replies, anxiety laced through his words. "I'm only waiting for my Shield."

His father's eyes scan him slowly, from head to toe, before finally settling on his eyes. "Waiting on others, your specialty," he says mildly. "Just like your mother."

Jeran says nothing to that. All of his cheery air has vanished under the scrutiny of his father and brother. My attention turns to Gabrien. He looks like the taller, crueler version: handsome where Jeran is beautiful, with wider shoulders and longer legs; his robes elegantly cut to resemble their father's Senate coat; his face similar to Jeran's but chiseled into something made out of stone.

He gives Jeran a pitying look that makes my blood run cold. "It's all right, Father," Gabrien says. "Jeran's strengths have always been physical."

Jeran shifts uncomfortably, head down. I find myself moving closer to his side, every muscle in me tensing to protect him.

"Well," Jeran's father replies to Gabrien. "A man is fortunate enough to have one son as high-achieving as you."

Aramin's expression doesn't shift at the subtle insult to the Strikers, that we are nothing more than brutes sent to hold monsters at bay, but I do see his folded arms stiffen, and his body turn subtly toward Jeran in a protective stance. Jeran doesn't look up at all. I'm reminded of the many times he'd be alone in a corner at the mess hall, nose buried in a book while the rest of us ate. I think back to how many times he'd taken the exams to qualify for a position in the Senate and please his father. How disappointed he'd been when he failed them.

Senator Terra turns his attention to Red. "So this is the prisoner who caused a scene in the arena," he says to Aramin.

"He *was* the scene," Aramin answers. He nods at me. "Although Talin seems to have stolen it."

"I see." Jeran's father glances thoughtfully at me before saying, "Is it wise to let a prisoner traipse around like this?"

"He's weaponless in a hive of Strikers," Aramin replies. "I assume he is a failed soldier of the Federation. Let Talin wear out her punishment."

Wear out my punishment—meaning until Red is killed, which will almost certainly happen soon, given his complete lack of training and weapons and anything resembling armor. He will be thrown onto a field in the warfront with me, and I will watch him die defenseless. That is, if I'm not killed first.

The same thought must have crossed Senator Terra's mind, because he replies, "In a few days, then."

"Don't be so sure, Senator." The Firstblade looks at me. "Perhaps she'll get some useful information out of her Shield by then."

The Senator sniffs and turns back to face his younger son. "When you finish here, Jeran, I want to see you back home. The gardeners need help cutting the roots of that dead oak."

"Father." Jeran clears his throat uncertainly. "I think I need to be at the arena until—"

It happens so fast. My hand has barely gone to the hilt of my sword before Senator Terra seizes Jeran by the hair and yanks him forward hard enough to throw him off balance. A strange, terrible giggle comes from Jeran, and when I glance at his face, it's blank from fear.

I start to pull out my sword, but the Firstblade acts before I can. One second, he's standing with his arms folded; the next, he's moved in between Jeran and his father. He grabs the Senator's forearm; his fingers close hard enough against the Senator's skin to wash it of color.

The Senator glances at him in mild surprise.

"Remember your place, Senator," Aramin says, his voice calm, but underneath it I can hear a dangerous edge. "Your son will be at the arena today for his training, at the request of his Firstblade."

The Senator doesn't look at him. All he does is hold Jeran tightly,

94

fist in his hair, until finally the pressure from the Firstblade's grip makes him let go. Jeran stumbles, dirt soiling the bottom of his coat. When Adena approaches him in concern, he just holds up a hand at her and shakes his head. He's still making that awful giggle.

"It's fine," he says to her. "I'm fine."

Even Red has tensed beside me.

Aramin meets the Senator's stare without a flinch. I imagine the man sneering, telling Aramin that he can do what he likes with his son. But the Firstblade outranks us all, even both Senators here, so at last, Jeran's father bows his head with a chuckle. "Shall we move on to the catapults?" he says. "My son and I are interested to see what the Senate's funding package has yielded."

He says this casually. As if he hadn't just attacked his second son a moment earlier. As if Jeran weren't still standing before him, trembling harder than he's ever done before a pack of Ghosts.

The Firstblade nods. "After you." He waits until the Senators have passed him before he turns to Jeran.

"I'm all right," Jeran says before Aramin can speak. "Thank you." He wears a tight smile on his face, but his brows are knotted and his eyes glossy. His voice sounds hoarse with the effort of holding back tears.

The fierce light has gone from Aramin's eyes, leaving a concerned expression on his face. He looks like he wants to say something more to Jeran, then hesitates and decides against it. Instead, he frowns at me. "Don't attempt to draw your blade at a Senator," he tells me in a low voice. His words are stern, but empty of anger. "I have enough to deal with, explaining away your antics in the arena. My power to protect you has its limits." Then he glares at Red and walks away.

I look at Red. Even though he couldn't understand everything that just happened, he isn't a fool—his eyes linger on the back of Jeran's father, dark and hostile, before jumping to Jeran in concern. My resentment of this prisoner gives way to something resembling approval.

As Adena walks over to Jeran and touches his shoulder, I'm hit with the realization that, if Jeran were ever to die, it would not be a monster that killed him, but his father.

8

I HATE THE PROCESSION WE ALWAYS MAKE
when we head out to the warfront.

It's no different this morning as we wind out of Newage's gates
and through the Outer City, our path pointed to the horizon. Teams
of cooks, servants, and metalworkers walk behind the supply wagons.
Then come battalions of common Maran soldiers, their armor scuffed
and worn, their faces gaunt. Strikers ride in pairs both at the front and
back of the procession.

Red rides beside me this morning. His presence is an unfamiliar
weight at my side, and I keep casting him sidelong glances.

He's still shackled, and chains still run across his chest, more for
show than any practical purpose. Though he hasn't been given a Striker
uniform, at least he has been allowed to change out of his prisoner suit.
No need for the Federation to hear about an obvious prisoner of war
staying in our defense compound.

Red's face is a cold mask of indifference this morning. He doesn't
look my way.

As usual, crowds have gathered to see us off. Most in the Inner City
are solemn, waving their respect to us as we pass. But I can feel their
expressions shift as they turn to me. The farewells dim, and in their place

is a din of mutters, hostile glares, snorts of disgust. I try to ignore their glances. As we make our way through the Outer City, I crane my neck in the hopes of glimpsing my mother in the throngs that have assembled along the muddy paths to watch us go. Maybe she's here, but I don't see her. The only ones clustered on either side of our procession are stall owners and their hollow-eyed children.

Finally, we leave behind the city and enter the open plains that dot our land. Towering ruins stand like silent sentinels as we pass. My gaze lingers on one of them, a fragment of steel three times taller than me, jutting out of a stream glowing with blue minnows. The sapphire light reflects off the metal in wavy patterns.

"Mara."

I turn around, still surprised to hear Red's gritty voice next to me, and see him looking up at the steel beam. He stares at it, then back at me.

"Different."

He's picked up a couple more Maran words since yesterday, but I still shake my head, unsure what he's trying to say.

He gives me a frustrated look and turns away again.

"I'll ask him." Jeran rides up beside me, then calls out at Red in Karenese.

I watch him as he goes. Gone is the strange, terrified version of Jeran I'd seen yesterday in the Grid, head bowed before his father and brother. Today he's the boy I know again, attentive and thoughtful, if a bit quieter than usual. A mottle of blue-and-purple bruising peeks out from the collar of his jacket.

He'd headed home immediately after practice yesterday, so eager was he to still help his father chop down their dead oak. He'd slept at home, not in his Striker apartment he shares with Adena.

have forged seems to fade again behind a curtain of suspicion. Jeran turns away at Adena's voice, eager to get out of the thick tension that's built back up between me and my joke of a Shield.

Red and I spend the rest of the day ignoring each other. By the time we reach the warfront, the sun has already crept below the horizon, casting the sky in hues of deepening purple. We settle into the defense compound in a mass of silence.

"Is Red not coming outside to join us?" Jeran signs to me as we gather around a fire.

"I don't really care," I sign back, still cranky.

Jeran hands me one of the bowls of stew he's carrying, then sets a second one beside himself after nearly dropping it. His eyes, always observant, linger on the tent where Red is currently hiding.

Across the fire, Adena leans on her knees from where she sits and uses a hunk of hard bread to push around the chunks of fish in the stew. She shoves the entire softened bread into her mouth. "Maybe he's plotting against us," she signs.

Jeran frowns at Adena and hands me a second bowl of stew. "You're suggesting he might be a mole?" he signs back.

"I'm saying he could be anything. We don't know. Do we?" She turns to look at me. "Is he clever when you talk to him?"

"Very average," I reply witheringly at the same time Jeran also signs, "He seems educated."

Adena snorts. "Maybe he's not a spy, then."

I glare darkly at the bird we have roasting over the flames. She's not wrong, although it would be foolish for him to try anything out here. What would he do? Break out of his chains and through the heart of our defense lines to deliver messages to the Federation? Either way, Red hasn't emerged since we arrived. As far as I know, he'll stay in there and go hungry for the rest of the night just to avoid having to see me again.

At the look on my face, Adena sighs and pats my knee. "I'm kidding. Just give it some time," she says aloud to me. "Maybe he'll be useful yet."

I watch the fire lick the night air, unwilling to admit that I'm looking for more reasons to dislike him. "He won't talk," I continue. "He won't eat anything except some stale dinner rolls. At this point, all I'm doing is waiting out the days until he gets himself killed."

"Adena didn't tell me anything for the first several years we were paired," Jeran speaks as he gingerly cuts a leg off the roasted bird and tosses it in her direction. She catches it in one hand, bounces it from the heat, and bites into it. "It took me six months to learn what part of the city she lived in."

"But you were the hardest to crack, Talin," Adena says to me, holding up a greasy finger. "And not because you're quiet. Corian came to me so many times for advice on how to get you to open up. Did you know that? He would ask me how I started conversations with you and what made you laugh."

I smile, remembering a time when Corian had dressed in a ridiculous shade of green because Adena had told him it was my favorite color. "I knew," I respond.

We all fall quiet for a beat, grieving over our own memories.

"Train with him for a few days," Jeran finally signs, nodding back in the direction of Red's tent. "Maybe you can help him prepare for a battle so that, if he does end up in front of a Ghost with you, he has a chance."

"Didn't he escape a Ghost at the warfront?" Adena signs.

"Word has it," Jeran replies.

"Well. Maybe he's a better fighter than we think. At least he has some muscle on him. Didn't you tell us about his unusual skin, Talin?"

I nod.

"Has he mentioned anything about what he can do?" Jeran signs at me. "Or why he's branded?"

I shake my head, thinking of the strangeness of Red's artificial body.

"If he's an experiment," Adena signs after a while, "then it's likely he isn't the only one. There might be others like him back in the Federation. Although who the hell knows what he's useful for."

A silhouette stretches over us, and suddenly our hands all freeze. I look up to see Red approach our campfire. His eyes are wary, his steps as slow and cautious as if he were hunting.

Adena's hand moves closer to one of the swords at her side, but Jeran reaches out to her without looking away from Red. He shakes his head subtly. Adena's hand relaxes, but her stare stays on my new Shield.

"So . . . ," she says, letting the word trail uncertainly into an awkward silence.

Red stands there, unsure of what to do. On the top of his shoulder, his mouse sniffs the air, tentatively heading down his arm at the smell of food.

I wave him over, gesturing to the bowl sitting untouched next to me. He stares at me, then at the stew, as if it might contain poison. The mouse doesn't hesitate. It scampers down to the ground and perches on the edge of the bowl.

Jeran looks like he might retch.

Adena makes an exaggerated cough at Red. "Just sit down and have some dinner," she says. "Jeran here cooked it himself. You should probably show some enthusiasm."

Jeran gives Red a nervous smile and says something to him in Karenese. Then he looks back at me and says, "I told him I'm a phenomenal cook."

"It's true," Adena adds to Red, waving at Jeran to translate for her. "If you ever end up lost in the woods, this is the one you want with you. He could cook a meal out of twigs and make you crave it."

Now Jeran is blushing and beaming at the same time. "Wild sugar-weed. It'll flavor anything, especially a good filet of white fish."

Red glances down at them. The expression in his eyes is so searing that Adena's hand rests back on her hilt again. The instinct that tickled the back of my mind at the arena flares up again now. What had the Federation been doing with him? What made him flee?

"No fish," Red then says, his accent thick.

We all stare blankly at him.

"Well, we're set," Adena says. "He can say 'no fish.' We'll all be chatting together in no time."

"Here," Jeran says to Red, cutting the other leg off the roasting bird and tossing it to him. "Try this instead."

Red catches the leg, steps toward me, and takes a seat. He pushes the bowl of fish stew carefully away and bites into the meat. I watch him curiously as he eats. He stops only to pull a few strips off to lay them next to his mouse. I look on as it grabs the meat with its foot-paws and digs in.

Finally, Red holds up the leg bone and gives Jeran an approving nod. Jeran's chest puffs up in pride.

"We're at the warfront now," Adena says as she studies Red. "You know anything about fighting?"

Jeran translates, and Red puts down the bone, eyes fixed on Adena as she talks.

"Yes," he answers on his own.

Adena smiles a little at the way he enunciates the word. "What kind of fighting?"

He doesn't answer, so I dust my hands of crumbs and stand up. My hand tightens around the hilt of one of my swords. I yank it out with a flourish—and the instant I do, I see Red tense, his body moving instinctively into what looks like a fighting position.

Adena notices too. "So you *do* have some training," she says.

"Decent training too," Jeran adds, nodding at Red's posture.

A warning buzzes in the back of my mind. We are skirting the edges now of who he must have been in the Federation, prodding at the mystery of the title they had given him. *Skyhunter*. What does a Skyhunter hunt?

I nod at him to get up. When he narrows his eyes at me, I hold my free hand open and give him what I hope is a trustworthy look. Then I pull out my second blade and toss it to him.

He catches it without hesitation, like it's an instinct he's been waiting to use. We all stare at him as he handles the first weapon he's had while inside Mara. He turns the blade in his hand, as if he can't quite believe I've given it to him, and then looks back up at me.

I get over my surprise quickly enough to lift my blade at him. "Practice," I sign.

Even without Jeran translating, Red seems to understand. He lifts the sword too, the weight of it effortless in his hand, and touches the blade to mine.

I twist my sword suddenly, attempting to disarm him, but he anticipates my move and spins his blade out, tossing it to his other hand with ease. He steps toward me with the blade raised.

He stops the sword an inch from my chest. I sidestep and yank out a dagger, pointing both blades at him, and spin low, ready to catch him on his legs. But he anticipates that too, shifting out of the way and bringing one of his boots swiftly down on my dagger. He moves much faster than his height would suggest. It reminds me uncannily of the size and speed of Ghosts, and I find myself swinging out at him less in play now, and more in defense.

He dances with me, parrying in sync, seemingly as used to a blade as any soldier I've ever fought. The others have gone quiet now as they watch us. Red is no Corian—we haven't had years together to train, to match up our every move. Nor is his style at all like a Striker's. He doesn't move quietly in the same way we do, doesn't test the sound that each of his steps makes. But he's good—really good. Good enough that I think he might be toying with me, intentionally holding his true skill back.

I make a final move, arching back to twist my dagger toward his neck. He catches my hand by the wrist. His skin is as shockingly warm against mine as it had been in the prison, as if he were running a constant fever.

I know immediately that, if he wanted to, he could break my arm with a single snap—but his grip is gentle enough that I realize he's only holding me in defense.

We stay still like that for a moment, our eyes locked, neither of us wanting to step down. From the corner of my eye, I can see Jeran's shocked expression and Adena's wary one. My cheeks flush in frustration at the strength of Red's grip. I've fought many much larger than me—but his brawn feels less like a human's and more like a steel vise. Why couldn't I be fast enough to stop him? How can he move so quickly?

In Red's eyes, I see a hint of the same amusement that had been on his face when his damn mouse scurried up my arm. Then he releases me and takes a step back, giving me a subtle bow of his head. My skin tingles where he'd held me, the warmth of him seeping into my bones. Is he mocking me now? He isn't even trying.

Again, I find myself thinking about what must have been done to him in the Federation. What had they meant him to become, before he escaped?

It's my last thought before the air splits with the wail of a battle horn.

We all turn toward the sound and draw our blades in unison. Guns appear in our hands. I look to the horizon, where a red glow sits low and angry, the telltale sign of fire on the plains. It's where our neighboring compound is supposed to be.

Before I can think anything else, screams go up from the front of our encampment.

The cease-fire is over. The Federation has crossed the warfront.

9

MY FIRST THOUGHT IS THAT IT'S IMPOSSIBLE.

Ghosts have never wandered this far into Maran territory—it would have to mean that two of our main defense compounds at the warfront have been overtaken.

And if those compounds have already fallen . . .

But there's no time to let this terrible thought sit in my mind. I'm already on my feet, blade in one hand and gun in the other, shifting into an attack formation before I can register exactly what has happened.

Red moves quickly into a crouch. Beside us, Jeran and Adena draw their weapons at the same time. Even from here, I can feel the inferno at the front of the compound. Soldiers rush by with blankets and buckets of water, while screams of agony fill the air. Outside the gates comes the gnashing of teeth and the shrieks of Ghosts.

I look sharply beside me to see Red's face drained of blood, his expression suddenly vulnerable.

I hurry with Jeran and Adena toward the side gate. Red keeps pace with me, his shackles clacking against his chains.

We rush out into a nightmare. The horizon is ablaze with fire, unmistakably coming from the two defense compounds at the edge of the warfront. Federation soldiers, clad in bold scarlet, have now doused our front gate in black oil. The flames roar a hundred feet into the air.

What makes me freeze, though, is the sight of a line of Ghosts at the crest of the nearest hill, their pale, hulking figures orange in the light. The sound of their grinding teeth, wet with the cuts on their mouths, fills the air. Heavy chains hang from their neck cuffs. They hold back, trembling, as their handlers sit on horses beside them.

"What are they waiting for?" Adena shouts.

My hands grip my blades so hard that my knuckles have turned bright white. I realize that my stance has turned instinctively, protectively, toward Red. His gaze is locked not on the Ghosts, but on one of the Federation soldiers on a horse.

Unlike the others, this soldier is draped in a long crimson robe, his arms and shoulders protected behind armor of black steel. At his side, two of the Ghosts lurch forward. Their neck chains clank, swinging, from where they are hooked onto the saddle of his steed. The fire outlines the young man's cheeks and sharp angles, exaggerating the bone thinness of him and the dark circles underneath his eyes. A bold slash of paint runs long and black down the right half of his face. All it takes is a single glance to know that he's sick, maybe seriously so. His skin is unhealthily pale, his head bald and brows scarce. Even so, there is an authority in his silent presence and regal chin, and most of all, a ferocious intensity in his stare. It is the expression of a conqueror.

I've never seen this man before, but I remember his profile adorning Karensan flags. This is Constantine Tyrus, the young Premier, son of the Federation's late Premier and leader of his regime. He is the one who brings armies into new nations and conquers them in his father's name. He was the one responsible for the destruction of my homeland and my flight into Mara, had rode into Basea's capital when he was only nineteen years old.

Beside me, Red's profile is lit from behind by the harsh yellow of the fires. His expression has transformed into one of stone. What has brought the Premier himself into our land?

Now he lifts his voice to address us as we face his troops. "Where is your Firstblade?" he calls out. I blink, startled by his near-perfect Maran accent in his rasping voice. "I'd like a word with him."

From the center of the line steps Aramin. He strides forward with a fearless gait, his long coat streaming behind him, and if I'm not mistaken, the ferocity on his face looks almost delighted by the prospect of the fight ahead.

The silence that hangs over us now is punctuated only by the crackle of flames from the gates behind us. The Firstblade looks at the Premier. "You are in Maran territory," he shouts. The growl in his throat rumbles low and angry. "And in violation of the Speaker's cease-fire agreement. Turn back with your troops."

Constantine doesn't smile, nor does he move. Beside him, his general raises his voice indignantly, speaking in Karenese as if to defend his Premier—but cuts off as Constantine waves his hand once. His voice is cool and bored as he calls out to the Firstblade.

"I'm only here for a bit of property you've stolen from us," the Premier says.

"What property is that?"

"You have something that belongs to me," he goes on. "An experiment. He crossed the warfront line between us, which has forced me here to look for him."

I know better than to glance at Red now, but I can feel his presence stiffen beside me as he moves deeper into the shadows behind our line.

Constantine scans the scene, then turns that calm, deadly gaze back to the Firstblade. "You wouldn't happen to have seen him, would you?" he asks.

I wait for the Firstblade to look in my direction. He has no reason to protect Red—he never even wanted him here. Returning him to the Federation in order to avoid this siege would be the wisest choice.

My hands rest on the hilts of my swords. Aramin will tell Red to step forward. What will I do, then? Why should I keep protecting someone who has been nothing but a punishment for me? I could step aside and expose Red, allow him to be taken back to the Federation. And good riddance. He has no desire to live, anyway, has shown nothing but scorn for me for saving him.

The Firstblade is quiet for only a moment. When he speaks again, though, he doesn't look our way. "Your deserters are your business," he says. "Get your soldiers off our land and back over the warfront. This is your last warning."

The Premier gives him a humorless smile. "No, Firstblade," he replies. "I think I will do the warning. I will give you another chance to return the Federation property you owe us. Think hard."

He shifts, moving his gelding forward, and the clanking chains of his Ghosts make the beasts snarl, snapping their jaws hungrily in our direction. The Premier stares at us all in the darkness, searching for the face he's come to retrieve. Red stays motionless.

The Firstblade is silent, and for a moment, I think he will point his sword in our direction. But he never does. Instead, he calls out, "You are in our land now, not yours. We don't follow the orders of a foreign ruler."

"It will be easier for Mara if you do, you know," the Premier says with a sigh. "You've seen the ruins of those who came millennia before us. I took a vow never to let that happen to Karensa." He nods around at us. "Your people are slowly starving to death in this tiny country. Why do you want them to keep suffering? We are powerful and organized, have strived to build a society so strong that it will never crumble. It will be better for your people if you just step aside."

The Firstblade straightens the lapels of his coat. He remains calm in his movements, but I can see that furious light appear in his eyes, the sign of an inevitable battle to come. "If your Federation is so powerful," he says, "and we are so weak, then why do you even bother?" His teeth flash with his smile. "Or do you still fear Mara? Perhaps we're not as small as you think."

A hint of annoyance shows on the Premier's face. "We are the rightful heirs to the Early Ones," he says. "But unlike them, there will never be ruins of Karensa. We were always meant to inherit their Infinite Destiny."

The Firstblade nods in the direction of the line of Ghosts. "Then come get your precious destiny."

Constantine doesn't look surprised. He just shakes his head. "So be it," he says.

Then he releases his Ghosts from their chains.

The realization surges through me. We are going to die here tonight.

Adena takes in the scene with a sense of eerie calm. The same thoughts must have occurred to her too, just as they must have occurred to every single one of us. But she doesn't show it on her face.

Beside her, Jeran—the same boy who had just been blushing earlier about his cooking—has already pulled on his black mask.

I pull on mine too. Beside me, Red shifts closer—and for an instant, I think he's going to attack me with his chains. But he doesn't make a move. Instead, his stance is turned in the direction of the Federation's troops, and his eyes have narrowed in rage. He casts me a single, steady look.

I twist my blade toward his chains. He flinches before he realizes that I'm freeing him. With two slices, the chain comes apart, and his arms snap free. I cut him loose from his leg bounds too.

He gives me a blank stare, as if not quite willing to believe that I've released him. And for an instant, I wonder if it's a stupid idea.

Then, he gives me a single nod. I return it, relishing this tiny moment where we can understand each other. If we're going to die here tonight, it doesn't make much difference whether my prisoner is shackled or not. Maybe he'll even fight alongside me.

It's the only thought I have time for. Then we fan out into an attack and charge straight into the jaws of death.

Adena is the first to reach a Ghost. She yanks out both her swords, twisting their hilts together so that they combine into a single deadly weapon—then she twirls it in an arc that cuts straight through the Ghost's front leg. As the creature topples forward, she untwists the swords and lands two heavy blows against the protective shackle clipped around its neck.

The injured Ghost is still frighteningly fast. It whips its head around and snaps its jaws at her. But Jeran wastes no time. In a single fluid move, he darts onto the injured Ghost's shoulder, swings up to its back, and yanks out his daggers. He stabs it before the Ghost even realizes it is fatally injured. As it falls, Jeran leaps from its body. His slender figure lands on the shoulders of another Ghost coming up from behind Adena. He crouches on its head, crosses his arms, and brings both daggers straight into the creature. It shrieks, trying in vain to throw him off. There is no sign of Jeran's sweet smile here, his gentle concern. He hangs on mercilessly. Adena whirls around and fires her gun at the Ghost's neck shackle. The bullet cracks it with a clang.

Nearby, Tomm and Pira press their backs together, guns out, and fire in a circle. But even as they cut their way through the monsters as fast as they can, more lurch toward us.

I crane my neck, searching for the Premier again. He's no fool on the battlefield—and that means he knows not to be in the thick of the fighting. Still, I look for him, hoping to have a chance to cut him down.

But he's nowhere to be seen.

I wave at Red to come with me, then sprint up the hill to the thick of the fighting. The ruins of the Seven Sisters rises ominous in the night, jagged black teeth of steel, seven tall and thin skeletons that tower above the seething masses of bodies. As I go, I pause at a Maran soldier who's been bitten by a Ghost. Without hesitating, I slash a blade at his throat. He lets out a startled gurgle. I don't dare stop to look at him. I just run on.

Beside me, Red's jaw is clenched hard. Our movements aren't synced in the way the others are—he is harsh and blunt in his attacks, uncoordinated, as if out of practice. We look like nothing more than a pair of people with absolutely nothing in common except the desperate will to survive.

I try to understand what kind of fighting style this is. He's stiff in a way that tells me he hasn't seen much open combat, but his movements are as quick and dangerous as they'd been during our practice spar. Had he trained at all in the Federation? Maybe he had only been a recruit and never seen a real battlefield. That would explain the awkward nature of his motions, like some kind of fledgling bird.

A Ghost comes charging without warning over the crest of the hill toward him. He turns in its direction, but I'm already moving, my gun hoisted. I fire three shots into its face and another round into its neck shackle. In the same gesture, I grab Red's hand and pull him behind one of the metal ruins. The Ghost, temporarily blinded, charges right over us. I stab a sword into its stomach as it goes. It flinches, rolling over and taking me with it. As it falls onto its side, I slash deep into its exposed neck.

There are at least three more hunting us. I haul myself up the side of the ruins, my feet finding shallow dents against the metal as I hop up to higher ground. Red presses himself into the shadows below. Another Ghost circles around us, listening for the sound of my boots scraping against the structure, but my steps are silent. It snarls, stalking away from me for a moment and turning its attention toward another part of the ruins. I reach down and seize Red by the wrist. His head jerks toward me, and our eyes meet.

I try to pull him up as quickly as I can, but he's even heavier than I imagined, his body a solid brick. He gives a mighty leap and joins me. His eyes sweep the scene of carnage around us. There are Strikers being taken down everywhere, their throats clawed out, mouths open in dying screams. Red's teeth are bared, and his grip against the metal ruin is so tight that his knuckles look like they might tear right through his skin.

I get a good look at the Ghost circling below us, its wild eyes, the teeth splitting its once-human face from ear to ear. Then I launch from the top of the wreck onto the creature's back. Before it can throw me off, I'm prying underneath its iron collar and jamming a dagger deep into its rotting flesh.

It whirls so hard that it throws me completely off, slamming me into a ruin. Stars erupt in my head. My ankle twists in a strange way and pain lances up my leg. Red leaps from the top of the ruins and attacks one of the Ghosts, but he's too far away to get to me in time. Four Ghosts close in on me, their jaws grinding, sensing victory.

The same scene is playing out all around us. The gate has collapsed at the defense compound. A battalion of scarlet-clad Karensan soldiers march through the inferno. Our dead are littered everywhere.

A stillness washes over me. My gaze settles helplessly on the monsters that twitch toward me now. I wonder if this is what Corian had felt when he realized it was too late. I wonder how bad the pain will be when a Ghost's fangs break my skin, when it tears my flesh until its poisons flood my own veins.

It occurs to me that I will never see my mother again. Strange; my next thought is that I wish I'd stopped to have tea with her.

The Ghosts stalk closer. I brace myself, ready to fight to the end. My vision blurs.

That's when I realize Red is no longer where I saw him last. He has vanished. I blink in the haze of night, searching for his silhouette. Maybe he's taken the opportunity to leave me behind and make his escape, test his luck elsewhere. It would be smart of him, something I might have done in his position. Or maybe he's even fooled us all and decided to surrender to the Federation, take his chances by begging forgiveness from his Premier. Maybe a Ghost had grabbed him—

A blast of wind cuts off my thoughts.

An impact shakes the ground so hard that I'm thrown to my knees. The shudder of it rattles my teeth. *An earthquake*, goes my first thought, like one I'd felt back in Basea that had rocked our entire house, leaving us to run out the door in terror. The world beneath me cracks and caves in, as if from a mighty force.

Something powerful lands behind me.

I flinch, dagger clutched so tightly in my fist that my fingers feel like they might break, ready to stab the creature about to attack me.

But when I glance behind me, I don't see rotting, ashen limbs—instead, I see the outline of a mighty figure in the night, black steel extending from either side of his back.

It's Red.

Except he is almost unrecognizable.

He crouches right behind me, close enough that his shoulder brushes mine. I have no idea how he reached me this quickly. His once-dark eyes now glow such a bright silver white that I can see neither pupil nor iris. Just light and fury. A low, inhuman growl rumbles in the back of his throat, and his teeth are bared, flashing a ferocious white.

And from his back . . . arch a pair of enormous black wings formed from blades of steel. They are the most massive things I've ever seen, easily forty feet wide, spread to form a protective shield on either side of us.

In ancient stories we salvaged from the Early Ones, there are mentions of figures called angels. They were mythical, winged humans, an order of armored supernatural beings that served some almighty god. Creatures with the power to both protect mankind and rain down destruction. Above all, the Early Ones seemed to believe in them as guardians. Warriors. Beings of incredible beauty, meant to be loved and feared.

It is the first thought that comes to me now. An angel of death.

For an instant, I think Red is finally going to reveal his true Federation nature. He is going to kill me.

Then I realize his face is turned toward the Ghosts, and his expression is that of sheer hatred. He hovers over me in a protective stance. I am a Striker, trained never to freeze in combat like a deer lost in its own panic—but now I do, unsure what I'm witnessing. Who do I defend myself from? The Ghosts, or him? Is he about to help me? With a jolt of terror, I finally remember what he said the Federation called him.

Skyhunter.

Their experiment. Their weapon of war.

He attacks.

I've trained with the most elite warriors of Mara since I was twelve years old. I have seen Strikers and soldiers alike cut down their enemies without mercy. I am not naïve about what we are capable of doing to one another in war.

But never in my life have I seen an attack like what he unleashes.

He moves like a bolt of lightning. I can barely see him through the blur of motion. The force of him launching forward at the Ghosts is so strong that the wind knocks me to my knees. The black blades of his enormous wings slice clean through the nearest Ghost as if it were made of soft clay, cutting the creature into bloody ribbons of flesh. He twists and shears through a second. A third. The Ghosts, riled up, scream and turn toward him, but they barely have time to blink before he cuts through them again. The tang of blood fills the air.

A Ghost towering a dozen feet high lunges at him. It doesn't even have the chance to open its jaws before he pushes his wings down. He surges into the air and spins. His wings expand to its terrifying span and then cut straight into the Ghost.

Like it's made of nothing. Like it's a ghost of the air.

He decapitates it and shreds the body into pieces. Across the battle-field, he soars and dips, expanding his wings and then contracting them like a falcon on the hunt, diving through packs of Ghosts, destroying them, littering the field with their blood. Federation soldiers in his way are slaughtered like sheep. Their terrified screams reach my ears.

I find my feet again. As Red—the Skyhunter—continues his rampage, I leap up and pull out my blades. They flash through the air, cutting, slicing, finding new life as I follow his path and make my way through enemy lines. A strange fervor hums through me. Miraculously, I can see Red scattering the Federation's forces, splitting their formations and sending them fleeing in confused clusters, right into the paths of our waiting soldiers and Strikers.

My body moves in a rhythm of its own, following the instincts that come with years of training. I fight my way back to where Adena and Jeran are pushing against a tide of Federation soldiers. The soldiers shrink away, knowing the reputation that comes with our sapphire coats, but Adena is in the throes of battle frenzy, her eyes alight with the fire of potential victory. Beside her, Jeran moves in sync with her every attack, his jaw clenched and movements lithe.

I can feel the tide of change in our moods. Before us, we cut through their troops like a scythe through wheat. The Ghosts are few now. The ones left are being called to retreat. A short distance from us, I see Red dive into a battalion of Federation soldiers. Blood follows in his wake.

And then I hear it. The horn echoes across the valley, the Federation's call to stand down.

A roar goes up from our soldiers. New strength rushes through my veins, and I throw myself into every cut and thrust, every spin and crouch. Their soldiers are retreating. Our men pursue them.

In the midst of our wild joy, I pause to see Red crouched in the middle of a bloodstained field. My elation trembles.

He is surrounded by our own soldiers, but he bares his teeth at any who attempt to come close to him. His eyes are still drowned in that silver-white light, so that there is no expression on him except pure rage. His fingers claw long lines into the dirt. His giant wings drip with blood. When he shifts, those wings move with him. The soldiers around him dart away like a school of fish, only to come back with their raised spears.

"You have to stop him," Jeran says, materializing silently beside me. His face is streaked with blood and dirt, and in this fiery night, it's hard to see the softhearted boy I know so well. "They're trying to rein him in. I don't think he can tell that they're Marans."

He's going to kill them. I break into a run, then slow as I reach the circle of soldiers surrounding him. His eyes dart from silhouette to silhouette, still glowing with white-hot fury. I don't know how much of them he can see. Perhaps everything looks like a smear of monsters to him.

There is no Striker training for this. No precedent I can draw on for pulling your Shield out of a trance. He hasn't known me long enough to recognize my gestures and habits. He might not even be able to recognize me if I approach him.

But I still turn toward Red and start to take steady steps in his direction. His glowing eyes snap to my moving figure. A low snarl comes from his throat, and his crouch tightens.

"Red," I sign to him. I pause, point to myself and sign, "Talin." Then, "Friend."

The other soldiers back away at my approach, their eyes wide. I know they think this is suicide. They may be right.

I stop again to repeat the signs I'd once taught him. "Red. Talin. Friend."

My head feels light. I barely know this prisoner. But I have given him my oath. He has saved my life, there by the ruins, when the Ghosts closed in and I knew all might be lost. I am sworn, until death parts us, to protect him, to lay down my life for him, to be there when he needs me. So I continue on. My hands are empty of weapons. The world around me seems to still and slow.

He watches me, his fingers digging against the earth. But he doesn't move. His wings arc black against the night sky.

I step closer and closer, until finally I stop a mere foot away from his crouched figure.

Everything about him screams of death. But my heart is steady, and I don't feel afraid. I take a knee before him, completely vulnerable to his steel wings, then remove my glove and press my hand gently against his tightened fist on the ground. His skin feels hot enough to burn.

His eyes turn narrower. He looks like he's going to attack.

"It's me," I sign to him, knowing he can't understand me, knowing I have no language I can use to speak to him. But I keep trying. "You can come back now."

He stares at me with his burning eyes. I wait for him to strike me, for those bladed wings to cut into my flesh. But he stays still.

"You can come back now," I sign again, gentler.

Then, gradually, the glow of his eyes begins to fade. His dark irises come back into view. For the first time, I realize that they are not black at all, but a deep blue, slashed with metallic gray. His wings droop, still dripping scarlet, their metal tips dragging lines against the dirt as they start to fold into themselves. Slowly, slowly, his posture loosens. As his wings retract entirely, slicing more lines into the shredded back of his coat, he blinks once, twice, then meets my gaze directly.

The light of rage fades from his eyes. He recognizes me.

Suddenly, his hands come up toward my face. Before I can stop him, he presses his palms against my cheeks and pulls me forward, so that my forehead touches his. His eyes close.

I try to pull away, but he holds us firmly together, and my body feels frozen in place, locked with his in an unbreakable grip.

A searing brightness in my head engulfs everything.

I wince and squeeze my eyes shut—but it feels like it's coming from *within* me, this overwhelming light. Pain lances through my body. The brightness feels white hot, so harsh that it's burning a hole through my mind. I gasp, trembling. It floods every inch of me before it settles into a narrow band that links me with him.

And all of a sudden, I witness a blur of landscapes. The glass walls of a room. A woman in a white coat and shining glasses, leaning over me while I'm strapped to a strange table draped in cloth. A lush garden with a man and a girl. A dense, foreign mass of buildings, all built in a series of circles. The Federation. A forest rushing around me as I run desperately through the trees, my throat dry with fear. And a grief so deep and yawning that it threatens to engulf my entire being.

Somehow, I know these are Red's memories. His thoughts. His emotions.

As if my mind has been cut open and flooded with glasslike clarity.

Red releases me. The painful brightness fades in an instant, replaced by what feels like the tug of a string connecting me with him.

What has happened between us?

I stumble backward. When I glance up, I see the Premier's horse silhouetted against the top of the hill, his figure turned in our direction. The heat from the flames distort the air around him, framing him in a halo of gold. He knows now that we have his weapon.

Red falters in exhaustion, then collapses to the ground. I'm at his side in a second. As the other soldiers step cautiously forward, I pull his head into my arms and hold him there. His eyes are closed. When I look up again to where the Premier had been, he's gone.

The strange link between Red and me pulses like a living thing. And as I stare at his blood-streaked face, I know. I know as surely as I can smell the sting of war in the air, as surely as the fire roars against the night. The Firstblade's words from days earlier come back to me now: *We need a miracle.*

He is it.

The miracle.

He is the weapon we have been waiting for.

10

THERE ARE NO CHEERS.

We may have forced the Federation to retreat, but nothing about this night is worth celebrating. We've lost two defense compounds. Our warfront has been pushed farther back. Our own defense compound is destroyed, the gates burned and blackened. The valley around us is littered with our dead.

I make my way into the fields where the main battle happened. Everyone is at work—black silhouettes fill the firelit night, clearing the space of their fallen friends. Blood has soaked deep into the earth, and the tang of its coppery smell hangs in the air like a cloud of death.

Nearby, two soldiers are holding down a Striker. Right away, I know what's happened. The Striker has been bitten by a Ghost. She's crying. Already her limbs are trembling with an unnatural strength.

My heart sits heavily in my chest as I watch the soldiers restraining her call for a Striker's help.

I recognize Jeran and Adena as they head to the scene. Jeran's slender figure is straight and unerring, his face grave with resolution. As he goes, he draws a sword with a single flourish. Adena walks in step beside him. The wounded Striker sees their long blue coats approach and starts to scramble furiously against the ground. She knows what comes next.

Jeran stops before her. For an instant, he bows his head and closes his eyes, bracing himself. Then he slashes his sword down in an arc.

It's a mercifully precise strike. The injured Striker trembles once, every muscle tight, and then slumps against the ground. Jeran nods to the two who had held her down. He looks exhausted, far too young to be bearing this, and when he turns away, Adena holds out an arm to make sure he doesn't fall.

I look down and help another Striker hoist a body into the wagon. Elsewhere, I can hear the Firstblade as he does a survey of our dead and injured, how much land we've ceded.

For a while, I lose myself in the work of clearing the fields. There are more who must be executed because they've been bitten by Ghosts, while others are given lethal doses of a tonic when it's obvious that their wounds are too great to bear.

Finally, as the blackness of the night sky gives way to a pale gray, I see the Firstblade striding toward me. He nods when our eyes meet.

"Talin," Aramin greets me, nodding toward the compound. His cheeks are streaked black with dried blood. "Your Shield is starting to stir. We can finish up out here. See to him."

Red had been brought to the makeshift infirmary hours ago. For the first time, hearing the Firstblade call him my Shield feels less like a jest and more like a formal command. Binding us together.

I bow my head and tap my fist to my chest.

Aramin lifts his head and surveys the field, ultimately settling his gaze on the ravaged compound's ramparts. "When he wakes up and starts to talk, tell me," he finally says. "Everyone wants to understand what happened tonight." He's quiet for a moment, and I wonder if there's an apology in that silence, his way of telling me that I was right to have saved Red's life. Then he asks, "Did he mention anything to you about his abilities?"

I shake my head.

"I've never seen anyone fight like that in my life," he mutters, and in this moment, he sounds less like the Firstblade and more like the fellow Striker we all used to train with. "He didn't even look human."

It's the same thought I had when I watched Red cutting through the Ghosts like they were made of nothing. Still, I stop short of nodding in agreement. His expression when he finally snapped out of his rage, when he blinked up at me in confusion before collapsing. That was *him*, the boy inside the war machine.

"I'll let you know when he's up," I sign, turning in the direction of the compound. "I'm not convinced he himself understands everything that happened."

As I go, I can feel Aramin's eyes on my back. He doesn't trust Red. I'm not sure if I do, either.

The infirmary is actually the compound's courtyard, now a mess of makeshift blankets lined up on the ground and ripped strips of cloth stained crimson. The low din of moans and sobs swirls around me.

Red is held in a separate room, a former officer's quarters at the back of the infirmary. The first thing I notice when I walk in is that they have chains on him again. Shackles sit heavy on his wrists and ankles, anchored to weights even as he lies on his side, unconscious on a cot. It makes me wonder whether he's done something in my absence that frightened the nurses.

I move without a sound to him. They've removed his ruined coat so that he lies in his tunic, the sleeves rolled up, the back of it cut up from his wings expanding and retracting on the battlefield. Now those wings are completely retracted into two slender strips of metal running flat against his back. He moves in a restless sleep, his fingers twitching slightly, his eyes shifting beneath their lids. His lashes rest long and dark against his cheeks. His hair, dark and tangled, fans out in a halo on the floor. A sheen of sweat gleams wherever his real skin is exposed, but he's shivering enough to make his chains clink.

Here, he doesn't look like the Skyhunter, the weapon I'd seen sweeping the skies, raining death down on any near him. He doesn't even look like the cold, suspicious prisoner I'd first met in the arena. He looks young and very human, in danger of breaking if bent too far.

I kneel beside him, then remove my coat. It's bloodstained, but at least it's warm. I drape it over his trembling body. As I do, my hand accidentally brushes against the skin of his neck.

He's burning with fever. I lift my hand, then tentatively touch his shoulder, where the black armor begins. Instantly, I jerk away. It feels so hot that it could scald me. In fact, when I look down at my finger, I see a red mark, as if I'd just pressed it against the stove in my mother's home.

I stare at Red's unconscious form in disbelief. Heat like this feels as if it should burn skin—but he seems completely unaffected. I pull my coat off him, wondering if the fabric will catch fire. As I do, something shuffles in his shirt pocket, and moments later his mouse pokes its head out and scampers down his body onto the floor.

The sight of the creature makes me smile in surprise. Had this thing been with him during the entire battle, hanging on for dear life inside his pocket? A survivor. In spite of myself, I reach out to rub its head. It lets me, leaning into my touch with its eyes closed.

Our movements finally make Red stir. His eyes flutter open, and I find myself staring down at the silver slashes in his irises. He looks back, brows furrowed. The mouse rushes up into his pocket.

Immediately, the strange feeling of clarity rushes through my head again, like the sensation of focusing down a bright, narrow tunnel. I wince instinctively.

Red squints with the same expression.

What I'd felt on the battlefield. The fragments of my memory, the moment when he reached for me and I felt the sear of a bond between us, linking our minds together like a bridge.

He tries to get up. His shackles clank loudly. He yanks on his chains, pulling them taut—a panicked light suddenly appears in his eyes. To my surprise, I can feel a trickle of that panic through our link, as surely as if the emotion were mine, followed by a rush of fragmented thoughts. In them, I think I hear a word or two—but it all sounds like a cacophony of noise.

I reach out to touch his hand, then shake my head at him. He turns wild eyes on me.

"The Federation," he breathes. "The Federation." It's all he can say, so he keeps repeating it at me, the words turning more urgent as he goes.

I squeeze his hand and gesture for him to lie back down. Then I shake my head, smile a little, and point at myself, trying to tell him he's still in Mara. Still with me.

"Talin," I sign at myself. "Red." I point at him. "Friend."

For an instant, I don't think he understands me. But his eyes settle on my moving hands as I repeat the words. A flicker of recognition appears on his face at my name. Then he finally sees who I am. His muscles gradually loosen. The wild panic on his face fades into exhaustion, and he collapses back onto his cot.

Perhaps he thought he'd somehow ended up back in his experimental chambers in the Federation. The way he reacted to the chains . . . maybe they kept him in shackles there.

A moment later, his head turns back toward me. His eyes go to the scarlet stains on my coat.

I give him a wry smile. "Not my blood," I sign, not expecting him to know what I said. "I'm too good a Striker for that." A part of me wants to go fetch Jeran and have him translate for us again, although Jeran must be in no mood for our company right now.

A rush of warmth comes through the bond between me and Red. Somehow, I *sense* him understand my words. He opens his mouth and responds in Karenese—but at the same time, I hear his response in my mind, something I understand so deeply and instinctively that it feels like I'm reading my own thoughts.

You look different, he's saying. *Without your Striker coat.*

I don't know how it works.

I can't begin to describe why I understand him without comprehending Karenese.

But through the new bond between us, I *know* what he's saying to me, as if his mind had fused with my own. All I can do is stare back at him, unsure how to react, stunned into complete silence.

"What did you do to me?" I finally manage to sign to him.

He lifts a hand, chains clacking, and taps his temple with a finger. *You don't need to sign to me anymore*, he says. *Think your words. I can hear you in my mind.*

It is his voice, except his lips don't move at all. Instead of hearing him out loud, his words echo inside my head, a trickle of his emotions accompanying it.

I stare at him, disbelieving. Then I tentatively try to do the same thing.

This is impossible, I think to him, my hands still moving unconsciously to sign the words.

Nothing is impossible, he responds in my mind.

Tears spring unbidden to my eyes.

The last time I'd ever said anything to anyone, I was eight years old and my mother was beside my sickbed in Newage, where we'd been sent to after we fled into Mara. She was holding my hand as I croaked to her, blood running from my nose, lungs seizing with dry coughs, blisters searing the skin on my face and arms. "I'm so sorry. I'm so sorry. I'm so sorry." Those were my last spoken words to my mother. I can't remember why I said it, what I'd been so sorry for. My eyes had darted wildly around, hoping to see my father walk through the door. He would have put a hand against my forehead and chuckled apologetically, say he hadn't meant to lose us in the mass exodus out of Basea. That he'd been right behind us. But he never appeared. And the next morning, I'd woken up silent.

I've gone so long without speech to communicate that I rarely think about it anymore. I spend my days in silence, signing to those who understand, steering clear of those who don't.

But here he is, Red, the Skyhunter, answering words that I merely think in my head, his voice so clear in my mind that it's as if I'd thought them myself.

And just like how he's able to catch a glimpse of my thoughts and memories, I now see something of his—a boy in a chamber made entirely of glass and metal, fiddling desperately with shackles on his wrists, screaming and screaming and screaming.

The image is there and gone in my head, so rapid that I wonder if I'd just imagined it.

How . . . ? I start to think, still unsure if my thought is being carried to him. But he seems to hear me as clearly as if I'd spoken or signed the word, because he nods and takes a deep breath.

In order to control their human weapons of war, he explains, *the Federation bonds with them through a mind link. It connects their mind to that of the Premier himself, who can control them.*

Again, I understand his words, even though I shouldn't. Again, I can hear his voice—deep, gritty like the salt of the sea—in my mind, as clearly as my own thoughts.

A bond with their Ghosts. A war experiment.

Are you saying you've bonded with me? I think to him.

The comprehension on his face reminds me so painfully of the way I felt when Corian had first signed to me outside the arena that I have to suck in my breath to calm myself. Red's expression changes to match my sudden wave of grief. He stares at me, and in a flash, I know that he has somehow managed to see the memory that I just conjured in my head, has managed to feel my rush of pain.

Your Shield? he asks.

I tighten my jaw, unwilling to discuss Corian with him. *Why does the Federation create this bond with their Ghosts?* I think instead.

To make their Ghosts obey, Red answers. *Attacking anyone from the Federation would feel like attacking themselves. Even if the Premier dies, the power of his mind stays, lingering in the Ghost as if the Premier's thoughts are its own.*

For decades, Mara has tried to explain how the Federation manages to keep their Ghosts from attacking their own troops. We have tortured captured Ghosts, cutting them open in an attempt to understand. Dozens of shops in the Grid are dedicated to trying to unlock this secret, whether by testing Ghost blood against that of humans or mixing the two in an attempt to find an antidote. And here, right in front of me, is the answer.

The Federation's Premier quite literally invades their minds.

But you're not a Ghost, I tell him.

I'm something worse. A new war experiment.

The thought sends such a shudder through me as I shrink away from Red. *And do you control me now?* I ask him, suddenly suspicious. *Did you link me to your Premier?*

He's not my *Premier*, he answers sharply, his eyes flashing. Then he softens and adds, *I'm his war machine. Others cannot obey me. I was supposed to obey the Premier.* He looks away from me. *Except they didn't finish working on me before I escaped. My link was only created, not bonded. Then I touched you on the battlefield . . .*

His voice trails off in my mind. He doesn't say it, but I understand. He's bonded with me.

Why me? I ask.

He hesitates for a long moment. *I don't know how it happened*, he says slowly, *but I think my mind needed to connect with someone who would be willing to understand.* Someone willing to understand him. He was crying out for help, I realize, and in his need, he reached out to me.

Engineered to obey the Federation through a bond. The Ghosts shackled during the battle until they were ready to be unleashed, the chains hanging from their necks—none of it was necessary. Ghosts are designed to not attack their masters.

Is Red the same? He was supposed to be bound with the same link. Except it hadn't worked.

The thought plays again in my mind, lighting sparks in the darkness. I hurriedly wipe the tears from my eyes and stare at Red. He fled before they could properly bind him to the Federation. And he has given to me the bond that he should have had with the Premier.

I picture Red racing through the Federation's capital, hiding in their alleys and then in their woods, surviving on his own as soldiers and Ghosts alike are sent to hunt him down. No—I correct myself—not Ghosts.

What if the Premier had recaptured Red? He would have taken Red back, and Red would have been his to command. But they hadn't linked. Red has bound himself to me instead, and now I have a direct bridge into the mind of a Federation creation who, for the first time I know of, doesn't obey.

If he can avoid being attacked by Ghosts, and if the Federation is capable of failing to bind Red to them, then it means their method for controlling their Ghosts isn't foolproof. It means that, somehow, there's a way to sever whatever bond they have with their creations. There's a way to stop them, and Red might be the key.

And now the Federation knows that Red has fallen into their enemy's hands. It's no wonder that the Premier himself came to hunt him down. They're afraid they've just handed their greatest weakness to us.

Did we win tonight? Red asks, his voice echoing in my mind and cutting through my whirlwind of thoughts.

I nod. How much of what I'm thinking can he sense? How much does he know? *We didn't lose,* I reply. *But our defense compound is severely damaged.*

He's quiet. There's another question hovering in his eyes, but he doesn't want to say it. I observe him, guessing at what it must be.

What did I do? he finally asks.

I think about not telling him. He's still recovering, after all. But when he gives me a meaningful stare, I find myself taking a seat on the floor beside his cot.

Do you remember anything about the battle? I ask him.

No.

The only reason we won was because of you.

His lips tighten, and he seems to sink back into himself, as if it were his way of retreating from a situation he doesn't want to be in. *Why?*

I try to recount what I'd seen. His wings. The light that consumed his eyes. The way he'd cut down the enemies around him like they were paper dolls. And then . . . how he couldn't stop, even when our soldiers surrounded him in the end.

You didn't attack our soldiers, I add. *You may not remember what you did, but you seemed able to understand which side of the battle you were on.*

I don't know if this is entirely true. Before he sank into my arms, his furious eyes and bared teeth had been directed at our men surrounding him. If I hadn't approached him, would he have cut them down too? Would Jeran and Adena and the rest of my patrol be lying dead in the grass right now, their bodies drenched in blood?

Finally, I tell him about the way he'd put his hands on either side of my face, how we'd touched foreheads and felt the burst of this bond between us.

His brows furrow, his eyes lost in thought. Does he remember any of it, the moment when he finally came out of his trance? Does he remember me walking toward him with my hands outstretched, the way he'd collapsed against me?

They are making others like me, he suddenly says. Tears glint in his eyes with a feverish light. I watch him take breath after shallow breath. *In their labs.*

Others. There are others in the Federation like him, who can rain down death such that the world has never seen. The fear of it claws deep into the folds of my stomach, sending a ripple of nausea through me.

Red had said that they never finished experimenting on him before he escaped. What will happen when the other Skyhunters are finished and fully equipped, their bonds to the Federation tight and uncompromising? How will any of us stand a chance?

The link between us pulses again, and suddenly I glimpse a few faces. An older man with deep-set eyes and a worried slant to his lips. A young girl, running through the grass. And Red, staring at a faint reflection against a glass wall. Some of the same images I'd seen flashing through my mind when he'd first touched my face, except now I understand what they are.

His father. His sister. I know this without hesitation through our link, as if the memory were my own.

What happened to them? I ask, dreading the answer.

Red doesn't reply this time, but the pain that comes through our bond now claws at my heart, ripping it open, filling it with the weight of grief and shame and failure. He won't say what happened to them. All I know is that this is the reason he didn't want to live, why he had despaired so much that he was willing to be executed in the Striker arena. This is the source of the haunting look in his eyes, the anguish burning deep in him.

I stare down at this weapon we have been handed, this young man who in many ways is still a boy. And in that moment, I know I must do everything in my power to protect him.

Red has started to shiver again. Even the little he's told me seems to have taken everything out of him, and already he seems to be sinking back into an uneasy sleep.

If the others come to check on him and notice him awake, they're going to want to interrogate him. More than that. He will be brought before the Firstblade, the Senate, and the Speaker. They may run tests on him. I can already hear the Speaker's command to send Red out immediately to fight at the warfront. Will they have the patience to understand this bond we have? Or will they consider him too great a threat to use? Will they want him dead?

Maybe there's a way we can help each other, I tell him. *But first, rest. We can talk more in a few hours.*

I pull my coat back over his body, and then start to get up.

His hand shoots up without warning and grabs my wrist. His skin is still feverishly hot. When I glance at his face, that undercurrent of panic has reappeared in his eyes.

Stay, he whispers in my mind, his voice hoarse with a sudden terror that I can't explain. *Please. Just for a while.*

I may not have known him for long—I'm not even sure if I like him—but I recognize everything about the fear now roiling in him. It's the way I'd felt in the months and years after my mother and I fled into Mara, the way I'd bolt awake in the middle of the night at the slightest sound, certain that the Federation's soldiers were breaking down our door. It's the way I'd stumble out of our shack to retch into the grass whenever I smelled smoke from the stove, because I thought it was the Federation lighting houses on fire, setting dead and living bodies alike aflame. It's the way I'd cling to my mother, crying, until she finally rocked me to sleep.

His fear is the same as mine, and it never really goes away.

I settle back down beside him, my hand still in his, and nod once without a word. The heat of his skin seeps into my palm. My eyes linger on his face, his dark, bloody lashes, the curve of his lips. The brows that stay knotted even in rest, never at peace. There is a beauty about him, in the same way that the Early Ones must have imagined their angels. I study him in wonder, my cheeks flushed. He mumbles as he drifts off. Whatever he's saying, he doesn't send it through our bond—but keeps repeating it as a mantra to himself until he slips gradually into sleep again. And I find myself thinking about whether ancient angels were actually real or not, and whether they were the reason the Early Ones vanished.

11

I STAY BESIDE HIM FOR SOME TIME AFTER HE
falls back into a fitful asleep. Everything about him seems enhanced now through our link, as if I'm seeing him clearly for the first time. He moves restlessly, his fingers twitching, his eyes shifting beneath their lids in an endless dream. He murmurs a feverish string of Karenese words.

"A hall with no end," he whispers. The language still sounds foreign to my ears, but through our bond, I know what they mean. "A day to live. A million ways to bridge the rift." He repeats this over and over again until it feels engraved into my memory.

The bond between us pulses steadily as he rests. I don't see his dreams, but I can feel the unease that seems to churn forever in him, the kind borne from a lifetime of fear. Now and then, a glimmer of his unconscious thoughts even seems to trickle through. I stare at him, trying to understand this new bond between us, until his eyes finally stop moving underneath their lids and he has fallen into a steady sleep.

At last, I force myself to stand and leave his side, then step out of the building. Every part of my body aches from the fight. Our link fades slightly, settling into a steady presence at the back of my mind. I glance back at him one last time before I head out of the compound.

With the dawn, the bite of winter eases slightly against my cheeks and lips. I turn my face up to the compound's fire-scorched ramparts, where tiny figures sitting along its ledge are outlined against the sky. The others must have headed up there. It's become a common ritual after each one of the Federation's sieges.

I sigh and run a hand through my hair, untangling strands knotted with dried blood, and head up toward the ramparts. The farther I go from Red, the fainter our link pulses, until the glimmer of his thoughts is replaced with the beat of his heart and a small, subtle current of his emotions, flickering deep and troubled as he endures his nightmares.

By the time I make my way up, the stars have winked out of existence. Jeran is already here, staring out at the dawning landscape with his arms around his knees, lost in thought. It seems like he's alone, until I spot who I'm looking for: Adena's tall figure perched some distance away on a stone ledge. She's always somewhere nearby, quietly watching over her Shield.

She glances up at me as I walk over to her. Now I notice that she's running the side of one of her daggers against a honing stone until the blade looks fine enough to carve a roast.

"It's one of Jeran's," she tells me as I sit down beside her and nod at the weapon.

I'd expected her to ask me about Red and what the hell happened during the battle. But even though I can see the question in her eyes, she doesn't say it. Maybe she's letting me mention it in my own time.

I nod at her, wishing everyone in the world had her heart. "I saw Jeran at the entrance earlier," I reply. "Saw him forced to cut someone down."

Adena pauses in her motions long enough to stare at the figure of her Shield in the distance. "You know Pietra, the Striker from one of the southern border patrols? Some idiot left a hunting snare intact near the edge of the compound, and poor Pietra stepped in it during the battle. Got stuck and bitten hard by a Ghost." Adena looks away from me and back down at the dagger. "She escaped the snare and got back to the compound by some sheer miracle. But we all could see the Ghost's bite on her. Her Shield had already been killed, so Jeran had to cut her throat."

So that was the Striker I'd seen begging for mercy.

Down below the ramparts, I glimpse the Firstblade surveying the field. He turns his eyes up toward us for a moment, and his gaze catches at the sight of Jeran sitting on his own. I'm too far away to make out Aramin's face, but he stays standing there for a long beat, watching his Striker, until he finally turns away and continues his work.

"Aramin will never say a thing about it," Adena says softly, and I turn my attention back to her. She nods down at the Firstblade. "But he always looks around for Jeran after a battle. To make sure he survived. Sometimes I think he would have been a better Shield for Jeran. He certainly cares enough for him."

"You and Jeran are a perfect match," I tell her.

She finishes working on the blade and switches to signing with me. "I let Jeran cut down Pietra because I couldn't bear to." Her furrowed brows cast a dark shadow over her eyes. "He knows I'm terrified of doing it. So he did it for me. What kind of Striker always makes her Shield carry that burden?"

I lean against my knees and take in the brightening horizon. "We all help each other in different ways."

"I'm a coward," she says, this time aloud.

"You're not," I insist.

"You were able to do what you had to do for Corian," she signs. "I'm afraid that if the time comes, I won't have the courage to do it for Jeran."

"You will." I pause, suddenly haunted by the memory of Corian's final sigh. "But Jeran's the best of us. Maybe you'll never have to."

"Maybe." She glances at me. "Just another day in the life, eh?" She taps on her swords. "The new hilts I designed for my blades? I put them on Jeran's too, and he said they worked like a dream. Let him cut down some of the Ghosts faster than he could have otherwise, and probably saved his life a few times." She forces a smile at me. "I took some notes on a few things I could improve. Remind me to add it to your swords too, Talin, and to your Shield's."

This is Adena sinking into her meticulous habits after a battle. But I don't mention it. I just nod wearily in return while she stares out at the landscape, silently contemplating.

"You know how Marans tend to use the ruins as places to meditate?" she signs after a while. "Like the Seven Sisters? The Morning Rose?"

"You always thought it was a waste of time," I reply.

"I do." Adena rubs her neck. "But sometimes you cope by wasting time, yes? I went anyway, right before we left for the warfront, to meditate in front of the Morning Rose. And the whole time, all I could think about was how meditation or prayer at these sites did absolutely nothing, because all that really matters is being able to steal as much of the Early Ones' technology as possible. That the only way for us to keep pace with the wicked is to do what they do, but better."

"We're not fighting the Federation only to become them, Adena."

"Said every nation before they fell to the Federation," Adena answers bitterly. "I'm going to beat them, Talin. They think they can take what they've learned from the ruins to build their own monsters? I can do it too. I have to invent better weapons, faster. I have to learn how to create like them. I am going to beat them at what they do best. Mara has to, or our dawns like this are numbered."

I stare out at where the first hints of gold have begun outlining the low-lying clouds along the warfront. When I was small, I would wake before my parents, climb out of my bedroom window, and sneak up to the roof of our house in Basea, where I could peek above the tree line and get a glimpse of the lightening morning sky. My father had caught me doing it one dawn. I remember starting an apology, only to see him crawl over to sit next to me on the roof.

What are you doing up here, pup? he'd said to me.

I gave him a sheepish look. *Just watching the clouds light up*, I answered.

He smiled and stared toward the horizon. *Did you know?* he said after a while. *There are a billion, billion, billion suns in the sky.*

The number was too large for me to comprehend. *What do you mean?* I asked.

Every star out there. The Early Ones discovered that. And do you know what that means? He threw a blanket around my shoulders as I shivered in the cool morning air. *There might be another you out there, another me and your ma, staring back at us and wondering the same thing.*

I snuggled closer to him and tried to imagine such a thing. If there was another me, what was her life like? Did she also live in a country fighting a war against a massive enemy? *What if there's no one out there at all?* I asked.

He shrugged and only said, *The world is too big a place for that, don't you think?*

A cold wind whips through my coat, sweeping the memory from my thoughts. After a few minutes, Tomm and Pira arrive to sit up on the ramparts. Others come too, until a smattering of sapphire coats sit along the ledge, here to watch the sun rise over a blood-soaked field.

I wait for Tomm to head over to us and stir trouble, but he doesn't. The two just cast glances in our direction without saying anything. Tomorrow, they will return to their sneers in my direction. Today, though, we sit in a row together and look out at the strengthening morning light, all of us searching for that little bit of peace. I don't know whether we'll have the chance to gather around a campfire and tell one another stories . . . but we, the only thing standing between Mara and the Federation, have survived another night. We've earned another morning where we can line up along the ramparts to watch the sunrise.

Why do I sit out here with them after every battle? Why do I risk my life over and over again for this country that is not my birth country, that still keeps my mother outside its walls, where some of my fellow Strikers call me a rat? My homeland's already gone. Why does this war matter so much to me? The question swirls in my mind, as it always does after a bad night on the warfront, and I spend the quiet moment trying to answer it.

Because Mara, for all its faults, had still taken me in. Because the alternative is the Karensa Federation, swallowing everything and everyone in its path. Because I have witnessed the deepest horrors their soldiers could inflict on other humans, and I've survived, and the reason I've survived is because of this last free nation, one that might soon also collapse. Because right now, we are all just young souls in identical sapphire coats, fighting to hold back the darkness. It has bound me together with them, whether they—or I—like it or not. It has to be the reason I stay.

But how many more sieges can we withstand before Mara falls? Every time, the Federation pushes a little farther into our territory. Someday, they will push past our walls.

Ahead of us, Jeran looks back our way and notices me for the first time. We exchange a wordless nod.

"May there be future dawns," I sign to him.

In this moment, Jeran's expression looks a century old rather than the twenty years he is. But he manages to give me a weary smile. "May there be future dawns," he signs back.

Adena does the same beside me. As she signs, I ponder on her words. Then I think of the link between Red and me, beating steadily between us.

"You say you want to learn how to create like the Federation," I finally tell her. "Well, I think you're about to get your chance."

She casts me a sideways glance. "Why's that?"

"It's about Red. I think we're going to have a problem, and the problem is that everyone is going to want a piece of him when we get back to Newage."

We both stare out at where Jeran sits. Adena doesn't disagree with my statement. After a silence, she signs, "Is the Skyhunter awake yet?"

Not Red. The Skyhunter, the monster she'd witnessed on the battlefield. "He was, briefly," I decide to tell her.

"Did you ask him what the hell happened in that battle?"

I hesitate, wondering how much to admit to Adena. "I did," I sign. "I still don't understand it all, except that he is the next iteration of the Federation's experiments. Red is a weapon of war. He says the Federation is developing others, but he is the first."

"Ah. That's why their Premier came here looking for him."

"The Speaker is going to want to use him immediately to fight in the war."

"Why shouldn't he?"

I hesitate. "Because as deadly as he was on the battlefield, that's not the part of him that will win this war for us."

For the first time, Adena turns her whole body to face me. She's caught something in my gestures. "You've discovered something else about him?" she signs.

I nod. "I don't think Red is just a weapon. I think he's our key to destroying the Ghosts."

12

THE NATIONAL HALL IN NEWAGE IS FESTIVE TO-
night. News of our victory at the warfront has cheered everyone, even
though every Striker knows that it wasn't really a victory at all. The
Federation has pushed farther into our territory. We'd lost dozens of
Strikers and soldiers in the fight.

Still, barely a week after we returned from the warfront, the National
Plaza is crowded with Marans dressed in their finest silks, laughing and
drinking as if death weren't perched right outside our walls. Where an
entire Outer City lies open and vulnerable. Where my mother lives.

"Of course they're celebrating," my mother had told me when I vis-
ited her after our return. "You're still alive, and Mara still stands."

I leaned my cheek against my hand and watched her crush eggshells
into her plants' soil as fertilizer. "Is it standing," I signed at her, "or is it
just falling slowly?"

She frowned at me. "How did I raise such a pessimistic daughter?"
she signed back.

"You raised one who doesn't like cheering when her mother's still
stuck outside the gates."

"Go," she scolded me in Basean. "Celebrate. If Karensa really is going
to march here, you might as well get your food and wine while you can."

"If I didn't know any better, I'd say you want me to be drunk."

"Remember me as a supportive mother."

Now I keep my head down as I head in through the National Hall's front doors. I've been in here before, of course, during banquets and ceremonies where Strikers have been invited, but all my senses are still alert, as if navigating among the wealthy elite of Mara is the same as stalking Ghosts in the narrow passes. The differences are minute.

My hands tug incessantly at the folds of my dress—one of Adena's that she'd lent me from her closets—as I search the crowds for the others. It's pretty, I'll admit, long-sleeved and a lush silky yellow, belted with a wide gold waistband that elongates my figure, and my dark hair is tied up in an elaborate series of braids, dotted throughout with bejeweled combs and dangling jewels. My skin is covered with a thin layer of oils that give it a subtle glow, and my eyes are lined with black powder, emphasizing the green of my irises and the darkness of my lashes. A choker of solid gold rings my throat.

The disguise of a rich Maran. The only element of me that remains true to myself is the Ghost bones studding my ears.

My lips move in a string of silent curses. Why can't Strikers just wear their coats to events like this? Without the weight of my guns and blades, I feel like I've been stripped of everything anchoring me to the ground. The unfamiliar swish of light fabric around my legs makes me scowl.

"I don't understand," I'd told Adena when she made me try on the dress in her room. "I'm sure everyone will take me seriously in my Striker uniform."

"No. You need to look like us," Adena had replied. "Like a rich Maran, not a soldier with enough physical strength to stand up to them. Your uniform will just remind everyone that you somehow managed to defy the Speaker's laws and become a Striker."

"A fancy dress can't hide my face," I signed awkwardly, my arms stuck in the air as Adena yanked the dress down my body.

"I mean, it would help." Adena gestured for me to close my eyes, then brushed my lids with an elegant line of black. "Look—the only people anyone will listen to tonight are other Senators and the wealthy. Make them take you as seriously as possible. Wear the damn dress."

I shake my head, smiling a little at the memory of her determination. Adena had refused to believe Red's connection to me—until, that is, I demonstrated I could understand Red's Karenese, repeating his words in Maran to Jeran's astonishment. Afterward, she paced back and forth across the floor of her Grid shop, while Jeran continued to quiz me. She'd stared so long at Red that he finally had to avert his eyes.

"What do we do now?" Jeran had asked, to no one in particular.

"We have to bring Red before the Speaker," I answered.

Adena whirled on us, the light in her eyes eager and impatient. "The bigger question is, *how* is this possible?" She pointed at me. "Red bonded with you. You bonded with him. He doesn't control you—the Federation must not have gotten to that step. Yes." She seemed like she was talking almost to herself, her words coming more rapidly as she thought. "If we can just figure those steps out, how this anomaly happened, we can stop the Federation. Hells! Can you imagine? Stopping the Federation with their own creation."

"I agree, but he's not our science experiment," I told her.

"He is *literally* a science experiment."

"You know what I mean. He's not *ours*."

I'm no one's. Red's voice had interrupted my thoughts, the tremor of it sending an unpleasant shiver through me.

I frowned at him, unsettled by this new sensation. *Of course not,* I said to him through our link before I signed to everyone. "But the Senate will have their own ideas for what to do with Red, things that probably involve using him for battle as our war machine." I point at Adena. "You and Jeran have to talk them out of it."

"Why do I have to do it?" Adena whined. "I hate talking to politicians."

"Well, they can understand you," I answered wryly. "And, somehow, I think the Speaker will be happier taking advice from other Marans than from a Basean."

"The Speaker will see him as a military weapon," Jeran agreed. "He'll want full control over Red and everything he does."

I nod. "Unless we want the Senate to use Red as their personal attack dog, we need to convince the Speaker that we know what best to do with him. That we can work best with Red to understand how his link works. This is a connection of our minds, not something we can physically see. We can't let them ruin Red before he can help us."

"Well, I'm willing to try anything, because somewhere here," Adena said, swinging a finger back and forth between Red and me, "is the secret to their control over their Ghosts."

As I now wander through the National Hall entrance and enter the courtyard, I hear Adena's words ringing through my head. *Somewhere here is the secret.* This is why we'd come to the National Hall tonight, to seek an audience with the Speaker of the Senate. To tell him how we can still win this war.

I can sense the stares from those passing me by, their eyes darting to the hue of my skin, the cut of my features. Some of the looks are hostile, from those offended by someone like me dressed in such a way. Other glances and smiles are ones of lust, their gazes running over me instead of meeting my eyes.

I think of my mother as I keep my chin high and my walk steady, but I can still feel the burn of unease flushing my cheeks. Has Red arrived already? Should I be able to communicate with him through our link here or do we need to be physically closer to do it? I try sending him a greeting. No response. Maybe he's too far away.

Word about Red's massacre on the battlefield has raced through the nation, and tonight everyone keeps turning their heads as restlessly as a line of birds on the Inner City's walls, keen on catching a glimpse of the so-called Skyhunter. Who is this stranger from the Federation, this weapon of war? I should have arrived at the National Hall with him, but instead he had been held at the hospital, where they are checking every inch of him to ensure he can't hurt the Speaker.

The thought almost makes me laugh. If he wanted to, he could kill the entire Senate before anyone could blink an eye. They didn't witness what I did. They didn't see the light of murder in his eyes that I saw.

Red. He had also been the young man who'd begged me to stay beside him, still weak enough on our return journey to Newage that he swayed heavily in his saddle. I'd finally hooked his steed's harness to mine, then tethered him securely into his saddle and draped a long blanket over him. He'd slept collapsed against his horse until we saw the walls of Newage.

I look down at my hands, now decked out in glittering rings, and flex my fingers, remembering the warmth of my palm tucked into his. Ever since the night after the battle, his face has lingered in my thoughts. I could feel the faint, steady rhythm of his heartbeat during our entire journey back—not from his body but through the strange new link formed between us. Even now, his pulse hums through me like the chirp of a distant cricket. It's a strange sensation, like my mind can see outside of myself, like there is another soul as alive and emotional as me, tethered to my own. He's in the crowds, somewhere. I try again to send him a thought.

"Look. Here she is."

The voice jerks me out of my thoughts.

Several elite Marans have paused in the arched corridor, blocking my path. My eyes dart quickly across their faces—there's Tomm and Pira, the trauma of the warfront now hidden behind a layer of makeup and luxurious robes, their lips settled back into smug curves. A couple of Senators I've never met before. Finally, there's Gabrien, Jeran's older brother. I have to hold back an instinctive grimace. Gabrien gives me a polite smile as he introduces me to the other Senators with him.

"The Basean Striker herself," Gabrien says. He doesn't bother mentioning my name.

I force myself to return his smile with my own stiff one, but my gaze already darts around him, as it always does whenever I know I can't defend myself, trying to find the best possible exit route. Gabrien sees me struggle. From the corner of my eye, I see his smile turn thin, menacing, then delighted as he realizes his opportunity to have some fun.

"It's not a rumor after all!" one of the other Senators exclaims, wagging a finger at me. The woman on his arm laughs, and behind him, his companions let out a chorus of chuckles. "She does exist."

"Some think she is one of our most capable Strikers," Jeran's brother says, his eyes fixed on mine, "although that's said more often by simple minds."

The other Senators murmur, chuckling, at Gabrien's teasing. He knows exactly how close I am with his brother and remembers how I'd shifted protectively toward Jeran that day in the Grid. He is not only sticking a thorn in me, but throwing an insult at his brother for being my friend. When I stare back at Gabrien, I can tell he knows full well how much this bothers me.

Tomm laughs with the others, although Pira simply looks away as if disinterested.

"They say Strikers learn how to dance, don't they, to practice their grace?" another Senator says, looking at Tomm.

He nods. "We do."

"Then perhaps the Basean once danced so well for the Federation's soldiers that they let her live," the Senator suggests mildly. Everyone laughs at the vulgar suggestion.

"A dancer?" The light in Gabrien's eyes turns teasing. "I wouldn't be surprised. She's very lovely." His smile widens at me. "You'll have to show us."

Does he really mean for me to dance for them? I hesitate, and at my pause, the Senators laugh harder. I stay very still, trying to understand the joke.

"I'm bored," Pira announces, irritated at the conversation. She tilts her head at Tomm. "Can't we get something to eat?" Tomm just waves her off, his face still turned eagerly in Gabrien's direction, as if for approval.

"She hasn't said a word," the Senator from earlier chimes in again. "She probably doesn't speak Maran. Perhaps we should go find your brother, Senator Gabrien." She waves a flippant hand toward the rest of the courtyard. "He speaks other languages, doesn't he?"

There's an edge to the way they talk without greeting me, a cruelty in the smiles they wear. Years of facing Ghosts at the warfront with my blades and guns and daggers, and yet the sharpest teeth are still here, on the grounds of the National Hall, where I have no weapons to defend myself. My hands clench and unclench helplessly at my sides. I can feel myself caving inward, feel them turning my silence into a weakness. While I fight for them at the warfront, they have their banquets and celebrate a losing war and taunt me, not realizing there will be a day when their world will suddenly collapse.

"Excuse me."

Red's deep, grit-rubbed voice makes me turn in surprise. I'd been so focused on the interaction happening before me that I hadn't noticed our bond sharpen and clear at his approach. His accent isn't bad. How long had he practiced saying that Maran phrase? He stops at my side and gives the nobility a single nod. Gone is the feverish, bloodied, frightened young man I'd sat beside at the warfront. His steel wings are hidden tonight beneath an elaborately embroidered black robe trimmed with shimmering yellow silk and dyed yellow fur, but even then, I notice that the back of the robe has been tailored with two trimmed slashes to allow his wings to unfold. Underneath it is a white silken shirt woven so fine that I can't see the threads. His expression is calm and bemused tonight, and his strange air of confidence suddenly makes me aware of how handsome he is.

Even if I could speak, I'd be at a loss for words. The only thing that breaks my stare is the sight of his mouse perched on his shoulder, munching on a bit of grape.

The Senator next to Gabrien makes a startled noise at seeing Red's pet, then clears his throat in embarrassment as he eyes the banquet tables, wondering whether other mice are scampering amid the food.

I'm sorry, Red secretly says to me through our link. *Is it considered rude to bring rodents to a Maran party?*

I lift an amused eyebrow at Red. He just shrugs, but the edge of his mouth lifts too.

Before me, the nobles' taunting banter quiets as they stare at him in stunned silence. Tomm's and Pira's sneers drop. Even Gabrien's smug smile fades under the hard eyes of the Skyhunter. The sight of the blood draining from his face sends a quiver of satisfaction through me.

Red doesn't bother to wait. He gives them a bow of his head so deep and proper that I immediately know it's sarcastic, and then pulls me from their group and ushers me down the corridor. I find myself feeling grateful for the now-familiar heat of his hand. Every conversation around us fades away. Behind us, the Senators exchange shocked whispers.

"That's him," one says. "The prisoner from the Federation!"

"The Skyhunter?"

"Yes. He's the one who massacred the entire Federation offensive at the warfront!"

Red gives me a sidelong look. *I thought you could use some help,* he says to me through our link.

I don't know whether to feel relieved for his help or annoyed at his comment. *You could have said something to me through the link, warned me you were coming.*

I didn't want to disrupt you during such a tense exchange.

Suddenly I remember that he can tell when I'm angry or anxious, that he must have known how the Senators' conversation made my heart contract. Can he also sense the way I'd admired his evening look? The thought burns my cheeks. *Have you been to formal events before?* I ask instead. *You seem so comfortable here.*

My father used to attend formal functions back in the Federation, he replies. *I know enough about how they work.*

I'm ready to ask him more, but then we reach the banquet hall, where the Speaker is in the middle of giving a toast. I stop and look away from him, trying to ignore the stares that follow our every step.

I heard Adena dressed you tonight, he says after a beat. *She did well.*

I search for sarcasm on his face. *Are you making fun of me?* I ask, irritated. *I'm not in the mood tonight.*

He frowns at me. *I'm complimenting you. Is that not it? You look decent.*

Decent. Maybe some things are lost in translation, even through our bond. I glare at him, wishing Adena was here so she could hit him with one of her customized weapons.

We step into the warmth of the banquet hall. Near the front of the chamber, the leader of Mara stands leaning over his table, an arc of his Senators on either side of him. Even Aramin has switched out his Striker uniform tonight for something more luxurious, a vest and coat of white and gold that highlights the subtle gold that lines his eyes. I relax slightly at the sight of Jeran, resplendent in his formal jacket, as he and the Firstblade talk in low voices. Beside him, Adena waves at us. We exchange brief smiles, then without a word turn to face the Speaker.

The Speaker pauses in his toast at our arrival. I've seen him before, but always from a distance. This close up, I can see the exhaustion behind his expression, the droop of his skin and the age in his watery eyes. His gaze skims first over me before darting away in disinterest, the edges of his lips thinned into a grimace. His attention settles on Red. "Well," he says, his voice laced with sarcasm. "Our guest of honor."

There's a shuffle as everyone around him shifts, jockeying with one another to be in the best position to observe the man that their Speaker has focused his attention on. Red stands stiffly beside me, but on the surface, he seems to accept the attention without complaint.

Jeran leans closer to me. "I've warned the Firstblade against provoking Red to the point of triggering his most powerful state," he signs, "but the Speaker will want to see a little of what you both can do."

I nod slightly in return, unsurprised, but the thought still makes my heart leap. We all know so little of Red's capabilities. What if this goes wrong? It doesn't take a link between us for me to sense Red's stiffness.

The Speaker waves a hand at the room. "A word with my Senators, please," he says with a curt nod.

The elites need no second bidding. They file out of the chamber in a hush of footsteps, but not before I hear them murmuring as they pass us by. Most of them step around Red as if he might lunge at them, while I merely get some hostile stares. I ignore the looks. Before long, the room has emptied, leaving us with only the Senators, the Firstblade, and the

Speaker. Guards at the entrances close the glass doors leading out into the courtyard. The noise from the festivities suddenly muffles.

I say nothing as we turn to face the Speaker. The silence stretches on for a moment as he studies us with suspicious eyes.

Finally, he looks at Red. "The Firstblade tells me that you almost single-handedly destroyed two of the Federation's patrols at the warfront," he says. "Along with some of the largest Ghosts we've ever fought."

Red waits for Jeran to translate, then nods once. "Yes, sir," Jeran says for him.

"Is that true?"

"Yes, sir."

He glances briefly at me, like he might say something about the rumors that float around me too. How I'd been the only one capable of approaching Red in the middle of his rage.

But when he addresses me, he merely says, "And you're the Basean."

I bow my head once.

"Who doesn't speak."

Appropriately, there's nothing for me to say to that, so I remain still.

A note of scorn enters the Speaker's voice. "A Basean Striker who doesn't speak, yet has the gall to call a meeting with her Speaker to propose an idea." He tilts his head at me. "Tell me why you decided to save this prisoner."

He isn't asking because he's curious. He thinks me a liar, that maybe I knew about Red's abilities when I asked to spare his life. Even now, he's studying my face, searching for something dishonest, something I'm hiding.

I bow my head again and sign with my hands. "Because I felt sorry for him, sir."

Jeran translates aloud for me. The Speaker regards me carefully. If he doesn't believe me, he doesn't say it. Instead, he nods at Red. "Let me see."

At that, Aramin steps around the table and comes to stand in front of us. He draws his blades. "With all due respect, sir," he says, "this may be dangerous."

"I can't very well discuss something I have no knowledge of, can I?" The Speaker lifts an eyebrow. "I want to see what this Skyhunter can do. Show me the physical transformation."

I nod at the Firstblade's hesitation. Then I take a few steps away from Red. Through our link, I send him a thought.

He wants to see your wings, Red, I tell him.

His lips tighten, and for a moment I wonder if he's unable to do it on command, that he can only transform if in an emergency. That if he does transform, it will be like that night, when he lost himself so thoroughly that he couldn't pull himself back.

But Red nods in response and turns to face the Speaker. I gasp. Through our bond, I feel the intoxicating rush of his strength. It's impossible. Where does it come from? It floods his every vein, as if replacing his blood with the ocean, the air in his lungs with a storm's gale. The sensation leaves me trembling.

Then Red's wings unfurl behind him in a ripple of black metal. I can only look on in horrified awe as they expand, wider and wider, each feather a deadly, dark blade, stretching to either side of him until they reach the edges of the chamber.

He no longer looks like a human. He looks like a machine, built for death.

Aramin takes a step back. Even his sharp frown wavers now in the face of Red's transformation. The Speaker watches with an unchanging expression, but I can see his hesitation in the stiffness of his posture.

Beside me, Jeran rests his hands on his weapons, while Adena's lips move unconsciously, as if she were already calculating how the Federation had managed to create such a thing.

I wait to see if Red's eyes will glow, as they did on the battlefield, but they stay dark and unblinking on the Speaker.

"It's true, then." The Speaker finally nods at Red. "The Federation has done their work on you." Then his gaze shifts to me. "What are you proposing?"

The link between Red and me tightens like a bowstring. I bow my head again, then sign my answer to the Firstblade. Jeran says my words aloud: "The Federation is capable of controlling their Ghosts. They attack only those who aren't part of the Federation's army. We've known this for decades. The same should be true for this prisoner—and yet, he doesn't answer to them. Instead, he holds the key to what we need."

Jeran nods here to Adena. She steps forward, her energy crackling nervously in the air. "Ghosts do not obey the Federation simply at their creation," she explains. "The poison they ingest permeates every inch of their blood." She takes a deep breath. "But this Skyhunter is proof that the Federation can make mistakes."

"What kind of mistakes?" the Speaker asks.

Adena glances at me, hesitant. "The Skyhunter tells us that the Federation uses a mental link between themselves and their creations to force them to obey. But Red escaped into our borders before his link could properly set. He has instead bonded with Talin, and in a way that does not involve control from either end. I believe this is because the Federation creates this link in a multistep process—first establishing the link, then asserting their authority through it. Red only experienced the first step. It means that even though neither he nor Talin control each other, they are able to communicate with each other through their link."

This surprises the Speaker more than Red's wings. He looks quickly at me, eyes narrowed in suspicion, and searches my gaze for evidence of something supernatural. "You're sure of this?"

I look at Red. *We have to prove ourselves*, I tell him without moving my hands at all.

He looks back at me and nods. Even in this small gesture, the others around us shuffle, and the Speaker eyes the air between us uneasily. They can tell that we have somehow spoken to each other without having spoken, that some kind of invisible communication has happened here that somehow managed to exclude them all. And even though I've talked to Red like this before, a new thrill hums through me at the public display of it. Here, I am not the one incapable of speech. I can talk in this world where others cannot.

Beside me, Red opens his mouth. He addresses the Speaker in Karenese. At the same time, I can *hear* his words in my mind, can instinctively understand the meaning of them without understanding the language itself. My hands come up; I gesture the same phrase to Jeran, who translates it aloud to the Speaker.

Then, I do the same with Red. I look at him, then think a phrase in Maran. I enunciate it in our own tongue, speaking it slowly and carefully through our link. As I do, Red repeats the words aloud, his eyes never leaving mine as he goes.

This is the more impressive feat, hearing this brute of a Federation soldier utter aloud the language of this nation, with all the correct intonations. The Speaker straightens, face stricken with bewilderment, his eyes darting back and forth between us.

When Red finishes, Jeran clears his throat and translates my signs. "Their minds are linked, as if one," he says. "If Red had fallen under the Federation's direct control, this link would be what they would have used to command him, to trigger certain emotional states and actions from him, to use him as precisely as a puppeteer does a puppet. But here, as you can see, their link went awry. It has fallen instead into our hands."

Silence. While the Speaker's eyes stay on us, still disbelieving, Aramin narrows his eyes. Behind his dark curiosity, I see an expression I would've never expected him to direct my way. Respect. I'm so taken aback that I look away, unable to bear it.

When the Speaker finally replies, his voice is thick with distrust. "How do we know this power between them won't be used against us?" he says. "A Karensan soldier and a Striker who comes from a nation now controlled by the Federation."

"You're saying they might still be working for the Federation, sir?" Jeran says.

"How do we know this soldier does *not* have a connection to the Federation?" the Speaker goes on. "That he will use this link he now has with one of our Strikers to feed the Federation information about us? How do we even know that this Basean is loyal to us, rather than some spy?"

He isn't wrong. We don't know, truthfully, if Red still has some kind of tie with the Federation's Premier. All we are really banking on is the fact that I have a history serving as a Striker, and that I have sensed nothing traitorous in Red's mind.

The Firstblade comes to my defense. "Talin has trained as a Striker since she was twelve," he says. "Since then, she has been loyal, has never done anything to arouse suspicion. If she says that this bond is what it is, that this Skyhunter is on our side, I'm inclined to believe her."

After the tense way Aramin and I had confronted each other in the arena over Red's life, it's strange to now hear him stand firmly by both of us. Nearby, Jeran smiles quietly to himself.

"Besides," Adena adds, "it's a dangerous game for the Federation to play, handing us one of their newer experiments like this. Would they let one of their own purposely lay waste to two entire battalions of their soldiers, with the risk of letting an open link like this fall into our hands?"

The Speaker has nothing to add to that, but the frown stays on his face.

"This is the first time we have an actual example of such a link," Adena goes on, trying to take advantage of the silence. "It's worth studying this in our labs."

"You're seeking to discover how the Federation creates such a bond," the Firstblade says, "and then learn how to destroy that same bond. Is that right?"

"Yes, sir." Adena is so eager now that she's leaning forward, hands gesturing along with her words. "It's the Federation's greatest strength, that ability to command their monsters. If we can sever it, we might have a chance to win this war and push them back. Maybe even to push them out of other nations already conquered."

The Speaker sniffs dismissively. "This can't be done," he says.

Instead of seeing this as a possibility, he sounds hesitant, fearful. Even annoyed. I frown at the tone of his voice. What do we have to lose?

Adena catches it too. "I think it's worth a try, sir," she answers defensively.

"You won't have long to work," the Speaker warns.

"We won't have long to fight, either," I answer with my hands. Jeran translates my words, and all eyes turn to me. "The Federation has pushed back our warfront. We have reached the end of our choices," I finally sign. "If we don't act now, we will fail."

So it has finally come to this. The Speaker looks around the room, surveying the expressions of the other Senators and the Firstblade.

They are murmuring to each other, but I can see the glint of hope in their eyes. The Speaker observes this for a moment, hesitating, then turns back to me.

"Very well," he grumbles reluctantly. He nods at Adena. "You have my permission to study this Skyhunter, but know that you'll be watched very closely. Report everything back to me, and leave nothing out. Do you understand?"

We all lower our heads to him. The marble floor beneath me glints cold in the evening light. Beside me, Red does the same. Jeran is right. The Speaker sees Red mostly as a weapon—I catch the glint in his eyes over the possibility that we might win this war. But even now, his distrust of me is woven into the air, that somehow this is all my elaborate ruse to take Mara down from the inside. I could hear it in his voice, the belief that we are not going to figure out what the Federation did to Red, and even if we could, we won't do it in time, not before the Federation sends their soldiers and Ghosts crashing through our walls.

But it doesn't matter what he believes. We have run out of options. And for the first time, that means that the Speaker of Mara will have to put his trust in a Basean rat.

13

ONLY THREE STRIKER PATROLS AND THE FIRST-
blade are allowed to stay in apartments on the National Plaza's grounds.
Our training in silence and speed means we make good bodyguards,
and so these Strikers act as the Senate's, tasked to protect them in a
rotating shift whenever they aren't training at the arena.

I've only ever seen the apartments as a set of distant towers along
one side of the Plaza, fortified on all sides by steel beams pulled from
the Early Ones' ruins. It never occurred to me that I'd now be setting
foot inside one—let alone living in here, and at the personal order of
the Speaker, no less.

Adena and Jeran take the first apartment in our new corridor, while
Red and I head for the one at the end of the hall. We step into a spectacular room, opulent far beyond anything I could have imagined. The
walls are creamy white and lined with ornate marble pillars that stretch
up to high ceilings. Morning light slants bright across a black-and-
white-marbled floor. Each of the windows stretches from top to bottom
and is bordered by white curtains. Furniture carved with curling details
decorates our shared central room, while our two bedchambers branch
off in opposite halls.

I let out a breath at the sight. This place is bigger than my mother's entire street in the Outer City.

Red stops in front of the glass cabinets located on both ends of the main room. They're weapons cabinets specifically designed for our Striker equipment, with secure slots for each of our blades and daggers and guns.

Fancy, I tell him through our link.

Unnecessary, he responds.

For what you're about to do? I raise an eyebrow at him. *This is the least they could offer.*

He doesn't answer, and when I glance at him again, he's already stooped down to appreciate the intricate construction of the cabinet. I just roll my eyes, a smile forcing its way onto my lips.

We each pick one of the bedroom halls to inspect, then pass each other by to look at the other. One of the rooms is noticeably larger, with a writing desk in one corner and a closet large enough to be its own room.

I want the bigger bedchamber, Red says through our link, his arms crossed as we stand together in the second one.

I scowl at him. *How chivalrous of you.*

What does that mean?

I don't bother trying to explain. *Besides*, I add, *I'm the veteran.*

I lived in a dungeon for a month.

I have more clothes than you.

I'm the one who got us these apartments. He gives me something that he seems to think resembles a smile. *Also, I'm larger. I need more space.*

I throw my hands up. *Fine.*

You and Adena are always doing that with your hands. Is that a Maran thing?

I glare at him before stepping out of the bedchamber and leaving

160

him to settle in. I walk back to my side of the apartment and into my own room, where I open my smaller closet.

Inside hangs a new uniform tailored specifically for me. I stare at it for a moment, my smile fading, and pull down the new coat. I hold it out before me, noting its perfect drape down to my knees and the sleek way it falls against my shoulders.

Red is, no doubt, doing the same in his bedroom, admiring his new uniform just as I am. Or perhaps he isn't—I realize I don't know exactly how he feels about officially becoming a Striker in our forces, especially when the Strikers had almost sentenced him to death just a few short weeks earlier.

Tentatively, I reach out to him through our link, a mental exercise as instinctive as squinting to see something more clearly, in an attempt to find out what he's thinking. As usual, there's a trickle of his emotions between us, accompanied by the dull, ever-present thud of his heart pressing against my mind.

Then I realize that the emotion I'm sensing from him is dread. It's something so heavy that I wince slightly at the weight it brings. I turn away from my closet and leave my bedroom to check on him.

When I step into the living room, Red is standing in front of the windows, his posture so stiff that he looks frozen solidly in place. Now the tension pours out of him in waves, violent and terrified, each hitting the shoreline of my mind like a nightmare repeating itself. I step over to him to see what's caught his attention. Down below, in the plaza outside the National Hall's front gates, other Strikers are gathered in loose groups on their way back from the training arena. Some of them look up in the direction of our new apartments, unsmiling.

Red doesn't acknowledge my presence. Nothing about him resembles the young man I'd seen just moments earlier, who had admired the cabinets and joked with me about which bedroom he wanted. Gone is his relaxed expression. I follow his gaze, puzzled, until I realize that he's not staring at the scene outside but at the window itself. At the glass.

Red? I think at him, but he doesn't respond. He doesn't seem to be aware of anything except for the windowpane. On instinct, I reach out to him. My hand touches his arm, and when he doesn't react, I close my fingers around his elbow and squeeze gently. *Red*, I try again.

The bond between us trembles, the disturbed surface of a pond.

All of a sudden, a flash of bright light blankets my mind. The apartment around me vanishes.

In its place appears a room around us made entirely of glass, set somewhere in a vast, dark chamber. I'm seeing the scene as if I were Red himself, strapped facedown on a cold metal table with a menagerie of metal instruments hovering over me. A cold, bright light overhead makes me squint every time I try to angle my head up.

This is one of his memories.

I swallow hard at the sight. When he looks at the reflection of himself against the glass, I can see portions of his arms and legs that have been cut neatly open, and two long shafts of steel being grafted into his back. A small portion of the brand on his upper chest is visible when he cranes his neck. The brand appears freshly done, the skin there a blistered, bloody red. His blood drips in lines from the sides of the table and stains the floor beneath him. I stare down at the near-perfect circles of blood as they expand, threatening to join with one another.

Red seems delirious in his half sleep, trembling and sweating from pain. I can even feel a faint spasm of that long-ago agony lancing through my own limbs.

Before him stands Constantine Tyrus, Premier of the Federation, along with a woman wearing glasses that catch the glare of light.

"I'm already giving him as much medication to dull his pain as he can take," she says to the Premier.

"He won't survive," Constantine responds in his rasp, his hands folded behind his back. "Give him something else."

"I can't—"

"Give him a *reason*, then," the Premier interrupts her, impatience lacing the edge of his words. "You're my Chief Architect. You figure it out." He casts Red a concerned frown before stepping around the woman and leaving the room.

The woman turns to look at Red with an aggrieved expression. "Is there anything else I can give you to make you hold on?" she asks him.

Red's parched lips part. He's obviously younger in the glass's reflection, but the shadows under his eyes make him look like an old, weathered soul. "My sister," he whispers. "My father."

The woman nods, turns toward the door, and hesitates. Then, in a quieter voice, she says over her shoulder, "I hope you'll find a way to forgive me someday, for what I've done to you. I hope you know that everything you've ever done to protect your family, I'm doing to protect mine. My little boy. My husband." She swallows. "So, I'm begging you, cooperate with the Premier. If you do well, I do well, and my family remains untouched."

Red doesn't respond, and after a guilty silence, the woman called the Chief Architect leaves.

Sometime later, a small figure approaches the other side of the glass wall. She stares at Red in fright. Her gaze wanders to Red's destroyed back, and she starts to cry.

"Laeni," Red whispers. A current of joy and terror rushes through him now—joy, at the sight of her, and terror, for what they might do to her. I notice a mouse sitting on her shoulder, watching the scene with its beady eyes. Red's old words come back to me. *My sister had a mouse for a pet.*

This is her.

The little girl presses her hands against the glass. "Red," she replies, "what are they doing to you?" Her voice is clear, small, and anguished.

"I'm okay," Red says, reaching his hand out in an attempt to touch the glass too. He tries to smile. "It doesn't hurt, I promise. They've given me medicine."

Finally, when Laeni manages to compose herself, she says, "Papa's here too. They've brought us both. They told us you can't leave yet, that you'll die. What can I do for you?"

"Just stay," Red replies. His eyes are closed now, and his lips move as if he's counting his breaths, one second at a time. "Tell me a story and distract me."

Laeni glances nervously at the guards before she sits down outside the glass and takes out a well-worn book. She opens it to a page. "Shall I read you my favorite?"

"Yes."

She clears her throat, then touches her finger to the page and scans the sentences right to left, the opposite of how Marans read. "A hall with no end. A day to live. A million ways to bridge the rift," she begins.

As rapidly as it came, the vision of his memory scatters in a burst of light—and I'm standing back in our new apartment, with sunbeams slanting against the floor and tall white curtains framing the windows and floors marbled black and white.

I blink, disoriented, and release his arm. Before me, Red has his hand pressed against the window's glass, the same way he'd attempted to in the vision. My heart races; my mind whirls again and again through the grotesque moment I'd witnessed.

Red glances at me, the glint in his eyes terrified. *You saw it*, he tells me.

There's nothing I need to say to him. I know it was a memory of him acquiring the wings on his back, the weapons that ultimately turned him into a Skyhunter.

All I can do is nod.

The terror in his eyes vanishes in a flash. His eyes shutter, and he takes a step away from the window, bringing his hand back down to his side. *I shouldn't have let her see me like that,* he says before he shoves past me.

I watch him as he heads down one of the halls toward his bed-chamber. Out of all of us involved in this mission to defeat the Federation, Red is the only one who will head back into a nightmare he'd experienced from the inside, a world so horrifying that he'd wanted to kill himself in order to escape its trauma.

And yet, he's still here. Still trying to help us.

A part of me wants to let him go and leave him alone. But he is no longer just a prisoner of war under my guard. He is my Shield, an official Striker wearing the sapphire coat, and that means I am to be here for him, I am to train with him in both mind and body, and that when we next fight together at the warfront, he and I will know the other's movements as surely as we know our own limbs.

More than that, I just don't want to see him like this.

So I find myself following him down the hall to the bedchamber, where he's pulling off his new Striker coat to hang in the closet. There, I lean against the doorframe.

He glares at me. *What do you want?*

I don't ask him about what had flashed through his—and my—mind. *You're in my room,* I think instead, nodding at the smaller space.

Red pauses, realizing his mistake.

Unless you want me to take the bigger chamber, I add.

What do you care, anyway? he mutters through our bond as he grabs his coat out of the closet again.

I stop before him, forcing him to look me in the eyes.

You're my Shield, and I am yours, I tell him. *It means I always care about everything related to you. It means we will spend every waking hour together, that I will show you how I fight and how I move, and that you will show me the same. It means you teaching me more about this bond.* I pause to point between us. *It means we are eternal companions, until death.*

I don't like companions, he replies, an audible growl in his throat accompanying his words.

There he goes again with the things he dislikes. This time, though, I sense fear behind it, fear of growing close to someone he could lose. Fear of what the future might bring.

Tomorrow, I continue. *We'll train. We'll start learning—really learning—about what links us. We'll take it one step at a time. But I'll always be there.* I meet his gaze with my steady one. *I'll see you in the morning. I promise.*

Red stares at me, annoyance on his face. Still, there is a sense of something new in the link that joins us—some kind of trust, the building of a bridge. Then he turns away and heads off to his own bedchamber, his shoulders suddenly hunched in exhaustion.

It is only then that something in my memory clicks into place with searing clarity. The brand on Red's chest, the one I'd puzzled over from the first moment he appeared in the arena. It is the same symbol emblazoned on the sleeves of the soldiers that had invaded my town in Basea, the troops specifically assigned to massacre us. It is the same symbol as the one worn by the young soldier who couldn't bring himself to shoot me.

And it is not just the symbol that is the same. It is his eyes. It is his face. Different now, as a grown man and as an experiment of the Federation, but still him. Now I suddenly understand why I'd felt so compelled to save him in the arena. The real reason.

Red is that twelve-year-old boy. The same one who had held the gun and failed to fire. The same young soldier from that night.

14

WE'RE QUIET AROUND EACH OTHER FOR THE
rest of the evening.

The realization that Red had been one of the young soldiers assigned
to invade Basea, that he had been the one standing over me the night
my mother and I fled, fills me with a nausea that keeps me from eating
dinner. All I can do is sit across from him at the cafeteria, my stomach
churning and churning, the memory of the boy with the gun clearer now.

The symbol. His face.

Jeran and Adena puzzle over our silence, but they occupy themselves
with their own talk, chalking up our tension to our usual discord.

Red ignores me too, likely because of the strange incident between
us in our living room. For the first time since our minds linked, I
can sense him resisting the open channel between us, the flow of his
thoughts bundled tight and hostile, as if he wished I could not sense
them. I do the same unconsciously, holding back until my insides feel
coiled tight as a snake.

When we finally arrive back to our apartment, we each head for our
bedrooms without a backward glance.

I turn restlessly in the darkness, struggling to sleep. Scenes from that
night in Basea so long ago play endlessly in my mind, moments that

had once been muddy now cleared. The twelve-year-old Red that I'd seen then, young and frightened, had clearly not been experimented on yet—no metal bands on his back; no wings; no strange, artificial skin. How did that version of him then become the boy I saw in his memory, lying trembling in the glass chamber?

Would Red have fired his gun at me that night if he'd been given more time? Why didn't he shoot? What happened to him after he refused to kill me? Did they punish him? He clearly doesn't remember me as a child—I've felt no sense of familiarity from him through our link. Does that mean, then, that he's seen so many victims of the Federation that we are all just a blur of faces to him? Before he'd been confronted with the idea of killing a child that night, had he killed any innocent people? *My* people?

Who had I saved? What have I done?

I spin and spin on these questions until I feel ill from them. What little I'd eaten for dinner now threatens to come up, but I force myself to slow my breathing, to concentrate on one thought at a time—the weak moonlight in my room, the curves of my blanket—until my stomach steadies. But my troubled thoughts continue as I finally drift off into sleep, my mind twisting them into a nightmare.

I am eight and my mother is facing the boy soldier again, her hand still gripping my arm tightly. The boy stares back at us with his gun pointed straight at my chest. I can see him willing himself to fire it, then failing, again and again. Now, in my dream, I can recognize that everything about him is Red, even though different from age and experimentation. His hair is light brown, without the strange metallic sheen it now has. His eyes are dark and wide, his face narrower and body leaner. His expression is less haunted, more frightened. The brand marring his chest isn't there yet; the same double-crescent insignia is emblazoned only on his sleeve.

He doesn't fire the gun. Then I'm fleeing with my mother and not looking back, not caring what happens to the boy or whether he will chase us. We run and run past burning homes on familiar streets, the roar of explosions and screaming. My mind obscures the worst of the horrors, but I know they're happening all around me—Federations soldiers doing unspeakable things to people I know.

Where is my father? Something terrible had happened to him, but even in my dream, I still can't remember what it is.

Poisonous gas clouds the only path we can take. Yellow mist fills my lungs. I cough violently, heaving, the burning indescribable as my throat feels like it's been coated in fuel and lit on fire. My mother yanks me forward, tears streaming from her eyes as she holds her hand to her mouth.

We enter a field of darkness. Blood trickles, then flakes, at the edges of my mouth. I cling tightly to my mother's hand and keep running. My vision blurs with hot tears.

We lose all sense of time. My nightmare runs on repeat for what feels like hours, days, weeks, as it had when we made our real escape. In this seemingly eternal night, the figure of us fleeing with thousands of other people is almost invisible, the grasslands we trample through nothing more than a black ocean. The only light comes from the full moon hanging in the sky, low and white and enormous, the stars behind it washed out in the brightness. We run and run as a horde of humanity, barely stopping, barely resting, trying to reach the edge of the warfront where we could cross over into safety. Into Mara, the last free nation.

When I look up at my mother, her eyes are wild and bloodshot, focused only on the bridges ahead of us. Maran snipers and archers wait on the other side of the ravine, alongside massive catapults, but they won't linger for us forever. Crates of explosives line the lengths of the bridges, and the archers' arrows are tipped with fire, ready to shoot.

Behind us, gaining quickly, are Federation soldiers and their Ghosts, their hulking shapes undulating on the horizon.

We reach the bridges. The sound of our boots against dirt suddenly changes to a hollow clang against metal. The bridges are impossibly thin. They shouldn't be capable of holding so much weight. I squeeze my eyes shut so that I can't look down into the dizzying darkness, with only a thin silver thread of a river thousands of feet below visible.

When I open my eyes again, I see lines of soldiers, the crest of Mara emblazoned on their sleeves, their guns hoisted and ready. Scattered among them are Mara's famed Strikers, their sapphire uniforms prominent against the firelight, their masks on, their guns and swords out, ready to face the Ghosts. I feel a sudden surge of hope. My mother's pace quickens, sensing the same.

We reach the other side. I nearly fall as the soldiers shout for us to move past their ranks. There, I cling tightly to my mother's hand and dare to look back across the chasm.

All around us, the other refugees are crying, some kneeling on the ground, retching up what little is in their stomachs after the exertion of the sprint. Most are still on the bridges, streaming to safety like a teeming mass of ants.

My mother collapses to the ground. She's weeping in pain now, her eyes shut tight, her hands pressed to her leg wound as if she can stop the agony from engulfing her. I kneel beside her, not knowing how to help her. Blood smears on her skin. There's so much of it.

Behind us, the archers fire at the bridges still crowded with people. Their arrows hurtle down. Some strike the refugees—others embed in the crates resting along the bridges' joints.

The crates explode as if they had been struck by lightning. Like the earth has split in two. And the bridges, the only trade routes Mara has left, buckle, tearing apart in a deafening groan of metal. A great wail of panic comes from those still crossing. I can see them climbing over one another, crushing their neighbors in their desperation to flee. On the other side of the chasm fly the Federation's red-and-black banners, their Ghosts letting out their piercing shrieks into the night.

"Don't look," my mother tells me. Her voice is a trembling murmur, and her brown skin is ashen pale. She shakes her head in despair, pulls me close to her, and lets me cry. *"It's okay, baby,"* she whispers into my hair. *"Keep your eyes on me. It's okay."*

• • •

It's okay, baby.

I stir in the night with the sound of my mother's voice still echoing in my dreams. The hallways of our new apartment are disorienting in the darkness, and for a moment, I can't be sure where I am. Gradually, my thoughts settle. I'm sitting upright in my bed, my body washed in silver from the rectangle of moonlight that spills into the room from the windows.

I stay where I am for a moment, letting the nightmare slowly fade from my consciousness and become replaced by the unease of my reality. On the other side of the apartment, I can still feel Red's low undercurrent of emotions rippling across my mind, trapped in a nightmare of his own that I can't see. The sensations of his dreams are more erratic than his waking thoughts—subtler, fewer whole scenes and words, but deeper feelings and shadows, with the occasional spikes of terror. And always the hint at the corner of my mind—just barely out of reach—of reflections in glass and the flash of scarlet uniforms in the darkness.

Maybe his nightmares had triggered my own, his fears leaking through our bond like water from a dam, soaking the walls of our minds.

Maybe his nightmare is even the same as mine, except from his point of view. From the boy soldier who couldn't bring himself to shoot.

If that's true, then perhaps the bond goes both ways. If I calm myself, will he calm? And subsequently—if I can calm his nightmares, will he stop triggering mine? I close my eyes and think of Corian, how we used to sit in silence across from each other in the middle of his family's garden and just let ourselves listen to the world around us. It is another daily Striker exercise, this meditation. I do it now as I turn in bed to lie on my back, imagining the ripples disturbing the surface of my mind, then letting them slow, still the surface back to glass. I let myself remember the sound of an evening forest, the call of the birds in the boughs. Then, gently, I send this meditation of thought through our link, slowly, slowly willing the ripples in Red's mind to still, the nightmares churning in his thoughts to fade back into nothing.

It's hard to tell if any of it is working, and for a moment I feel foolish for even attempting to understand this link between us.

Then I feel the subtle rhythm of his breathing even out. The shadows flickering across the back of his mind slowly fade, until all I can sense through our link is a low, steady pulse of a person in deep sleep.

Red had told me that the Federation originally created this link so that their Premier could control his mind, keep him from attacking their own troops. They may not have had the chance to finish linking him to the Federation, but the fact that I can use my own mind to calm his is both fascinating and unsettling. Maybe he would be able to do it to me too. Maybe there are other small, subtle things we are capable of controlling about each other. The thought makes me shiver. How had he gone from that scared boy pointing the gun to the experiment pinned down on a table in a glass room? How had the Federation turned him from a child into a war machine?

What a cruel sense of humor this world has, to join me with a soldier partly responsible for the destruction of my old world. A soldier who nevertheless spared my life.

Eventually, I fall back to sleep. But the nightmares continue again, casting me this time as a puppet controlled by the faceless form of a soldier bearing an insignia on his sleeve. He tells me to point the gun at myself, sobbing, on the ground. He tells me to shoot. And in the nightmare, I do exactly as I'm told.

15

THE WINTER SUN SHINES BRIGHT AND SEARING against rain-dampened paths. As the other Strikers head to the mess hall, Red and I cross the National Plaza with Adena and Jeran at our sides, on our way to the prison.

As we enter and head down, the dampness seeps through our clothes. It chills us, although Red doesn't shiver at all. Through our bond, I can sense his sheer exhaustion from the day before. He'd spent a good part of the afternoon hurling his guts in an alley of the National Plaza, then skipped dinner to head to bed early. Whatever his nightmares had been last night, they'd kept me awake and restless.

"We keep a Ghost down here," Adena whispers to Red as we approach the lowest level of cells. "It's been alive here for over a year. We've subjected it to enough starvation and experiments that it stays mostly quiet now."

Red stares at Adena after Jeran translates, but he doesn't flinch at the lack of mercy in her words. When Red casts me a questioning glance, I just shake my head. I should tell him about how Adena had lost her brother, but I don't want to mention how Adena had also stood in the stands during Red's execution and shouted for his blood to be spilled.

My own sympathies for Ghosts are limited, anyway.

174

The cell, unlike others down here, has two layers of doors, with torches lit in the tiny corridor between them. They're the only light source that filters through the inner door's bars. After the guards step aside for us, we go through the first into a dark corridor that ends in a second chained door. Here, Adena takes out a different key and unlocks it. My hands are already resting on the hilts of my swords, the blades partially pulled out of their sheaths.

The ceiling is low, barely tall enough for Red, the largest of us, to stand fully upright. There are no windows. The Ghost doesn't make a sound, but I know it's here the instant we step inside. I can hear the faint, incessant grinding of its teeth in the dark, the chilling tang of its rotting flesh that presses against my senses like a dagger.

My gaze rests automatically on the ashen figure crouched in one corner of the cell, the bones of its spine an uneven silhouette in the torchlight as it keeps its back turned to us. It rasps weakly with each breath. Patches of its white, cracked skin have peeled off, revealing the decay underneath. Shackles around its wrists keep it chained firmly to the wall. Based on how tight the cuffs are, I can tell the Ghost has grown larger since the last time it was fitted.

I'm surprised every time I'm in here that a Ghost can possibly be subdued. But even a monster has its limits, I suppose, and its figure stays slouched even as it can hear our entrance, knowing soldiers have come to deliver another round of torture.

Adena steps forward first. A small metal kit is in her hands, and when she opens it, I see the glint of a long syringe.

"I'm going to take its blood," she signs to us. It's so dark in here that I squint to make out the movements of her fingers. "When it turns around and sees you, do not attack it. Let it come." She glances at Red. "To him."

Jeran looks back at the Ghost. "Those chains don't look stable enough," he signs.

"I've been in here enough times," Adena replies in silence. "Trust me."

Now she steps closer to the Ghost. She moves with confidence, but I can see the slight stiffness in her shoulders, the nearly imperceptible tremor in her hands. She reaches the beast, then holds out the syringe toward the bones of its spine that jut out. We remain still, not daring to breathe as she approaches it. Beside me, Red's emotions stir slightly, and through our link, I sense a rising tension in him that almost feels like anticipation. Like he *wants* to see this Ghost approach him.

Adena hesitates for a second—then injects the syringe deep into its spine and pulls a vial of blood from it as fast as she can.

The creature whirls. It moves so fast that at first I think it will catch Adena in its jaws.

Its eyes are still milky white like every Ghost I've ever seen, its teeth still long and bloody around its ruined mouth. But its scream is hoarse and liquid, like its throat has almost completely rotted away. I notice that one of its eyes is missing, and it only has two or three claws per hand.

That doesn't stop it from lunging at Adena. Hate burns cold in its eyes.

Adena spins smoothly away, slicing back with her dagger as she goes. It cuts a long ribbon into the creature's upper arm—a piece of flesh comes away from its body at the action. This Ghost is falling apart.

I realize that she's trying to lead it toward Red. Jeran whips out one blade and spins forward, cutting the Ghost hard enough on its other arm to force it to turn. It bares its overgrown teeth at him, then lunges again. Like water, Adena moves out of its way and cuts it once more, bringing it closer to Red. The two of them work together in a seamless pattern of movement, goading the Ghost toward one, then the other, then finally close enough to where I'm poised with Red for it to sense his presence.

I tense. Somehow, in this darkness, I don't remember that Red is the one beside me. Instead it's Corian, still bent on one knee on the forest floor, paying his respects to the Ghost he had just killed, unaware that this will be one of his final moments. My blades are in my hands before I can think, and I take a step toward Red, baring the steel before me as if his life might depend on it. The logic in me struggles against the tide of my memories.

Hold back. This is not the forest. He is not Corian.

Beside me, Red stills. For an instant, I'm afraid he'll transform right here in the cell. Or, worse, he won't—and the Ghost's chains will break and it'll sink its teeth into him.

The Ghost reaches Red—its chains pulled taut, its arms stretched tight behind it—and it screams in frustration. At first, it doesn't seem to treat him any differently from how it treats us. But when its milky eyes meet his, it halts. Its teeth are still bared, and it still glares at him with an inhuman curtain of fury—but instead of lunging, it continues to stare, tilting its head at him in confusion. A low growl rumbles at the base of its ruined throat.

To my horror, I can tell that Red has a strange kinship with this Ghost. I sense the surge of emotions from him—that he and this creature were both birthed from the same place, created from the same nightmare. Then I realize that this is how Red feels—there is an understanding that sparks between them, and whatever that is, it keeps the Ghost from attacking him.

The Ghost snaps out of its hesitation. It gnashes its teeth at Red, then turns away from him and shifts its attention toward me.

I'm ready for it. I yank out one of my knives and stab it into the Ghost's arm before it can lunge at me. The creature screams. Unlike with Red, it looks at me with familiar hatred, then shifts to attack again.

Suddenly it shrieks, slapping at its neck as if a bug has stung it. Behind it, Adena pulls another syringe away from its neck and steps back.

It takes less than a second. The Ghost blinks twice and sways on its feet, then backs up a few steps. The snarl in its throat morphs into some kind of whine. Those eyes flutter again. It tries to focus on Adena, its teeth still gnashing, but then it collapses to its knees. Its muscles flex as it struggles to stay awake, but it's no use.

I look on as it goes limp and splays unconscious across the stone floor.

Adena's forehead gleams with sweat. "It didn't attack you," she signs, nodding once at Red.

"It's as if it knew you," Jeran adds, materializing out of the darkness to join us.

Red stands his ground. *It isn't trained to attack me*, he tells me through our link. His voice in my mind sounds hoarse and exhausted, weighed down with unspoken grief.

I repeat Red's words to Adena and Jeran, signing with my hands.

We step out of the Ghost's cell, and Adena carefully locks each layer of the cell's doors behind us. Only when we're completely out and standing back in the dungeon's corridors do I let my shoulders loosen.

"I've never seen anything like that in all my years of studying Ghosts," Adena exclaims, trying to keep her voice down and squeaking in the process. "The way it reacted to you? It didn't even try to attack." There's a bright light in her eyes as she holds up the vial of blood she'd taken from the Ghost.

Jeran has a glint in his eyes too. "We are going to figure out what the Federation tried to do to Red," he says. "And we are going to figure it out soon, before they can take us down."

"What *do* we do now, though?" I sign, my eyes going from the vial of blood in Adena's hand to the dark silhouette of Red's figure.

Adena takes a deep breath. "Now you're going to help us get around the scrapyards in the Outer City. Because I need some good magnesium."

16

"I JUST NEED ENOUGH OF THE METAL TO TEST
Red's blood against that Ghost's," Adena tells us as we head out of the
Inner City gates and into the muddy paths of the shanties. "Magnesium
metal doesn't do much when dropped in water. But when mixed with
Ghost blood, it froths and turns pale. Ghost blood is wild. The result
is a sample where the froth trails let us see the movement of the blood
inside the mixture."

Around us, people cast Red nervous glances. Even without his fearsome wings, he looks taller and stronger than most here.

"You'll have to help me gather it," I tell her and Jeran. "It's not
the easiest metal to find. Would be better if we all searched for an
afternoon."

Before I became a Striker, I spent most days twisting my way through
the scrapyards littering the Outer City. You can see them towering in
the distance, beyond the jumble of makeshift tin roofs that make up
most of the shanties—the silhouette of stacks and stacks of discarded
metal, artificial mountains behind wired fencing that rise every dozen
or so blocks.

The one closest to my mother's home—the one I now lead the
others to—is no different: an acre of useless dirt and mud, piled high

with a random assortment of everything. Old parts from ruins left behind by the Early Ones, pieces of engines or buildings or machines, things that regularly turn up on farmers' land and out in the valleys. There are also discarded metals from the Inner City. Broken carriage parts. Pieces of buildings that have been taken apart and rebuilt—roofing, cladding, doors, and window frames. Old pots and pans and cans, chairs with three legs and tables without any. Wheels. Screws. Pipes. Forks and knives and spoons.

It sounds like a broken, ugly landscape, but in reality, I find the scrapyards one of the most beautiful places here.

People in the Outer City scavenge in the scrapyards all the time. My mother and I certainly did. Most of the shanties are built using rusted metal sheets found here for their walls and roofs. My mother learned how to identify the strongest steel for resale, though, and with my help, we would haul the pieces to the gates of the Inner City's wall and barter them to the Grid in exchange for money. I learned too how to crawl between the stacks of wreckage, my delicate fingers fishing for wire to strip from machinery and my body squeezing through dangerous narrows to find pieces valuable enough to sell.

But as we draw closer this afternoon, I see that the scrapyard has been temporarily transformed into a betting stage. There is a crowd of Outer City folk here, all shouting up at a series of daredevil games in play.

"What the hell is going on?" Adena asks me as we stop at the fencing to stare into the yard at the crowds.

"The Scrapyard Circus," I sign, pointing at the games set up.

Someone has strung a series of wires high between two metal stacks, and now several are balancing their way precariously along the lines while people down below exchange coins and cheer them on. Elsewhere, people are competing over how far they can throw iron sewer caps or how accurately they can shoot down cans lined along the fence.

They are makeshift games that change every time, a circus of spontaneous entertainment that pops up now and then and offers the populations out here something to distract them from their troubles for a night.

"Is it safe for us to head in?" Jeran asks. "Should we wait?"

I shake my head. "No less safe than any other time. People look happy enough." Then I push my way in through the fence's open gate.

Red's curiosity comes in through our bond, and when I look over at him, I see his head tilted up at the high-wire walkers, watching them wobble and hesitate as people down below shout encouragement. I remember staring up in awe at the competitors when I was small. I've seen people make it across on their first try; more often, I've witnessed people slip on the wires and go plummeting to the ground, hitting the sharp edges of protruding metal sheets along the way. The memory of the accidents makes me cringe, my muscles tense as I will the current walkers to make it across.

Red looks at me. *Did you ever try?*

I shake my head. *My mother did. She never let me. But the circus is good for distracting others while you dig for parts in the piles.*

"How do you know where to find magnesium?" Adena asks as I lead us away from the main festivities toward the back of the scrapyard, where the piles of metal cast long, quiet shadows across the land.

I point at the stacks. Magnesium was something I occasionally searched for as a child. Metalworkers in the Grid paid a good price for it because they liked mixing it with steel and iron. It's lightweight, good for tools. You could fetch enough from even a small haul of magnesium to buy bread and flour from the markets to feed you for a week.

"The Early Ones sometimes used it in their tools and machinery," I explain as we reach the stacks. I reach into one of the piles and pull out what looks like a flat, rectangular machine. When I turn it over, exposing its innards, I can see that it's already been salvaged hollow. I hold the object out to the others. "Look for similar ones that haven't been taken apart." Then I point out a massive cylinder of an ancient flying object. "They used them to fly once. You'll find it sometimes in these hulls, although most have been stripped clean." I turn my head up. "And the best, of course, will be up high, where fewer people can reach."

Adena and Jeran look somewhat lost for a moment, like they always do when I explain pieces of my past life to them. To their credit, they don't question me.

"How did you stay alive climbing these stacks as a child?" Adena grumbles instead as she starts moving her way up one of the stacks. Even trained in the footwork of a Striker, she's unused to the way the unstable metal shifts and groans with every turn of her body.

Farther up, though, Jeran is already hopping from stack to stack, nimble as a goat on the edge of a cliff, his face intent on the task before him.

I wedge myself in at the same time Red regards me. He starts to unfurl his wings. *I can carry you higher*, he says.

I hesitate, imagining the thought of being in his arms as he hoists me into the air. It would make the entire process faster, and if I'm being honest, I've wondered how it must feel to soar through the air the way he did on the field. Then the idea embarrasses me. It's probably best not to draw that kind of attention out here, anyway. So I force myself to shake the idea off and frown at him.

You take to the skies here, I tell him instead, nodding toward the crowds, *and we might spend the rest of the afternoon trying to quell the panic.* I point up to one of the stacks. *Just watch for me. If you see any of us slip, feel free to rescue us.*

Red scowls. *So I'm going to stay down here?*

You're too heavy to climb these stacks, I tell him, then start making my way up the side of one.

It's been years since I've climbed stacks in the scrapyards, but the muscle memory of years spent here comes rushing back to me, and I find my footing as naturally as I always did—gingerly shifting my weight along the edge of a metal sheet until I find the stable spot, knowing where to hop to get to another stack, feeling the body of it move beneath me like a living thing. You had to make decisions quickly out here. I wasn't the only child scavenging, but often I was the smallest. Other children formed roving gangs, teamed up to both take the best metal and beat down anyone else trying to prowl in the same areas. So I learned how to squeeze my body tightly between the stacks, how to hide myself inside hollowed-out carriages and rusted roofing.

Later, I'd taken Corian here, taught him how to navigate the terrain. We'd chase each other through the stacks, hopping back and forth, me saving him on more than one occasion from crashing down to the ground. We practiced first by daylight, then by moonlight. The Firstblade considered the exercise beneath that befitting a Striker, that we didn't belong in the shanties. But there was a reason why Corian and I had once been considered the most nimble pair in the forces, and the reason was this.

The memory of his voice teasing me to find him in the stacks brings me up short. I stop midway through digging in the skeleton of a carriage, then close my eyes and try to steady my breathing. I can hear Corian's laugh echoing around me, still feel him squeezing in beside me as he tried to wedge himself into the same hiding places I could find.

Then the wave passes. I open my eyes. Down below, I catch a glimpse of Red pacing beside the stacks, unused to doing nothing. His usual frown stays on his face.

Every day since his death, I have missed Corian so much that his absence feels like a wound in my side. Red could never replace that, no matter how long we end up knowing each other. Still, the longer I stare down at Red from the privacy of my vantage point, and the longer I feel the glimmer of thoughts through our link, the more curious I become about him. I find myself watching him the same way I used to watch Corian, in fascination over this human from a world so different from the one I was used to. In awe.

He stops pacing for a moment and glances up in my direction. I duck down into the husk of the carriage, my heart suddenly pounding. It takes me another second to remember that he, too, can sense the emotions flowing from me to him. He'd probably felt my mixture of grief, pain, fascination, and curiosity. Probably noticed the way I was watching him in interest. And now he is aware of the wave of embarrassment hitting me too.

I grit my teeth, irritated again at being forced to open my heart to this stranger and simultaneously ashamed because I'd been snooping on his feelings too. Through the bond, I can tell that he's puzzled and even a bit bemused at my reactions, and trying to figure out exactly why I'm feeling such a wild jumble of things.

Time to put an end to that. Everything in me wants to look back out from the carriage to see whether or not he's still looking up at me, but I force myself to turn my mind to something else. To the task at hand.

Magnesium. Right.

I let myself fall into the motions I used to do daily—find machines that haven't yet been gutted, cut through their containers with shears and scrape through them until I find bright silver bits of magnesium, strip the metal out, toss it into my pockets. As I go, Red falls to the back of my mind. It isn't until I've made my way through at least a few skeletons of carriages that I realize he's stopped thinking about me too. I'm strangely disappointed.

Soon my fingers are raw from the work. I stand up, stretch, and note the changing light. It must be late afternoon now, the hour right before sunset. In the near distance, I can hear Jeran calling out something to Adena and Adena's answering laugh, while the circus continues in the front of the scrapyard. I look at my arms, satisfied with the small amount of magnesium I've collected, and let myself search the grounds for signs of Red.

When I see him, I pause.

He's seated on the ground, his face turned slightly away, and his wings are out in full display, stretching dozens of feet to either side of himself. But he's not in a state of fury this time. A gaggle of children have wandered away from the circus to cluster around him instead, squealing at the black steel blades of his wings and tugging on his hair to inspect the rough, metallic texture of the strands. He has folded his wings in such a way that the blades stack carefully, so when the children touch the feathers in curiosity, they don't slice their hands. Standing in an arc some distance away from them are adults, all too timid to approach him and hanging back instead to whisper among themselves.

My first reaction is annoyance that he's completely disregarded my advice about keeping a low profile while in the scrapyard. But then I watch him tilt his head sideways to let a small girl play with his hair. When he shakes his head, she jumps back with a wide grin, giggling, before hurrying back to him to do it again. Red keeps his movements slow and careful as the children run around his wings and attempt to climb on top of their arches. His face is still, gentle. Joy pulses from him through our link, but underneath it is layered a level of grief so deep, the weight of it presses against my chest. And within those emotions, I see glimpses of a memory. It's of a little girl with the same dark hair he once had, the sister who had been on the other side of the glass. Then she fades away, as if Red were too afraid to let her loose.

Corian. When I look at this scene, all I see is my dead Shield. It is always the gentle ones I fear for the most, those willing to bare their hearts, who grieve for others and feel happy for others' happiness. Corian had been that, and I had failed to protect him. I hadn't thought of Red, alternately grouchy and teasing, as such a person—but here, watching him stay perfectly still as children climb all over him, as he stretches out a wing where a boy is dangling from the end and deposits him carefully back on the ground, I'm filled with the same sense I used to have with Corian. A wish that I could be like him. A fear that I will lose this person.

I shake my head firmly. Red is not Corian. He never will be. And no matter what I'm witnessing right now, I have to remember that Red is still the boy soldier who had helped conquer Basea for the Federation, had been conscripted into fighting for the Federation as a child. I have to recall the light of murder on his face as he ripped through the Federation's battalions without a single hesitation.

Can you be kind and a killer? Can you be gentle and a weapon of war?

By the time I climb back down from the stacks, Jeran is already waiting for us with a handful of magnesium chips, while Adena is gingerly making her way down a wobbly structure of leaning steel. By now, almost everyone has left behind the circus to watch Red make his slow movements, his majestic wings sweeping in slow arcs across the dirt.

When Adena approaches us, she brightens at the sight of our stash. "Good enough, good enough," she mutters, inspecting the quality of the metal. "I can work with this. Oh!"

She'd been so busy with her gathering that she hadn't noticed Red at all. Now, as she watches the way he treats the children, her rapid words fade away and her smile thins into a serious line. I know she must be thinking of her brother and the anger she'd first held against Red. But this sight has turned her quiet.

All I can think about is how the Federation can transform people like this, with hearts and minds and thoughtful moments, into monsters. All I can remember is how little time we have to fight against their darkness snarling at our borders.

· · ·

As night settles into place and we turn in the direction of my mother's home, I cast a glance at Red. He's quiet, but his mind roils, sending me fragments of thoughts—of the same little girl I'd seen in his previous memory, a woman watching him from a garden window, and a door, creaking open to allow in something terrible.

I didn't know you were so good around children, I finally tell him through our link.

He gives me a small smile. *My sister was much younger than me. I'm used to it.*

Your sister, Laeni. I think of the little girl from his nightmares. *Was that her?* I ask him, knowing he can tell what memory I'm referring to. *You think about her a lot.*

Red doesn't look at me and doesn't answer right away. When he does, it's a quiet voice in my head, full of sadness. *Yes. And I do.*

I swallow, unable to keep my next question from going between our link. *What happened to her?*

Red is silent for so long that, when he finally replies as we turn onto my mother's street, his voice in my mind startles me. When he looks at me now, his eyes are filled with the most terrible weight in the world.

The same thing that happened to my father, he tells me. *They turned her into a Ghost. And I had to kill her.*

17

ADENA TAKES SEVERAL VIALS OF RED'S BLOOD
later that night, enough that it makes him weak. Even without that, though, he seems quieter than usual, and through our link, I sense the presence of memories that cloud his mind with fog.

After we retire to bed, Red's nightmares are no longer just shimmers in the darkness. No longer just a glimpse of humanity. No longer a portal into another world. This time, his nightmare materializes as a vision so clear that I feel like I'm living it.

In the dream, he is dressed in a thin white shirt and pants and standing before a woman in a white coat, his young head bowed. He must be the same age that he was during the night of the Basean siege. I recognize the woman too. She keeps appearing in Red's dreams, her face long and gaunt, lips thin and eyes framed by glasses.

This time, I realize that they're back in the glass room. "Do you know where you are, Redlen?" she asks him.

He shakes his head, eyes wide. I can see the brand peeking out from under his shirt, except this time it looks freshly done, the wound still bloody and swollen. It's the same double-crescent insignia that had been on his uniform sleeve during the invasion.

"You're in the Laboratory of Cardinia," the woman tells him.

Cardinia, I think, the name registering in my mind. The capital of the Federation. "Do you know why you were sent here?"

Now Red is trembling, his lanky twelve-year-old frame bent like a willow. I can tell he knows exactly what she's talking about, but the woman tells him again anyway, as if she feels sorry for him. "Soldiers of the Federation are to, above all, obey the command of their Premier. You are very young, Redlen, but that's never an excuse to fail at your duty in battle. I heard that you were shadowing your captain in Sur Kama. He gave you a direct order to shoot, and you refused. Your hesitation cost him his life." She sighs, sounding sad, and looks down at the floor. Then she asks him a fateful question. "Did you understand that it was a direct order?"

Red hangs his head and nods quietly. "Yes, ma'am," he murmurs.

"Of course you did, because you deliberately disobeyed."

Red suddenly looks at her with an expression of desperate intensity. "I didn't mean to. Can you please help me get an audience with General Caitoman again? I'm not ready to go. Is my sister all right? My father? I . . ."

The woman gives him such a look of pity, of deep understanding, that I immediately wonder who she had also lost before, and who she fears to lose. *My little boy*, she had said in the last vision I'd seen from Red. *My husband.*

"This is beyond my power," she replies apologetically, as if she'd told this to dozens of others before. "Federation law dictates that soldiers in violation of their oath be branded with their failure and then permanently separated from their family. Your family will suffer similar consequences. You knew this when your disobedience lost the Federation a valuable soldier. Yes? The Federation tells you no lies and keeps every promise. Isn't that right?"

Red doesn't look like he wants to agree, but he does anyway, as if it might help. "Yes," he repeats.

So this is what happens to soldiers in the Federation, why they stay loyal. Obey the Federation, and it will reward your entire family. Disobey, and not only are you branded and punished, but your family will suffer similar fates.

His sister. His father. I remember the small girl I'd seen in Red's first memory, her look of fright.

"You have now forfeited your life into the hands of the Federation," she continues, "and since you have proven to be unreliable in the field, you must serve your nation in another way. Do you understand?"

"Yes, ma'am," Red says, even though he doesn't look like he does.

"That is why you're here, Redlen. Here, I've been tasked with putting you to use for the Federation." Her eyes are weary and full of sorrow. "The Premier himself saw something very promising in you when he reviewed your training videos. Not every soldier in violation of their oath gets sent to me, you know."

"And what will you do with me?"

"Have you heard of the Skyhunter Program?"

At that, Red's eyes widen. He backs up to the edge of the glass, and the color drains from his face. He knows what it is; he must have heard about it before. But my heart is still in my throat as I witness this nightmare go on, feel the terror that surges through his chest.

"It is our most ambitious program yet. The Skyhunter will become our most fearsome weapon." She bends down to look him firmly in the eye, and in that gaze, I see a silent apology for what she's about to do to him. "You should be very proud of yourself. You will soar, Redlen. But in order to do that, you must first be broken."

Then she steps aside. On the other side of the glass wall, I see a panel rise slowly to reveal a second glass room directly opposite Red's. And as the panel rises, it reveals a girl inside. Red's sister. Her eyes stay trained on Red, wide-eyed with terror.

The nightmare shudders, then shatters, as if the entire vision around me were made of glass, and the shards exploded into fine dust. I jerk awake in my bed, breathing hard at what I'd just experienced. My eyes dart wildly around the bedroom, settling first on the moonlight spilling across the floor, and then the display of my weapons hanging against the wall. I'm drenched in sweat.

So that is how Ghosts are chosen. You, your family, your loved one makes a mistake that insults the Federation. And you are all sent away to their labs, to be broken and remade as monsters in the Federation's image, ones unable to rebel against your leader.

And in Red's case, his mistake had been to spare my life.

• • •

I'm shaken out of a restless sleep early the next morning by a fist rapping on our front door.

It's Adena. Heavy bags hang under her eyes, as if she'd stayed up all night like I did, but a wide smile covers her face. Her hair sticks straight up, barely held back by the goggles pushed up on her head.

"Is Red awake?" she says in a breathless rush before peeking over my shoulder into the apartment. Then she blinks at me. "Hells, you look exhausted. Did you sleep at all?"

I shake my head, unwilling to explain Red's memories. His nightmares kept me awake for most of the night, so that every time I closed my eyes, I saw the horrible images of him and his sister being held in opposite prisons, secured behind glass. Even now, I can feel the churn of it in my mind.

"I could ask the same of you," I reply instead. "Anyway, Red's still asleep."

"Your mother's in the Grid with me. I've been working with her on something."

My mother? I come alert now. "What happened? What's wrong?"

But one look at her tells me that nothing is wrong. Her eyes are so bright, so eager, that I know immediately she's discovered something. It's the same look she gets when she has designed something no one else has ever thought of, when she sees something that no one else can see.

"I think Red just ended our war," she says.

18

IT'S EARLY ENOUGH THAT ADENA'S SHOP IS
one of the few in the Grid that has its torches lit and machines on.
Early morning light filters across the dusty floors, dotting the scattered
piles of tools with patches of sun.

My mother is still there when I arrive, hunched over a series of
identical glass vials all lined up in a wooden box, each of them with a
different label. She waves at me when she sees us arrive. There are faint
bags under her eyes too.

"Your friend's been awake all night," she tells me in Basean, touching my wrist and nodding at the display. She raises an eyebrow at me.
"She came knocking on my door at some ungodly hour. I almost hit
her with a pan before I realized she wasn't a soldier or a thief. It's as if
I have two daughters."

"Why?" I sign back. "What for?"

My mother takes one of the vials out of the container and hands it
to Adena. "You explain it, child," she tells Adena, switching now to her
accented Maran. "You discovered it."

Adena beams at her as if praised by her own mother. She takes the
vial and holds it up to the light. "You know that no one has your mother's hands," she tells me. "I asked her to help me prepare these samples

in the most sterile way. You see, this contains Red's blood. The same that I collected yesterday."

She hands me the vial before she takes out the second. "And this contains blood from the Ghost in the prison."

I look closely at the two vials. Although the Ghost's blood is darker, they're both a purple-black hue that sometimes looks blue under the right light. I glance expectantly back at Adena.

Adena nods at my mother, who takes a slender glass pipe, fills it with a bit of the Ghost's blood, and then carefully drops a bit of the liquid onto a flat tablet. Her movements are so sure and refined that I'm immediately reminded of when I was a child, when I'd watch her administer medicine to her patients.

Here is when one can see the true difference between their blood and our own. The Ghost's congeals immediately into a tight circle and then expands out as thin as it can go, as if the rage contained in a Ghost shows up even in their veins, moving outward in a hungry pursuit of unaffected blood. I stare at the unnaturally flat sheet of blood that's stretched itself thin, my stomach roiling at the sight.

"Ghost blood has low surface tension," Adena explains to me when she sees my face. "It likes spreading itself out." She opens a jar of the magnesium flakes we'd collected the day before and drops a few into the blood sample. "So you can see what's happening," she says. The circle of Ghost blood suddenly shimmers with bright bits of dust, the metallic flecks winking in and out of existence. After a while, the magnesium dissolves into the blood, leaving the liquid a shade lighter.

My mother holds a vial of Ghost blood near the sample on the glass tablet. As I look on, the froth in the sample stays completely still, reacting in no visible way to the presence of the vial.

"As you can see," Adena says as she goes, "Ghost blood is obviously uninterested in itself. Ghosts have no interest in attacking one another, or anyone else with the same poison in their blood."

She nods at the Ghost's blood. "Now watch what happens when I put my own blood beside it."

My mother takes another red vial from the container. She puts a few scarlet drops of Adena's blood right next to the sample of the Ghost's on the tablet.

The color of the sample blood almost seems to move toward the vial, forming a gradient with darker blood on the nearest end, as if drawn by an invisible force.

"Ghosts hunger for us," Adena says, pointing at herself, my mother, and me. "Their blood wants to bind with ours and consume it." She pauses to point at the Ghost's blood. "The blood has a gradient now because it has likely gathered against the side, as if yearning toward my blood, wanting to mix its poisons with mine. Until they're killed, Ghosts are designed to seek us out."

I nod at Red's vial. "What about his, then?" I ask.

Adena brightens. "Take a look at Red's blood."

This time, my mother puts a few drops of his blood on a clean glass tablet beside drops of the Ghost's. The Ghost's blood doesn't react at all to Red's blood. Neither does Red's. It's as if both were completely uninterested in each other, as still and unaffected as if two samples of human blood were side by side.

"I think," Adena murmurs, "that the Federation wanted Red to be the more advanced iteration of their Ghosts. A far more intelligent war machine, a more unstoppable one. Ghosts aren't designed to attack him, because they see him as one of their own."

Adena then puts a sample of Red's blood beside her own on a new tablet. No reaction either.

She smiles at my mother and me. "Now, for the best part. Are you ready?"

I nod faintly.

First, Adena mixes Red's blood with the Ghost's blood. Then she puts another sample of her own blood beside this mixed sample.

None of the blood samples move. The Ghost blood mixed with Red's stays floating in its own circle. There is no eerie, hungry movement that the pure Ghost's blood originally had.

I look quickly up at Adena, not trusting myself to understand what she'd just done. "Wait. Does this mean what I think it does?" I sign.

Adena's smile is so large and so full of hope that I'm afraid to believe it. She nods. "Red's blood causes the Ghost's blood to stop reacting to ours, to stop hungering for ours."

It means that Red, the Skyhunter, is the walking, living, breathing antidote for the Ghosts' hunger for attacking us. His blood is the key to breaking the bond between the Federation and their monsters.

I'm in such disbelief over what I've seen that a part of me thinks this is when I'll wake from this dream. My eyes dart from Adena to my mother and back again. "Why would the Federation create their Skyhunter to do this?" I ask.

Adena crosses her arms. "I don't think they meant to," she replies. "I think they made a mistake. Maybe it's because they didn't finish working on him before he escaped. Red doesn't respond to the Federation's beck and call. He doesn't stay trapped under their commands like the Ghosts do. Whatever it is that the Federation put in their Ghosts' blood, poisoning it, they failed to do with Red." She leans closer to me, feverish with hope. "And when Red's blood is mixed with a Ghost's, that Ghost can do the same. That Ghost can stop responding to the Federation's will. Somehow, it interferes with whatever bond that exists between their minds and the Federation."

"So where does this all leave us?" I ask. "We take Red's blood and figure out how it can inoculate the Maran population?"

Adena shakes her head. Her eyes are intense and serious now, and all signs of smiles have vanished from her face. "Red's blood works best with Ghost blood, not our own. At any rate, Mara has too many people. Red can only afford to lose so much blood before it endangers his life."

"What do you propose?"

She points at us. "We head into Federation territory. You, me, Jeran, and Red. We get into the heart of their capital, into Cardinia, where their lab is. We'll snake our way into the heart of their darkness, where they create all their monstrosities." She nods at me. "And we find a way to infect their Ghosts with Red's blood. If the Ghosts are corrupted with what his blood contains, they'll stop obeying the Federation. They'll become useless. And we'll break the most fearsome weapon they have."

"What about new Ghosts they create? Surely they'll just fix the problem."

"Yes. But it will cost them time, money, and effort. Meanwhile, our soldiers can, for the first time, mount an offensive attack at the warfront into their territory. Push the Federation back. Give us time to find a way to make enough serum to protect us all against their Ghosts. All of this might just set them back enough that they'll think Mara isn't worth the trouble of invading."

Now my heart has started to beat rapidly with the thought. Destroy the Federation's monster machine. Destroy their Ghosts.

Impossible.

But then, I just witnessed the impossible right here in Adena's shop.

This is a suicide mission in every way—maybe none of us will return from an expedition like this. Red, with his traumatic history and strange relationship with the Ghosts, might even refuse to be used in this way. But maybe he'll agree, *maybe* it could work, and we could all return having dealt the Federation a heavy blow.

My eyes return to the vials in Adena's container. Then I stare at my mother. In her eyes, I see my father's gentle face, the way his absence turned her hair white, the pain and suffering that has plagued us ever since we fled our homeland. I see everything that my patrol mates and I have lost, all the grief from Corian's death. It's hard to believe that it stems from something as small as this. A sample of blood.

If we can sever the Federation's control from its war beasts, we'll end all of that suffering. It is worth the sacrifice of a few lives.

My mother touches my hand. "You don't have to do anything," she signs to me. "You have no obligation to this world. But if you do, my heart will go with you." There is an urgency in her watery expression now. She's afraid, I realize, because she knows what this means for me.

Adena has the same expression mirrored in her eyes, the near inevitability of our deaths. No more summer days working in her shop here. No more afternoons arguing at my mother's home in the Outer City, with the smell of hand-rolled noodles and soup wafting around us. But I see no signs of hesitation in Adena either. She knows, as well as I do, that we don't have a choice.

"I didn't want my brother to become a Striker," Adena says quietly to me. She leans against the table, her eyes distant. "I woke up in a sweat one night and ran into his room, certain he was dead. He just laughed and hugged me. I asked him if he was willing to give anything in order to stop the Federation. He said he was. I asked him if he'd be willing to sacrifice me to achieve that. And he stopped to give me the strangest, most wounded look." She shakes her head. "I'll never forget that, as long as I live. Because to him, not being a Striker *was* sacrificing me. He told me he couldn't control the future, only what he could do to alter it. He knew that my future couldn't exist unless there were those willing to fight to protect me. Now that he's gone, I carry his promise." She lifts her eyes to me. "If you go, I go. This is the future we can alter."

My hand tightens against my mother's. I'm silent for a breath. Then I let go, and my hands start to move.

"It has to be a fast mission," I sign. "Get into the Federation's capital. Get into their labs. Do what we need to do, get out." My eyes narrow as anger surges through me. "And when we've accomplished it all, we destroy their labs. Burn them down."

Adena nods grimly. In her eyes is the reflection of her brother. "We will leave them with what they leave behind for the rest of us. Nothing."

19

NO ONE BELIEVES US. I CAN HARDLY BELIEVE us myself.

So the next day, the Speaker calls the Senate to gather with us in the Grid, where they form a ring around the large, muddy square of land that we use to test our weapons. A patrol of Strikers stands evenly spaced out before them, masks up, gloved hands resting on the hilts of their weapons. I stand with Red, Jeran, and Adena. In the crowd, I pick out Jeran's father and brother, the former's face stony and expressionless, the latter's looking almost bored. The Speaker himself looks disinterested in the whole experiment, as if expecting it to fail.

Guards bring out the Ghost from the prison, snarling and squinting under the sun after many months in darkness, its fury turning frantic as its ears pick up the shuffling and voices of so many humans nearby. It tries over and over again to lunge, but its handlers hold tight to the chains radiating from its neck.

Red cuts a small line in his arm and lets some of his blood drip into a large bowl of water in Adena's hands. Then Jeran steps into the circle with the Ghost, and the guards let the Ghost free. It dashes for the Senators—who part for it like terrified fish—but Jeran slices wounds into its side, forcing it to focus its attention on him. They say Ghosts don't have much capacity for higher thought, but I think this one recognizes Jeran's scent from our last visit to its cell. It narrows its eyes at him in a sense of familiarity, then snarls and crouches, clawing at the dirt. The Ghost tries to bite him again and again. Each time Jeran spins away, the Deathdancer in his flawless state, expertly guiding it around the ring so that it never attempts to attack the audience.

Then Adena darts forward and injects the Ghost with a serum she created using Red's blood. The Ghost whirls, shrieking, and shakes its head, licking its lips as if tasting the poison.

At first, it continues to lunge for Jeran, now freshly enraged. Jeran dances away each time, his eyes narrowed in concentration. I lower my eyes, unable to bear the disappointment. Something must have gone wrong in our testing yesterday.

Adena is shaking her head beside me. "Maybe I diluted it too much," she mutters to herself under her breath. "The serum worked yesterday."

Then the Ghost shudders. It turns to Jeran with a bewildered snarl, sniffing at him, tilting its head this way and that. The Senate murmurs, shifting their feet.

And as I look on with disbelieving eyes, the Ghost growls low at Jeran and turns its head away from him. It stares around the ring, growling, twitching its head as if it doesn't understand why its appetite for us had suddenly vanished.

"Oh hells," Adena breathes beside me. There's a glossy sheen in her eyes. Her words tremble. "It's not attacking. Hells. It's not attacking."

I can only stare. My hands feel numb from the shock.

The Ghost has been subdued, by nothing more than a serum made from Red's blood.

In my numbness, my gaze turns to Aramin. He's watching Jeran stand unmoving beside the Ghost, who now seems to want nothing to do with him. Who now seems to have lost its purpose. The Firstblade and Jeran lock eyes, exchanging some unspoken realization between them. In Aramin, I see a glint of fire that mirrors the hope stirring in my own chest.

I thought I knew what kind of weapon Red could be for us. A vicious killing machine, exactly what the Federation wanted him to be. But instead, it is this gift that he has given us. The key to the Federation's downfall.

Beside me, Red is frozen like a statue. When I reach out to him through our link, I feel a wave of . . . something.

Not joy. Not relief. Not even vengeance.

Only anguish. Because all this Ghost reminds him of is the moment when he had to stop his own family's suffering by ending their lives.

• • •

I don't know where Red goes after we're dismissed.

For a while, he trains in the arena, where maybe he wants to be alone after the demonstration. I think about following him to make sure that he's okay—but the hollow, haunted look that was on his face stays with me. It's the kind of expression that begs to be left alone. After all, it won't be long now until the Federation shows up at the front of the Inner City's gate. Our training arena will be theirs soon. Might as well use it while we still can.

So I return to the apartment without him, the distance between us making our bond fade until we can no longer send our words back and forth. Even though I miss his constant presence at my side, I decide to head out to the baths. The stench of the Ghost's blood from the Grid's yard seems to still hover in the air, as if the strands of my hair had absorbed the smell and made it part of me.

I make my way down the spiral of marble steps that leads to the baths. Newage had been built near a cluster of hot springs; a circle of Early Ones ruins told us that those ancient people had also used this place as a bathhouse. This particular spring is reserved for the Strikers, and whenever I'm exhausted after a particularly hard rotation at the warfront, I'll come down here amid a sprinkling of other Strikers to wash away the memories of blood and battle.

The baths are empty today. I'm not surprised. Most of the other Strikers went to the mess hall for lunch. I reach the bottom of the steps and head into the hazy, steam-tinted air. Archways made of creamy marble, restored and polished from the original ruins, are juxtaposed with newer stone pillars, forming paths that lead every which way, each ending in a long, rectangular pool of hot water. Windows cut high into the walls let the late afternoon sun stream in, illuminating patches of the marble floors and pools with golden light. It's quiet and peaceful down here, so still that I can almost forget about the revelations we'd seen today.

I remove my long Striker coat and toss it onto the floor near one of the steaming pools, then strip off the bandolier for my daggers, the belt and blades at my hips, my vest, and finally my linen shirt. Finally, I let myself sink into one corner of a pool. The steamy water caresses away some of my ache. I let out a quiet breath, closing my eyes and letting myself luxuriate for a moment in the soothing heat.

In the darkness, I sense Red's bond with me tense up, then sharpen and strengthen as if he's nearing me. My eyes open in time to see his silhouette approach the bottom of the spiral marble steps.

I stiffen and duck down in the water to my chin. He pauses there at the first archway, blinking in momentary confusion at the sight of the baths, and then turns in my direction.

The Strikers bathe here? he asks me through our link.

I nod toward the pools at the far end of the hall. *Usually the men go to a different*—I start to reply.

Oh. He hesitates, looking farther down the hall, and starts walking toward the most distant pool. With half of his body in a beam of light and half in the shadows, he looks like a mirage that might melt into the darkness. I listen as his steps lead him away, and for a moment, I feel a strange sense of disappointment.

He pauses. *Did you not want me to?* he asks, and I curse his ability to sense my moods.

I scowl, blushing. *No. Keep going.*

He continues on. There's silence for a while, followed by the faint sound of rippling water as he eases himself into his own steaming pool.

We can't see each other from opposite ends of the bathhouse, but he's close enough to talk through our bond, and that means he's also near enough to send me glimmers of what he sees. I catch a glimpse of him looking over his bare, scarred shoulder at his wings, unfurled, the black steel blades of those feathers slicing down through the water's surface. A patch of light from a nearby window halos his body in the afternoon's glow.

My cheeks redden. It's been too long since I've been with a man, and I can't help but linger on the vision of his bare skin dewed with water. I take a deep breath, trying to still my thoughts. Even though I know he can't actually see me, I stay ducked low so that all he can potentially see through our link is the bobbing surface of the pool. We stay quietly like this for a while, until I gradually start to relax again.

We can only speak from a certain distance, I tell him.

Yes, he replies.

When we're far enough apart, I can still sense your emotions and see glimpses of your world. Can you do the same for me?

Yes, he replies again. *But it seems the farther we get, the fainter that becomes.*

What happens if we're miles apart?

I don't know. He pauses. *The Federation tends to keep their soldiers and* captains close to their Ghosts, so there is always someone within several miles of a Ghost.

What about a Skyhunter?

I can feel him shaking his head. *I'm the first, and I am unfinished. I don't know.*

I imagine our link fading as we walk away from each other, first the words and communication between us, then our emotions and visions, our dreams, and then, finally, nothing but the beat of our hearts. Somehow, the thought of being completely untethered from Red sends a wave of unease through me. Have I already lost the ability to be alone? Or do I just not want to be away from *him*?

If we really can destroy the Federation's bonds with their Ghosts, he now says, *the war will end.*

Not forever.

No. Not forever. They will try to find a way to repair it. Red grimaces. *But they must first protect themselves from their newly freed Ghosts. Sometimes, all you need to fracture a regime is to exploit its moment of weakness.*

There is a growl that rumbles deep in his answer, the sound of all the rage built up inside of him over the years, and I find myself called to it as much as he's called to mine.

We each soak in peace for a long while. I think back to the memory of the invasion of Sur Kama, and then to the vision of young Red standing over me, his hand on the trigger of his gun. This time, I don't tense at the thought—I wait as it drifts through our link to Red, then at his answering emotion of dread.

You must have sensed this thought from me before, I tell him. *Couldn't you?*

I could feel the sudden hostility from you, he replies. *I saw fragments of it in your dreams.*

So he's been able to glimpse my nightmares as surely as I could see his. It suddenly occurs to me that perhaps he soothes my dreams with his consciousness, just as I do for him. There's another long silence before he speaks. *I didn't know you were the girl from that night.*

The question I've been waiting to ask him finally comes out now. *Why didn't you shoot? You just stood there.*

He doesn't reply right away. *I'd never shot a child before,* he finally says.

Before. That means he must have already been forced to kill adults, perhaps women, mothers, sisters.

You knew what it would cost you, I continue. *And yet you spared my life anyway.*

It wasn't honor, he answers, and in that answer is a lifetime of bitterness and regret. *It was fear. I . . . just pictured nothing but the carnage in my head, of you as a small girl lying on the ground, your face bloodied. I couldn't bring myself to do it.*

Do you regret it? I ask him quietly.

It's a difficult question for him, and I can feel him struggling against it, his emotions roiling at each possible outcome. He could have put a bullet in my head and spared his father and sister their fates, could have gone home to them instead of to the labs.

Finally, he says, *I always did what the Federation told me to do, because I was afraid of the repercussions. So I killed others in order to protect my family.* His words are laced with sorrow. *But then you kill again and again, and each time the threat builds, the pressure to keep them safe. They escalate their demands. You first shoot a war criminal in the back. And then they tell you to kill a soldier who is innocent. And then they tell you to kill a civilian, and then a young girl. And you realize that if you keep agreeing, it will keep spiraling down, down, down, until you've killed your own soul.* He shakes his head. *I just couldn't do it anymore. I don't know if I regret it. I don't know. I don't know.*

To have someone you love held like bait, to forever deprave yourself more and more in the hopes of protecting them until you realize you can't rescue them. Red had known the fate he would seal for everyone if he let me live, and yet he had stopped anyway.

When my mother and I first crossed into Mara, I tell him, *I felt like I would never survive the horrors I'd witnessed during our escape. But then the days pass, turn into years, and we are still here. Somehow, you find a way to make it.*

I am still here because of you, he answers.

It is a fact, a truth, because I had rescued him from his execution. But within his answer is also some other emotion from him, something intimate and secret that turns my cheeks warm again.

I'm glad you are, I tell him.

The afternoon sun has begun to fade, dimming the glow that streams into the baths. The air around us takes on the chill of a blue winter evening, made mystical by the haze of steam. The only sound is the lap of water against my skin, subtle ripples hitting the pool's tiles in rings. I stay still, wishing we were close enough to touch each other, embarrassed that he might sense my thoughts, hoping secretly that he does anyway. The bond between us brightens and brightens until I think I can see it in the darkness, a thread of blinding light, like everything in the world that is good has concentrated right here.

For a moment, all I want is to stay here forever, hidden away where nothing ever changes. Where there is no Federation. No Mara. No Ghosts or Skyhunters or war machines. Just this, the curious, quiet, intimate companionship between us. The desire for something more.

It's evening by the time I finally dry myself from the pool and step back out in my full gear. Red says nothing as I go, but when I exit the bathhouse, I feel something shift in our bond. I can't quite put my finger on what it is, but as I head to the apartment, I find myself lingering on what has changed between us, and why I find myself trying to picture his face there in the dimness, the air around him still haloed in light.

20

RED. MYSELF. ADENA. JERAN. IT IS A MISSION
that no one wants to be on.

Red will knowingly let himself be captured by Federation forces, and through our link, we'll track him back into the heart of the Federation, to the laboratory complex where they'll take him. He will find a way to open the complex for us from the inside. According to him, each Ghost at the complex has a syringe embedded in its arm at all times, feeding it nutrients and medications that come from a central control room. If Adena can get into that room, she can contaminate their concoction with the serum. What happens after that is an open door. Perhaps the newly freed Ghosts will attack no one at all, be as confused and stripped of bloodlust as the Ghost we tested. Perhaps we'll find a way to escape, or die fighting our way out of those labs. Or perhaps our tactic won't work, or we won't be able to do it effectively enough, and the Ghosts will react in a way that's entirely unpredictable. Perhaps, in their confusion, they'll try to attack anyone near them, including Karensan soldiers.

We have to wait until the Firstblade approves of our plan—but honestly, there's not much of a decision to make. We can all see that this is our only chance.

The plan spins endlessly in my mind tonight as the four of us walk past the mess hall, where Strikers currently fill the long tables, eager to celebrate before we rotate out to the warfront again. Jeran and I sign to each other in conversation, but Adena and Red are both quiet and exhausted—Red from being bled as much as he can bear and Adena from making and packaging crates of serum to be shipped to the warfront. Still, the new companionship between the two of them is encouraging. The air carries with it the sharp cold of winter and the scent of hot cider and tea. Outside the mess hall doors, they've already started hanging up wreaths of pine and berries for the first day of Midwinter's two-week-long festivities. The windows are lined with dangling droplets of golden cones and shining metal scraps. They cast a kaleidoscope of light against the cold streets. Even in a grim year like this one, we still try to scrape up some good cheer.

We continue on past the hall and out through the double walls, until we're in the Outer City's paths headed toward my mother's home. Most other nations celebrate Midwinter too, and along the narrow corridors, bright strips of fabric hang from clothing lines between the stalls, while others burn circles of candles and lanterns outside the doors to their shacks. I can smell the cooking wafting from each tiny home, peppers and spices and sauces foreign to Mara, and the aromas make my stomach rumble. We ignore the stares we get from the vendors, this group of four Strikers out patrolling through the shanties. They duck nervously when I notice them. You'd think they'd know me by now—that my intentions here have nothing to do with them. But for some, our uniforms are enough to keep them hidden. And the way the guards treat them here, who can blame them?

My mother is already outside when we arrive on her street. She's pieced together a haphazard set of crates, barrels, and giant metal tins in front of the open door, creating a jigsaw of a table and chairs for us to sit on, and covered the entire spread with an old blanket. On top is what would be considered a feast out here in the shanties—fragrant hand-rolled noodles tossed with herbs from her garden, fried minnow cakes, flat seaflour bread, and tiny squares of a sticky treat sweetened with sugarweed and honey.

When she sees us coming, she straightens and breaks into a smile.

"Thank you for dinner, Mother Kanami," Jeran says to her in excellent Basean, bowing his head. My mother beams at him and pats his cheeks.

"Prettier every time I see you, Jeran," she tells him, and he blushes so pink that Adena laughs.

Adena greets my mother with a bow and a hug, and I embrace my mother tightly. Already, though, I can tell her eyes have fallen on Red. Her smile fades, and her stare turns sharp and piercing. For his sake, I can only hope he left his mouse at home.

"I know you," she tells him in Basean. And even though Red can't technically understand her, the emotion he feels from me through our link tells him what he needs to know. That my mother recognizes him from the night of the invasion.

He stands stiffly there, not sure what to do.

Then my mother pulls him forward. She doesn't try asking him why he did what he did that night, or why he didn't shoot. Why he fled the Federation. Instead, she reaches up on her toes to give him a hug, and when she does speak again, she says, "You need to eat more, if you plan on being much good out there."

Soon, others from the street have gathered in the dead end in front of my mother's house too. Nana Yagerri brings platters of corncakes soaked in green chili sauce. The Oyanos and their son, Decaine, bring a bowl of ripe persimmons and pomegranates from their two trees. Kattee, who lives with her parents and sister at the intersection between our street and the main stall shops, comes with them, bearing potatoes seasoned with garlic and thyme.

Others come too, bearing no food at all. They stare uneasily at the Strikers in uniform seated at the table, particularly at Red, whom they seem to recognize as the Skyhunter. But their eyes are hungry, their bodies less fortunate than the rest of us have been in finding food, so my mother calls them over. At first the conversation's awkward, but soon the chatter turns into loud debates and laughter as bowls and plates are passed around.

"You're so quiet," Adena says as she watches Jeran fill his plate again. She nudges him hard in the shoulder. "Speak up a bit. Everyone here's going to think you're a spy."

Jeran swallows a piece of flatbread soaked in my mother's stew and heaves a sigh. "If we might be heading into Federation territory, I'd like to spend my last days in Mara eating as much as I possibly can."

Decaine smiles awkwardly at me as I pass a basket of bread to him. "I'm glad you're here tonight, before you leave," he says in Basean.

I can't help smiling a little. "Me too."

"Maybe, when you come back, I could make you a potato roast," he adds, his ears turning pink.

Decaine has tried to impress me for years. And even though I have no interest in him, there are times when the idea of being with my own people appeals to me, calls to me until I remember that I'm different enough to be unable to bridge the gap. So I just shrug at him and offer him another smile.

"That would be really kind of you," I decide to sign.

Laughter catches my attention. I glance to one side to see Kattee smiling at Red, who stares hesitantly back at her before he returns to eating potatoes.

I feel a strange sense of something unreasonable—annoyance?

exasperation?—before I catch myself. Why do I care if she flirts with Red? Wasn't I sitting here myself, dealing with Decaine's awkward attempts? Red looks uncomfortable, and through our bond, I can tell that he doesn't quite understand what to do with the attention. If he had been walled away by the Federation since he was twelve, then it's likely he's never known how to recognize flirting or how to return it, let alone been intimate with anyone before.

I jerk out of my thoughts to see Jeran studying me with curious eyes. Adena looks like she's about to eat me with the way she's leaning forward with her chin in her hands.

"What?" I scowl and shake my head at them, then purposely turn my gaze away.

"I think it's sweet, how you look after him," Adena signs with an innocent shrug, her round eyes never leaving mine.

I raise an eyebrow at her. "Is it not normal to worry about your Shield before he has to infiltrate the Federation's lab complex?"

Jeran nods solemnly. "That's what I prefer to do before I head out to certain death," he signs. "Scowl in a chair."

I sigh at his teasing and throw my hands up. Beside me, my mother casts glances between me and Red.

She hasn't spoken again to me about the mission we're proposing, or about whether I'm going to go. It doesn't matter, because we both already know. She has seen the heart of what the Federation can do. She knows the depths of what we're facing, and why I have no choice but to do this. Even though Adena has suffered the grief of losing family to this war, she's never been over the border, never seen what it's really like to be inside the Federation when they're swarming over you, swallowing your world whole. She and Jeran are children of a free nation. My mother and I know better.

Another ripple of murmurs crosses the table, followed by a few scattered grins from the other Baseans. I snap back to the conversation around me.

"Hm," Mr. Oyano is grunting at the end of the table, casting glances at Red. "So what if he's a prisoner of war?" he says aloud in Basean, shutting my Striker mates out of the conversation. "Doesn't make him less of a Karensan. Besides, why aren't these Strikers all at their mess hall inside the city? Who wants to spend a night out here?"

My mother glares at him. "Is it strange to you that my daughter wants to see us on the first night of Midwinter, before they set off to the warfront?"

"I think it's strange that the rest of them are here, yes."

"They're here all the time," his wife intercedes, shooting me an apologetic look.

"So?" The man shrugs and leans toward us, pointing his flatbread at me. "What kind of Basean is allowed to become a Striker?"

"Pa," Decaine mutters, his face turning beet red. "Stop."

"What?" Mr. Oyano ignores his son and continues. "They don't even permit us past the walls, let alone into some prestigious uniform. But I'll tell you this. Last week some guards came and took my neighbor Pason for questioning. Thought he was hiding tax money behind his business in the markets and confiscated a canister of cash he'd buried under his doormat. How would they know that?"

"What's going on?" Adena signs to Jeran as she nudges him.

"They think we're spies," Jeran signs back to her.

Mr. Oyano narrows his eyes at them. "And stop doing that," he snaps, pointing at their hands. "Using that spy language of yours. Speak to us. I know *you* can," he adds to Jeran.

Nana Yagerri rolls her eyes at him. "Maybe you should just learn theirs," she says to him as she signs the same words.

"Talin isn't a spy from the Inner City," Kattee speaks up, in Maran so that we can all understand, and I feel guilty for being annoyed at her interest in Red. "Can't we just enjoy their company? I never get to see so many Strikers up close."

Mr. Oyano doesn't pay her any attention. He just grabs another slice of flatbread and dips it in his stew. "It doesn't matter much anyway now, does it?" he grumbles, although now he switches to Maran too. "We're all going to be under his rule soon." He glances at Red as he says this, but seems too intimidated to keep his eyes locked.

"If you don't feel comfortable at this table," my mother says stiffly to the man, "you're welcome to leave."

The silence settles over us as we all wait for Mr. Oyano's answer. He stares at each of us in turn. Decaine looks like he wants to disappear. I glance at Adena, who's currently leaning her head close to Jeran as he whispers translations for her about everything happening at the table. Red has stopped eating, and even though he doesn't know exactly what's been said, he senses enough of the tension hanging between everyone to know we aren't exactly celebrating. He looks uncertainly at me.

I nod back, then reach for his hand under the table. Our fingers touch, his skin always warmer than mine. *Thank my mother for her cooking,* I tell him. *She'll appreciate it.* Then I pronounce the words in Basean to him.

He listens through our link, ignoring the others at the table who watch him communicate in silence with me, and then turns to my mother.

"Thank you for our food," he says to her in halting Basean.

Everyone at the table murmurs at the sight of this former Karensan soldier speaking our language.

My mother gives him a tight smile back. "You're welcome," she replies.

"His accent sounds funny," Kattee's mother says before Kattee nudges her into silence, but it's enough to make a couple of the others at the table chuckle.

Nana Yagerri leans forward on her elbows and puckers her lips slightly at Red. "Thank you for our *food*," she says for him, emphasizing the correct pronunciation.

Red tries again, getting it a little closer, but his enunciation is so exaggerated that now everyone laughs. He blinks, startled at the sound, and smiles. I nudge him teasingly under the table for it, and this time, he reaches for my hand and laces his fingers with mine. I try not to react, but heat creeps into my cheeks at the intimacy of his touch, and I realize that we're sitting so close that my body presses slightly against his.

"I could do better than that," Adena says with a raised eyebrow, and then goes on to completely butcher the Basean intonations. Everyone groans.

"Marans always make the *r*'s too heavy," Kattee says to her. "You have to roll your tongue."

Adena tries again, this time with different phrases that everyone throws at her and Red.

"Merry Midwinter to all."

"To *all*. You say it like that and it'll sound like you're saying, 'to *hit a wall*.'"

"Have a good night."

"Good luck on the warfront."

The phrases go back and forth, quicker now, and slowly, the tension at the table eases. Mr. Oyano still doesn't look thrilled by our presence at the table, but even he grunts a few times at Red's sillier pronunciations, shaking his head at Red's attempt to say "This food is delicious."

As Adena tries the same phrase, Red grins at me. *I think I'm getting it*, he thinks to me, and the outrageous pride in his emotions is enough to make me laugh.

A few hundred more dinners here, and you'll be speaking fluently, I reply.

He glances at me, lips twitching with his amusement. *I accept, then. A few hundred dinners here with you.*

I hesitate, suddenly unsure I understand him correctly. Maybe he'll have the chance to sit here with me, at my mother's home, for dinner after dinner, year after year. Maybe, if we're lucky, we'll get to grow older at each other's side like this. As Shields, perhaps. Or as something more.

It's an arrangement, I respond, unable to resist smiling back at him.

My hand is still entwined with his under the table. What a silly assumption to make, I scold myself in embarrassment, to fantasize about some distant future that might never happen, with someone I've only begun to know. But in his eyes, I see a hesitant mirror of my thoughts. It's the wild hope of someone who dares to think we all might live long enough to be here again. That it's not foolish to want.

"Your turn," Adena says to him now, breaking the moment between us. "It's only fair. What do you want to ask us, Red?" She's relaxed now, her plate empty, and a glow seems to cast her dark skin in warmth. "Tell us something in Karenese."

There's a slight pause at the thought of hearing the Federation's language at the table, but no one stops her. Instead, everyone leans in.

I look at Red. *You don't have to say anything*, I tell him, but he shakes his head and returns Adena's stare. Then he says something in Karenese.

Jeran clears his throat and looks quietly at Adena. "He asked why do we fight," he says, "as Strikers. Why we risk our lives."

The merry tone at the table turns somber at that. I wait, watching Adena's face dance through several different emotions before she straightens to respond.

"For my brother," she says. When silence follows, waiting for more from her, she continues, "My brother's name was Olden, and when I was a little girl, he would tease me about my name. Adena, you see? In Maran, it means 'the curious one.' My mother used to say that my eyes were wide-open when I was born, hungrily drinking in the world. She said I tilted my head early on to show my interest in things, so my brother would tilt his head exaggeratedly at me all the time. It made me laugh like crazy, so I hear. I don't remember any of it—I was so young when she died." She shakes her head. "After she was gone, my brother started taking me to his Striker practices, to keep my mind off things, and when I became interested, he helped me train. I was jealous of him for a long time, you know?" She fiddles with her hands. "I was my mother's baby girl, but he was my mother's favorite. I think I always resented him a little for that, until he was captured at the warfront and held hostage with a dozen other Strikers." Here she looks at Red, and even though I can tell she's trying to hold back her hatred for the Federation from him, there's still a small part of her that blames him for being Karensan. "They were never going to let him live, you know, but they let us believe it anyway. I could tell the instant they let the prisoners try to run across the border. They shot him twice in the back, took their time with each hit so he could still try to run. He died before I could reach him."

Adena looks down at her hands. "So," she says in a loud voice, taking a deep breath, "I fight because I like the idea that my random talents and interests, the things my brother encouraged in me, can now be used in the hopes of avenging his death. That's why I do it."

Her shoulders slump when she finishes, as if this had taken all her strength, but she offers Red a weary smile. He gives her a grave smile in return. It's an acknowledgment, I realize, that Adena understands what Red might have gone through. That they're on the same side.

Red nods at Jeran. "And you?" he asks.

"My father once said that the Senate was the place for the most esteemed young men," Jeran replies, looking at his hands. "He had high hopes for Gabrien, my older brother, to join him in the Senate. Gabrien has a sharper mind than I do. He remembers things more quickly and can deduce the intentions of people before I can, so when he took the qualifying exams for Senate candidates, he scored high. But I kept failing my exam. No matter how long and hard I studied, I couldn't do it. After my third try, it became clear that qualifying to become a Senate candidate wasn't going to happen for me. It was frustrating for my father, who thought me a disappointment. So I tried out for the Strikers instead. I thought that if I could prove myself among the Strikers' esteemed ranks, it might put me on a footing that could rival my brother. Maybe footing that my father will love." He cleared his throat uncomfortably. "I'm decent at it, fighting Ghosts, but it's not my natural state. I still get sick after every battle. Still can't eat for days after a visit to the warfront. So there it is. I love my country, will gladly die to keep us safe for as long as we can—but that is my honest reason."

He doesn't mention a word about his father's abuse or his brother's constant, cruel jests. I look at Adena, but she just appears resigned. It's a conversation she's had a dozen times with Jeran. *Your father beats you, Jeran,* she's told him before, gently, then firmly. *Sometimes to the point where you can't walk across the arena. You have to stop trying to earn the love of a monster.*

But there are only so many times we can say it to him. Jeran waits, bracing himself for the rebuke from Adena and me, but Adena just shakes her head and looks away.

Red's eyes fall on me. My reason to fight.

And I hesitate. I'm not sure why I do it, to be honest. Here we are, eating a Midwinter feast in front of a shack in the mud, when my mother should be living in somewhere dry and warm. Mara refuses to let her into their walls. They call us rats. We are seen as the invader.

But Mara had been the country to open her doors for us when we were at our most desperate, when she had a nobler leader. She had saved us from our fates in the Federation. We may be rats here, but we are alive. And here I am, wearing the sapphire coat of a Striker. Mara is imperfect, but it is not the Federation. I had seen the fires of hell on the night they invaded Basea, have witnessed what they are capable of. And if they cross here into Mara, if they swallow this nation too, then what will they do?

"I fight because there are good people in Mara," I finally decide to sign. "Because when we all left Basea and came here, we brought with us everything and everyone we loved the most. They're here." I look pointedly at those around the table. "Doesn't our presence make Mara home? Isn't that worth fighting for?"

The table is silent as Jeran translates my signs aloud. No one speaks for some time after he finishes. We refugees had all seen the Federation's darkness firsthand. Perhaps everyone is imagining what this place will look like when their red-and-black banners hang over the walls, when their Ghosts are led, chained, through the streets in victory, and when our families are split apart and sent to various destinations inside their territory.

It's during this silence that a messenger arrives from the National Hall. I turn at the sound of steps sloshing along the path and look up to see a young Maran grimacing at the grime of the shanties. A look of relief crosses his face at the sight of us.

"From the Firstblade," he mutters, thrusting an envelope at Jeran with the Firstblade's seal. Then he turns around without bidding any of us farewell, as if he couldn't wait to wash the infection of the Outer City from his body.

Jeran leaps up before anyone else can say a word. He breaks open the seal and pulls out the letter. Then he reads it in silence, his eyes fixated on every word.

My heart contracts at the expression on his face. A cold sweat breaks out on my brow.

"Tell us, Jeran," my mother says in the silence.

Jeran folds the letter and looks around the table. "The Speaker has refused our mission," he answers quietly.

Red hisses through his teeth at the same time Adena leans forward on the table with a slap of her fists. "What?" she says.

"There must be some miscommunication," I sign.

Jeran shakes his head. Then he unfolds it again and reads it aloud. "'Jeran,'" he says, his voice hoarse. "'The Speaker and the Senate have rejected your mission to take the Skyhunter into Federation territory. They believe we will be handing the most invaluable weapon we've ever gained back into the hands of our enemy. They have ordered you and your team grounded within the Striker complex, while Red has been ordered to the labs to be bled in an attempt to inoculate as many soldiers as possible. You have until morning to comply.'" His voice drops to a near whisper. "'Eyes forward, my Deathdancer. Yours, Aramin.'"

Signed not as the Firstblade, but as his own name. Jeran blinks back tears as his hands tremble against the letter. He doesn't even seem to care that, in reading this letter aloud, he has all but revealed to us the feelings between himself and the Firstblade.

I curl my hands into fists so tight that my nails threaten to cut through the skin of my palms. The Senate is unwilling. Unable to see. Too afraid to take a chance, even when the solution is right before their eyes. This is the same kind of irrational decision that has kept other refugees from serving in the Striker ranks.

"This is idiocy," Adena snaps. "The Speaker has sentenced Mara to death. Every child. Every civilian. This country will burn down in flames." She whirls, holding her hand out to Red. "The potential answer to defeating the entire Federation, sitting right here with us. And the Speaker is going to turn his back!"

"More than that," I add, and the others turn to me. "They're essentially arresting us. We're confined to the Striker complex until further notice."

"They won't even let us fight," Jeran says, pale. "They think we're going to resist the order and they're going to keep us from helping on the warfront. They really think Red can survive our labs and then take on the entire Federation army."

Red narrows his eyes. *I will not bleed for your Speaker*, he says through our bond. *Not like this.*

No, you won't, I reply.

He glances quickly at me as I stand. I point to the Firstblade's writing on the letter. "Don't you see?" I sign. My finger underlines his sentences. "You have until morning to comply." I look up and meet Jeran's eyes. "The Firstblade cared enough about you to write this," I sign gently. "What does he mean?"

"Aramin is warning us," he signs back before running his fingers carefully over the Firstblade's signature. "He's risking arrest himself by having this message delivered to us twelve hours early. He's telling us in the hopes that we'll escape while we can."

"Escape? Where?" Adena says before the realization dawns in her eyes. She meets Jeran's bleak gaze. "You don't mean—"

The Firstblade is trying to give us a head start to the warfront, buy us a night to travel there and cross into the heart of the Federation before the Senate sends troops to arrest us. But there is more in his message. He knows, in doing this, that his letter may be his final words to Jeran.

Eyes forward, my Deathdancer. He is giving us his blessing and bidding him farewell.

I look at my mother. We exchange a silent, knowing gaze. As a Striker, I have had a hundred moments that might have been the last time we see each other, but this time, I'm not just heading out with my patrols to face the monsters. This time we are the hunted, by ally and enemy.

Something in my mother's eyes reminds me of the way she'd looked on the night we'd fled into Mara, that light of panic and desperation. I wait for her to tell me not to go, for me to argue it with her, but it never comes. She doesn't flinch. She can see that it will do no good, because my mind is already made up.

"We're going on this mission," I tell the others. "We are going into the heart of the Federation. But we have to leave now. Tonight. Before they come for us."

The rest of the table watches in silence as the reality sinks in for each of us. Even Mr. Oyano, who moments earlier had sneered at Red, now says nothing. I know, without speaking, that these Basean refugees will protect us and pretend that we never received such a letter, that they never saw us here tonight.

Finally, Jeran speaks. "To honor Mara, then."

"Honor is a thankless thing," Adena mutters. "They'll hunt us in the morning, like we're criminals."

"Sometimes a crime is an act of heroism," my mother answers quietly. She looks at me as she says it, and I know she is telling me she loves me.

I force my breathing to steady in order to keep my tears from spilling out. Her words ring around the table, silencing us all, and Adena lowers her eyes for a moment at the truth of it. I look at my mother and suddenly wish I hadn't decided to go, that I didn't think this was the only way to save us.

Red stands first. The waning fire highlights his towering figure. He nods at me, ready. I'm grateful that at least we've come here directly from the training arena, that we are wearing our gear and weapons. And that Adena has been carrying a pouch with vials of Red's blood since our demonstration.

"My shop," Adena breathes. "They'll ransack it. My tools. I need them."

I shake my head. "No time."

"They'll send soldiers after us," Jeran says. "We need to cover most of our ground tonight."

"I'll gather as many provisions as I can." I stand up. The night is not cold, but my hands are trembling. "We need to leave within the hour."

21

THERE'S NO FANFARE FOR US THIS TIME, NO crowds gathered on the sides of the streets to see us go. There is no Striker coat streaming from my back, and I don't ride tall on the back of a horse.

Instead, we steal out of the shanties like thieves in the night, in the back of a Basean wagon driven by Decaine, as if bound for one of Mara's smaller cities to try our luck in the shanties of Spiderfang or Reedhollow. We've all stripped off our Striker coats and removed the harnesses looping around our shoulders, taken off our conspicuous weapons and strapped them inside canvas bags instead. I shiver in my inner shirt. The only blades I still wear are the daggers inside my boots. I find myself keenly aware of Red's body hot beside me, his legs bumping into mine with every jostle. Jeran and Adena sit across from us, their figures outlined by faint slivers of light from a slit in the canvas.

I don't like feeling this unequipped when threatened. But we're all still the deadliest fighters in the country. If they want to capture us, they'll have some of their blood spilled first.

The wagon itself is made out of rusted steel, full of holes, and as it goes, it creaks and groans, the faint metallic scrapping from Decaine's cycling drifting to us and tricking me repeatedly into hearing footsteps or the draw of blades behind us. Through the slit in the wagon's canvas top, I can see the Outer City's jumble of scant lights fading away, and beyond it, Newage's walls fading into the black. Soon, we're in total darkness, with nothing but a sheet of stars overhead to guide us. It reminds me too much of the night my mother and I had fled into Mara. I have to stop myself from hearing the panting of thousands of fleeing refugees beside me, and the grinding of the Ghosts coming for us in the distance.

No one says a word. I don't know how much time has passed before I hear a soft humming in the wagon. It's Adena, her voice low and throaty, the tune jerky from the terrain that we bounce over. Eventually I recognize the song, though. It's a song Strikers sing during the end of practice every day, when everyone is tired and ready to head to the mess halls.

Jeran joins in after a while, and I'm content for the moment to listen to the two of them filling the silences between the bumpy wagon with a reminder of who we are and what we fight for. Even in the darkness, I can make out Jeran still folding and refolding Aramin's letter, the paper crunching slightly with each crease.

"I lied during dinner," he suddenly says, very quietly, so that I lean forward to hear him better.

"About what?" Adena asks.

"About why I fight." There's a pause before Jeran continues. "I mean, what I said was true, but it wasn't the real reason."

"Because you actually care about Gabrien?" Adena sounds surprised.

"No. When we were small, Gabrien would find me in the house—playing on the rugs, or by the front door, or in my room—and play a game of telling me what to do. Fetch him water. Fetch his slippers. Sing for him. He said he wanted to practice what it'd feel like to be a Senator, ordering others around. If I did it, he'd think of something else. Eventually I'd stop or complain. Then he'd grab me by the hair and haul me off to the water trough outside, where we kept our horses, and shove my head in until I choked." Jeran hesitates again. "Sometimes the surface of the water would be frozen in winter, and he'd smash my head through the thin ice to the cold water underneath. But I hated it more in the summer, when the water would fester with mosquito larvae. I'd go back inside smelling like horse spit and mold."

"So you became a Striker to learn how to fight back," Adena mumbles. "Jeran. You've never told me this before."

"You loved your brother so much," Jeran replies. "I thought it'd be unkind of me to be so ungrateful for mine."

"Gabrien's not a brother, Jeran." Adena's voice is low with anger now. "He's a monster, same as the Ghosts in the valley, just disguised in silks and smiles. Like your father."

Jeran doesn't argue with what she says, but he doesn't agree, either. It takes another long silence before he finally adds, "They're my family, Adena."

"So? Your family can also be the poison in your life."

I wish there was enough light for me to sign to Jeran. Instead, I just listen. Beside me, Red shifts, sensing the sadness in Jeran's voice.

"And did your father know?" Adena adds.

"Gabrien learned it from my father," Jeran adds softly. "He said Gabrien couldn't hurt me if I was smarter about his games."

"And did Gabrien stop attacking you after you became a Striker?"

Jeran's voice is quiet, but I can make out the silhouette of his head shaking. "No."

Because he doesn't fight back. I know it, because I've witnessed how he changes in the presence of his father, shrinks into his skin and erases all signs of the graceful, confident Jeran I've seen at the warfront and at practice in the arena. The Deathdancer. And I understand why too.

It's the way I contract into myself at events like the National Hall's banquet, why I become a silent, withdrawn shell of myself, questioning my instincts. It's how we protect ourselves.

"What does Aramin think of it?" Adena asks quietly. She's the first of us brave enough to bring up the Firstblade's name.

Jeran hesitates for so long that I think he won't answer her at all. Then, finally, he says, "Aramin once asked me to be his Shield."

Our heads turn in surprise to him.

"What?" Adena says.

"He did?" I sign, even though I'm not sure anyone can see my hands.

"You were still paired with your brother," Jeran tells Adena. "If I agreed, I would move into the Firstblade's quarters in the National Plaza. My rank would surpass both my father's and my brother's." He looks at his boots. "Even though I was inexperienced at the time, our fighting styles paired well. But more than that, he hoped to protect me from my father and brother."

As he tells the story, I picture how it must have happened—Jeran meeting Aramin at the Firstblade's office in the Striker complexes, the Firstblade offering him the position, careful to keep his tone unemotional, telling Jeran he has no obligation to comply. Jeran, mouth open, wanting more than anything in the world to say yes, yet unable to make a sound. Him bowing his head to the Firstblade, then getting up and walking away.

"Why didn't you agree?" I ask him.

Jeran turns his eyes to me. "It wouldn't have stopped Gabrien or my father. None of this was ever about my rank." He looks down. "I didn't want the reason I became Aramin's Shield to be because of my family. As if they are the reason why the Firstblade approved of my fighting skills."

A part of my heart resonates with his answer, and the words of Corian's father come back to me. *He felt sorry for you.*

Adena reaches out to touch Jeran's shoulder. He flinches, his mind far away. "Well, you're *my* Shield," she whispers. "You should have told me."

At that, Jeran gives her a wry smile. "Why? So you could scold me about it?"

"That's exactly right," Adena replies.

Jeran laughs, and in spite of it all, I can't help smiling a little. At least they have each other; at least we are in this together. Red shifts against me, and I feel the trickle of his thoughts turn in my direction, enveloping me in its warmth. He doesn't let on exactly what he's thinking, and I can't read it, but I do pick up in his emotions a sense of yearning. I stay quiet, too afraid to reach out through our link to ask him what he's thinking. He doesn't say a word either. Instead, we let the wagon fall back into its creaking rhythm as the horizon yawns ahead, each of us lost in thoughts about those we love.

We travel in silence until the first hints of dusk cast the landscape outside our wagon in deep blue. Adena is snoring softly, and Jeran's head lolls from side to side in sleep, but Red stirs awake beside me.

"The warfront," he says, in accented Maran, another word he's learned in the past few weeks.

And sure enough, I can see the outline of one of our defense compounds in the distance. There's another, farther in the valley, but even from here, I can see Karensan flags flying over it. A few more big pushes from them, and they'll break past the last lines of our defense compounds, making it into the soft belly of Mara and the open lands between here and Newage. Sickness roils in my stomach.

The wagon finally lurches to a halt here, and an instant later, Decaine's face peeks in at us through the canvas slit. "You'll have to go on from here," he whispers. "There's a checkpoint I can't cross."

I nod, my bag already slung over my shoulders. Across from me, Jeran shakes Adena awake. "Thank you," Jeran tells Decaine for me.

He shrugs, but his eyes are already darting nervously around, eager to unload his illegal cargo.

The four of us ease out of the wagon without a sound into the tall grasses, where our shirts and pants blend us into the surroundings. There, we watch the wagon rumble away, Decaine hunched over his cycle as he pedals it back in the direction of Newage. I turn my attention to the defense compound some distance away. There's a fence with a narrow rampart running all the way from one compound to the next a mile away, and the top of it is patrolled by the occasional soldier. Right now, it's empty. We should have plenty of opportunity between here and the next checkpoint to sneak into Federation territory. I'm about to map out the route we should take when an image tacked up against the fence makes me blink.

It's a sketch of the four of us, along with words written in bold black ink:

WANTED: FUGITIVES
Speaker offers 100,000 meins for the
Capture of
Talin Kanami
Redlen Arabes
Adena Min Ghanna
Jeran Min Terra

No one caught our wagon on the way up, but news about our escape has beaten us to the warfront.

I duck lower into the grasses, my heart racing. The defense compounds usually have lookouts with telescopes, scanning the area for Federation troops and Ghosts, but no doubt they're now also searching for us.

"Now what?" Adena signs.

Jeran nods toward the woods, where the valley leading into the Federation's territory begins to slope. "If we can make it into those trees," he answers, "we should be able to get over the border before they can catch us. We just have to cross this grassland first."

"The snipers will be aiming to injure us," I add.

Adena nods back at Red. "Not him. He's valuable."

I'm not even sure if snipers *can* hurt Red, not with his unnatural, armored skin and his weaponized body and mind. He may move so quickly that he can dodge the snipers' bullets, could kill everyone at both defense compounds. But massacring our own side is not the goal we have today. Mara can't afford to lose more Strikers.

Red. I nod at him, speaking through our link, and brush my fingers against his arm. He turns his dark eyes to me, and my chest tightens in fear for him. *I'll go first. Stay beside me.*

He seems to know what my intentions are before I can properly articulate them. *Stay beside me; shield us with your body so the snipers don't try to hit us. Help us get through the valley into the Federation's territory, while I keep an eye out for Strikers or guards that spot us.* I can see the understanding in his eyes as he takes in my thoughts and makes sense of them as if our minds are one.

His gaze turns to the woods ahead. We begin to move.

It's slow going through the grasses as we try not to move through them quickly so that the swaying grasses draw attention. But as we go and no responses come our way, I begin to hope that we can pass through uneventfully.

Then, abruptly, something shines from one of the compound's towers. I freeze in my tracks like a deer. My heart jumps. It's a sign to the second compound.

They've spotted us.

No later than I think this, a shot grazes through the grass and zips past me, dangerously close to striking my neck. The bullet hits the dirt so hard that mud splatters onto my face.

Instantly, Adena flattens herself to a low belly crawl and speeds up. "Move," she signs back at us with a cutting hand gesture.

We copy her and cut through the grasses as quick as we can. Even now, our movements barely register a sound. But when I glance up, I can see the first hints of figures emerging from the nearest compound gates. Strikers with their masks up.

I've been hunted before by Ghosts and by Federation soldiers, but never by Strikers. Never my own. So now, for the first time, I'm on the receiving end of the terror of seeing those sapphire coats heading silently in my direction, and the Strikers' dark, ominous eyes above the veil of their masks. Friends and allies I've sat with in the mess hall. Killers trained in everything I know. One and the same.

"They see us," I sign to everyone. "It doesn't matter now if we hide. We just need to move fast." So I straighten and start sprinting.

The others do the same. We cut wildly through the grasses, keeping our heads low and bodies tucked in close so that the snipers firing at us have a harder time. A second bullet hits a foot away from me, a third so close to Red that it grazes his arm, leaving a burnt streak. He doesn't even flinch.

The Strikers are closing the distance between us. I wipe sweat from my brow and keep my eyes ahead.

Then the clearing before us suddenly parts, widening abruptly into a valley thick with trees. We dart for the dim paths of the woods—

—and run right into a patrol of Strikers.

If we'd been hunting Ghosts, Jeran, Adena, and I would never have stumbled into enemies like this. We're trained to track Ghosts and Federation troops, know the sounds and mistakes they make. But pitting

Strikers against one another is something else entirely. I didn't hear them coming, and neither did they hear us.

There's the smallest fraction of a second in which we all look stunned at the sight of one another. Instantly I recognize two of them as Tomm and Pira. The other four are faces I know from the arena. They have simply materialized through the dim light of the forest, their silhouettes rippling in the dark.

The light of recognition hits their eyes at the same time. Then Tomm narrows his eyes and lunges for me.

Every instinct trained into me now surges through my veins. My body reacts—I duck down and seize the dagger in my boot, then bring it up in time to block his hit with the hilt of his blade. Another Striker aims for my other side, but Jeran's already there. Somehow he manages to knock the blade from the second Striker's hand and turn it on him. Adena is fending off the two others, all the while trying to get into her canvas bag of weapons.

My eyes sweep desperately over to the edge of the forest. The end of the warfront—and beginning of Federation land—is just beyond us, so close I can taste it. If we could just get over, we might run into enemy troops, but at least the Strikers won't follow us.

Then I see Red. His teeth are bared. In one mighty sweep, his wings unfurl to their full expanse. He turns his rage in the direction of the Strikers fighting Adena.

Panic surges through me. I shove Tomm back and send a thought barreling through my link with Red. *Don't hurt them!*

His head whips toward me.

They're Strikers, I tell him as Tomm hits me again. This time his hilt catches me in my side and I dart away, pain lancing up and down my body. *Mara needs them.*

As soon as I think this, Pira's blades flash before my eyes. I flinch.

There are just too many of them, and I don't have my other weapons with me. They'll capture us at this rate unless we spill their blood. Unless—

—and then I realize that Pira isn't attacking me, but clashing blades with Tomm. She shoves her Shield back before giving us an angry glance.

"Stop playing games and get the hell out of here," she signs to me with rapid, cutting gestures. Then she whirls to face Tomm as he gives her an incredulous stare.

"What are you doing?" he signs furiously. "Firstblade's orders!"

But Pira just shakes her head. There's no time to explain, and we're too close to the border to risk speaking out loud.

I don't linger, even though I want to meet Pira's gaze and ask her why she's helping us. There's no time for questions or conversation. Nearby, Jeran breaks away from the Strikers he's fighting. Adena has managed to wrestle out two of her blades from her canvas bag and connected their hilts together, turning them into a new double-bladed weapon, and slices a deep gash into one of the Striker's legs. He stumbles, wincing. Still silent, as trained to be.

I dart for the border with Red. Jeran sees my movement and breaks away from his Strikers long enough to make a run too. Adena stumbles backward, but Jeran reaches her and catches her as she's about to fall, yanking her upright again and pulling her forward. We all run.

Red drops back behind us. As we gain speed, he whirls around and bares his wings at the oncoming Strikers. They shrink back slightly, hesitant to attack him. He turns around and tilts his wings down, lifting himself into the air, and glides over us in a single sweep.

We're almost there. The forest feels like it parts for us as we sprint. The trees start to look unfamiliar.

And then I realize, in our mad dash, that the Strikers are falling

behind. No, they've stopped. They've reached the edge of Maran territory, the no-man's-land where our warfront shifts to our enemy's, the
limit of where they can go.

I look past the forest to where a clearing slopes down into the valley
that leads into unfamiliar land. This is what finally makes me slow to a
stop. My ears ring with a high-pitched buzz, and my breaths come in
labored gasps. The look on Pira's face still hovers in my mind, haunting
me, and I realize that I'm so unused to her acting on our side that her
help frightens me. It means she knows just how desperate our mission
is, and how much we need it to succeed.

I should feel some sense of relief that we've escaped the Strikers
chasing us, but all I feel is the unfamiliar dirt under my feet and the
chill in the wind that whips through the clearing. Jeran and Adena halt
beside me too, shivering, neither uttering a word, their faces turned
down toward the valley, where the oncoming evening stretches long
shadows across the land. Red comes last to stand on my other side. In
him churns an old fear, a terror borne from firsthand knowledge of the
kind of darkness that we've just entered.

We have officially stepped into the Federation.

THE
WARFRONT

THE KARENSA FEDERATION

22

IT DOESN'T TAKE LONG BEFORE WE STUMBLE
across the first evidence of enemy soldiers making their rounds through
this newly acquired territory.

Prominent on the forest floor are the telltale signs of soldier tracks,
the shape distinctly different from ours, the toes rounded while Maran
boots come to a sharper point. There are few at first, one here and
another twenty yards away, but gradually they become more regular
until there's a solid path through the woods, made by soldiers clearly
confident that no one is using the prints to track them.

We move invisibly in the lengthening twilight. Jeran and I stay in
the trees, scouting ahead, while Adena makes her way on the ground,
blending in so well with the tall, thick ferns crowded beside tree trunks
that sometimes I completely lose her. Red moves with her, the most
conspicuous by far, his muscled form a dark shape in the shadows of
the trees. I keep a constant eye on his surroundings, ready to throw a
warning if there are any signs of soldiers nearby.

We must have traveled for several miles by the time we come across
tracks more regular and numerous. Here, the trees grow more sparsely
too, and we find ourselves approaching the section of the valley that I'd
glimpsed from the top of the hill as we crossed the warfront.

Red is the one who stops us first. He halts abruptly, then narrows his eyes in the direction of the clearing. I feel a tug in my mind from him, as if he's calling out for me to slow down. I look down at him from my vantage point in the branches to see him nod at me.

Careful, he tells me before looking ahead. Then he says a Karenese word that I've never heard before, for which there's no equivalent in Maran. *Trains incoming.*

I frown down at him at that. *Trains?* A thought in his mind spills into mine, flooding me with the image of a black engine billowing smoke into a blue sky, giant metal wheels churning in sync with one another, and a series of dozens and dozens of metal carriages chugging one after the other into oblivion.

Now I know the word *trains.* I've seen wreckage of them before, part of the Early Ones' ruins. We assume that they were once a mode of transportation, when there were things like ships in the sky as surely as in the water. But I hadn't thought the Federation had them, functioning ones, these enormous monsters that belched ash and soot as they roared across the land.

But Red says it again. *Train station*, he tells me, nodding at the clearing up ahead.

I sign the same to Jeran, struggling to explain what it is, and then down at Adena. We pause, listening for sounds of soldiers, before slowing our pace and inching forward.

Then I do hear it. The sound of soldiers' voices, speaking Karenese, coming and going as if busy with something or other. From several trees away, Jeran crouches low in the branches and points in one direction, through the trees and into the clearing.

I move along my branch until it crisscrosses with that of another tree, make my way onto it, and then peer toward where Jeran's pointing.

There, before me, is a sprawling sight. Several Federation campsites dot the space where the trees thin out, and then, a short distance from them, is a building with lanterns twinkling against its walls, built in front of a long metal track that snakes far off into the valley until it disappears over a hill. Sitting in front of this building, partially obscured by a curtain of steam, is a great black engine lined with silver paint, its enormous wheels extending back to a second compartment, its trail of carriages running far down the track.

A train station.

Soldiers bustle everywhere there, and from this distance, they appear like a swarm of black ants—their uniforms and shadows melting into one another—as they load boxes and crates onto carts and then head back to the station, unload, and then head out to the campsites scattered across the land. Elsewhere on the land are plots already churned into dirt by workers, upon which are unfinished buildings with long fences coming up around them. Defense compounds, I realize with a sickening start at the sight of half-constructed watchtowers. The Federation is already beginning to strengthen their presence here in the new land along the warfront.

Jeran glances questioningly at me, then points down at the nearest campsite, where a small patrol of Federation soldiers have set up their tents within the last few lines of trees. They're perfect for what we need.

Red, I say through our link. When he looks up at me, I nod through the trees. This close, the link between us tugs sharply at my mind, and I can feel the rapid rhythm of his heart and the rumble of breath in his throat.

We'll be watching you, I remind him.

He nods. *Keep close as you can when you trail me,* he responds. *The train will lead us back into the capital. All the trains converge there.*

The capital of the Federation. My heart squeezes tight. I can no longer tell if it's anxiety from Red, for having to return to the darkness he'd emerged from, or if it's my own, for venturing in for the first time.

Good luck, he says. I startle at the final words from Red through our link, and when I look down at him, he's pressed his hand to his chest in a Striker's salute.

And in this instance, I am overwhelmed with the fear that I'm going to lose my Shield again, just like I'd failed to protect Corian. I'm about to let Red walk back into the Federation that had twisted him into this half-man, half-machine weapon.

How strange that, not long ago, I'd been facing him in the training arena, staring at him in shock as the Firstblade named him my Shield. I'd hated his every step then, loathed being tethered to him. Had been terrified of what he could do. And now here I am, entirely capable of betraying him and leaving him behind, and I cannot imagine doing it.

I find myself tapping a fist against my chest in return. *I'm not going to leave you behind*, I tell him quietly.

Red looks away from me and down toward the train station. There's something in the link that tells me he doesn't quite believe me, but he nods anyway without responding. Then he turns away from us, and we watch as he walks into the woods in the direction of the tents until he's lost among the trees.

I straighten and force my eyes away. Time to get into position. My boots find their footing against the edges of broken bark on trees, and in a few seconds, I'm crouched among the gnarled branches that almost overlook the campsite. Adena has disappeared into the brush, while Jeran perches on light feet in a tree opposite me. There, we wait.

From here I can make out laughter echoing from below. There must be a dozen soldiers down there, all sharing a bite of lunch as they clap one another on their backs and stamp their feet in an attempt to warm up cold toes. One of them points and laughs at a mate struggling to load a heavy crate onto the train at the station. The fury rises in me from somewhere deep. Karensan soldiers, able to laugh even after all they've done. What had they been doing before this? Were they torturing hostages? Killing Strikers at the warfront?

Then I remember Red's story of how he'd been punished by the Federation for failing to shoot me during the Basea invasion. I think of how his family had been separated and then individually destroyed, how he was made to participate in it. And I wonder how many of these soldiers have been trained into their cruelty, whether or not they're like Red, out here laughing around a fire at the warfront because if they don't, their families will be torn apart.

Crack.

All of us freeze at the sound. Down below, Red had purposely stepped on a twig and made the sound. It echoes from where he's hiding, crouched in the ferns.

The noise around the campfire pauses. There's silence, followed by murmurs. Then I see a scarlet uniform making its way down the path through the trees. One of his friends calls out at him, looking exasperated, but the first soldier waves him off and keeps walking in the direction of Red's hiding place.

In the trees, I rise into my fighter's stance.

Red shifts just enough to catch his attention. The soldier freezes at the sight of him, then jumps back instinctively with a shout. Immediately, the others at the campsite hop to their feet. The first soldier pulls out a gun and points it at Red. With his other hand, he frantically waves the others over.

Red avoids looking in our direction, but I can hear his thoughts. *There's some confusion among them*, he tells me as he glares at the first soldier. The troops are wary around him. Like we'd been when we first saw him in the arena, they can tell that he's built strongly, like a horse, muscled in the chest and arms, lean in his torso, as if he'd trained as someone who can fight. But he doesn't look like a Maran, and his silence unnerves them. I look on as they mill about before forcing him to get to his feet by waving their guns at him.

Then a call goes up among them, echoing from one soldier to the next, each repeating the same word as the next.

It's the Skyhunter, Red translates for me in his mind. *They know who I am now.*

They must have been briefed on how Red looks on the chance that they stumbled across him in the wilds. I wonder if they'll relay word of this back to the capital immediately.

Below us, Red turns around and feigns an escape. If I didn't know our plan, I would have believed him. Maybe it's not all false, either—the fear in his eyes is tense and sharp, the same that I'd seen on him during the siege at our compound. He starts retreating down the path that leads back into the forest, away from the soldiers—but his movements are purposely slow, a pretense that he's been injured or weakened by exhaustion.

They fire something at him. In an instant, Red collapses.

My every instinct screams at me to leap from the tree and attack the soldiers. I'm a better fighter than any of them, even with their more advanced guns and weapons, and if I take them by surprise, I could kill every single one before they could figure out where I'd come from.

It takes all my strength to hold myself back—to recall that Red reminded me that the Federation has no intention of killing him when they've invested so much in him, that they would bring him back to their lab complex and continue their work on him.

Through our link, I feel his consciousness shudder, his heart slow, and his body suddenly cool. He tries to reach out to me through our bond, and I grasp for him, but he's gone before I can, and on the path below us, I see him go limp against the forest floor, surrounded by soldiers.

I watch in silence, trembling from the act of keeping myself still and hidden, as the soldiers approach to capture him. Underneath the steel mesh of their nets, Red looks surprisingly vulnerable, not a war machine but a human caught in their trap.

The soldiers exchange rapid words before one of them goes running back to the train station. Two of the remaining clap each other on their backs with a laugh, while several others point at one another, arguing. They look shocked, shaken, and even elated by their find. Their movements remind me of when prizes are won during Midwinter celebrations back in Mara, and I wonder if maybe there was a bounty put on Red, some reward for the capture of him alive. Perhaps these soldiers are arguing about how to split it, or imagining what they'll do next with it. It must have been a significant prize. Each new thing they do sets my teeth on edge.

Only one of them looks up at the trees in our general direction. I still myself into invisibility, barely daring to blink. Several branches away, Jeran slowly inches farther into his hiding place so that even I can't tell he's there. The soldier frowns thoughtfully to herself, but she doesn't seem like she wants to interrupt the others. And who would? They act like they just won the jackpot of their lives. Why question how it happened?

I hold my breath as her eyes wander from one tree to the next. But we've given her nothing to see except shadows and bark.

Finally, one of the others shoves her arm slightly and gestures toward the train station. More soldiers are coming now, bringing with them some kind of sled to pull Red back with them. They struggle to get his dead weight onto the sled, and then they're dragging him away toward the train. The woman who had been searching the trees goes with them, whatever concern she might have had disappearing as she keeps pace with the others. Their excited shouts fade into the distance as they go.

I don't move a muscle until they're well out of earshot. Then I shift forward in the branch and survey our surroundings one more time. The other campsites are farther away, and there are no signs of Ghosts nearby. It seems like Red's capture has gotten everyone at the station worked up, with soldiers swarming back and forth to the train as Red is loaded into one of the metal carriages.

Still, I wait a few more minutes before I finally drop to the ground, making no sound more than a soft hush against the dirt.

Jeran's already down, his figure barely perceptible among the ferns. I don't even notice him until I see his hands moving in the darkness. "For a second, I didn't think they'd take him back," he signs as he brushes leaves from his shoulders. Behind him, Adena emerges from the shadows without a sound.

"They would have," Adena answers, her fingers moving rapidly. "I've seen them carefully load up Ghost corpses to take back with them. No Karensan patrol would be instructed to leave behind something that can be studied."

Something that can be studied. I think of the vision of the glass chamber I'd seen in Red's thoughts. When they get him back to the lab complex, the first thing they'll want to do is find a way to establish the link between him and the Federation. Make sure he obeys the right people and never tries to escape again.

"I don't know how that train works," I tell them, nodding in the direction of the station, "but smoke is starting to pour from its front."

Jeran nods at me. "Do you still feel his pull?" he signs.

Even unconscious, Red's mind sends a faint, steady pulse that touches my thoughts, just as when he's asleep or dreaming.

"Yes," I sign.

Jeran looks off toward the train station. "Let's go, then."

The night has set in fully now, so that the only light floods from the station lanterns and the train itself. Steam pouring from its chimney drowns it in a fog that hides the silhouettes bustling around its base. Good. It'll help us hide too.

We steal closer to the station under the cover of darkness until we've reached the long line of carriages sitting on the tracks, and then slide underneath them to wait for soldiers to hurry past. They must be in the process of laying down more tracks, I realize, given the steel and wood piled high on the side of the station. And then it occurs to me that they're doing this because they're preparing for the day when Mara falls, so they can continue expanding their world into ours without interruption. The realization leaves me cold.

Finally, we see an opening as soldiers step away from the train. A whistle blisters the air with its shrill shriek, and for an instant, my heart jumps in the way it does when a Ghost is near. Then Adena is tapping my shoulder quietly and gesturing at the carriage nearest us, now loaded with wooden crates.

"They're about to move," she signs, before we steal out into the shadow cast by the train on the side facing away from the station. Through the sea of steam obscuring the ground, we make our way along the side of the train until we find the nearest carriage with its door slid open. Jeran pulls himself up into it without missing a beat, then reaches down to grab Adena's arm. He hoists her up. When he reaches to help me up, the train jerks forward. The movement makes me stumble as I land inside with them. We readjust our footing as the train begins to pick up speed, then push ourselves back into the darker recesses of the carriage, where the scent of wood and pine and metal fill the space.

I've been in wagons and on horseback. But seeing this enormous contraption of steel move from a crawl to a steady roll to a roar is like something out of a bad dream. The stench of black smoke makes my eyes water. The train station behind us vanishes rapidly as we speed into our enemy's land. Jeran curls up beside Adena in an attempt to keep warm, while Adena reaches into her canvas bag to hone some of her blades.

I settle near the edge of the carriage, partly shielded from the cold night by crates in front of the door, and let myself lean against the wall, feeling the sway and jostle of this strange machine. I have no idea how many times or where it will stop, if at all—and at this pace, I have no idea how quickly we'll arrive in the capital. The night swallows everything outside the door, swathing it all in black. Now and then, I see a flicker of light in the darkness from some cluster of lonely country settlements. What kind of technology will we find once we arrive deeper into the Federation?

I hold my trembling hands out in front of me, turning them this way and that, missing the warmth of my Striker coat and gloves. Suddenly, home feels achingly far away. Is it even home now? If we return, will we be imprisoned or executed?

The only thing that steadies me is the constant, quiet pull of Red on the other end of my link, a sure sign that he's in another carriage on this train.

My jaw clenches tight. I'm not here to save him, but to find a way to take down the Federation before the Federation can take Mara down. Still, the entire mission now suddenly takes on a personal tint. I couldn't promise Red that we would help him escape back to Mara. I couldn't promise that we would live through this. But now, as we make our way inland, I tell myself that promise. I'm going to get him out of here.

And it's only here, in the shadows of a strange land, that I realize I'm finally thinking of Red as my Shield.

246

23

I'M NOT SURE WHAT I EXPECTED THE FEDERA-tion to look like.

The farther we travel away from Mara's borders and into foreign territory, the warmer the climate gets. The next afternoon, as the chill of Mara's winter winds fades away into lighter breezes and clearer skies, we stop shivering beside one another, and the landscape switches to rolling hills dotted with bushes and tiny towns. Here too are ruins from the Early Ones peeking out everywhere—rusted hulls of hulking structures and flying craft, some draped in greenery, others still standing stark against the sky. There are old, hollowed-out buildings of crumbling stone that have never been rebuilt. Small towns circle other ruins, stripping those structures down to their barest bones so they are nothing more than piles of rock in the center of a dozen buildings.

Then, by late morning, we cross over a hilltop and find ourselves pausing at a station inside a small city.

It's only here that I realize something that turns my stomach. We're traveling through Basea.

I barely recognize it. The town where I'd grown up was a landscape of green, rows of plants lining the edges of neat grids of houses. But this place where we've stopped looks nothing like what I remember.

The land around it has been stripped of the forests from my child-hood. It now lies bare and yellow, and beyond it is a thick, half-built jumble of civilization—the wooden lattice of buildings under construction leaning against old steel bones of ancient cities, dirty roads churned into mud, logs sliding down their paths to the workers below, stacks of apartments leaning on either side of the rows. Beyond the unfinished borders of the city rise towers crowded one next to the other, their windows hung with lines of drying clothes. Lines of steel slice through the ground, along which run smaller trains filled with people. Signs written in Karenese hang over window fronts.

Baseans bustle in the streets. They hunch their shoulders nervously as they pass Federation soldiers standing idly on the intersection corners. Maybe there's some sort of curfew in place.

A weight sinks in my stomach. It's a childish fantasy, but somehow I'd always imagined a day when Basea would win back its independence and my mother and I would travel back to our old home, then see it still standing there the way it does in my memory. That, in my wildest dreams, we might even stumble across my father, as if he'd just gotten lost wandering through Basea and was waiting for us to return. Of course we couldn't—I'd seen this land burn with my own eyes. But how could so much strangeness pop up here in the years since I've been gone? What would my mother think if she saw this?

I'm glad she can't. I'm almost even glad my father isn't around to witness what has happened to his nation.

This is a different land. This is Karensa.

Adena's hand on my arm makes me startle. I look up to see her face pointed grimly out at the scene. "Best we get back inside," she signs at me. "I think they're checking the carriages."

I rip my eyes away from the scene and scoot into the shadows with

Adena as soldiers hurry by, carelessly glancing inside to make sure their cargo is there before patting the side of the train and moving on.

A short time later, the train's whistle cuts through the air and I feel the carriage lurch forward again. We leave Basea behind. Soon, we're traveling through wide stretches of alternating farmland and wilderness. Jeran and Adena don't speak at all. Our Striker training has embedded in us the need to stay quiet in hostile surroundings, so here we use the occasional sign, nothing more. I find myself oddly comforted by our shared silence. When my stomach squeezes in hunger, I take out hunks of cooked yam and flatbread from my canvas bag and share it with the others as they pass me cold strips of chicken.

Through my link, I can tell that Red is still unconscious. They'll probably keep him this way until we arrive at the capital, and I'm glad he doesn't have to be awake for this journey, but I find myself missing his voice all the same.

Rain slants down across our carriage's opening for the second night. The next morning, right as the first rays of light peek out over the horizon, we finally feel the train slow around a bend. I stir out of an uneasy sleep, uncurl my body, and make my way over to the entrance. Jeran's already there, crouched, his entire body tense. He nods out at the scene without looking my way.

I glance out to see Cardinia, the capital of the Federation, sprawling before us.

The smaller city we'd seen now seems like nothing more than a construction project next to this place. Bridges of black steel radiate from the city's edges in regular intervals, arching over a deep trench of a river that acts as a protective moat. The buildings stretch into the sky with brutal elegance, eight or ten stories high, their sides draped with banners trimmed in scarlet. Their interiors are flooded with so much light that I wonder how they prevent their buildings from burning down. Other trains run in and out of the city via the bridges, huffing their steam behind them in long trails.

I duck farther back into the carriage's shadows as we now head along one of these bridges into the capital. My eyes tilt up at the structures towering over us. As we cross the river and enter the city, the roar of life fills my ears. There are people everywhere, spilling out from storefronts, packed into marketplaces, squeezed onto small trains that cut through the Karensan cities we'd passed before. They look like they come from every nation that the Federation has swallowed, although their clothing has changed to align with Karensan style—long, straight coats and trousers on the men, short coats on the women with loose pants that are so wide they look like dresses swaying with their steps.

Horses pull wagons through the crowded streets. The roads are paved with the same smooth black rock we have in our streets, a creation from the Early Ones. There are sights of beauty—enormous fountains surrounding elaborately carved statues, wide expanses of lush gardens, long roads lined with shops selling every variety of goods.

I focus on these shops the most. Fish, meat, and vegetables. Shoes. Soaps. A store with cans and jars piled high, selling preserved foods. Then there are stores displaying yards of fabric of all kinds, from silks to cottons and wools, as well as ammunition and weapons, knives and blades and guns, cakes and breads, cigars, hats, and medicines. The sheer variety makes my head spin. Along the banks of two rivers cutting through the city are dozens of factories, each seemingly powered by the churning of enormous water wheels. We have a few factories in Newage, right outside the Grid, all of them dedicated to creating uniforms and weapons for our soldiers, but here they seem to make everything. I see every manner of goods leaving their doors in carts.

I always knew, as did everyone, that the Federation was more advanced than Mara, that they had managed to learn a great deal more from the Early Ones than we did and put those inventions to use. They have always worshipped everything the Early Ones created, certain that they are the chosen ones to carry on that legacy. But seeing it all here with my own eyes leaves me feeling overwhelmed. How can we hope to defeat a nation this much more developed? What are we going to do?

Everything feels run with overwhelming efficiency—and yet, I can't help but feel that things are off, that there's an underlying tension beneath this bustle of economy and productivity. A moment later, I realize that tension comes from the imposing number of soldiers in the city, armed with guns at every corner, watching every interaction around them. And not just soldiers . . . ordinary citizens watch one another too, their eyes darting from one person to the next, as if no one can be trusted.

Adena points at the people. "Will we draw attention here if we stay dressed like Baseans?" she signs. She gestures down at the clothing that my mother and neighbors gave us, our high boots and linen shirts.

"We'll attract more if we dress as anyone else," Jeran signs back. "See how often the soldiers are stopping people on the streets?"

Right as he says it, we see a pair of guards gesture at a girl who looks lost at an intersection. She obeys, and when she does, one of them holds her hand out. The girl gives her a paper. The guard looks at the girl again, then nods and points down the street as if to show her the way.

"Basea has been conquered long enough that the soldiers shouldn't be surprised to see some of us in the crowds," I sign. "Jeran can translate. If anyone stops us, we'll say we're in the city to shop for supplies and ask for the nearest clothing store."

As the train pulls to a stop, we slide out immediately and duck down underneath the train before the guards start coming around to unload their supplies. At first I wonder if the soldiers will do a close inspection of each carriage, but then we notice their boots hurrying past us all in one general direction. Somewhere farther up the train is a commotion.

My link shudders, and then a steady trickle of emotions—bewilderment, anger, a dull pain—pour into me from Red. Through it, I glimpse flashes of what he must be seeing. The dark interior of a carriage now flooded with light. A dozen hands reaching for him. He's awake. I know immediately then that the commotion must be for him.

Are you here? Are you safe? Red's voice echoes in my mind a moment later, and I close my eyes, overwhelmed with relief at the sound.

Yes, I tell him. *Where are you? What are they doing to you?*

There's a pause before he answers with an image. And there, I see as if through his eyes a steel-bar cage yawning before me. His vision is shaky as soldiers shove him inside. Red tries to stand, but something they've given him has weakened his muscles, and he struggles to stay on his hands and knees. The bars close behind him, and then he's locked inside, chains shackling his body tight to the cage so that he can't veer in one direction or the other. All around him, soldiers shout in Karenese, and through Red, I can understand them.

"Back away, back away!" one yells, waving at the others with both arms. "He's not completely drugged."

"Straight there?" another asks.

A third nods. "Orders direct from the Premier. Don't keep the Architect waiting."

The mention of him sends a jolt through me. Of course, word of Red's capture had been sent ahead of the train, and Constantine himself would be impatiently expecting the return of his prized possession. But their mention of an Architect brings me up short. We know so little of how the Federation's experiments work. All I'm sure of is that this must mean they are going to take Red to their lab complex. Anticipation courses through me at the same time I feel a stab of fear.

What if we can't get Red out in time?

We're right behind you, I tell him. *I promise.*

He doesn't respond, but I do feel a flicker of hope come through our link from him. Then they're taking him away, and the images vanish from my head as Red's concentration switches to something else.

It doesn't take long for the soldiers to follow in his wake. The ones remaining settle into the task of unloading items from the train, starting from the very back. As they work, we find a moment to slip out from the tracks, and in the clouds of steam, we vanish into the city.

It's too easy to get lost in this overwhelming place, this maze of streets and alleys and plazas, of towering buildings lined with severe columns and harsh lines. Here too are what look like ruins—except they don't resemble the Early Ones' ruins that we have in Mara. Curves of steel that might have once been the side of a ship, an exquisitely carved wall that must have held up a beautiful building, uniform steel structures that look like rib bones, stretch up to the sky in dizzying patterns. Unlike in Mara, though, these ruins do not look like they originally belonged here. They're not embedded in the ground as if they've been there for a thousand years. They look freshly planted here, then fenced off and marked with labels.

Jeran stops to read one of the descriptions. Then he clears his throat, careful not to use sign language here in public, lest he give away our Striker status. "Wall of the National Courthouse," he translates in a low voice. "Larc."

And then I realize that these are not ruins from the Early Ones at all—but pieces of destroyed buildings and structures taken from the nations that the Federation has conquered, then brought back here to display as trophies.

I take a step back from this open-air museum of graves, suddenly queasy. Soldiers stroll past us with leisurely expressions, as if they're not concerned at all about the war happening at their far border. They're the faces of those who know that the war is all but won for them. Who are ready to march through Mara's steel walls and plunder it, bring our ruins back to this capital and put them on display for their enjoyment.

The night when their soldiers had raided my home in Basea now comes flooding back to me. I no longer feel like I'm walking down a manicured path in the Federation's capital. I see Basea around me, falling. Screams filling the air. My mother, seizing my hand and telling me to run. My father, already disappeared, whose memory I still cannot recall from that night.

What former Basean landmarks will I find displayed here? What will they take from the ashes of Mara, once they invade and burn us to the ground?

"Look," Adena whispers as we make our way down another street.

Her voice cuts through my rising tide of thoughts, and I gratefully turn in her direction, eager for the distraction. My eyes settle on what's caught her attention. In sconces on either side of each building's entrance are torchlike objects. But when I look closer, I see that they're not flames. At least, not candles or torches in any form that I recognize. The golden glow from them are contained inside small glass bulbs.

"I don't understand. How do they light?" Adena murmurs in fascination, reaching a hand tentatively out to touch the surface of one glass bulb. She jerks her hand away, as if it burns the same way a flame does, but then goes back to touch it again, tapping delicately against the glass, her eyes wide.

"Doesn't it burn?" I ask her, standing closer so that others near us don't see me signing.

She shakes her head. "It's hot, but bearable. Not like a flame." She squints at the fixture, and I can tell she wants to take the whole thing off the wall and bring it back to Mara to study.

I touch the glass too. The light inside the bulb is so steady and warm, like a frozen flame. I frown, tapping the glass the same way Adena had done.

In Mara, we'd learned from the Early Ones how to make guns and buildings out of their leftover steel, fortified our estates with their other-worldly metals and stone. But what kind of technology is this? Fire that doesn't burn, light that gives off heat but no flame.

In the back of my mind, Red's presence tugs at me. I look away from the strange invention and out into the street in the direction he must be.

Jeran watches me. "It's him?" he murmurs.

I nod, listening for a moment. Red is too far away for words to pass between us now, but I can feel his unmistakable presence as well as a trickle of images he sees. Rows of trees, lined too neatly on either side of him. A circle of buildings, all draped in tall banners. Curious crowds gathered around his cage. And a festivity of some kind, a fair being set up, all colorful tents and grass sectioned off with rope.

"Something is happening in the city," I tell the others. "A sort of celebration."

I turn and lead us down a narrow road that opens onto the lawn of a large circular building in the center of a square. Now we start to see banners hanging from the metal poles around the city.

"Midwinter, maybe?" Adena murmurs.

"It's possible," Jeran replies, "although my language classes taught me that the Karensans don't celebrate Midwinter. Perhaps a difference in decorations?"

"Less white, more desserts?" Adena suggests at the sight of carts lining the streets, selling food on sticks.

As we walk around the circular building, still following Red's pull on my mind, we reach an area where we get a better vantage point of this part of the city. A wide river slices through the roads, and over it

255

curve steel bridges. Beyond it is a section of the city that appears less crowded, with none of the towering apartment buildings that we had just passed. Instead, there are tall hedges and shorter buildings arranged in neat courtyards that span at least a dozen blocks in each direction.

And then I see the array of colorful tents rising beyond the hedges in a wide, open plaza.

I nod and point toward it.

"Let's go join the fun," Adena says.

I step forward and am about to head down the terrace when a voice makes me freeze in my tracks. It's cool and steady, one full of authority borne from a lifetime of power. It's the same voice I'd heard on the night the Federation pushed past Mara's warfront, when I'd witnessed Red's terrible strength.

I whirl around and come face-to-face with the Premier of the Federation.

24

GONE ARE THE HARSH LINES OF HIS ORNATE battle uniform. Today, he's dressed in a simple but luxurious robe of flint gray. His face is as sickly and gaunt as I remember but washed clean of the black paint, the dark circles under his eyes like bruises against his white skin. Under his faded brows, though, his eyes gleam like the edge of a blade. He smells of rose water and soap, and I realize that the circular building we're beside is a bathhouse, where he must have just come from. All I can think is that he's far too young to be ruling this regime in his father's stead. Far too imperial for his delicate body. Far too ill for his age.

He regards us curiously.

The three of us kneel before him in sync. I keep my head lowered so that he can't keep staring at me, so that I don't have to reveal my silence. As I stare at the ground, my mind whirls. We'd been so intent on locating Red that I never even noticed him nearby, hadn't even considered the possibility that the Premier would merely be wandering the grounds of his city. From the corner of my eye, I can see the boots of a small patrol of his bodyguards gathered in an arc around him, along with admiring—and fearful—citizens looking on a distance away. Maybe this bathhouse is a frequent stop for the elite of Cardinia, which means they must live nearby. The luxurious plazas on the other side of the river, near the festivities, must be the official government halls. Perhaps that's where the Premier's home is too.

As this jumble of thoughts rushes through my mind, the Premier shifts and addresses us again. His voice stays calm, but I can hear the sternness in it, the expectation of a proper reply.

Jeran finally answers in an apologetic tone. I glance up at the young man, only to find his eyes again locked on me. He seems to consider Jeran's words before he tilts his head and repeats them, his voice hoarse and rasping.

Jeran looks at me as he tries to keep a calm façade too. "He says he knows you, Talin," he murmurs at me.

I keep my face passive, but a cold sweat breaks out on my back. I wonder if he can sense the tension in my muscles. He's only seen me once before—in that single, brief moment on the battlefield during the Federation's failed raid, when he'd made his ultimatum and then witnessed Red's display of power. He'd been watching us from a distance as I tried to calm Red down. And when I'd looked up again, he was gone.

Does he really remember my face from that small moment, from so far away? But I shouldn't be surprised. Even now, I can tell that his sharp mind is whirling, trying to place the familiarity of my face.

I shake my head and look down so that I don't have to talk.

The Premier leans to rest his elbows on his knees, then regards me closely. I have no choice but to stay where I am, my eyes lowered.

When he speaks again, it's in Basean.

"You must be in the capital for the national fair," he says. "I suppose you're interested in seeing our Ghosts up close."

His words have a slight Karenese accent, but otherwise he speaks Basean so well that I glance up at him in surprise. There is something breathtaking about his grace, the straight lines of his neck. Against his robe, his eyes take on a deep gray hue, like a storm reflecting against sunlight. He studies me carefully. I tense, waiting for him to recognize me.

Then one edge of his lips quirks up at my reaction. "My father always told me that I needed to speak all the languages of the nations I'd someday govern," he tells me. "Learn your habits and cultures. How can I rule, otherwise?" He looks casually at his bevy of bodyguards, who chuckle in unison in response. "You need to understand your people, what they're trying to tell you, what they're saying to one another." Those piercing eyes return to me. "Isn't that so?"

He has trained in every language so that no one can sneak secrets by him in a foreign tongue. I shiver at the serenity in his voice as he tells me this in unspoken words. A part of me wants to test him on this, to sign to him and see if he can respond to that. But letting him know my muteness will only give him one more clue as to who I am. So instead I swallow my defiance and lower my head again, as if I were nothing but a stupid Basean terrified of her new Premier.

He's silent over me. Maybe he notices the tension in my muscles and is piecing everything together. If he raises the alarm and calls for his guards to arrest us, we'll have to try to kill him here. But that will be near impossible. The only weapons I can reach immediately are the knives in my boots, and his guards are so close that I don't know if I could move quickly enough to end his life before they pounce on us. There might be more guards watching us right now, waiting in the shadows to protect him, ready to fill us with bullets before any of us can make a move. Even if we could—the Premier of the Federation, murdered in broad daylight in the capital? We will die here alongside him, and Red will remain forever trapped in their labs. It won't stop their war machines or their invasions.

Then one of his companions speaks up with a terse laugh. I can't understand him, of course, but I glance up to see that the speaker is a young man dressed in the garb of a Karensan general, standing strong and healthy in contrast to the pale, thin Constantine. He'd been at the warfront siege.

My tense moment with the Premier breaks. Constantine nods at the man's words without looking at him. His gaze shifts from me to Adena, and then finally back to Jeran. "You've picked up the Karenese tongue quickly for a Basean," he tells him. "Well done." He straightens and gives us a nod of dismissal. "The fairgrounds are on the upper side of the city, across the bridge. Enjoy yourselves tomorrow."

Then he's gliding away from us with his guards in tow, falling back into conversation with his general, moving as steadily and gracefully as a Striker through the streets. A cluster of spectators watch him and whisper from a distance. They bow in a wave as he passes. I watch him go, still kneeling, my emotions tumbling from relief to rage. From wherever he is, Red must feel it too, because I sense his alertness heighten, followed by worry in my direction.

"What did that general say?" Adena whispers to Jeran.

Jeran's eyes follow the retreating figures. "That was General Caitoman Tyrus," he whispers back. "The Premier's younger brother." He glances at me in sorrow, his voice hollow. "He told Constantine to stop harassing the survivors from his conquests."

His conquest: Basea. A cold rage churns in my stomach. I tell myself to calm down, that we are here to take all of this down from within.

Adena leans close to me, her head still bowed. "Constantine said the Ghosts will be out for the national fair," she whispers. "That means they'll open the lab gates to take them outside."

Her words cut through my fog of emotions like a beam of light.

I look quickly at her. She's right. The Premier himself had said it, as casually as if it were common knowledge. Whatever this national fair is, it sounds like their Ghosts will emerge for the public to see.

Which means tomorrow is our chance to get into the Federation's labs.

25

THE COMMOTION BEGINS EARLY THE NEXT morning, when the sky is still sleet gray.

Shouts from a guard on the streets stir me out of an uneasy sleep. Then comes the steady pull from Red somewhere in the near distance. I lie still for a moment, trying to remember where we are—wedged underneath an awning in a narrow alley between an apartment complex and a store selling soaps and cigars, where others in the city too poor to rent a room for the night have also camped. There are dozens of others here too, living in makeshift tents or simply sheets propped up with poles. The smell of unwashed winter bodies hangs musty in the air.

I concentrate for a moment on Red's emotions. He seems groggy this morning, as if his mind were swimming in a fog. Have they injected him with some sleeping drug?

Adena groans as she stretches out her back. "I dreamed about my bed back in our Striker quarters," she complains in a whisper so that others don't overhear her speaking Maran. "And I never dream about that bed."

"At least it was a warm night," Jeran whispers in return.

I just shrug. For me, who's used to life in the Outer City, this almost feels like a slice of home. As I look on from under our awning, a line of these people is already snaking out the alley to crowd outside the factory entrances near the river, where they seem to be hoping for work.

A low hum of activity buzzes in the streets. Adena scoots over to the edge of the alley to peek out at the bridges. Sure enough, packs of people are already starting to head across toward the colorful tents, their voices alert and excited. Young workers are sprinkling a mixture of flower petals and squares of crinkled, colored paper along the road.

We share some of the last of our cooked yams and flatbread between us for a meager breakfast, and then dust ourselves off as best we can and head out of the alley into the street. As we go, Red's mind hums through our link, pulsing weaker and then stronger whenever we veer near the river. It's easy to get lost in the throngs across the bridge, and as the morning wears on, the space only becomes busier. The national fair seems to be held in a circular series of plazas all connected to one another with walking paths, a collection of green open spaces surrounded by Cardinia's government halls. As we go, we start to pass some of the colorful tents, each growing in size the farther in we get.

"This is a fair displaying their latest inventions," Adena murmurs into my ear as we stop before one of the tents. She nods at the display, her eyes bright. "Look."

Under this tent, they're demonstrating the glass bulbs that contain the flameless light we'd seen the day before. A woman cranks a lever connected by wire to one such glass bulb, and as she does, we see the bulb glow bright. People clap as the woman gives them all a brilliant smile.

At another tent, a man lifts an enormous metal plate imprinted with what looks like thousands of letters against steel, then presses it down against a sheet of paper to produce a large print of the embedded words. He then steps away as the machine works on its own, printing multiple copies of the same print over and over. Over the noise of applause, he hands out some of the printed pages to young children in the crowd.

Each tent exhibits some unusual invention, each more impressive than the last. Along the walkways, street stalls are already set up at regular intervals, selling fried meats and sweet snacks, fresh fruits and paper bags filled with candied nuts. Other stalls sell fruit too rotten to eat and bread too moldy to keep, little sharpened sticks and pebbles with sharp edges to them. These confuse me for a while before I realize they might be things meant not to be eaten or used, but to be thrown.

Finally, we enter the main plaza where the largest tents loom. Here we come to a stuttering halt. Towering several stories in the air is a massive structure built almost entirely of steel and glass, with a grand curving roof letting in the light. One look tells me immediately that this was built on top of a ruin. The Early Ones' influence is everywhere— symbols carved into the stone floor look reminiscent of those on the structures in Mara, and the tall pillars of black steel that circle the edges of the plaza are jagged on top, as if once part of something bigger. But the glass itself reminds me of Larc, one of the nations that the Federation had conquered long ago. They must have swallowed their artisans and engineers as much as they'd swallowed the land.

Beyond this impressive building, near the end of where these government halls line the city, I see a courtyard surrounded by hedges and walled by a long gate, around which dozens of guards now stand. Red's presence pulses in my mind. He's somewhere in that direction, my instincts tell me. Perhaps that is the Federation's lab complex.

Now I walk underneath the giant glass entrance with Adena and Jeran, trying hard not to let my temper get the best of me. Hundreds of guards are inside this building, pushing crowds back and forcing clear pathways between exhibitions. There are displays of enormous machines, some with wings, humming with wheels running as if they might take off into the sky. I think instantly of some of the ruins I'd seen before in Mara, the Early Ones' winged machines, and realize with a lurch that maybe the Federation has begun to figure out some of those ancient inventions and have remade them. Other displays are of new guns that advertise to be faster, more accurate, and more devastating than ever before. There are huge cannons, as well as parts of ships and new styles of experimental armor modeled by soldiers. Children squeal in delight as one of these soldiers pretends to lunge at them, his movements shockingly fast behind plated metal that must be light as air.

Suddenly, Jeran touches my arm. I look in the direction he's focused on.

And there we see the cages that are currently drawing the biggest crowds—along with the creatures contained inside them.

The first cage holds a Ghost as I know them. It's lying against the cold, metal floor of its cage, its body cut with lines of shadows. If it stretches out, its hands and feet touch the opposite ends of the space. The cage's bars are painted gold, and as it stirs, it squints under the sunlight beaming down through the glass atrium. It turns its milky eyes feverishly at the crowds surrounding it, gnashing its teeth, but unlike the Ghosts I know, it doesn't lurch at the audience. Instead, it's subdued. I think of what Red had told me about the Federation's link with its Ghosts, how it can command them into rage or calm, and realize that it's not attacking anyone in this crowd because it has been told not to.

Children mew in fright and clutch their parents' hands. Older boys and girls laugh and point in delight, some of them tossing the rotten fruit I'd seen being sold at stands into the cage. Adults give it looks of awe and fear. I can see their expressions change as its cage rolls by, the way they nod knowingly to one another as if they're studying a specimen in a zoo.

264

Standing on either side of its cage are pairs of guards, hands on their guns as they watch both the creature and the crowd.

The next cage features a Ghost too, but something about it also seems different from those I've fought on the warfront. Its features are less twisted, its limbs less stretched and cracked. Its eyes even seem less milky, and it turns its head from side to side as if it can see us more clearly, stopping to focus on each of us. It still gnashes its teeth against its bloody mouth, but the teeth are shorter too. Even its voice, still gritty and raw, sounds less like a Ghost's and more like a human's.

In horror, I look at the next cage. This Ghost looks even less like a monster, with limbs only stretched a bit long and its stance like one that is used to walking on two legs. It has hair on its head, white strands clinging together in greasy clumps, and its eyes look more bewildered than enraged, with a spark of something left in them.

One after another, the cages display Ghosts less and less like Ghosts, until finally I see a cage containing a young man, his skin not ash white but warm with pinks and yellows. His arms already have deep, bleeding cracks in them, but they are the length of normal human arms, and his fingers look like my hands instead of clawed fingers that have been broken and regrown. His hair is long and unkempt, shaggy with sweat. He grips the bars of his cage and peers out with such a heartbreaking look of fear that I feel my heart swell in pain.

They are displaying the progression of a man into a Ghost. Even now, as I look on, I can see each of them transforming gradually, their bodies twisting painfully into what they will ultimately become.

My arms and legs tingle from the horror of the sight. I think of Corian, how he used to kneel beside the bodies of dying Ghosts and offer them a few final words. *May you find rest.* And now all I think of as I stare at this nightmare of an exhibit is the sound of those dying Ghosts, the piteous, humanlike cries begging for mercy.

Beside me, Adena's eyes are hauntingly dark, and as unsympathetic as she is toward most things related to the Federation, she looks as sickened by this sight as I am.

Red's foggy mind still lingers through our link. For a horrible moment, I wonder if they're going to have him out on display too, their Skyhunter, to be observed like an animal in captivity. But I reach out tentatively through our link, asking him where he is, and when he doesn't reply, I realize that Red is still too far away for me to hear his voice. He can't be right here in the glass atrium.

Two people are standing in front of the row of caged Ghosts. One is a bearded man with a wicked smile so bright that it would seem he's showing off a gold statue instead of experiments in cages. He now taps on the bars of the nearest cage, making the half-formed Ghost inside jump in startled anger.

"In the span of fifty years," he says to the audience in a loud, clear voice, "we have used what you see here to conquer nearly every nation on our continent. By the end of this winter, we will finally overtake Mara. Then we will stretch from coast to coast, an unbroken land. This is only the beginning of our Infinite Destiny, as ordained by our ancestors." He stretches his arms wide. "Here before you is a treasure trove of inventions, gifts given to us by the civilizations that came before us. Unlike them, though, we have improved on what they've created and learned from their mistakes, so that we will never fall into darkness and obscurity. This is our Premier's promise to you. There will be no ruins of Karensa!"

It's similar to the words I'd heard on the night they attacked our warfront. No ruins. Infinite Destiny. This man speaks it with such reverence that it almost sounds like fear. In the midst of the crowd's riotous applause, he sweeps his hand up at the balconies overlooking the atrium, and there I see the young Premier standing with his guards, dressed now in a full scarlet outfit and coat, his bald head sporting a heavy band of gold. He waves at the crowd, a proper smile on his face, and the audience cheers him. He must have someone else address the people for him, because his own voice has the rasp of someone deeply ill. I instinctively shrink behind the silhouettes of taller people, hoping he doesn't spot me in the crowd.

The second person standing beside the announcer, a long, lean woman with a slight hunch in her shoulders, looks more reserved. She wears a white coat, and her eyes are so deep set that the light beaming down on her swathes her gaze in shadow. Although she doesn't speak, I sense the tension in her, the tightness of her posture and the stiffness of her muscles, frozen like a rabbit before its predator.

It's the woman from Red's nightmares.

"And now," the man continues, offering a formal hand in the woman's direction, "a demonstration of the Chief Architect's abilities."

She startles a bit at this sudden introduction. Then she steps forward, turns her back to the crowd, and faces the cages. As she does, the crowd instinctively shifts to murmurs, their faces intent on her.

"Bow," the Chief Architect says to the Ghosts. Her voice is not loud, but it carries clear and unmistakable across the room.

In the cages, every Ghost seems to freeze. They bend, bowing to the audience seemingly against their will.

The crowd gasps at the spectacle. Even I gape at the sight of these monsters on their knees, their heads lowered before this woman. They don't look up once, don't snarl, don't gnash their teeth. They do exactly what they're told.

This is it, the Federation's real power on full display: the ability to take a human being and twist body and mind into a monster—a creature capable of such severe hatred that it would then kill others just for the need of it—and the ability to then manipulate those monsters' minds to do the Federation's bidding.

"That's enough," the Chief Architect says. This time, the Ghosts rise in unison out of their bows and go back to their crouches, their twisted, destroyed faces subdued, if unsettled. The audience gasps again in approval, then claps and whistles.

They don't think of the Ghosts as machines of death, mutated from humans like themselves. They think they're fun. Entertainment.

The Chief Architect watches the crowd without reacting, her expression as blank as a hollowed soul.

"Do you ever feel power over Red like this?" Adena whispers beside me, her eyes riveted on the Chief Architect. "Or him over you?" Every fiber of her being seems fascinated by the control this woman has over her monsters.

I shake my head.

Adena chews her bottom lip as she thinks. I know she's picturing the samples of blood that she'd experimented with, how Red is the key to severing this powerful bond. "Tonight," she finally murmurs. "We'll get into those labs. We'll change all this."

Everything in me wants to bolt out of this crowd and aim for the woman standing before those cages. The one responsible for creating these monsters that have destroyed so many lives. I could kill her, even with only my knives. I could do it so quickly that no one would know until she lay dead at my feet.

Of course, I don't. Adena is right. We have come here for a plan bigger than that. So I take a deep breath instead and wait with the crowd, enduring their cheers.

It's only then that I pick out some of the downcast expressions and anguished eyes in the crowd. Here and there, I spot a man looking anxiously from one cage to the next in search of something, or a woman hugging a child to her with a pained expression. Near me stands a little girl leaning so far out to see the cages that she looks like she'll fall any second. She continues to strain at the edge of the crowd until someone pulls her back.

The families of those who had been mutilated into Ghosts. Those permanently separated from one another and then condemned to this half death. They're here too, silent and helpless, looking on at all the people around them who don't seem to care. Searching quietly for something familiar in the faces of these creatures. Trying to find the lost pieces of their families and terrified that they will get their wish. Those who have felt firsthand the true cruelty of the Federation, their tool for keeping their military mighty and their people under control.

Red's sister and father.

As I think this, I feel a shock of pain come through our link. Perhaps he can sense that they're on my mind. And suddenly my anger at this crowd dampens, replaced by true sorrow. How many of them applaud and cheer because they have no choice, because not doing so invites the risk that the Federation will come to their doors one night and rip their families apart? How many of them, then, have faked this glee so often that they now believe it?

Even though I know he can't hear my words from this distance, I send him my thoughts anyway.

We're not leaving this place without you, I tell him. *And all of this— these sick games, this awful display, the torment of these souls—will come to an end. We will avenge your family, and mine. I promise.*

I don't know how much of that promise Red can feel. But the thread of emotions between us turns dark, determined. My eyes lock on the

Premier still standing casually up on the balconies, his cool eyes turned down at this hall. We may all die by the end of this mission, but so long as I'm alive, I'm going to bring this Federation down. I'll tear down every brick of this place if I have to, until there is no breath left in my body.

26

ALL THROUGHOUT THE DAY, I FEEL RED'S PAIN shoot through me. It's a knife in and out of my mind, coming and going, until finally it fades away with the sunset. I don't know what is happening, but either they've stopped what they're doing to him, or he's collapsed into unconsciousness.

His agony leaves a sheen of sweat over my brow as dusk falls and the fairgrounds begin to quiet. Fog settles into the corners of every street, haloing the city's lights and blurring the crowds like a dream. We linger with the people, watching and waiting, until finally the guards unhook each of the Ghosts' cages from their platforms in the glass exhibition hall and start to pull them out of the space. As they do, the remaining crowds jostle to watch the procession.

We join them. Adena nods in the direction of where the hedges wrap around a gate, the same luxurious courtyard we'd seen earlier in the morning.

"I think they're going to parade them down the paths toward there," she whispers.

Jeran glances at me. "Red?" he asks.

I nod, my eyes fixed on the hedges too. I jut my chin in its direction.

"Do you know what he's doing? Can you see anything?"

"No," I reply. "We're too far away. I'll try when we're closer."

The crowd begins to disperse as the procession rumbles toward the complex gates. In the misty twilight, the Ghosts stir, gnashing their teeth, their eyes turned on the hedges with what I think is almost fear. Several of them, the ones still somewhat humanlike, avert their gazes altogether so that they don't have to see. The lone human among them is curled into a tight ball on the floor of his cage, his shoulders shivering with sobs.

I close my eyes for a beat, concentrating. Red's pulse feels shallow, a nervous and flittering rhythm. Gradually, as we edge closer to the far side of the government halls, our link begins to take a more distinct shape. I sense more of the pattern of his emotions, followed by the faint haze of thoughts, so vague that they feel like dreams forgotten by the first light of dawn, hovering just out of my mind's reach. Then, as we pass another bridge toward the hedged gate and the crowds turn sparser again, Red's mind sharpens—I'm finally able to focus on some blurry memory.

I see glass walls and the glint of light against them. Somewhere nearby, whimpers echo.

We're close enough to the complex now that the gate emerges from behind tendrils of fog. The procession continues on, and as it goes, several of the guards at the gate move to open them. As I look on, one of them heads to what looks like a rectangular lock on the side of the entrance. He turns dials on the lock that I can't see from here, and then twists the entire lock in a full circle until it completely inserts into the wall. The gate groans open.

Adena watches all of this from the corner of her eye. "It's a code they're using," she murmurs as we continue to walk, "although we're not anywhere near enough to see it."

The first of the Ghost cages reaches the opened gate. More guards come around the perimeter to look on as the cage is ushered inside.

They keep guns out and drawn, visible for the spectators to see, so that the remaining crowd gathers in an arc around the outside of the gate while each of the cages heads in. We stop here too, clustering with the others as each cage rumbles by.

The open gate is so close. Inside, I glimpse only a few trees and the wide expanse of a grassy courtyard leading up to a series of windowless buildings.

There's a sudden commotion on the other side of the gate. One of the people in the crowd has broken free from the others with an anguished cry. He steps forward as the cage holding the untransformed young man rolls in, and for a few seconds, his foot crosses the threshold inside the gate.

Then the soldiers are on him. He disappears in a scuffle of uniforms, still struggling wildly.

"Bena! Bena!" he's shouting, but then his voice cuts off abruptly. When the soldiers step back, I see the man lying unconscious on the ground, a thin trickle of blood leaking from the back of his head. Two guards pull him up and drag him unceremoniously across the dirt path to deposit him on the other side of the bridge.

I swallow hard and try not to fixate too much on the stricken face of the young man as his cage wheels into the complex's inner courtyard. He uncurled himself from his fetal position at the sound of the other man's voice. His face already looks unnaturally pale, and sweat glistens on his body. I know this phase well, have seen it on many Strikers who had to be killed. By midnight, he'll be well on his way into his Ghost transformation.

Adena forces herself to stay focused on the lock. "If I knew the code, I could figure out how to input it," she whispers. "Are we close enough to Red yet?"

I clench my teeth and look away from the procession to concentrate instead on Red.

His mind has sharpened in mine again, so that now I can feel the details of his emotions—a prickle of curiosity at the fact that I'm nearby, then the stir of his heart as it beats more rapidly. Then, his voice.

You're outside the gates, he says in my mind.

The gate has a code, I tell him. *Do you know it?*

No, he tells me. *They've changed the rotation of their guards. There have been more of them here ever since my return. Do not come back at midnight.*

When, then?

Come at the hour before dawn, and use the entrance meant for servants, on the side facing away from the main path. There is a different code there, but the same lock mechanism. It's where they took me inside yesterday.

Do you know the number?

I can feel his mind at work as he recalls the numbers he'd seen the day before. The last of the procession enters the gate, and the guards begin to pull it closed again. A part of me longs to bolt inside the courtyard before they can seal the complex off from the rest of the world. But I stay where I am, until the gate locks again with a clang, and the guards shout at the remaining crowd to disperse. People begin to wander off, some elated by what they've seen, a few children dashing about with excited chatter.

Then Red's voice comes back to me again. *Four, five*, he says. *Two, six. Nine, four.*

He says the numbers slowly, as if struggling to remember them from when he'd been returned to the complex, and I can tell that he's hesitant about them. *Once you're in*, he finishes, *I'll guide you.*

We'll see you then, I tell him anyway. I know he can sense my uncertainty, but he doesn't respond to it.

Then it's all over, and we go with the last of the crowd so we aren't the final few standing in front of the gates. I look behind me to see two women and a little girl lingering at the gate, as if hoping it will open for them. Maybe they had been the ones in the audience who recognized a loved one in the face of one of the Ghosts. What they hope to find now by staying here, I don't know, but I doubt it will bring them any peace.

I force myself to turn to Jeran instead. He doesn't look at me as we cross the bridge. "Will Red be able to get us in tonight?" he whispers.

I nod once. So it's finally time for us to execute the mission we'd come all this way for.

Jeran nods back, but he doesn't smile. Neither does Adena. We stay mute the whole way back through the main plaza until our expressions are hidden by the night's shadows.

Because we all know getting in is not the hard part. Getting out will be.

• • •

We wait through the night until dawn is approaching.

The air has a bite of cold at this hour, and I shiver in the thickening fog as we perch in the trees lining the banks of the river. I miss the heavy coziness of my Striker coat. The fog will help conceal us, but the thin shirts we left Mara in don't do well on a cool night like this, and I find myself thinking up new curses in my mind as a way to distract myself.

The guards should change soon. Red's voice comes to me again, echoing in the quiet of my thoughts.

We're waiting at the side entrance, I tell him. My eyes dart from one guard on patrol to the next. *They don't appear to be in any hurry to change.*

Adena glances at the side of the wall. We're still two buildings away from the entrance where we'd seen the procession of caged Ghosts enter. She absently touches the pouch tucked securely at her waist, where she keeps the vials of Red's blood that she's going to add into the complex's water system.

They used to stagger it differently, Red answers. *Then I escaped during one of their windows. They changed the hour to just before dawn because of it.*

Why?

Because it's when both night and morning rotations of soldiers are in the streets, and the capital is under the heaviest guard. We'll have the smallest chance of escaping out of the city.

From here, I can see a hint of guards standing near the side entrance. A series of shrubs obscures our line of sight, though. I glance at Adena, then look up at the buildings' roofs.

"I'm going to get some height," I sign. "Better vantage point."

She nods silently back.

In the night, my boots don't make a sound. Every ounce of my Striker training comes forward now as I move like wind through the shadows. At the edge of the building, I get a foothold against the wall and reach up for the roof. My gloved hand closes around it.

I grit my teeth and pull myself up into a crouch on the edge.

There are guards patrolling up here too. I can see a couple making their rounds on the top of the gates that surround the complex. I wait quietly until they've turned their backs to me, and then melt into the night by blending into the branches of a tree that leans over the roof.

From here, I get a better view of the main entrance. There are two additional guards we hadn't seen, each posted at the far edges of the building.

I tell Red this.

Good, comes his answer. *They keep watch when the rotation happens. It will be soon.*

And almost like clockwork after he tells me this, the other guards around the perimeter pause in their usual routes as another set of soldiers comes to replace them. There is some shuffling, and for a while, the place seems to crawl with their uniforms. But in this there is a slightest sense of chaos, exactly the window we need as the only soldiers with their minds entirely on their watch are the pair at the side entrance, doing temporary duty.

Now is our only chance.

I bite the inside of my cheek and glance toward the trees. No one else would be able to see where Jeran has hidden. But after a beat comes a low trill, followed by the sound of what seems like a clicking beetle. Only a few seconds later, I hear a faint rush through the air. Down below, one guard at the side gate suddenly touches a hand to his neck before his knees give way. He slides slowly to the ground. On the west side, the guard makes the same gesture, then hunches as if he'd sighed. His body crumples without a sound.

As always, the Deathdancer never misses.

For the briefest moment, a flash of doubt sparks through me. This is it—this is too easy, but it will become difficult very soon. We are going to fail in what we do, we will die for it, and the fear of that fills me with sudden hesitation.

But then my training kicks back into gear, and my body acts before my mind can decide.

I'm sprinting as the second guard hits the ground. We have to move fast now. They'll know within minutes that something has happened. I dart to the edge of the building, take a silent leap, and land on the building next to the main one. In my mind rush the exercises I'd done through the rooftops of Mara's Inner City—how Corian and I would race together, side by side, from the double gates to the National Hall without alerting any of the city's soldiers. If we failed, we'd start over. It would go on for hours.

Corian's laugh still echoes in my mind from whenever he had beaten me. If he were here with us now, no doubt he'd take down the guards before I could even make my way off the roof.

Now I cushion each of my steps the same way I'd done during our training. Down below at the side gate, Adena materializes from the shadows of the trees to drag the guards' bodies into the darkness. She moves quickly—one blink and they're there, another and they're gone. I stop in the trees right above the gate as Adena emerges to look at the lock. Another guard walks by on the complex's gate. He glances in my direction, then looks right past me, and continues.

I slide a knife out of my boot and give myself only a split second to aim. The knife flies down at the guard, burying deep in his throat.

His eyes pop open as his hands fly to his neck. I'm already down from the tree before he can see me as anything more than a shadow in the night. My hand wraps around his mouth and I snap his neck hard. He goes limp in my arms as I lower him to the ground, collecting my knife and his weapons in one swift motion.

Well, look at you, Corian would say to me with a smirk if he saw me now. *So light on your feet.*

Adena pulls her face mask down as she studies the lock. There are a series of six tumblers against the rectangular grid, each with the numerals 0 through 9 on them. She turns each, realizes they don't just move like a simple tumbler, and fiddles with the first one until she figures out that it requires a twist to the left and then a twist to the right. Her eyes dart occasionally to me as I sign the numbers to her as a reminder. Her fingers move quickly, feeling the weight and clicks of each tumbler.

"What a design," she whispers to herself.

Four. Five. Two. Six. Nine. Four.

Then Adena tries to turn the lock in the same circle as the guard had done.

It doesn't budge.

Her eyes dart immediately to me. "Wrong numbers," she tells me. Her eyes go frantically to the edge of the gate. The new guards will come around the bend soon.

"Try again," I tell her.

She runs through it again. Again, it fails.

What if Red remembered them incorrectly? He had sounded so hesitant. He must have gotten one of them wrong. I close my eyes, willing myself into calm, and think.

Then, through the fog of my memories, I think of one incident with sudden clarity. The moment after the battle, when Red was feverish and near delirious on the floor of the makeshift infirmary. He had called out words from a Karenese story that his sister had once read to him.

A hall with no end.

A day to live.

A millions ways to bridge the rift.

According to my vision of that moment between Red and his sister, she had read the lines from right to left, the Karenese way, not left to right as Marans typically do. Maybe Red had told me the code in the same way, meant to be input right to left.

I wave urgently at Adena. "Four. Nine," I sign. "Six. Two. Five. Four."

Adena starts again right as a guard comes around the bend in our direction. She spots us. I see her hesitate, shocked, and then get into a fighting stance. She's going to raise the alarm.

But then a blur comes from the trees. Jeran. His knife sinks deep in her chest. She utters a gurgle, but I know the wet sound of her voice means her lung was punctured. She staggers against the wall, then slides down with a whimper.

It's a messier kill and none of us can go over there to hide the body. But there's no time.

Adena finishes putting in the new numbers and tries turning the lock again. This time it works. It spins in a full circle before sinking into the wall, and the gate clicks open.

We dart inside.

There's little time to take in our surroundings. I turn my attention to the main building and then to the trees around it, hazy in the mist. At the same time, Adena pinches my arm, nodding quietly to the pair of guards at the far end of the courtyard. We make for the trees. As I reach them, I skip up the trunk to grab one of the branches that arches close to its roof.

My mother had been the one to teach me how to move through the trees. As a child, I used to watch her from the ground in awe as she crept along the branch with both hands and feet, as silent and smooth as a leopard. Squirrels wouldn't even know she was coming until she speared them from behind.

I creep along the branches now, my boots firm against the bark. I gauge my distance from the main building and take a silent leap. My boots hit the roof with a muffled thud. I crumble and roll immediately, cushioning the rest of my landing.

Down below, one of the guards glances idly up at the trees, as if unsure he'd heard the wind through the branches, then goes back to listening to his companion complain.

I go to the edge of the roof and look over toward Adena. She's ready and waiting. We exchange a brief nod.

Then we jump down at the same time. Daggers flash in both of my hands.

The guards don't have time to look up. They don't even have time to widen their eyes or utter a sound. My gloved hand clamps across one's mouth. My dagger comes up to his throat. I press hard into his skin and cut.

Gentle Talin, my father always said to me whenever I cried at the sight of my mother culling a chicken for our dinner. He'd chuckle in sympathy and hug me to him. I'm glad he never got to witness me doing my job.

Adena doesn't hesitate in her movements either. She chooses instead to stab the back of the other guard's neck at the same time I make my move.

Both soldiers collapse. We catch them before they can fall to the ground, then lower them carefully into the bush surrounding the complex.

Then we hear it—the alarm going up outside. There's a shout, followed by a second one. They've discovered the body we were forced to leave outside along the gates.

We exchange a silent look of understanding. Adena pats the side of her belt, where she has the samples ready. There's no smile between us—only the option to move forward. Through the darkness, I can feel Red's pull beating strong in my mind. He can probably sense that we're here too.

They may try to take everything from you, my mother had said to me on our first night in Mara's Outer City, huddled over a fire. Her eyes were locked on mine, sharp as flint. *But you can take from them too.*

Then we face the main door of the building and smash the glass.

This is enough to stir the hornet's nest. Instantly, the courtyard and the gate come to life with guards. I see their shadows running along the top of the wall, then figures in the darkness of the courtyard, heading toward the shattered door.

Adena and I both dart inside. I find myself staring at a hall that branches into darkness.

The guards are on us, I tell Red.

His voice comes back instantly. *Head down the hall,* he tells us. *Stop two doors from the end and make a left. It's a more private corridor that will take you deeper into the building.*

Outside, Jeran sends his call again. He'll be waiting for us to emerge again ... *if* we come out at all.

I've never set foot inside a laboratory at the heart of the Federation. I wouldn't know what kind of architecture they have. But I *have* been inside the Early Ones' ruins, seen the way they structure their strange metal walls and their machines.

This place looks like it could have been taken straight from one of those ruins. The walls are smooth and high, formed from metal, and within the grooves in the floor comes a faint glow of light behind glass, the same flameless filaments we'd seen on display in the city.

Soldiers come behind us. Adena and I dash to the end of the hall until we're two doors away, then follow Red's directions and swerve left. The halls echo with the shouts of soldiers as their boots land on the floor.

How far in? I ask Red.

You'll know when you've reached the main room, he tells me.

We break into a sprint. Shadows pass us by. Then the narrow corridor ends, and I halt in my steps. Before me yawns a room larger than any I've ever seen in my life.

At first glance, I think the room is full of mirrors, their edges catching the strange, sterile light shining from the ceilings. Then I realize that I'm staring at glass walls, dozens of them, each partitioning the vast space into separate rooms and chambers.

I think of the way that Red had stared at the windowpane in our shared apartment, his eyes distant with an ancient wound. I remember the vision I'd seen flash between us, of him lifting his fist and pounding it repeatedly against a glass wall. He had meant this place.

And now, as I keep looking, I realize that within each glass room is a figure hunched under the light, their limbs and silhouettes almost—but not quite—human. Ghosts.

I watch in horror. Beside me, Adena sucks in her breath. This place is exactly what we thought it was. The birthplace of the Federation's experiments.

Inside each glass room is either a Ghost or one in the process of changing. Some, I can tell, have just been transformed days ago. They look like people—a few still have deep bite marks on their arms or legs, where they'd been attacked by another Ghost. Many of them stay shivering uncontrollably in the corners of their spaces, agitated and scratching at their skin, which has already started to split. Still others are already long-lost, hulking figures of ashen, cracked flesh and bleeding jaws with sharp, overgrown teeth, swaying in uneasy pain as they wait for the Federation to use them for another battle. From here, I can see another section of the complex that leads outside, where there are more glass chambers. They're bigger. Those must hold Ghosts that are older, ones who have grown into beasts.

Sure enough, embedded in each Ghost's arm is a syringe connected to a thin tube. Currently, nothing seems to be flowing through it.

The control center, I say to Red through our link. *Where do we go?*

Head to the back of the room, he replies. His voice is even clearer now, his pull strong as we enter the space where he must be kept. Now, instead of speaking the directions to me, he sends the mental image. I see before me the entire space, only through Red's eyes, with the same knowledge and familiarity of its layout that he has.

Guards are beginning to run down the aisles of this space. Some of them hold lanterns, their light flickering through the darkness, and as they go, light floods first one section of the chamber, then another, and so on down the line. It's the same flameless light, and soon we'll be bathed in it.

Adena and I dash to the back of the chamber, then head against the wall to another corridor that leads to a hall of doors. We run right into a pair of soldiers. Their mouths open in surprise and they grab for us—but I disarm one of his gun and then seize his blade with the other. I use the weapon to slice him hard across the face. He collapses. Adena twists out of the grasp of the second guard and hits him so viciously in the jaw that it knocks him unconscious.

We go on grimly.

Then I pull to a halt before a final door. Through our link, Red tells us to open it. I do, and we find ourselves standing in a room full of machines and cylinders.

Adena seems to know immediately that we're in the right place. She grins, but doesn't waste another second. She crouches down beside one of the cylinders and inspects the machine.

"I'll handle this," she signs to me. "Go! Hurry!"

I don't bother asking her if she'll be all right on her own here. Without a second's hesitation, we exchange a quick fist against our chests before I run to find Red. The strange lighting of this place casts long shadows of Ghost silhouettes against the floor. The creatures stir restlessly, snarling and gnashing their teeth as soldiers dash past their displays, knowing that something has gone wrong.

I crawl to hide as best I can behind one of the glass panels. My mind shifts instinctively in Red's direction, from where his steady pulse is now beating through our bond. How had he survived life here for so many years? Had he spent all his time growing up among these tortured, gnarled beasts?

I sense a change in Red's pulse. It quickens, followed by a surge of warmth, some sense of fear and delirium. It's the only thing that brings a determined smile to the edges of my lips. He's close. If Adena does what we came here to do, then soon these Ghosts will be breaking out of their confines in a rage.

I wait until there's a clearing, and then dart to hide behind another glass room. I can feel myself edging close to Red now. I turn to look down the aisle of glass chambers—until my gaze rests on the creature inside the room I'm crouching behind.

Inside is a Ghost. No, it's a silhouette I recognize all too well. A human, crouched, half transformed, with blood trickling down his arms and legs as they hyperextend into the elongated limbs of Ghosts. But it is his eyes that catch me off guard.

They are a bright, searing blue, surrounded by cracked, bleeding skin.

Corian. It's Corian. It must be him.

Everything in me freezes. Corian's body, lying in the middle of the forest after I'd been forced to end his life. He's here—the Federation took him and brought him back to their labs. I stare in horror at his face peering back at me, those blue eyes now bloodshot and twitching with pain and anger.

I had not just failed Corian on the battlefield. I'd failed him in the final vow of a Striker to his Shield—to make sure that he dies a clean death, that he doesn't end up in the hands of the Federation, doomed to be twisted into a creature that is no longer human. To become a war beast of the Federation itself. And suddenly I'm there in the forest again, standing over my Shield's fallen body, his blood dripping from my blade. I'm kneeling in the dirt beside him and sobbing in silence, willing him back.

Corian is here. It has to be him.

But no! I'd carried him back to the defense compound myself. I'd seen his body laid to rest during his funeral, had been one of those to light him with fire.

I close my eyes, willing my heart to calm.

When I open my eyes again, I realize that the Ghost inside the chamber isn't Corian. His eyes are different, the tormented features of his face are slightly longer, his cheeks deeper set than my former Shield's. Through his nearly unrecognizable frame, I now can see that this Ghost was once someone else.

Not Corian.

The hairs on the back of my neck stand on end. Everything here feels wrong. Through my link with Red, I can sense a rivulet of what I think is terror. I realize that his heartbeat through the link isn't rapid because he's anxious about our presence here.

He's trying to warn us.

Red, I call to him. *Red, what's happening?*

His answer slices through my mind. *Get out.*

Then the space where I'm crouching suddenly floods with brightness. I'm momentarily blinded by an intense, white light.

Through our link, Red's warning heightens into horror.

"Well. You're here now."

A familiar voice over me makes me look up. Through my watering eyes, I see the silhouette of a gaunt young man.

It's the Premier. The silver thread of his collar shines in the light, and his eyes are narrowed at me in curiosity. A faint smile plays on his lips.

"You're the one I saw at the bathhouse," he says in that rasping voice. He speaks to me in Maran this time, which is how I know he's figured out who we are. "And you're the one bonded to my Skyhunter."

27

RED SENSES THE INSTANT I'M CAPTURED. IT'S A merging of his fear and mine.

I wince at the sudden brightness. All around me, the Ghosts stir out of their uneasy sleep. Snarls and the gnashing of teeth surround me.

Red, I try to call through our link. But it's no use. All I feel through our bond now is extreme terror and despair. Somewhere else in the space, I hear the sound of blades scraping hard enough to cut lines into glass walls. He's not far now. I can feel his rapid pulse increasing.

The Premier watches me closely. It's as if he were searching for evidence on my face that I can sense Red through a bond, and when I meet his eyes, he gives me a smile.

I grab for a dagger—but my fingers barely brush the blade's hilt before someone hits me hard in the neck, and a searing pain shoots through my limbs. Then guards are on me, pushing me hard to the ground. The Premier's security is even tighter than I thought. I grit my teeth and twist in their grasp. All of my instincts are firing now. I feel like I'm no longer fighting against humans, but a pack of Ghosts in the forest. I whirl hard enough so that one guard loses his grip on my arm, then stab at him with my dagger. He lets out a choked shriek and falls.

The Ghosts around us stir into a frenzy at the scent of blood in the air.

But there are far too many soldiers here. I'm brought down hard to the ground again. My cheek strikes cold marble, and the force knocks me unconscious.

. . .

I don't know how long I'm out. Seconds? Long enough that when I open my eyes again, my cheek is throbbing and their guards are dragging me across the floor. Ahead of me walks the Premier, his black boots clicking against the ground and his coat streaming behind him. Beside him is the woman with the white coat I'd seen from Red's memories. The Chief Architect.

I struggle, but my coordination is slightly off after my bout of unconsciousness.

Talin.

Red comes through our link, his voice clear as a dove's call. I hang on to his thought. *Talin.* Now that I hear him speak again in my mind, I can tell that he's struggling to send his words to me, as if my name is all he can manage. And then, abruptly, we stop in front of a giant glass wall.

I've never seen an enclosed room like this. It's a structure of glass so thick that I couldn't hope to shatter the walls. Inside, the space is bare except for a series of chains hooked to the floor and ceiling. And there, in the center of it, crouches a figure I've come to recognize anywhere, his wings unfurled so that they stretch the full length of the room.

Red.

In the darkness beyond him are similar rooms to his, and when I look inside them, I see the shapes of two others. Strapped to flat tables. Chained to the floor. Wings of deadly steel grafted onto their backs. My breath leaves me.

They are already making more Skyhunters.

The soldiers drag Adena forward from the darkness too, stopping in front of the glass wall. She struggles between two soldiers before one of them hits her hard between her shoulders. She lets out a pained gasp and slumps slightly. Everything in me wants to protect her, but I see the guns in the soldiers' hands and force myself to stop. They might shoot her dead. Had she managed to inject the serum into the control room's containers? What if they'd caught her before she could?

The Premier casts her a dismissive look. Beside him, the Chief Architect has her hands folded behind her back and head turned down, as if none of this feels out of the ordinary.

I sway on my feet. My cheek throbs from where I'd hit the floor. We've missed our rendezvous time with Jeran, I think, trying to concentrate on how many minutes must have passed. He'll know that something has gone wrong, that our mission has been compromised.

The Chief Architect says something to Red, and Red glares back at her with rage that simmers hot through our link.

"No answer?" the Premier speaks, the Maran language as eerily smooth on his tongue as Basean had been. He looks at me, then nods at the guards.

I'm shoved forward hard enough that I stumble. I barely manage to catch myself. Red stares at me. I know he can tell that my balance is off, because a fresh current of worry ripples through our bond. Then the guards force me to my knees, and my hair flops over my eyes, obscuring my view. Splatters of blood dot my shirt.

Behind the glass wall, Red utters a long, low snarl. It's the sound he makes before his mind goes blank, before he transforms.

The Chief Architect notices his reaction and says something to the Premier. He, in turn, smiles at me. "Ah," he tells me. "He's afraid for you. You're communicating right now."

They know. My eyes go back to the woman, whose gaze darts nervously away.

"Perhaps we should test your link," he says, then turns to the woman and speaks Karenese. Beside him, one of the soldiers draws a dagger in anticipation.

A surge of fury from Red sears through me, threatening to push him over the edge. I glance sharply at him. *No*, I think, sending the word as strongly through our link as I can. If Red reacts to my pain, it will be the proof that the Premier wants to see.

One of the soldiers holding me down doesn't wait. He grips my right arm tightly and positions his dagger.

Then he digs the blade in against my skin and cuts one long, jagged line.

Pain blooms in my mind. I suck my breath in sharply as blood trickles hot down my arm.

Behind the glass, Red's eyes flare, glowing silver white. Through our link, I see a flash of his memories. Suddenly, I'm staring into the eyes of his sister and father as if I were he, looking over my shoulder at their wide-eyed stares as the Chief Architect leads him away from his home.

The Premier nods in grim satisfaction. "So silent, this one," he murmurs to himself.

I keep my head bowed, my body trembling, my mind filled with Red's seething thoughts. The Chief Architect says something to the Premier, and he looks at me curiously.

"My Architect tells me this bond you have with my Skyhunter shouldn't be possible," he says. "She tells me that severing the bond by force may damage my Skyhunter's mind. It may make him impossible to bond again." He frowns. "That would be a waste."

He bends down to my eye level. I want to cut through his body with my blades. But all I can be is helpless as I watch his lips thin into a line.

"You don't speak, do you?"

I don't know how he makes this assumption about me, but I only scowl back at him. It makes his lips tighten in satisfaction.

"A gifted killer," he says, rising back to his feet. "I was wondering when you and your companions would actually show up here at the complex."

His words take a second to sink in. I look up at him, startled, trying to understand. Had he been expecting us?

As I puzzle over this, one of the soldiers asks him a question. He shrugs, shaking his head, but his eyes never leave mine. "No," he says, "I'd like to keep her." He tilts his head toward Adena, who is slowly stirring back to life. "And that one seems gifted enough to apprentice to our Architect here. She'll learn quickly."

Then several things happen at once.

A boom sounds from the front of the lab complex, accompanied by shaking earth. The lights flicker violently, setting off every single Ghost in the room. In an instant, soldiers form a protective barrier in front of their Premier.

Adena twists free from her guard's grasp, one of her knives held at the soldier's throat and another pointed at Constantine. She gives him a smile.

And in that glorious instant, I know she has succeeded in her mission.

28

EVERYTHING SEEMS TO HAPPEN IN A BLUR—THE
Ghosts stirring to life all around us, their snarls triggering one after the other, the soldiers drawing their guns in unison.

Adena's daggers flash in her hands. Before anyone can react to her, she whirls and slashes one of her guards hard across his chest. She looks so alive in this moment that I wish I could shout. Adena, our savior.

From the corner of my eye, I see a shadow dart through the corridor.

Then I'm moving before I can even register the thought. I spring up from my crouch on the floor. My guards, taken aback for an instant by everything around them, aren't ready for my lunge. One of my arms comes free from their grip—I seize a dagger from my belt and stab it straight into one guard. I yank my other arm free and jam a dagger hard into the second guard's chest, then dart toward the Chief Architect, who's standing the closest to me. Before any of the other soldiers can stop me, I throw an arm around her neck, pressing a blade against her throat hard enough to draw blood.

Before me, the Premier stands stiffly and watches me. When he holds up a hand, the guards advancing on me freeze.

"You think you can threaten my Architect," he says to me.

I tighten my grip and press the dagger harder. In my grasp, the

Architect trembles, then shuts her eyes and mutters what might be a prayer. Is it my imagination, or is there a subtle smile on her face? As if she were almost relieved for death.

"Go ahead, then," the Premier continues. His eyes glitter like a pair of gemstones, hard and refined. "You think the Federation cannot continue without her? Take her. I will not be held hostage by a filthy Maran scout."

The Chief Architect is the creator of everything that has made the Federation the sprawling dynasty that it is. She is the inventor of its war machines. If I were smart, I'd kill her right here without hesitation. A life, for countless lives.

And yet, I feel her trembling in my grasp and remember the things she'd said to Red in his nightmares, that she too fears for her young son and husband, that she does terrible things in order to protect them. I wonder if my own mother would work for the Premier if she knew he held my life in his hands. It's this image—my mother standing in the Chief Architect's place, quivering in my grip and pleading for her family—that makes me stall.

I know the Premier is bluffing, daring me to do this thing that I know he can't afford. But I stare back at him, search his gaze, and see no hint of uncertainty at all. His expression is unforgiving, his back straight and chin high. Even if he was dressed in rags instead of his lavish coat, I wouldn't doubt his confidence. He has played this risky game before, and he has always won it.

He smiles grimly at the look on my face. "There's fear in you. It drives everything you do. I saw it in you when you first crossed my path at the bathhouse. But fear is a good thing. It breeds insecurities, which then breed ambition. And I always admire ambition." He folds his arms. "You are too good to fight for Mara. Do you know why?"

Within his words is a deep arrogance that digs at me. I can hear in it everything that the Federation stands for—the belief that they deserve to tell us how to live our lives and what we should be sacrificing to them.

When I continue glaring at him, he gives me a thin smile. "Do you wonder how I knew you would come here, and that you can't speak? It's because your Speaker—yes, the leader of the nation you defend—sent me a letter warning of your approach."

His words fall off me at first, then hit me again. He must be lying. They make no sense.

He lifts an eyebrow at me. "You think your Speaker has not thought about the coming collapse of Mara, and his inevitable execution once the Federation conquers his country? That he's too noble to cut a deal with me, telling me about your mission to destroy my Ghosts in exchange for his life? You think I wouldn't presume this about your leader and take advantage of it?"

Nearby, Adena hears his words and stumbles in her fight. A guard almost cuts her with his blade, yet she manages to dart away, but not before I hear a broken cry of disbelief come from her. I struggle to keep steady as the room seems to spin. The Speaker has always struck me as a coward, a weak man—but even I'd thought he would stand by Mara until the end.

"What do you think our cease-fire negotiations have really been about?" the Premier says archly to me.

The cease-fires at the warfront, the negotiations. All the Strikers who had given their lives for Mara. All the people, Inner and Outer City alike, who struggle in the throes of our losing war. We have been preparing to make a final stand, while our Speaker has been making plans to save himself all along.

In grief and fury, my knife digs deeper into the Chief Architect's skin.

Then, all of a sudden, I see the first Ghost shudder.

It's the one closest to us, so tall that its head nearly comes up to the ceiling of its glass chamber. Barely a moment ago, its bloody teeth had been bared in my direction, and its milky eyes were full of the rage and pain that I'm so used to seeing on a Ghost's face.

But now it looks away, seemingly confused. Its eyes wander in a restless attempt to settle—and then it shakes its head violently, as if trying to rid itself of something toxic, and lets out a piercing shriek of agitation.

Adena grins. For the first time, the Premier's confident expression wavers.

Another Ghost follows suit—then another. It ripples through them in rapid succession, the confusion and the rolling eyes, until each one is writhing in agony. I narrow my eyes in satisfaction. Perhaps the Speaker's betrayal hasn't stopped us, after all.

Adena's serum. Her infiltration of the lab's control room. All of her theories and experiments. It worked—the Federation's grip on its Ghosts seems to be breaking down.

The soldiers beside the nearest Ghost turn toward it. One of them makes the mistake of rapping his gun against the glass, yelling at the Ghost to calm down. But the noise just startles the creature—it throws itself at the glass with such force that it leaves a trickle of blood on the surface. The glass shudders.

These Ghosts' fixation on us may be broken, but they are still creatures motivated by some sense of survival. If they break out of their prisons, they may go on a blind rampage in self-defense.

"We have to go," Adena hisses at me.

Red shudders in his chamber. His lips curl into a snarl as the soldiers turn their attention on him.

The Chief Architect struggles in my grasp. I don't have time to wrestle with her—I release her instead and lunge toward Red's cage. A sword and gun are in my hands now. One, two shots—I hit a couple of the soldiers hard and they crumple.

It's too late to take a shot at the Premier now; he's retreated behind a phalanx of soldiers. Everywhere in the lab, chaos reigns—the Ghosts are shrieking now, each of them ramming into the glass walls as hard as they can, so hard that some of them crack their heads from the force.

I'm about to dash into the fray of soldiers by Red's chamber when a slender young figure lands right in front of us in a perfect crouch, his face half covered by his mask. It's Jeran. He barrels into the soldiers like a possessed madman. All I see is the flash of silver blades and blood.

I dart through the crowd like water. Inside Red's chamber, he's already in position near the entrance and bracing himself against the glass. His eyes lock on mine.

I reach the door and break it open for him. Instantly, he bursts out through the entrance, his wings extended and eyes glowing.

All around us, glass shatters. Ghosts break free.

More soldiers are pouring into the space, their attention turned on the Ghosts—but for the first time, I see the Ghosts, blind in their fury, turning indiscriminately on whoever is blocking their path. I rush to help Adena, who's fighting off a dozen guards in one corner. Daggers appear in my hands. I throw them and they hit true. Two of the soldiers collapse.

But there are so many of them. Overhead, Red cuts a line through some of the soldiers as we make a dash for the exit corridor we'd used to enter earlier. All around me, Ghosts are shattering their glass walls, some of them injuring themselves so badly in the process that they crawl, shrieking, on the ground.

It is a scene of madness.

Had we truly succeeded? It seems wildly impossible that this mission may actually end with us crippling the Federation—that, despite every-thing the Speaker did, we may have destroyed their hold on their war beasts.

The corridor comes into view. At the end of it, though, is a line of soldiers, all with guns drawn and waiting for us.

Beside me, Adena yanks out one of her daggers and flings it at the soldiers. She catches one—but there are still too many of them. As they head toward us, I draw the blades I'd taken from the soldiers and give Adena a nod. Somewhere behind us, Red is fighting in his weakened state through the throngs. The Ghosts are all loose now, their blood-curdling screams filling the air. I face our enemies and brace myself.

Jeran glances back once at Adena, then darts ahead at the soldiers. Watching him attack is like watching a perfect storm in action—everywhere at once, cutting down all in his path. He arcs and bends, his blades deadly in their efficiency. Adena wastes no time. She falls right into place beside her Shield, moving in sync with his every attack, weaving around him whenever he ducks to slice through soldiers' calves, stepping forward whenever he shifts back. Even without our full arsenal of weapons, they are a sight to behold.

I cut forward as we force ourselves through the corridor. I hear Jeran suck in his breath in pain—an arrow has pierced straight through his side. Adena immediately pushes him behind her as two soldiers lunge at them. Her swords whirl.

I don't feel the slashes through my sleeves and vest. I don't feel the pain from the bloody wounds I'm accumulating. If we are going to have any chance of getting out of this place alive, we can't afford to stop and think.

I feel like I'm back in the dark field my mother and I once ran through, only now I'm running the other way, *into* the throngs of the Federation's killers, cutting through their ranks just like they had once cut through ours. *Don't look back, Talin.*

And then, suddenly, I feel the shock of cold air against my cheeks. We've made our way through to the outside of the lab complex.

It looks nothing like how it'd been when we'd broken in. Now the courtyard is full of soldiers trying to keep the Ghosts from escaping. One glance across the space tells me that we may not make it out of here alive. There are too many soldiers for us. We number four. There are dozens of them.

Still, I move forward. Somewhere behind me, back in the complex, Red is wreaking havoc. Even with his strength contained here, he is a fearsome sight, his teeth bared and flashing. I cannot turn around to get him. All I can do is sense the bond between us as I continue to fight, to push forward.

I'm here, I tell him. *I'm here.*

He answers back with a fierce tug.

A blade catches me on my leg and slices deep through my thigh. I gasp in pain—through the link, Red senses my wound in alarm. I stumble, but slash out even as I fall to one knee. My sword catches the soldier who had tried to cut me down. My blade stabs hard into his stomach. He grunts in shock. I twist my blade, then stab him again. He collapses.

Suddenly, a giant fist closes around my neck.

My eyes pop open. The fist belongs to a Ghost—the monster narrows its milky eyes at me as it lifts me off my feet. Its cold, cracked fingers tighten around my throat.

For an instant, I'm a child again, being dragged by rough hands out of my home. For a moment, I forget who I am and how to fight back. I claw helplessly at the Ghost gripping my neck.

Through my panic, I hear the rasping voice of the Premier echoing in my memory.

You are too good to fight for Mara.

Then he is here, standing near me as the Ghost holds me still. The tips of my boots barely touching the ground, forcing me to stare at him. He's on the back of his horse now, surrounded by a patrol of soldiers as he surveys the damage around us. The cheekbones of his thin face jut sharply in the light, and his eyes glint like a predator's.

"Your reflexes are remarkable," he says, tilting his head at me.

I clench my teeth. *You've lost your war beasts*, I want to say. And yet, here is a Ghost beside him, doing as he bids.

He only gives me a grim smile in return. "I didn't think anyone could engineer something to disrupt the links formed between our Ghosts and Skyhunters, and our Federation. Yet here you are, with your team of allies." He narrows his eyes. "You don't think my Architect didn't make plans to fix our Ghosts after the Speaker told us about your mission?"

His words blur through me as I continue to struggle against the Ghost's grip on my throat. It continues to obey him, despite the serum Adena had created.

To save his own life, the Speaker of Mara had destroyed our only chance to take down the Federation.

"No one can sever the bond completely between two linked souls," he says. "It's the same trouble we ran into with you and my Skyhunter."

And that is when I finally realize that we've failed.

There in the courtyard, I can see glimpses of a changing scene. The Ghosts that had seemingly been released from their links with the Federation . . . already, some of them have started to back away from the soldiers they're supposed to obey. Their erratic, blind attacks have ceased. The Ghosts aren't tearing free of their bonds with the Federation. They're gradually snapping back into place.

The serum that Adena had created only worked temporarily. Our mission had failed before we even arrived here—the Chief Architect must have injected the Ghosts with something to counteract Red's blood.

No. Everything around me spirals. We'd always known this mission's success would be a miracle. But I had still hoped.

Jeran whirls into an attack against a Ghost that has targeted Adena with wide-open jaws. He cuts it hard in its legs, then stabs deep into its neck as it stumbles, severing its crucial vein.

The edges of my vision are turning dark. We've failed. And now we are going to die here, on the soil of the Federation's capital.

Through my fading consciousness, I hear the Premier issue another command and shake his head once in my direction. Two advancing soldiers halt in their steps, their guns still pointed at me.

From the sky comes the sound of wind. Through my bond, I feel Red's presence turn overwhelming, his strength surging through my weakening body and filling me with heat. I instinctively tilt my face up to meet his, even though I can no longer see.

I'm here, he tells me.

Then he really is, a maelstrom of black metal and fury. I hear the Ghost scream as he barrels into it—and an instant later, I'm falling through the air to collapse to the ground. *Get up*, I command myself. I struggle to my feet, then stagger. My surroundings have become nothing but a streak of scarlet and night.

Suddenly, a force lifts me from the ground. Wind rushes against my cheeks. I can feel Red's firm grip on my arms.

We've failed. The thought spins over and over in my mind until I can't understand it any longer. It's the last thing I remember before the world finally fades around me.

29

OUR ESCAPE SEEMS TO HAPPEN IN A SERIES OF still moments.

I recall the long corridor of the lab complex, crawling with soldiers and blinded Ghosts. There is the Chief Architect and the Premier, surrounded by their bodyguards. The courtyard is a scene of Ghosts, blind and enraged, corralled by their guards.

The world comes and goes for me. I remember Jeran helping Adena through the yard. I remember Red cutting through the soldiers, his wings extended, raining death on everyone in his path. I remember the fog, which had settled thick into the city the night before, now giving us merciful cover.

In the heavy mist, Red comes back to me, guided by our link. Then I recall the cold air whipping past us, the shroud of fog hiding our bodies in the air.

I remember silence, the weight of it pressing in all around me.

Through my flickering consciousness, the Premier's words to me repeat again and again. My bond with Red can never be wholly severed. It is the only way he could have found me through the chaos.

The reason for our mission's failure is the same as the reason for our survival.

. . .

The next time I properly wake, it's almost dawn, and I feel the earth cool and damp beneath me. There's a faint memory playing in my mind of my mother and father, the last remnants of a dream: My mother cuts fat slices of fruit, and my father rolls up my sleeves for me as we paint together. My father dips his brush into ink and sweeps it down the paper in an arc, and I coo under my breath, thinking it's the most beautiful thing I've ever seen. I try to copy it, over and over, until he laughs at me. *Create what you want*, he tells me. *It will be even better.* My mother walks over with the plate of fruit and feeds a slice to me, smiling at the juice that dribbles down my chin.

They vanish now, replaced by darkness. The cold is what must have stirred me, because I'm shivering uncontrollably. The air here is noticeably icier than what I remember from the capital. Yet it's blissfully still. There is the sound of birds in the trees, then the splash of them fishing in some nearby stream. I let myself listen until the ache in my heart from my dream eases.

I shift, then regret it as pain lances down my arms and legs. Grimacing, I rub my limbs and take stock of my surroundings.

We're out of the city—the oppressive smell of it, the throngs of people in the streets, the towering apartments and narrow alleys crowded with tents—nothing of Cardinia anywhere to be seen here. Instead, a cool mist hangs in this forest, and when I sit straighter, I glimpse a valley sloping in the distance through the trees.

Beside me, Red sleeps, still unconscious. He is covered in blood, some his, some from the soldiers that he'd killed. Now his breathing is slow and even.

My eyes dart around the makeshift campsite. Where are Jeran and Adena?

Then I spot Adena up in one of the nearby trees, her back against the trunk, looking idly out at the valley. At my movement, she glances down—her hand whipping immediately to the dagger in her boot—and then she breaks into a smile. It isn't the smile I remember, though; there's no joy in it, only weary relief. She nods down at me, and I nod in return.

"Sorry about the cold," Jeran signs to me as he takes a seat beside us. "We're about fifty miles out of Cardinia. Red helped guide us a bit on what routes to take into the forests. Try to stamp your feet a little, once you feel up to standing." He reaches into his pocket and offers me a handful of fresh berries.

I take one gingerly, my fingers caked in blood, but when I try to open my mouth, my tongue is so dry and my throat so parched that I cough, barely able to swallow a single berry.

Jeran offers me some water as I run my hand along the makeshift bandages now wrapped tightly around my wounded arm, the fabric soaked through with blood. The pain that had jolted through me when the soldier cut that arm had also rippled through Red, just as his agony at the guards spearing him during the procession had coursed through me. Now, even in his sleep, he stirs slightly, scowling at the twinge of pain that comes through our link. His eyelids flutter.

"Talin?" he whispers, not through our link, but aloud. His voice sounds hoarse from lack of use. His eyes crack open, and I find myself staring into those deep, dark irises. Then, to my surprise, I glimpse a familiar quiver of fur and whiskers emerge from inside one of his sleeves. His mouse pokes its head out to investigate its surroundings, its tiny claws gripping tightly to Red's shirt.

If I could laugh, I would. Somehow, against all odds, this damn mouse has managed to survive Mara's prison, the warfront, the Federation, the labs, the fighting. Just like Red.

Red smiles at me while his hand goes instinctively to pet the mouse's head. "Hello," he murmurs to me in his rough Maran.

Before I know it, there are tears on my cheeks. Maybe it's because the mouse is still alive. Maybe it's the relief of seeing Red awake, of feeling the bond pulling strong between us, of the certainty that I hadn't lost another Shield. Or maybe it's because we have failed in our mission. That all of Mara's hopes had rested on our shoulders, and yet here we are, returning empty-handed. That my mother may never again live in a free land.

Red props himself painfully into a sitting position. Then he reaches into his pocket and takes the mouse out, lowering his hand gently to the ground. The creature sniffs the air eagerly, lured toward the scent of berries nearby.

"Go," Red tells it gently.

The mouse doesn't look at him, but when it catches sight of bushes of berries off in the distance, it hurries off toward them.

A long moment of silence passes. As he watches it go, I can tell he's thinking about his little sister.

The light around us strengthens, touching the distant hills. Somewhere far beyond them lies Maran territory. None of us speak. What is there to say to one another now, anyway? So Jeran, Red, and I just sit, startling at every breeze through the trees, quietly eating berries until they're gone. I bite my lip, trying to ignore the raging hunger that this meager meal has awoken in me. It brings back memories of darker years, when my mother and I first settled in the Outer City.

Dark circles haunt Jeran's eyes. His shirt is also splattered with old blood, but he seems mostly unharmed. None of us bring up the miracle that we are still, somehow, alive after our failed mission.

Failed. My heart twists as the memory of everything that had happened now comes flooding back.

After a while, Adena comes, picking her way along the forest floor. "I see a train track running to the west," she signs to us. "We should steer clear of it."

She sits down and immediately pulls out her two daggers, then rubs the back of one against the other to sharpen it. For a while, all we do is listen to the sound of water and birds nearby.

"What do we do now?" Jeran signs in the silence. His eyes stay on the valley peeking through the trees, in the direction of Mara, and his jaw stays set in stone.

I know he doesn't mean what route we take next, but what happens when we arrive home. "I don't know," I sign.

"If we return," Adena signs, "they'll arrest us."

It's more than that. If we return to Mara now, not only will the Firstblade be forced to put us in chains, but they will probably execute us in the arena, in the same fashion Red almost was, for our treason to the country. Killed for trying in vain to save us all.

The thought is almost comical to me, and I have to force a bitter laugh away. Treason. Mara has suffered a worse betrayal at the hands of its very own Speaker.

"What do you want to do?" I sign to her.

Adena leans back slowly, wincing. She must be just as sore as I am. Her eyes fall on Red, and her lips move in silence for a moment, trying to find the right thing to say.

Finally, she looks at me. "Do you think the Federation's Premier is right?" she signs.

"About what?"

"About the Speaker."

I'm still for a moment as Constantine's words to me return. *You are too good*, he had said. He'd meant I was too good to fight for such a leader.

"We don't have to go back, you know." I take a deep breath. "I can get my mother. We can flee. We've done it before, and we can do it again."

"To where?" Jeran signs.

There are no choices left, but Adena still tightens her lips. "Into the woods, maybe," she signs back. "We know more than anyone how to survive. I can make everything we need. I might even be able to sneak into the Grid for some of my tools. Then, when the Federation finally breaks through the warfront—as they will in weeks, maybe days—we'll be safe in the trees, hiding. They won't know to look for us. We can stay there, even strike back later, when they're least suspecting it."

Red looks questioningly at me, understanding only some of her signs, and I turn my focus to him, translating briefly to him through our bond.

He frowns. *They'll find us eventually*, he tells me, his gaze falling on Adena. I sign his words to her, but she just grimaces, not wanting to believe it.

"The Federation stretches in every direction," Jeran signs. His lips have stretched as tight as a string. "They'll find us."

I can hear the warning in it, but Adena plunges on anyway, too exhausted to care. "Well, maybe the Federation will even treat us better than they do in Mara. What are we going to do—sit in prison cells until they come?"

Jeran glares at her. "Because we'll soon be under Federation rule, anyway?"

"It doesn't matter either way, does it?" she signs. "If we stay or if we flee."

"Then why did we do any of this?" he hisses aloud, his voice low and angry. Fury rolls off him like mist, and it is so sudden and dark that both Adena and I pause. "Risk our lives? Give up our honor and our standing and go barreling into the heart of the Federation on a fool's mission? What was the reason? Why do this?"

"Why, indeed!" Adena is furious now too, her eyes flashing, her voice a sharp whisper. "You think it doesn't affect me? I tried. I *tried*, Jeran." Then her voice catches, and she stops herself, too embarrassed to let out a sob in the middle of her argument. She looks away so that we don't see the well of tears in her eyes. "It's all the same," she signs. "They'll come for us in the end."

I can feel the way this has broken us, deep in our bones. Maybe we are all too good for Mara. Would I be a fool for stepping back into their territory, to be the one arrested when the true criminal is our Speaker? Why do I still feel a pull to return?

"We have to go back," Jeran signs.

"Why, Jeran?" Adena signs, leaning toward her Shield's face in anger and anguish. "*Why* do we need to go back?"

"The Firstblade would stay and fight," he signs. "Even after what the Speaker has done."

And then I finally understand Jeran's reason. Back before we fled into the Federation, when we were gathered around my mother's table, he had told us that he fought as a Striker in order to prove himself to his father. Then he told us he fought because of his brother, because he wanted to learn how to defend himself from Gabrien's vicious attacks. These must all be true reasons—but they are not the final one. They're not the reason why he went into the Federation with us, why he fought so hard to get out, and why, even after the knowledge of what the Speaker had done, he wants to return.

It's because of the Firstblade. Because Jeran, young and kind and forever loyal, would rather return and give his life alongside Aramin than live knowing he had turned his back on the man he loves.

Isn't that why I fight too? Because of Jeran. And Adena. And Corian. It's because of that dinner at my mother's table, with everyone's faces reflecting warm in the evening light. It's because of the children I see running through Mara's Inner City, their bones sharp and jutting from all the years of war. Someone has to stand for them.

"I'm going back," I sign. I look at Red and repeat it through our link. *I'm going back.*

Red taps his fist to his chest in the Striker salute. *If you go back, so will I,* he tells me.

I look at him, feeling that tug between us, knowing I would kill for him, and that he would for me. How strange it is that the Federation had given us this gift, the bond that cannot be broken.

"For Mara?" Adena signs.

"For the idea of Mara," Jeran replies.

"Ideas are nothing but air," Adena mutters.

"Then we're truly lost," I sign.

We don't say anything after that. The sun shifts until its light spills warm over us through the forest canopy, then blankets the valley in pink and purple. After the last rays vanish over the horizon, we pack up our campsite in the twilight and move on, using the night to protect us.

It is evening on the fifth day of our flight from Cardinia when we finally cross the warfront from the Federation into Mara, our hands up, weapons sheathed away. The Maran soldiers who fetch us from their defense compounds come bearing rope, shouting between one another, and I know they already recognize us.

Strikers. The deadliest fighters in the land, the pride of Mara, the only thing standing between freedom and annihilation.

It doesn't matter. We are still led back to our country as criminals.

NEWAGE

THE NATION OF MARA

30

OUR RETURN TO MARA IS A SOMBER, SILENT
one.

We are all wounded and exhausted, shadows of ourselves from when we'd first left the country.

The Strikers who ride back with us don't talk as we go. Their eyes shift uneasily in Red's direction as he rides in silence, and they leave a wide berth between him and the rest of us, a circle of guns pointed in his direction should he so much as make a single unexpected movement. Adena, Jeran, and I are transported with our hands and feet bound, escorted on our own horses. It's impossible to ignore the weight in the air, as if we're less Marans and more enemy soldiers.

None of us utter a word to the other Strikers about what we know of the Speaker. Saying so here, now, as criminals arrested for treason, will only make us sound like liars. Who would believe such a claim? They would just tell the Speaker, who might have us assassinated before we can even stand trial in the arena.

Red's eyes stay forward, but I can sense his attention on me. He's wondering if we should try to break free. I wait until he glances in my direction, then shake my head once subtly. Even Red, who can slaughter an entire battlefield, can't survive a bullet to the head. There are so many guns trained on him. Besides—if we killed Strikers in an attempt to free ourselves, then they can no longer protect Mara.

As we crest a hill and the familiar sight of Newage comes into view, one of them turns to me. She's a girl I'd trained with since the beginning, and one of the few who seems willing to communicate with us.

"Did you see what the Federation does to their prisoners?" she signs hesitantly to me.

Her eyes are wide, the expression in them almost desperate in their hunger. I realize immediately that she's asking because she knows someone who had been captured once and never heard from again. My mind skips to the Ghost I'd seen in transition at the labs, with eyes so piercing I'd mistaken him at first for Corian. I think of the parade of Ghosts on display at their national fair.

Instead, I just shake my head. My hands twist in vain against their bonds.

Like any good Striker, the only real fear she shows is a tightening of her jaw. She nods back at me and returns to concentrating on the city ahead.

The Speaker is waiting for us at the entrance to the gates with the other Senators. I meet his eyes as we go and notice that he tries to avert his own gaze by nodding with approval at the other Strikers bringing us in. Along either side of the gates are a cluster of people all craning their necks for a look at us. Inner City citizens gather, searching our faces for some sign of hope. Refugees from the Outer City watch us with their hollow eyes.

After a while, they turn their eyes away. Perhaps it is better not to know the truth.

Suddenly, I spot my mother in the crowd. She has her hands together, wringing them unconsciously, and her gaze stays on mine without wavering. I can tell from the mud splattered on the hem of her pants that she ran all the way here from her home the instant she heard of our approach.

She looks like she wants to say something, but her words catch in her throat. The chains on my wrists feel unbearably heavy. When the Federation comes over our border, who will protect her without me there? What will happen to her?

As we enter the Inner City, I expect to hear a round of jeers, something loud and mocking from people who have always wanted to see me fall. But to my surprise, they greet us only with silence. A few bow their heads in our direction as we pass by. Some still refuse to meet my gaze with anything but sneers—but most look somber, even respectful. Many of them know Jeran and Adena. They recognize all of us, and it occurs to me that perhaps they are grateful for our return, even in the face of certain imprisonment.

Our procession continues to the National Plaza, where the Firstblade is waiting for us at the entrance to the prison.

There is no satisfaction on his face. At the sight of Jeran, his eyes soften, but he doesn't move as we are helped off our horses and made to stand before him. I sneak a glance at Jeran. He's careful to keep his head down, but his body seems to lean instinctively in the Firstblade's direction, as drawn to the man as he's been since the days when Aramin used to train with him.

The Firstblade studies each of us in turn. I wait, wondering if he'll cut us down right here.

Then he bows his head to us, long and low. "I'm glad you're alive," he says.

"Glad enough to imprison us?" Adena speaks up, and the rest of the Strikers go still.

But Aramin doesn't look angry. He seems exhausted, worn down by decisions out of his control. He looks at Adena without saying a word, because there's simply no good reply to her question. Adena just stays where she is, staring the Firstblade down defiantly.

"You will each be confined separately." His gaze goes to Red. I know Red could kill him, without question—that no one here can physically restrain Red or keep him in any bonds—but there's no fear on Aramin's face. "The Skyhunter will return to his old cell."

Red glares at the Firstblade in disgust before shifting his eyes away.

We're brought down the circular depths of the prison, lower and lower, to the damp floors where only meager shafts of light illuminate the darkness. Here, we're each placed in a separate cell. Mine is small, smaller than my mother's home, with a grating the size of my palm on the floor and one on the side of the wall. Through the floor grating, I catch brief glimpses of Jeran in the cell below me, pacing incessantly from one corner of the room to the other. There's no telling where Adena is being held.

I lean back against the wall and close my eyes. Red is on the bottom floor, but he's near enough that I can see fragments of his world through my own point of view, glimpses of the small army of soldiers surrounding him in a wide circle, watching him in his cell with their guns pointed at him.

Red, I try to say to him through our bond. He's too far away to hear it, but I do sense his mood flicker with a ray of something light at my attempt.

Somehow, I savor the thought of him being able to sense me but not hear my words. So I decide to continue. *I'm sorry you've ended up exactly where you began.* The thought gets a bitter chuckle out of me, and as if in answer, I feel a brief spark of amusement come from Red. *Well, I'm glad one of us is pleased by this*, I tell him wryly.

He's silent, but the space between us doesn't feel empty, and I let myself sink into the comfort of his presence in my mind.

I'm sorry, Red, I tell him after a while. *We wanted to avenge your family. You gave everything you could and withstood returning to the place that held you captive. We still failed you.*

The weight of that realization sits heavy in my mind. I let myself stay very still in the darkness, trying to keep my feelings down, glad he can't sense everything.

I don't know what to do, I confess. *I don't know how we're going to survive all this. Maybe we won't.*

His mood shifts again, somber now, but there is a current of something else there. Gratitude. And then . . . what?

Love? The thought makes me blush, but instead of pushing it down, I feel a surge of courage.

I'm most sorry that I won't get a chance to know you better, I say. *Maybe, in another life, we could have taken our time with each other. I* . . . I hesitate, my pulse quickening. *I would have liked that.*

He doesn't answer, of course, but his emotions sway with mine, warm and close. I imagine him pulling me into an embrace, his arms strong and steady, wrapping me tight. And somewhere through these walls, in a prison down below, he answers with a vague image of his face close to mine, eyes lowered.

The door to my cell groans open. I startle out of my reverie to see a soldier give me a brief nod. "Your visitor," he tells me. Then he steps aside to let my mother in.

She's carrying a small cloth package. From the messy way it's tied, I know that the guards must have undone her careful knots to inspect everything inside the sack before tossing it back to her. She gives me a grim smile, her eyes roaming the chains shackling my limbs, before sitting across from me and unwrapping the cloth.

Inside are her handmade meat buns, still warm, and a large bowl of noodles with roasted chicken and carrots. There are ripe apricots from the tree beside her home, as well as sweet sticky cakes made from pounded seaflour and sugarweed.

My throat tightens with emotion at the sight. Chicken is not an easy meat to get, not even in the Inner City, and neither is the beef for the meat buns. I don't know what my mother must have traded in order to make this food for me.

She waves a hand in annoyance at my expression. "The first thing I thought when I saw you led back through the city," she signs, "is that you haven't eaten enough the past few weeks. Your last good meal must have been the one we had before you left."

Now I genuinely laugh, the sound coming out as a hoarse whisper. We had risked death on a train into Cardinia—I had looked the Premier in the eye, had broken into the Federation's lab complex and lived to tell of our escape, had fled through the woods bordering both sides of our warfront. But my mother's main concern is that I didn't eat enough while in the Federation.

I want to hug her. "Thank you," I sign before picking up one of the buns, then offering her the second one.

She frowns and shakes her head. "For you," she says in Basean. "I just want to see you eat."

I finish one of the buns and half of the bowl of noodles and chicken before my mother speaks again. "I've asked the Firstblade what they plan to do with you," she signs. "He won't tell me. No one else will give me any information." She pauses to make a disgusted face. "They can't do anything to you. Not with the Federation about to push past the warfront. They need you in your Striker coat, defending us."

My best guess is that they will execute me, because the Speaker couldn't care less about whether Mara survives the next attack, and he will want me silenced before I start spreading the truth about his treason. But I don't want to tell my mother this, especially not with the knowledge that the Federation is going to invade soon. What good would it do for her to know about the Speaker's betrayal, anyway? It will only give the Senate a reason to punish my mother if they find out that she knows too.

"They haven't told me any more than they've given you," I answer instead. "But it doesn't really matter, does it?"

She stares at the cold, damp stones of the floor. "No, I guess it doesn't."

The grief in her posture is the acknowledgment that, no matter how hard she had tried to keep us out of the Federation's rule, we're going to fall to them anyway. When we do, anything the Maran Speaker chooses to do with me will be nothing compared to what the Federation's Premier will inflict on me.

"You have to hide, Ma," I tell her now. "When they come. Do you hear me? At the first sign, make for the forests. Stay there for as long as you can."

"While you stay and fight?" she scoffs aloud in Basean. "I'm not running again. It didn't do much good the first time." She pauses for a long moment. "What did you see in there?" she whispers.

I know what she's trying to ask. What kind of fate is in store for us all?

"Darkness," I tell her. "Disguised as light."

She doesn't answer. After a while, she says, "I hope you bury it in the back of your mind. Sometimes, it's better to forget."

I look her directly in the eyes. "I love you," I sign.

My mother takes my hands in hers, then kisses my fingers. "I love you," she signs in return.

The words are foreign in our house, as unnatural a part of our lives as it is a part of Basean culture. The rarity makes it carry that much more weight, though—I can feel it in the strength of her grip and linger of her stare.

"Don't give up," she says to me in the tongue of our homeland as the guards finally return to escort her out. "You haven't lost yet."

$$\bullet \ \bullet \ \bullet$$

As the afternoon stretches on, I fall in and out of a light slumber. Rumors overheard from the guards outside my door tell me that the Firstblade is going to visit each of our cells before the night comes. Maybe it's to tell us what our fates will be.

Finally, as the afternoon dims into evening, I hear a commotion in Jeran's cell below me. I come out of my half sleep, then crane my neck so I can peer through my grating to see Jeran rise to his feet. He taps his fist to his chest and bows low at the figure that strides through his door. In the torchlight filtering into our cells, Aramin's face is washed in hues of blue and gray.

He doesn't waste any time. "The Speaker has ordered me to arrange for your execution," he signs to Jeran. I squint, paying close attention to the silhouette of his hands moving.

Jeran doesn't reply at first. He keeps his head bowed, waiting for Aramin to say more. When he doesn't, Jeran seems to swallow and nod. "And what about Talin and Adena?" he asks aloud.

"They'll receive the same sentence," Aramin replies.

Jeran narrows his eyes. "What's their crime?"

"Disobeying an order from the Senate and crossing enemy lines without authorization."

"Aramin," he says. It's the first time I've heard him address the Firstblade by name since Aramin gained the position. "You know they don't deserve their sentence."

I can tell that Jeran's words affect Aramin. He blinks, and suddenly, the energy between them seems to shift from a superior and a subordinate to two young soldiers, once ranked the same, once comrades in war.

"And why is that?" Aramin says tightly.

"When we became Strikers, we took an oath to protect this nation with our lives."

"It was a direct order."

"Sometimes you have to disobey an order to protect what you love."

This is the closest I've ever heard Jeran speak against his Firstblade, and I can tell that Aramin feels the weight of it. He considers Jeran quietly. Finally, he says, "And what about you?"

Jeran hesitates.

At his silence, Aramin scowls. The black bones piercing his ears glint in the weakening light. "You've used all your strength and passion to vouch for someone else. What about you? Do you think you deserve your sentence?"

Jeran is silent for a long time before he finally answers. "No," he replies. But he says it quietly, so quietly that I think even Aramin can barely hear him.

The Firstblade sighs and then draws one of his blades. He points it at his subordinate. Then he tosses the blade to Jeran and draws a second one of his own. "Disarm me, then," he tells Jeran.

"What?"

"You're nicknamed the Deathdancer for a reason. Disarm me, fight for your life that you deserve, and I'll order your release."

Jeran shakes his head. "I won't fight you, Aramin."

"We used to fight each other all the time. You were the best I ever sparred with."

"Then I suppose I'm going to disappoint you," Jeran says.

Aramin's lips tighten. "You won't even fight for your freedom?"

Jeran stays quiet, struggling against the words he wants to say.

Without warning, Aramin darts forward. His blade cuts toward Jeran in an arc. There is no mercy in the movement—but Jeran deflects it with ease, bringing his blade up in a flash and clashing once with Aramin's before spinning out of the way. Aramin lunges again, this time striking high. Jeran ducks low and twists his blade with a smooth flick of his wrist. Again, Aramin's hit only glances off Jeran's blade.

Aramin scowls at Jeran's flawless technique but his reluctance to retaliate. "Why won't you fight back?" he says through gritted teeth. He aims to hit Jeran again, but again Jeran deflects the blow. Again, Jeran doesn't lunge for Aramin.

There's a grief in Aramin's voice now. "You defend others, fight for their right to live. But you don't defend yourself against those who want to hurt you. You won't fight for yourself."

"Just as you don't raise your voice against a Speaker you disagree with?" Jeran snaps.

Aramin pauses in his attack, taken aback.

There's a flash of something wild and fierce in Jeran's eyes. "The Speaker refuses to allow refugees to join our ranks," he continues. "He keeps rations secured only for his wealthy friends. And as we discovered, he's willing to sell his own country to his enemy in exchange for his own safety. But you still fight for him. Are those the orders you want me to obey?"

The Firstblade is silent, his blade still. He's staring at Jeran as if he's seeing him for the first time and not recognizing him at all. I hold my breath, watching.

"What do you mean?" he says in a low voice. "About the Speaker selling his own country to his enemy?"

"Ask Talin," Jeran responds. "It won't change anything, regardless. What good is our word, as a group of treasonous Strikers? The Speaker will stay in power as long as Mara still stands." He shakes his head. "Sometimes you have to disobey an order to protect those you love."

"And who do you love?" Aramin asks him quietly.

Jeran says nothing. Instead, he throws down the blade Aramin had given him and bends his knee. He puts his fist back against his chest. His hair has loosened slightly from its knot, and messy, red-gold strands hang on either side of his face.

"I came back here," he replies, "for you."

Aramin doesn't answer for a long time. When he finally does, his voice is subdued. "You should have stayed in the woods, out of the Federation's reach."

Even though Jeran doesn't move, I can see the impact of Aramin's response shudder through him and the tremor it leaves.

"I'd rather you stay alive than die at my side," Aramin adds.

Then he turns and steps out of the cell, leaving Jeran kneeling alone on the floor.

• • •

I don't know how much time passes after the Firstblade leaves Jeran's cell. The night settles in earnest, and my cell plunges into darkness, lit only by the faintest trace of moonlight spilling down from the grating in the side of the wall. For a while, I try to count the hours in my head. I fall into a doze sometimes, but nightmares keep me from sinking into a real sleep. I can't tell if the dreams are mine or Red's.

Finally, at some strange hour of the night, my cell door opens again. This time, when I straighten myself against the wall, I see no guard accompanying my guest inside. Instead, Aramin emerges alone from the darkness to stand before me.

He doesn't speak aloud. Instead, he kneels to my level and gives me a strange, severe look. It's a warning that what we're about to discuss is as dangerous as if we were hunting Ghosts at the warfront.

"What do you know about the Speaker?" he signs to me.

I search his gaze and see the young man he was before he became the Firstblade. This is the person Jeran had awakened—someone so brave and headstrong on the warfront that he'd been tapped to lead us at an unusually young age. I remember the letter he'd written to Jeran, warning us all so that we could flee for the Federation. Now Aramin has come to see me in secret, risking his standing in an attempt to get the truth.

Aramin sees my hesitation, but he doesn't comment on it. Instead, he waits patiently.

"Our mission failed," I sign, "but it would have succeeded. Adena's discovery would have disconnected the Ghosts in the Federation's lab complex from their masters. And for a while, we even saw it in action."

"What happened?"

"The Federation knew, somehow, that we were on our way, that we had entered their territory and were on a mission to destroy their links with their Ghosts. Their Premier told me they had been expecting us, all along. He had been informed of our arrival."

The Firstblade's eyes pierce mine. He already knows what I'll say next.

"Aramin," I tell him, "our Speaker made a deal with the Federation's Premier in exchange for his own life being spared after Mara falls."

He looks away, pale with the realization, and fixates on the torches flickering outside my door. "What deal?" he asks.

"The Speaker warned them that we would try to disrupt their links with their Ghosts. He told them what we had discovered, and it gave the Federation enough time to create an antidote to Red's blood."

"You're sure about this?"

"The Federation's Premier himself told us."

"Have you told anyone else?"

"No."

"Good." Aramin's lips tighten. "If the Speaker hears about this accusation against him, there will be nothing I can do to save you."

"Will you save us now?"

A wry smile appears on his lips. "Perhaps my chances are better."

I return the smile with a somber one of my own. "There's nothing you can do, is there?"

He's quiet, and for the first time, I think that this soldier, who I've never seen weep, who is somehow capable of bearing the weight of leading us all, who gave me the chance to escape the Outer City, looks helpless.

"I'm sorry, Talin," he signs.

I just shake my head. "We're going to lose, anyway," I respond. "Maybe it's better to die at the hands of Marans."

Aramin searches my gaze. Then he rises to his feet. "Well," he responds, "if we're going to lose, then perhaps we should do it right."

31

THE NIGHT PASSES. I TWITCH IN A RESTLESS
sleep. Every sound outside my cell door—echoes of the guards' boots
as they change shifts, voices and distant shouts from other prisoners—
makes me stir, thinking that the Firstblade has returned to see me or
that the Speaker has sent someone to have me killed. But no one comes.

Red. I reach out again through our link. I've been calling for him
regularly through the night, in the hopes that he might somehow hear
me, but if he does, there's no answer. I imagine him breaking loose of his
bonds, cutting through all his chains and slaughtering the guards. But
he won't do such a thing, not when our lives might be at risk, when we
need everyone to push back against the oncoming Federation.

What will happen, though, if they do choose to execute us? Will
Red be forced to save us and carry us to safety in the wilderness, aban-
doning everyone we know here?

Even though Red can't hear my exact words or thoughts, I summon
the hope that he can feel what I'm thinking. A moment later, I sense
the push of his emotions through the bond, his undercurrent of anger
at the thought of us being led out to the arena to be killed. He would
do it, I realize. He would stop at nothing to protect us.

The day drags on without any visitors. I start to wonder if something has happened to Aramin. What if the Speaker had him arrested—or murdered? In the cell below me, Jeran paces, his wrists flicking as he practices his forms. Sometimes he glances up through the grate, his eyes searching for mine. When he finds me, his gaze is hollow with despair.

"No news?" he signs up to me.

I shake my head, and he turns away to continue his pacing. He must be wondering the same thing about Aramin.

Another night comes. Then a third day, a fourth. Jeran's pacing turns more frantic, and the bond between Red and me ripples with unease as we continue to wait. None of the guards who visit my cell can understand signs, so I am powerless to ask them if they have any news for me.

I dream about Aramin appearing, coat flapping, to unchain me from the wall and lift me to my feet. The dream occurs over and over again, so often that I start to have trouble distinguishing when I'm dreaming from when I'm awake, waiting for him to come through my door. The reality only settles in when I realize no one is coming.

And then, on the fifth day, the guards storm in. They don't say a word to me—they don't even meet my stare. I'm instead hauled to my feet as one of them unlocks the chains from around my wrists and ankles. I manage a glance down through the grating on the floor. Jeran, who had been leaning against his wall, has already leaped to his feet at the sound of the commotion in my cell. All we can do is lock eyes before they drag me out.

We make our way through the dark belly of the prison upward, spiraling into the light until we finally emerge back on the grounds of the National Plaza. Red's presence seems to be growing more distant. I can feel the beat of his pulse dimming with distance.

Is he not being brought out here with us?

Only moments later, I see Jeran emerge from the prison, flanked on either side by guards with their guns trained on his head. Adena comes next, her hair tangled in a mess. She exchanges a silent stare with us.

A sinking feeling fills my stomach. Somehow, something in me had hoped that the Firstblade would find a way to save us, that he'd ordered us up here to free us and reinstate us in the Striker forces. As if we could go back to the days when we practiced in the arena and headed out to the warfront. But the warfront is going to collapse soon, and we are now enemies of our own state.

And Red. Where is he?

Red. Red. I call for him again, but he's too far away. Still, I can sense his emotions rise, fury amid his confusion. He knows we've left the prison.

The feeling grows stronger, tipping into nausea. They're not going to kill him. Are they going to keep him alive for their own purposes?

The Firstblade is already waiting for us in the center of the space, his arms folded behind his back. In the stands are the other Strikers of our ranks, quietly waiting, while standing behind the Firstblade is an arc of Senators, the Speaker in the center of them. Jeran's father and brother stand at one end of the half circle, their eyes trained on Jeran. I wonder if I'll see only cold disdain on their faces, but even though Gabrien looks satisfied to see his brother's fate, their father appears grave.

Maybe here, in the end, even a monster can recognize that he's about to lose his son.

Across the arena, Jeran's and Aramin's eyes meet. They hold each other's gaze for a moment, some silent acknowledgment of what they had learned about each other in the prison. Then it's gone, and Aramin looks away. Jeran lowers his head. I look on in disbelief. After everything, will Aramin really allow the execution of the person he loves?

As we approach, I see the Speaker lift his chin to stare at us, satisfied to see that we'll soon be facing our justice.

There is a range of Strikers standing in a block formation before the Firstblade, their guns out. It takes me a moment to realize that they have been chosen as our executioners, Strikers being the only ones trusted to take the lives of other Strikers. I see Tomm and Pira among them. When once I would have imagined them doing this with glee, I instead see no joy on their faces. Pira bites her lip at the sight of me and averts her gaze.

My heart begins to pound.

Aramin, to his credit, meets my gaze without looking away. "You have been brought before us to answer for your actions," he says. It is the same speech he gives before every execution of a traitor or prisoner of war, and I remember the echo of it from the day when they'd first brought Red out here and into my life. "Because of your betrayal of your nation, the Senate has sentenced you to death."

I look around the arena, wondering if here, at the end, anyone will vouch for us. Many of the Strikers had loved Jeran, had admired Adena for her ingenuity. Will they watch now as they're executed for trying to save Mara? I stare at them in the stands, my fellow Strikers. As stony as we're trained to keep our faces, I see sadness there, resignation. Even some anger. For who executes soldiers like us, soldiers willing to fight, before the Federation comes tearing at our gates?

But no one moves forward.

Beside me, Adena and Jeran exchange looks with each other.

Then I turn to Aramin, a silent question in my eyes. What will he do?

Whatever secrets are in him, he doesn't say. But the Speaker steps closer to him and utters a few words, then moves away, and the First-blade continues.

"When a betrayal to Mara happens on such a grand scale," he says, "it is only right that the consequences be witnessed by those dedicated to protecting this nation."

He looks at us. Then he turns to face the Senate.

"Let this be the witness stage, then, for the Speaker's treason to Mara."

The Speaker's face bleeds white.

I blink, stunned for a moment into stillness. Around the Speaker, the Senate shuffles their feet, unsure what to make of the Firstblade's declaration.

Jeran's eyes jump back to Aramin in shock.

The Speaker frowns, unable to speak. But Aramin doesn't back down, doesn't act like he's somehow misspoken. He just stares coolly at the Speaker as he holds out a blood-flecked letter.

"I sent a hawk after your messenger birds last night," he says to the Speaker, loud enough for the entire arena to hear. He begins to read the letter:

"'Constantine Tyrus of Karensa, it is my pleasure to inform you that your Skyhunter has come back into our territory. We will arrange for his return to you as soon as the invasion is over. Regards, Ramel An Parenna, Speaker of Mara.'"

Even from a distance, we can glimpse the unmistakable flourish of the Speaker's bright crimson stamp on the letter. They were going to return Red to the Federation, so that they could continue their experiments on him.

"This is treason of the highest order," the Speaker says to the First-blade, his lips curling, his eyes dark with rage. "This is a lie, and you know you have signed your own death warrant with it."

But Aramin doesn't look concerned at all. When I glance up at the stands, I don't see surprise on the faces of the other Strikers either. The shock reverberates through me. They already *know*. I am witnessing a coup.

Only the other Senators buzz, enraged and confused. "What is this theater?" one of them scoffs with a frightened laugh.

The Speaker narrows his eyes at the Firstblade. "Arrest this man," he calls out to the guards with him.

They turn their guns toward Aramin.

Then I see the Firstblade's hand flicker, and in a single trained movement, every Striker in the stands rises and draws their guns. The sound is thunderous.

I stare at them, surprised by the sting in my eyes. They had not spoken for us earlier because they already knew that Aramin would turn on the Speaker.

They are standing for *us*.

And then it happens—here, in this tense standoff, the sound we've all dreaded to hear suddenly pierces the air.

It is a sound we have trained to hear since we were children, a sound that has haunted our thoughts and given us nightmares. It is the sound of the alarms on the Inner City's double walls, designed to warn us that the last of our defense compounds has fallen.

Speaker, Senator, Firstblade, Striker—in this moment, we are all the same. We turn our heads toward the walls. As if on cue, the earth shudders in the distance. And then comes a new sound—one none of us has ever heard before, and one so chilling that it raises every hair on the back of my neck.

Fists. Thousands of them, pounding desperately against the gates in a ripple of thunder, accompanied by the screams of Outer City refugees trapped outside and begging to be let in.

The time has come. The Federation has arrived.

32

ALL MY THOUGHTS VANISH, REPLACED BY A single, searing goal: Find my mother and get her inside. If the city falls tonight, she won't stand a chance out there. Already, I can smell smoke in the air, the telltale odor of burning metal that I remember from the shanties.

The Speaker is still screaming for the Firstblade's arrest—but with the blast of one alarm, his power has been stripped away—and suddenly all I see standing before me is a small, weak man with expensive robes and a shrill voice. Every Striker turns instinctively to Aramin, awaiting his next order, while the guards and soldiers freeze in their motions, unwilling to lay a hand on the person we need to lead us into battle.

The Firstblade ignores the Speaker. Instead, he nods toward us. "Unchain them," he calls out, "and get them into their gear. We don't have time."

And just like that, hands are on me, loosening the shackles around my wrists and ankles and letting them clatter to the ground. Guards do the same to Adena and Jeran. As they do, the Speaker keeps shrieking, his voice rising higher and higher.

"You damn traitor, you damn traitor!" he repeats at the Firstblade, his spit flying as he shouts. "I should have you beheaded for this! I should have executed you long ago! I—"

Then he lunges for the nearest soldier. He manages to get his hands on the butt of a gun and raises it at Aramin—but before he can fire, a bullet hits the gun and knocks it out of his hand. The Speaker yelps and shoves his hand in his mouth, hopping a little from the sting.

I look to see Pira pointing her gun at the Speaker, her lips turned down in a scowl, the barrel of her gun still smoking.

Aramin casts the Speaker a cold look. "You'll be fine," he calls out to him. "The Federation will be sparing your life anyway, won't they?"

The Speaker stands there, frozen, as the Firstblade turns his head to his Strikers and lifts his voice, as if he had been ready for this attack all along. "Form your ranks!"

Their fists go to their chests in unison, and as one, they stream from the stands and run out of the arena, off to take their positions in front of the double walls. At the same time, the Senators, finally realizing the full extent of what's about to happen, break into clusters and run too, hurrying for their homes.

Tomm and Pira are the only ones who run with Adena, Jeran, and me as we hurry to the supply halls outside the arena. Through my link, I send frantic messages to Red.

The Federation is here. The attack has begun.

He still can't hear my words. I curse to myself, try again in vain, and then hope that he can feel the desperation pounding in my mind as I sprint to the supply hall. Here, dozens of weapons line the cases. One by one, we strap them on without a word as Tomm and Pira look on.

Six daggers each, their edges ready and sharpened, into our bandoliers and halters.

Two long, curved blades, tucked into their sheaths with a flourish.

Two guns each, strapped securely to our belts, a cloth bandolier of bullets around our waists.

Our crossbows slung over our backs.

Not long ago, Corian counted our weapons with me every morning. Now we do it without him, in what might be the last time we ever strap on our weapons.

Beside me, Adena finishes first and turns momentarily to face Pira. "Why'd you help us that day?" she says. "Out at the warfront, when you caught us running?"

She still wears that sneer on her face, the same one she'd always turned on me, but this time she looks away toward the walls. "They said you were going to destroy the Ghosts," she replies. "I thought that was worth it."

Beside her, Tomm yanks out a blade and a gun. He frowns at us, but this time, his wrath is trained not on us but in the direction of the gates.

"Are you done?" he snaps at me. When he sees my full arsenal, he nods. "Hurry up, then."

Adena turns instead toward the Grid. "I'll meet you all there," she calls at me over her shoulder. "There are some supplies I need to grab."

Then she's off before anyone can say otherwise. Jeran dashes after her, the two of them soon running in sync as they disappear past the Plaza.

I call out again to Red as I run with Tomm and Pira. Still no answer, but I feel the rumble of something buried deep in him, that power he calls when his true fury rises. It sends a current through me, and I shudder with anticipation.

By the time we reach the edge of the Inner City, a fire is burning at the top of the outer wall, where a flaming rock hurled from a catapult had ignited a store of our own explosives and collapsed an upper portion of the gate. The rest of the steel gates seem to be holding, but I can feel the heat of the flames even from the ground, and the soldiers on the walls are running frantically, shielding their faces from the inferno as they attempt to put it out.

We run into Adena in our rush down toward the gates. Her eyes are wild, her face smeared with oil and grease, and when she sees us, she wipes a hand across her face.

"I don't know what they're using to hit us," she says breathlessly, "but the fuel igniting the walls is burning hotter than any flame I've ever known. It's strong enough that I can see some signs of it melting the steel along the ruined area of the outer wall. You see that?" She points to where some of the steel has started to warp. "It's a reaction I haven't seen."

That makes me blink. The walls were built by the Early Ones, their steel near impenetrable. "What?" I sign. "That steel has resisted every kind of attack."

"I know. And yet, here we are. Have you seen their Ghosts at the wall?" The fear in her eyes seems to hollow her from the inside out. "They're enormous. The size of beasts. I've never seen so many."

I think of the Premier and the two he had brought with him during the siege weeks ago. Then I picture my mother out there in the panicking crowds, trying to escape the Federation soldiers by hiding in her home. Or maybe she's not hiding at all. She might be helping others escape, trying to gather them into areas of the shanties where the Federation's soldiers aren't looking.

"I have to get out there," I sign grimly to Adena.

"You won't be able to do it before we all head out together," Adena replies. "The Firstblade's going to send us out through the gate tunnels, and then they're going to collapse them the instant we get out."

That means there's no retreating for us tonight. Once the Strikers head out to fight, we're not coming back.

"And the citizens?" I ask.

"They're fleeing through the tunnels in the back of the city," Adena says as we stop at the inner gates, where other Strikers have spaced themselves out into a long line of orderly rows. "We're going to try to hold the Federation off as long as possible while the citizens escape."

There are hundreds of thousands of people in the Outer City with nowhere to go, no tunnels to use to get to the forests safely, no walls to hold back the enemy that will soon be on them. And they will be left to fend for themselves.

I draw my blades. As I do, another flame streaks through the sky. It's so bright that I pause to stare at it. This one soars high—high enough to clear the walls. A deep dread lodges in my throat.

And right as I think it, the streak lands in a cluster of metalwork stalls along the edge of the Inner City, behind the protection of the double walls. Everything explodes in a shower of light. We're all thrown to our knees by the impact.

High in the sky, through the smoke, I see the first silhouette of a winged creature.

The fear burning in my chest turns into terror. Red? But it isn't him. It's someone else, clad head to toe in black armor, his face shielded behind a mask, steel wings expanded to their full size.

It's a Skyhunter. Then, flying behind him, another.

The memory of others in Cardinia's lab complex with wings grafted to their backs overwhelms me now in a sickening wave. The Federation has been busy creating more like Red—but unlike him, these are fully under the Federation's control. Red's feverish words to me in the infirmary, right after the warfront invasion, come flooding back.

I tremble at the sight of them and remember the carnage Red had left on the battlefield in just a few minutes. How many of them are there?

The ground beneath us rumbles. I feel a shock jolt through my link with Red. Suddenly, the images in his head—murky and undefined until now—turn sharper for an instant, and I see him break out of his cell amid a scene of fleeing guards, then walk to the center of the prison's cylindrical pit. He looks up. His eyes are glowing, and I can no longer see his pupils. His lips curl. I can sense his rage welling up and spilling over, forcing him into blinding fury. His steel wings unfurl behind him in a rush of sliding metal. He bends his knees.

Red, I say again through our link.

And then there's a blur of motion. I shudder once, violently, as a blast comes from the prison below the National Plaza. I look behind me to see a winged soldier burst into the sky, all black steel and metallic hair, his figure silhouetted against the sky.

I let out a breath at the sight of him. Maybe we can have a chance. With Red, I dare to believe it.

Our bond pulls tight. Then he vanishes over the wall.

Out by the front gates, another fireball comes hurtling over the edge of the gates to crash into the Inner City.

"Steady, Strikers!" the Firstblade calls out, holding his gun aloft. His eyes are fixed on the shuddering gates. Beyond them come the shrieks of Ghosts driven into a feeding frenzy from the sounds of hundreds of thousands of human voices.

In unison, every Striker fans out until we form an arc facing the steel walls. Our conversations die as we each pull on our masks.

I find myself lingering for a moment on Aramin's image. Around us, some other Strikers are pale with terror, a few of them pausing to retch before hoisting their weapons and preparing themselves for our last stand.

Aramin must know that none of us will return from this night. But even now, I see no hint of fear on his face, no sign of doubt or uncertainty, no wavering in his stance. His head stays held high; his eyes flash in a fiery, almost insane defiance. A smile even plays at the edges of his mouth.

This is why he is our Firstblade, why he was chosen so young. Here, with his hair up in its fierce knot, he looks every inch the leader I've seen cutting through Ghosts on the field. He seems to relish the coming battle and the chance for us all to strike back, one last time, against our impossible enemy. On my other side, Jeran has his head turned in Aramin's direction, his jaw clenched tightly shut.

Then he, Adena, and I exchange a final look. In the sky, I feel Red's pull, the rage in him pouring ceaseless and unending.

"Weapons!" the Firstblade shouts.

I pull out my swords in unison with the others. The sliding of metal against hilt rings out across the night.

There's a moment of calm.

"It's been an honor, Strikers," the Firstblade calls out.

We lift our fists to our chests and pound out a final Striker sign.

Then Aramin lowers his blade at the wall. "Attack at will!" he shouts.

On instinct, I step forward in sync with everyone else. My attention focuses on nothing but the steel walls and the shrieks coming from beyond them. In my periphery, I see Adena and Jeran on my left.

We march outward in a ring to our deaths.

As we glide through the city streets, I see crowds of people teeming along the roads in a panic, heading in our direction and away from the walls. Marans. They're fleeing by the thousands, their faces pale with terror, cringing every time they hear the scream of a Ghost come from beyond the walls. Some of them clutch children in their arms. Others carry prized possessions—everything from clothing to gold to family heirlooms.

When we reach them, they stream past us and run toward the back of the city, where tunnels lead into the forests on the south side of Mara.

It's useless. But I keep my eyes forward and let them flee. We are surrounded by thousands of their bodies, crushing upward against us in a panic. Children wail in their parents' arms. Families call out for one another over the chaos. Over the walls hurtles another fireball. It barrels right into a set of buildings and explodes in a shower of flames. Dozens of people are caught in its inferno.

The Strikers don't flinch. I don't stop moving. We go on as the citizens run behind our line.

Suddenly, I see familiar faces as I continue to push forward. Some of the people running with the crowd are the same Senators who had been waiting in the arena for my execution. Among them, I see Jeran's father and brother.

How powerful they'd always seemed. How cruel. But now they are no different from the rest of the crowd, disheveled and desperate. Their eyes flash with fright. Jeran's father is coated in a film of mud and dirt, as if he's already fallen several times in his mad rush. In his arms are an assortment of gold and silver—bracelets, cuffs, necklaces, candelabras, and shoes. He snaps at his wife to keep up with him, but has no spare hand to help her along. She runs several paces behind him, her face red and swollen from crying, smoke, and exhaustion. Jewels drip from her arms. Gabrien runs alongside them, ignoring the others around him, elderly and young alike, uninterested in anything else except the path they're taking.

As they draw near, they see Jeran. Their eyes lock for an instant with his.

Jeran's father winces, and for a moment he looks like he wants to avoid his son in his path and find some other way to get to safety. There's embarrassment in his gaze along with his panic.

But Jeran doesn't stop moving. Instead, he points wordlessly behind himself with one of his swords, telling him with the gesture to get back behind the Strikers' moving line.

Gabrien glances at me, bewildered, as if unwilling to believe that I will let him pass. I just stare back at him, this man who had smirked at me at the National Hall's banquet.

You have spent your entire lives sneering at the ground I walk on. The style of my clothes and the tint of my skin. The food that I eat. The language of my people, the signs I use because I cannot speak aloud. You have wished for the death of my loved ones by barring them from the safety of your doors, even as you take from them what you like—their jewelry, their customs and food, their traditions. You have taken advantage of my silence in every way, robbed me of my dignity and my pride. You have used me for your own gain.

Now, in your hour of greatest need, you will use me again.

And yet, I will still risk my life to save yours. I swore an oath to this country on the day I donned this coat, to protect you and every other citizen from harm so long as there is breath in my body. While you try to escape through the tunnels, I am going to turn in the direction of danger and head out beyond the wall. I've done it my entire life, and I will do it now. One final time.

Jeran's family rushes by. As they go, I see how their heads hang low as they scramble behind me—this Basean rat—for safety.

Why would you do this? they seem to ask in their gazes.

Because my mother taught me that, in spite of everything, I must choose goodness.

The moment passes. The people scramble past us and in the direction of the tunnels along with everyone else. I don't bother watching them go. I already know that they'll survive this onslaught. Somehow, people like that always seem to get another chance.

It doesn't matter now. My eyes narrow at the wall towering before us. My hands tighten against the hilts of my blades. I've trained my entire life for this.

Ahead of us, soldiers standing by the one-way tunnels leading to the Outer City and the battlefield rush to raise the vertical gates. Steel grates against the ground as they crank giant levers against the wall, and inch by inch, the gates lift to reveal dark passages.

I take a deep breath. Beside me, Jeran breaks into a run. Adena draws the crossbow from her back, secure with her favorite weapon in her hands. She has some kind of new arrow notched to it, yet another one of her contraptions.

She winks at me when she sees me stare. "People are going to remember us, Talin," she says. "I'll make sure of it."

Her grin is so infectious that I find myself smiling back. My attention returns to the tunnels before us, their mouths now gaping open. Through them, I can feel the rush of cold air funneling in from the other side. My walk breaks into a run too.

If we're going out, then I'm grateful to be alongside this team. Rats, orphans, disgraced children.

We are Mara's saviors.

33

THE OUTER CITY'S SHANTIES ARE ALREADY ON
fire when the other Strikers and I emerge from the tunnels leading
from the Inner City. Behind us, a series of explosions shake the darkness we just came through. When I glance over my shoulder, I see the
tunnels each collapsing one by one, permanently sealing us out of the
city.

There's nowhere for us to go now except into the battle.

The scene before us is a nightmare. Ghosts tower over the shanties' shacks, their faces twisted with cracked, bleeding skin and scarlet,
fanged mouths, their shrieks a mix of fury and agony. They turn that
anger and pain onto the shanties around them.

My attention homes in immediately to the east shanties, where my
mother's house stands. Would she even still be there? My mother is no
fool. It's likely that she fled the instant the Federation's flags came into
view—but there's nowhere for her to go that would be any safer. The
house is located on the far side of the shanties, a good distance from
where the soldiers are now striking. Anywhere else in the shanties will
be more dangerous.

People run screaming down every mud-strewn street. As I pass them
by, their eyes flicker to me with wild, desperate hope. *The Strikers are*

here! I can see the light on their faces, as if we're some sort of miracle that can hold the Federation at bay.

One man with his baby slung around his chest even runs up to me and clasps my hand in desperation, speaking rapidly to me in a language I can't understand. I shake my head vigorously at him and point to the outer rims of the shanties, away from the Inner City gates.

Some refugees are trying to head to the open plains beyond the Outer City, only to run headlong into approaching Federation troops. The enemy is marching in from all angles now, a line of red along the horizon growing steadily closer. Other refugees clutch their children and belongings and stream toward the back of the Inner City walls. They know that there are escape tunnels installed underground. If the nobles are fleeing through there, then they might have a chance too.

I want to tell them all to turn back. Even if they made it there, Maran soldiers wouldn't let them in, not without letting the Inner City's residents go first.

But there's nowhere else for the refugees to go. So I try to ignore their terrified faces and keep running in the direction of my mother's house.

As I reach her street, I see a couple of her neighbors still frantically grabbing their belongings. Nana Yagerri is one of them. She drops the pans she's holding and then runs up to me, waving her arms.

"Talin!" she signs as she reaches me. Her figure is bent double, and she's wincing from her sprint. Her gnarled hands clasp mine in a trembling grip before her fingers move wildly. "Your mother isn't here. She's already left. She wanted me to go with her, but I couldn't leave all this—" She pauses to look at the humble shack that she's poured so much love into maintaining.

My mother already left? I put both hands firmly on Nana Yagerri's shoulders and squeeze them once. "Where?" I sign.

"She ran toward the walls," she signs in response. Another explosion rocks the ground somewhere in the shanties behind us, and she lets out a startled cry. "They're setting everything on fire, Talin! What will we do!—"

She's going to die out here, with her few pots and pans and precious belongings. I take her hands in mine and start pulling her away from her house.

She resists at first. "Talin, my things!—" she starts to wail.

I shake my head sternly at her, then hoist her up onto my back. There's no time for any of this. With her still crying, I push away and hurry along with her toward an area of the Outer City that still hasn't been burned yet.

Is that where my mother might be too?

A patrol of Federation soldiers appears at the end of the street. I see them tossing torches on the roofs and shooting anyone nearby who isn't clad in Karensan scarlet.

I dart sideways into an alley, but not before one of them sees me. He whistles loudly—I hear their voices as they shout something to one another.

He's calling for a Ghost. I don't bother to wait.

As I dart off with Nana Yagerri clinging to my back, I hear the unmistakable shriek of a Ghost round the corner behind us. Its voice changes pitch when it sees our fleeing figures, and I hear the click of its claws as it starts to chase us. Nana Yagerri screams at the sight.

I won't be able to outrun it. So instead, I skid to a halt, ease the old woman off my back, and turn around to face the Ghost. My eyes narrow—I draw a long blade in one hand and my gun in the other. The Ghost snarls as it lurches toward me. Someone has stabbed clean through one of its eyes, leaving nothing but a ruined socket and blood dripping down the side of its face. Shreds of blue fabric hang from its fangs.

I lift an arm to rest my gun against, then aim straight at the creature's neck cuff. I fire three times in rapid succession.

They all strike true—once, twice, thrice. The cuff shatters, leaving its neck exposed. I shoot again, but the Ghost darts away from my line of fire and breaks into a low, jolting sprint.

I push Nana Yagerri out of the way and crouch. My muscles tense. The Ghost draws frighteningly close.

At the last instant, I break into a run, aiming headlong at it. Its mouth opens wide—it lunges at me. I leap up and kick off exactly against its open jaw, then twist in midair. I land squarely on its upper back, then whirl around and wrap my arm tightly around its neck.

It lets out a bloodcurdling scream, then thrashes in an attempt to throw me off.

No time—I have to move fast. Already my grip is slipping. I bring my drawn sword down hard on the back of its neck, burying the weapon so deep in its throat that the blade comes out the other side. Somewhere from the alleys, Nana Yagerri screams.

I still haven't severed the Ghost's main artery, though. The creature twists around in fury and tries to claw me off its back. I duck, avoiding its poisonous nails, then yank out a dagger and saw it across its throat as hard as I can.

The skin breaks with a sickening rip, and then I feel the blade cut the vein. Blood gushes in a torrent onto the ground.

The Ghost lets out a hoarse, choked cry, stumbles, and collapses. I leap off its back and land nimbly beside it. I don't bother watching it in its death throes—I instantly run toward where Nana Yagerri's voice had come from.

When I turn the corner, I freeze. She's struggling against the grip of two Karensan soldiers who have already found her. One of them hits her hard across the face. She cries out, blood on her mouth, and stumbles backward. Her eyes meet mine in panic.

I have no time to stop them. Even as I lift my gun, the other soldier is already slashing out with his sword. He shoves the blade through the old woman's back. It cuts through her fragile body as easily as a needle.

Nana Yagerri's eyes go wide. She collapses forward as the soldier shakes her off his sword.

And all I can think of is the night I'd run with my mother, trying to ignore the sounds of others getting cut down behind us by Federation troops. All I can remember is my mother lying on the ground, weeping and holding my hand, telling me everything was going to be okay even as she dripped blood along the ground.

I'm attacking before I even realize it. My gun swings up at the first soldier—I shoot him straight between his ribs. He grunts and falls. As for the soldier who'd killed Nana Yagerri, I grab him by his hair before he can even think to swing his sword at me. I yank his head back, then cut him as I just cut the Ghost.

He grabs at his torn throat, his eyes wide with terror at the sight of my face, before crumpling in a heap.

All I can spare Nana Yagerri is a wave of grief. She had taught me how to sign, had given me back the gift of communication. Now she's gone.

There are so many Federation soldiers nearby, swarming through so many streets. Everyone will die here tonight. I clench my teeth. And yet, I have to keep fighting. We don't have a choice.

My mother.

Where could she have gone? My eyes scan the darkening shanties, now lit with flaming shacks. If she'd run from our home, then which way—

I haven't finished my thought yet when an arrow comes slicing through the air and embeds itself in the ground at my boots.

I draw both my blades and whirl in the direction it came from. My eyes go up to the roofs.

And there I see my mother crouching, armed with a crossbow and a dagger, her eyes ferocious in the twilight. She gives me a grim nod.

Mara will fall tonight, and the Federation will sweep over the land. But right now, I can't help staring up at her in awe. This is my mother, the huntress, the doctor. The one who would come home to her village with a kill slung over her back. The one who had somehow managed to flee with me into Mara and kept us alive all these years.

"Where did you go?" I sign up to her.

She hops down to the ground and comes up to my side. "The metal yards," she replies, holding up a sheet of old steel that she's transformed into a shield.

The scrapyards. Of course. The Federation has no reason to raze the yards the way they're destroying the Outer City. They'll salvage the metals there for their own use. It's a brilliant hiding place, at least for now.

My mother hoists her crossbow on her back. "But first, I think you could use some help," she tells me. Her eyes tilt skyward, to where the silhouette of a Skyhunter sweeps. "Your Shield seems to be busy with his own fight."

Red. Even now, I can feel the fury pulsing through our bond as he attacks the Federation's troops.

I can't help but smile. My mother has been through invasions, conquests, and poverty. She can do this too. I nod at her and start running back in the direction of the other Strikers defending the gates. My mother runs easily beside me.

This battle isn't finished yet. And even if the Federation wins in the end, we're going to make sure they feel the cost.

34

I SEE RED THE INSTANT WE ROUND THE BEND
of the Inner City walls. He's fighting a pair of Ghosts guarding the
Premier on his steed—but to my surprise, he's not attacking them in
the efficient way that he usually does.

As this realization hits me, I feel a jab of pain through our bond.
One of his wings is severely injured. The way he slices through the air is
uneven. As if on cue, another rivulet of agony seeps through the tether
that binds us. This time, it's so sharp that I wince.

Beside me, my mother frowns. "What's wrong?"

I nod up in Red's direction, then see the silhouette of a winged figure
gathering to protect their Premier. Another Skyhunter. The sight chills
my blood. They're going to make a strike at Red if we don't get help
for him.

My gaze scans the rest of the battlefield. Strikers are converging
near the gates in an attempt to hold off the overwhelming tide of Federation troops, their silhouettes dark and exaggerated behind the veils
of smoke and flame that blanket the Outer City shanties. Others have
turned their attention up to the ramparts, where a Skyhunter is sweeping among them, cutting Maran soldiers into pieces as though they
were made of air.

I turn my attention back to Red. He's decided to take aim at the Premier. If we can help him, if we can secure the slightest chance at taking him down—maybe that alone would cripple the Federation in this battle.

I point to Red and give my mother a meaningful look.

To her credit, she doesn't flinch for an instant. Instead, she picks up her pace and motions for me to follow. "We can cross through the metal yards," she says as she goes. "It'll give us some cover, so they don't know we're coming."

I run beside her at a steady pace. Ahead, a patrol of four Federation soldiers stumbles upon us—but my mother's already moving, lifting the crossbow in her hands and aiming it directly at the nearest soldier. At the same time, I yank out my gun and fire twice at a second soldier, then flip the weapon into my left hand and fire at the third.

My shots hit the second soldier square in his chest—the third manages to duck, but a bullet catches him in the leg. I dart out of his line of sight as he falls, swearing, and lifts his gun to fire blindly toward us. My boots move without a sound as I climb up the side of a burned-out shack, the destroyed metal shifting unsteadily beneath my feet as I go.

Below me, the soldier doesn't even know that I'm now running above him. I feel like the phantom that I've trained all my life to become—a Ghost killer, a weapon of destruction, an invisible outsider in every way. The wind rushes beneath me, blasts of heat accompanying it from the fires that rage all around us, and for a moment, it seems like I might be lifted into the air.

Then the soldier turns his gun toward my mother. I pivot off the side of the shack at the same time. My body twists in midair—efficient and practiced—and my blades are instinctively in my hands before I can register what I'm doing. I slash out at him in a whirlwind. Once, twice—

—scarlet sprays against the ground. The soldier collapses.

I land lightly on my feet and start running again without looking at the carnage I've left behind. My mother runs beside me, her breathing steady. She nods to my left.

"Horses," she gasps as she goes.

I see the panicked steeds left behind by the group of soldiers we encountered. We swerve from our path to secure them. Their eyes roll, showing their whites, and when I approach, they rear up.

I dodge past their hooves, grab the pommel of a bay's saddle, and swing myself up effortlessly. Then I lean over and seize the reins of a horse for my mother.

Part of being a Striker means having the ability to project a deathly calm, to use anything and everything around you to your advantage. Now, I can sense the horse steadying in my grip, relieved to have a master again. My mother climbs on hers.

I turn the horse in the direction of the scrapyards, then urge it into a gallop.

The battle scene blurs past us. Smoke has thickened so much that it's difficult to see anything through it except the red tint of silhouettes, of Federation soldiers clashing with Marans, and of Ghosts ripping through the bodies of fleeing refugees. Ahead of us, Red's figure is a dark, airborne speck surging around the enormous Ghosts.

An explosion near the gates makes our horses scream. I look over to see the gates finally starting to crumble—an impossible sight, something that should never have been able to happen. Those gates that had never before been breached will soon be reduced to rubble. A great roar goes up from the Federation troops, and the first of them begin to flood in, charging into a mass of somber, waiting soldiers.

I tear my gaze away from the scene and focus on our plan at hand:

Get to the Premier. Kill him at all costs. Our horses speed up, their hooves pounding against the ground.

We've barely reached the scrapyards when a Ghost charges into our path. It turns its bleeding eyes toward us, enraged, and then bares its gaping jaws.

I pull the crossbow from my back and aim at it—but before I can fire, another arrow blooms right through its clavicle, making it shriek and twist around. A blur of sapphire flies through the air, landing on its shoulders. *Jeran.*

He grabs his gun and fires at the creature's neck cuff until it gives way. From his side materializes Adena, blades spinning. She slices through its vulnerable vein, and blood sprays on the ground before us.

I break into a smile. They're still here, still fighting.

Jeran hops down from the falling Ghost to land nimbly on the back of his own steed. He shoots my mother and me a questioning look. "Red?" he signs, nodding back toward where my Shield is fighting for his life.

I nod once.

Adena smiles. Her expression is fierce, her eyes alight with the anticipation of war. "Don't want to miss the party, then," she signs at us, and then they nudge their horses into a gallop too.

We ride through the carnage and the smoke and the flames. Past the burning gates of the outer wall and the massacre happening within. I see Ghosts lurching in through the charred entrance, while archers on the inner wall's ramparts still try to hold their ground.

Mara has always been the last beacon of freedom. I'd crossed over into this country with my mother thinking that now we would be invincible forever, that somehow, Mara's impenetrable capital would never fall. But the scene before me looks eerily similar to how Basea had looked when it finally crumbled to the Federation. There is no difference.

My attention zeroes in on the Premier, still stark against the sky in his armor astride his horse. Overhead, an enemy Skyhunter dives down, aiming for Red. He has finally killed the two Ghosts guarding the Premier, shredding one's calves and cutting its tendons, slicing clean through the second's throat. But it doesn't matter—more Ghosts, massive ones that must have been converted decades ago—converge on the battle. The pain that comes through our tether sears me to the bone.

I think of Red's memory that had once flashed through my mind, of him seeing his sister as the Federation gradually transformed her into their Ghost and him into their next weapon. I think of Corian, his eyes turned up to me as I take his life so that he will not walk this land as a Ghost. I think of my mother as we huddled on the other side of the cliffs, watching refugees fall into the abyss as the bridges collapsed.

This is what the Federation does to us. It plants these horrifying memories in our minds until our hearts have turned hollow.

I clench my teeth at the sight, my heart burning from Red's fury, then crouch lower against my steed's back as we surge toward the fight. The rest of the battle around us dims into the distance. Even now, my Striker companions don't make a sound beside me. My mother stays silent. We ride as a phantom team, accompanied by nothing but the pounding of war hooves.

Mara will fall. But maybe we can take the Federation's Premier with us.

Through our tether, I reach out to Red. *You're not fighting alone.*

His attention flickers to us. Our eyes find each other through the chaos and hold for a precious moment. I linger on him for as long as I can. It might be the last time we ever get to see each other.

Then I narrow my gaze on the closest Ghost and pull my gun out of its holster. My other hand yanks out one of my blades.

For a moment, I think I can feel Corian's spirit riding beside us, his smile fierce and his hair wild. It's as if nothing had changed since the day we headed out together into our first battle.

See you after the carnage, he'd sign to me, then vanish into the melee.

I hurtle toward the Ghost and then jump high into the air. I aim at its neck and fire.

The bloodlust in me blinds my concentration to anything else. I am death now, steel and sword and bullet. I am one with my weapons. The world blurs around me—I see Adena and Jeran throw themselves into the fray, aiming at the other Ghosts. My mother has her teeth bared as she fires arrows into a nearby Federation soldier. And overhead, Red clashes with another Skyhunter, their wings a maelstrom of death as they spiral and spin.

Ahead of me is the Premier.

The Ghost I'm attacking claws for me, shrieking. I arch out of its way, hit the ground and roll, and then dart underneath it, moving as quickly and silently as I've ever done. I have to get close to the Premier. He has his own weapons out now, pointing his gun at Maran soldiers nearby. His weapon swings to where Adena is cutting down one of her Ghosts. He fires.

The bullet hits Adena hard in the leg. I bite my tongue at the sight until I taste blood in my mouth, but I don't dare scream out. All I can do is watch as my patrol leader cringes and collapses to one knee, losing her balance. She topples from the Ghost's shoulders, blades still spinning as she goes. Even now, she doesn't cry out or utter a single sound.

I force my attention back to the Premier. He's going to fire again. He doesn't see me coming.

Another Ghost lunges for me. I skid beneath it, roll, and keep going. Another horse runs past me—I grab its saddle and swing myself up onto its back, forcing it to turn toward the Premier. Closer, closer.

All I need is one good shot. The gun in my hand tightens as I aim for him.

This is for what you've done to Red. To his family. For what you and your father have inflicted on every nation you've conquered and brought under your fist. For my mother. This is for everything and everyone and all of us.

I fire.

At the same time, the Premier sees me.

One of his soldiers lunges forward, knocking him off his horse. My bullet hits the sacrificial soldier in the chest.

The Premier lands on the ground—hurt, but alive.

Guards swarm to him, hiding him from view.

I'm forced to swerve away as they point their crossbows and guns at me again. As my horse gallops underneath a Ghost, I throw myself off its back and land in a roll. I have to try once more.

Then pain explodes through my body.

I glance down, dazed, to see a thick arrow protruding from my side. The angle of it makes me turn my eyes up. There, I see a Skyhunter bearing down on me, his eyes glowing with the determination to kill.

A second arrow—a bullet?—hits my leg. I wince and fall, my blades still in my hands.

Everything seems to slow down. From above, a dark shadow falls over me.

Red strikes the Skyhunter before he can reach me. There's a loud crunch of metal, followed by the shrieks of Ghosts. A second Skyhunter has sealed off my path to the Premier—and as I stagger back, I see one of them land in front of his horse, wings outstretched protectively before him.

Red lunges again and again at his own Skyhunter assailant. Too late, I see a second one swing a chain in his direction. They're going to capture him.

Red. I reach for him through our tether as I force myself to my feet and strike out at the nearest Federation soldier. *Behind you!*

He turns and looks down at the second Skyhunter just as the chain the Skyhunter throws strikes him. Red's quick enough to dart to his right, so that the chain misses his torso—but it catches one of his legs and whips tightly around it. He winces. The spark of pain shoots through our link and I wince too. The weight makes him lurch sharply to one side.

Everything around me has turned into a smear of blood and fire. Between the fighting bodies, I see the silhouette of Mara's Inner City burning. A lone scarlet flag flies over the ramparts of the inner wall.

The city has fallen.

A third arrow strikes me in my other leg. I barely feel the pain of it this time—only its force thudding through me, then my body betraying me as I fall again. From the sky, I think I hear Red calling my name through our link.

Talin!

Perhaps he's shouting with his real voice. I can't tell anymore. My arms swing out, still fighting. My blade runs straight through a soldier's chest, and he falls with a hoarse groan.

Blackness threatens my sight. Is Jeran still fighting? Adena? I turn my gaze skyward to Red and lift my gun at the chain binding him. If they take him back to the Federation's capital, they'll finish transforming him into a full Skyhunter, and I'll lose him. We can't afford that. *I* can't bear it. If Mara must fall, then let him go free.

With the last of my strength, I take aim and fire three shots—my last bullets—at the chain.

At least my aim is still accurate. I hit it once, then again in the same link, then a third time. The chain snaps clean with a clatter of metal, and Red suddenly lurches free into the air again, the links falling to the ground beneath him.

He whirls immediately around to look at me. His eyes are engulfed in silver-white light, but behind that glow, I know his expression is a stricken one. A trill of rage shoots through our tether as he starts to lunge for me—only to halt when the Premier's Skyhunters gather between us, cutting us off. He's far too outnumbered here.

Go, I think, as clearly and sharply as I can. There are tears on my cheeks now, but my resolve stays unwavering. *Get out of here. It's useless for you to die here too. Stay free and get help. Strike back another day. Please.*

He doesn't want to leave me. I can feel the desperation coming back to me from him, and for an instant longer, he stays there, hovering in the air. Then the other Skyhunters move toward him, and I send my thought more harshly.

You have to do this for me. Go!

Finally, Red tears his gaze away from me and pushes down hard with his wings. He soars up, out of the range of the Skyhunters, and dives into the chaos of the battle, disappearing behind the giant silhouettes of several Ghosts. Behind him, the other Skyhunters give chase for a moment before they stop. Two remain on Red's trail, while the rest return to protect the Premier.

I look around the battlefield for other Strikers, but see no flash of sapphire coats. Everything is a sea of scarlet. Again, I try to rise to my knees and swing out at the soldiers now approaching me. This time, though, I just crumple again.

My mother? Where is she?

Finally, my arms feel too leaden to fight. Every part of my body weakens, even as I try to force it onward. My breaths come in gasps.

For Mara, for its citizens, for the wealthy and the wicked and the poor and the suffering, I am going to give my life today on the battlefield. And maybe it won't even matter. It'll be like every other country that has fallen before the Federation—the soldiers that stood up against it forgotten, ash blown away in the wind.

It will be as if I've never existed. Will every Striker fall tonight? Will the world even remember that Mara once had such an elite fighting force?

Red. Red. What will happen to him? Will the Federation capture him and take him back to their labs and finish their work on him? I reach for him in my mind as I fade, trying to hang on to the quiet moments we'd shared. I think of the first time I ever saw him, in chains as Maran soldiers led him out into the arena, willing to die, yet exuding a strength that I couldn't ignore.

Red.

I have no idea if he can hear me call for him through our link, whether I'm too weak to reach him or whether he's still alive himself to hear it. I think I feel the pulse of him on the other side, and everything in my heart yearns toward him, wishing for one last moment before it all ends.

At least we tried. At least we gave our everything.

I wait for the sear of another arrow to pierce my chest and end my life. As the world around me dims, the last thing I see is a scarlet figure striding toward me. It's a young man. The Premier, Constantine Tyrus. There is a slash on his cheek, and blood smears his hands, but he still holds his head high. Uninjured.

We've failed to take him down. Constantine will remain and rule over the Federation.

My eyes meet his as he kneels down to my dying figure. He recognizes me now. I can see the flicker in his gaze.

"You're the one from the capital," he says.

I wish, more than anything, that I still had a voice in this moment, just to spit an answer back at him. Tell him that everything I've ever done was to destroy him and his father. That he had taken so much from me—my words, my home, my world—and yet could not take everything.

But instead I stare at him in silence, and in that silence, he gives me a grim smile. "It's better to forget this," he tells me. "You're a part of the Federation now."

It's better to forget.

His words trigger some small, old part of my memory. I flinch, wincing at the sudden recollection. Something about that phrase, something about it paired with this surrounding of a world destroyed by the Federation. It is too familiar.

It's better to forget, it's better to forget . . .

And then, just like that, the fog in my memory—the blur surrounding the night that the Federation had first invaded Basea, the mystery of what had happened to my father that night—clears, burned away by the familiar sight of yet another home of mine collapsing to the same enemy.

I see myself as an eight-year-old again, on the night of the invasion of Sur Kama. My mother and I were curled beside each other in a trapdoor underneath our carpet. My father had dug this space out under the house—it's tight and dark, no bigger than ten square feet wide and four square feet deep. We had originally intended to use it as a cool pantry to store some of our harvest. But then the Federation came to the borders of Basea, and we'd turned it into our hiding spot.

My mother's arm wrapped tightly around me. Her entire body trembled.

Outside, we could hear the shattering of glass as Federation soldiers smashed our neighbors' windows with the hilts of their blades and the butts of their guns. Screams pierced the night air. Already, there was a hint of smoke permeating the air as the Federation began to set fire to homes.

At the door stood my father. When I lifted the trapdoor enough to let in a tiny slit of light, I could catch a glimpse of his tall figure pressed against the wall, listening intently for the approach of soldiers. I could see every detail of his face cut into sharp relief—the same cheekbones I inherited, his angular nose, the soft brow and green, slender eyes. Sweat dripped down his temple, but his face stayed as it always was, serene and still.

No, no. I don't want to remember this. I don't.

"Get down, Talin," my mother hissed beside me, and I lowered myself a little, but I couldn't help watching my father stand there.

"When is he going to come hide with us?" I whispered to her in the dark.

A loud knock made me jump. My mother clamped a hand over my mouth and forced us to crouch lower into the hole, but through the slit in the floor, I could see my father move to stand calmly in front of the door. Earlier in the afternoon, he had rushed in with family heirlooms in his arms—a copper ring, a set of bracelets from my grandmother, a series of rare coins from my grandparents' time—and flushed them all down the toilet. The Federation wants things, he'd said to us, his voice dark with fear. Things, and people.

People. I'd heard this about the Federation, the way they fixated on the most efficient uses for their people—as soldiers, as weapons, as experiments, as labor—as well as the rewards lavished if you did well and the punishments given if you failed.

Maybe we could just do well for them, and they would let us keep on living.

The soldiers shouted something I couldn't understand. My father cast one glance in our direction before they burst inside, guns already drawn. One of them asked my father questions in harsh words, but my father just shook his head calmly. He lifted a hand and touched his fingers to his lips. Instantly I knew it was a gesture meant for us.

"Silence, my little love," my mother whispered to me in the darkness. My heart hammered so loudly against my ribs that I thought they'd hear us for sure. *But what about my father?* I kept thinking. *How would he save himself?*

Then one of the soldiers pointed a gun directly at his face.

I was eight years old, and I couldn't stop the squeal of terror that burst from my lips. "Pa!" I squeaked, before my mother clamped a hand over my mouth.

Oh no—what have I done? The thought flashed through me at the same time as my shout.

At first I hoped the soldiers couldn't hear it over the chaos—but they all turned simultaneously in our direction. My father's face turned sickly white in an instant. The soldiers headed toward us and threw the carpet aside. The trapdoor flung open over our heads. Light flooded down over us.

My father moved so quickly. He lunged forward, tackling the closest soldier to him and knocking the gun from his hands. Shouts went up. There was a scramble. It couldn't have lasted longer than a minute, but to me it felt like hours and hours. I saw a second soldier lift his gun to my father's face. This time there was a blast of sound, a burst of sparks.

My father fell and didn't get up again.

I screamed and screamed as hands hauled my mother and me out from our hiding place and dragged us toward the front of the house. As I went, I caught a glimpse of my fallen father's ruined face. Then we were out in the night, and I was thrown to my knees. My mother struggled against her captor—she managed to escape him. And I knelt, sobbing, before a twelve-year-old Red, helpless as he stood over me and weighed the risk of punishing himself and his entire family against murdering the little girl in front of him.

My lost voice. My hazy recollections of my father. My inability to remember his face.

The Federation's poisonous gas permanently scarred my throat, yes. But that was never the true reason why I stopped speaking after that night. If I hadn't called out for my father, they likely would have offered him and my mother the chance to join the Federation's ranks, keeping me as insurance that they would stay loyal to their new nation. We would have lived.

But instead I had raised my voice. And my voice had killed my father.

Oh, Talin, Talin, my mother had said to me. *Sometimes, it's better to forget.*

That's what I'd done. I'd buried that memory along with my voice.

Until the Premier's words echoed my mother's from that night, against a backdrop of similar carnage.

I feel myself slip away. The world around me fades to nothing but the face of the approaching Premier. Then he fades away too, until all I know is the ground cold beneath me, my mother's words echoing into the darkness.

Better to forget.

35

IN MY DREAM, I RUN AFTER MY FATHER. ALL
around us tower columns of fire, and behind that, the burning silhouette
of a fallen Mara. I'm trying to call out to him, and in my dream, I have
a voice, the voice of a child right before it is stolen from her.

Maybe everything that had happened was one long nightmare.
Maybe Mara still stands, with her flags flying blue and free over the
ramparts.

There's a familiar voice that calls to me in the dream, and it does
not belong to Red. It sounds like the most beautiful and horrible voice
in the world, at once soothing and dark, the sound of bells in a temple
of death. I find myself turning toward it, curious to hear it again at the
same time I push away from it, repelled.

"Wake up, Talin," he says in Basean, and the sound of my native
tongue stirs me out of the blur of my dream.

The towering flames fade into gray, and the image of my father
before me turns to mist. My heart lodges in my throat. I reach out for
him, desperate for him to stay. But of course he can't hear me. His figure
turns lighter and lighter until it disappears altogether, replaced by this
voice that keeps calling for me from another world.

"Talin, it's time to wake up."

Pain starts to lance down my arms and legs. There's such a sharp agony in my side that I can't take a full breath. I think I'm standing, but I can't possibly have enough strength to be holding myself up alone. The pain turns acute and real now. Tingles run through my limbs as I try in vain to move. Something is securing my arms tightly behind my back, and the way my weight seems to hang tells me that I must be chained upright. There is no gag on my mouth, but with the way my hands are bound, I'm as good as silenced.

Slowly, I open my eyes.

The Premier of the Karensa Federation is standing before me, resplendent in a brilliant yellow coat. The kind of outfit a king would wear to his coronation. When he sees me awake, his lips curve up.

"There she is," he says encouragingly to me, again in Basean. Hearing the language on the lips of the man responsible for tearing my life apart . . . I want to reach out and rip the words out of his mouth.

I see that we're in the banquet room of Mara's National Hall, the same chamber where Red and I had once stood before the Senate and demonstrated to the Speaker what we could do.

The Premier ignores the anger on my face, nods behind him, and lets me see everyone else in the room. A ring of his personal guards circles the space around us, their hands resting on the guns at their belts, their scarlet uniforms emblazoned with the Federation's double crescents. My gaze stutters to a halt on the Speaker of Mara, who now stands in a corner with guards on either side of him, his hands behind his back. He clears his throat at me, but something in my stare must unnerve him, because he quickly averts his eyes.

Then I see her.

Chained and kneeling, with two guards on either side of her . . . is my mother. Bloodied, but alive.

I come fully awake now, and every muscle in my body screams in pain. A cold sweat breaks out all over my body—I struggle to catch my breath as the wound in my side and my leg flare to life. My eyes stay fixed on my mother, who stares back at me in anguished silence.

One of the soldiers steps forward, the ornate trim of his sleeves distinguishing him from the others. His gloved hands go to the sword at his belt.

The Premier just holds a hand up and shakes his head. He takes a few steps away from me and folds his arms across his chest. "Have you trained as a Striker all your life?" he asks me, this time in Maran.

I only nod at him.

"So, starting when you were twelve."

Another nod.

"They say you can't speak," he muses out loud, "but I can arrange for my Chief Architect to fix that."

My eyes narrow at his words. He doesn't understand that scars can be invisible, that his soldiers—that *he*—was the one who'd broken my voice. His words are so dismissive, so confident in his assessment and control over my own body that I resolve, in this instant, that I'd rather die than give him the power to force me to speak.

Beside him, one of his soldiers steps forward and bows his head. General Caitoman, the Premier's brother who I'd first seen in Cardinia. He says something in Karenese, and the Premier considers me as the man talks. When he finishes, he nods at me. "I'm told you're one of the best in Mara's forces," he says. "Your Firstblade tended to put you on the warfront, and I can see why."

Aramin. Did he survive the massacre? What about Jeran, and Adena? What about Red?

The Premier strides in a slow circle around me as I continue to tremble from my pain. "I heard you took down more of my Ghosts on your own than anyone else out there on the field. Your Firstblade must have seen a great deal of potential in you."

I hate that, in spite of everything, my heart jumps at his words. *A great deal of potential.* Not because Corian had taken pity on me, had spoken for me. Is it a cruel irony that the respect I've ached for comes from my worst enemy?

He stops before me again, the rings on his hand clinking as he holds his hand out. "Given your resemblance," he says, "I'm assuming the woman chained behind me is your mother. Yes?"

A surge of strength jolts through me, and I lunge at him before I can stop myself. The chains holding me back pull taut, sending fresh pain lancing through my arms. Around the chamber, all the soldiers immediately lift their guns at me in a unity of clicks.

The Premier doesn't flinch at my movement at all, nor does he smile. "It's up to you," he continues, "whether or not your mother lives."

I don't know if he can see the hatred burning in my gaze. My hands are trembling so hard behind my back that my chains rattle.

He looks grave now. "I know how hard everything must be for you," he says. "How difficult it must *always* have been. You never had a chance to know your homeland of Basea, and when you and your mother fled into the borders of Mara, you ended up in a country that both sheltered you and insulted you."

The manipulation in this man's words. *How would you know?* I want to say to him, the thought barbed with rage. How could you begin to care about the pain that you have inflicted on this world?

Constantine smiles grimly at me, as if he can guess what's going through my mind. "I know you see me as the source of your pain, that I take from you and your people without mercy. But the truth is that I am here to build a better country for Mara. Do you know, Talin, what ended the Early Ones' civilization?"

In spite of myself, I lean forward, suddenly curious to hear his answer. No one knows, I thought. It's the mystery of their disappearance that's always added a near-spiritual element to their ruins.

"I know. We found evidence of it in the ruins in our territory. They had built such a powerful society, had been poised to leave this world and travel to the stars. But they were careless too, in the way they lived and created. And when a weapon they built escaped from their control, they paid the price with their lives."

I listen, my heart in my throat.

"This weapon caused a sickness. They tried to stop it, built massive walls around their cities to contain it." His eyes stay unwaveringly on me as he speaks. "Their best and brightest scientists raced to find a cure. It didn't matter. Nature has a way of moving faster than any of us. By the end, the few survivors fought one another in bloody wars for the scraps of what remained. They turned on one another and tore one another apart. You would be surprised at how quickly a society can fall and forget itself, how they can regress from a period of enlightenment into one of darkness. Thousands of years of progress lost, after they made a simple mistake: They couldn't control what they had built. That was their fatal flaw, Talin, and one I don't intend to make."

The Premier then pointed out beyond the chamber and in the direction of our prison.

"Before Karensa, wars erupted frequently between every country on this land. Everyone knows this. It's the way of our kind, war. But I believe in rebuilding a unified, advanced society. We can rise to the former glory of our ancestors by bringing all of our fractured nations under a single rule. And a single rule—absolute control—brings peace. Each of us can contribute something greater to a whole." He leans forward.

"You see, Mara is rumored to hold the ruins of an ancient technology mightier than anything we've ever discovered. It is a weapon buried in the ground, deep in their old silos. It is the power, they say, contained inside the hearts of stars and the cells of man, a source of incredible energy that can carry us all into the next millennium. Now, finally, we are all under the same rule. With the new peace that brings us, and with Mara's help, we can advance together. Stretch our ambitions further than the Early Ones ever did." His smile now is cold, searing. "After all, there are other lands to conquer across the seas."

So this was the reason behind the Premier's determination to conquer Mara. To end war, in his twisted way. Then to claim this myth of an energy source in Mara. I think of the displays of ruins I'd seen in Cardinia, taken from fallen nations. And then, suddenly, I remember the prison under the National Hall. The cylindrical pit winding down into the darkness, originally dug by the Early Ones. How Adena had always complained of the chemical smell down there. A weapon buried deep in the ground.

Horror rises low and nauseating in my chest. My hands clench and unclench against my bonds. I watch the Premier from behind a veil of hate and fear. Was there more to that ruin than we ever knew in Mara? What terrible power buried under Mara's surface has drawn the Federation here?

The Premier's eyes dart to my shaking chains, then back to me. "Did you see Mara as a country that loved you?" he asks. "When you first entered, you were grateful for her embrace of you and your mother—but did this nation give you back everything you gave her? You were willing to lay down your life out there on the battlefield." He leans closer. "And yet, Mara wouldn't even let your talented, educated mother live within the walls of Newage."

I don't know who he talked to or forced information out of, but he must have been paying close attention to me.

"Tell me, Talin," he says. "Is that the kind of country you want to defend? Was that worth your life?"

Behind him, the soldiers force my mother onto her feet. She struggles up, wincing, and for the first time, I see the lashes along her legs, wounds bleeding on her arms. She shakes her head almost imperceptibly at me.

"You loved Mara, clearly, as much as you loved your own," the Premier says to me. "But do you see these soldiers behind me?" He motions to the others standing in the chamber. "They are all willing to lay down their lives for me without hesitation—because not only do they believe in defending the Federation, but because they appreciate how they are valued. Because *I* value them. If you fight for me, I can promise you that all your loyalty and love will be returned to you tenfold. I do not take my soldiers for granted. I can't unite this world in peace without first waging war, and I can't wage war without my army at my back. I make sure they have everything they need, that their families are provided for. In return, they are willing to lay down their lives for me. Do you see?"

My eyes stay on my mother. They are going to kill her right before me—or worse, do what they did to Red's family. I can feel the threat permeating the air, winding through the hollows of my bones.

"I can give you anything and everything you've ever wanted. Your old home back? I can gift you ten thousand acres of land and a title in the heart of Basea. Wealth? The Federation overflows with gold—have as much wealth as you can stand." He watches the way my shoulders tense. "Prestige? I can transform you into a greater fighter, a more formidable assassin, than you've ever been. Whatever you were capable of as a Striker for Mara, you can be a hundredfold under the Federation. I've seen you fight, watched you make your kills. I can tell you that no soldier I've ever worked with has ever started off with half your talent. Not even Redlen."

Red. His name on the Premier's tongue sounds hostile and chilling. My gaze shifts from my mother to Constantine. There's an intensity etched into his face now, as if he were truly *seeing* me for the first time, and the way it pulls me in is unnerving. I can sense the words he's about to say next.

"I'm offering you the chance to become a Skyhunter for the Karensa Federation," the Premier says. "My personal Skyhunter, to shield and protect me at all times."

A Skyhunter. The most advanced warrior the world has ever known. The deadliest killing machine I've ever witnessed.

A Skyhunter, bringer of death, servant to the Federation. Servant to the regime that stole our home. Servant to the Premier, at his every beck and call.

What he'd intended Red to be.

My limbs tremble harder now. This is not an offer. There is no choice in this.

"It's difficult for you to see the benefit of becoming a Skyhunter right now, when you've suffered such a loss as your country has," he continues. "Someday, you'll understand why an unbroken Karensa Federation, stretching sea to sea, is the greatest gift for all humanity. Why I will not make the same mistakes our ancestors did. But if not for the treasures I can offer you, perhaps you will do it for your mother's sake, and for the sake of other Marans we now have captive."

He glances back to where the soldiers have forced my mother to her feet. "Your mother was in the thick of war," he explains, "and showed a great deal of courage in the way she fought. I see where you inherited your skills. Unfortunately, this also makes your mother an enemy of the

Federation, a soldier who took the lives of some of my men." He nods at me. "By law, I must make her a prisoner of war, and she must stand for her crimes against Karensa. She will be executed for her actions. You know this, don't you, Talin?"

One of the guards holding my mother pulls out a dagger.

They're going to cut her throat here. Her blood is going to spill against the marble floor.

Constantine nods at the soldiers standing beside me. "Let her loose," he says. "It's all right."

The chains over my head clack as they move to unlock me. I feel the weight of my shackles shift, then the slack of the chains as I'm released from them. Immediately, my legs buckle, but I manage somehow to fight for balance and stay standing, swaying in place, my shoulders hunched and my arms still secured behind my back.

The Premier watches me as I fight to stay upright. "Your mother will die, unless you consider my offer. I won't make it a second time. If you choose to become a Skyhunter to the Federation, I promise you that your mother will be pardoned of her crimes. I will release her and give her the chance to earn a place for herself in the new society that the Federation will establish in Mara. She wasn't allowed to live inside Newage, but perhaps now she can have a proper home, and some sense of dignity."

I stare at him, quietly inspecting the soul in his gaze. He knows he will run out of time soon, die young. His weakening body will eventually return to dust. But before then, there is a searing determination in him to *build*, an urgency to leave behind his legacy before whatever illness he has claims him. A belief that only he is capable of creating an unbroken empire, that *he*—more so even than the Karensa Federation—is the one destined to inherit the world. All this time, what drives him isn't fulfillment of the Early Ones' mantra. It isn't Infinite Destiny. It is instead what drives all tyrants.

It is his fear of death.

He studies me for a second longer. When I don't move right away, he looks back at the soldiers holding my mother and gives them a nod.

The guard holding the dagger grabs my mother by the hair.

And I sink to my knees.

There is no other choice I can make. It's my turn to become the Chief Architect, pledging my loyalty to the Premier, promising to do terrible things for him in exchange for my mother's life. Here, I am a child again, clutching my mother's hand and looking over my shoulder in terror as the sound of Ghosts comes steadily closer. I can feel the way my mother squeezed me tightly to her that night, can see the sad smile on her face as we watch the bridges collapse behind us.

And in this moment, I finally, finally understand why I fight for Mara. It is because my mother sacrificed everything to bring me here, went hungry so that I would not, lived in squalor so that I would not. Mara is the gift she gave me. And I'll be damned if she did that for nothing. I'll be damned if I don't fight for that gift.

I'll be damned if our enemy now spills my mother's blood on these floors, erases the life from her face.

So I lower my eyes before the Premier. Everything in me feels numb. In vain, I try to reach out through the bond that connects me to Red, aching to feel the reassurance of his presence on the other end. Tears well against my closed lids. *Red*, I call out to him, searching sadly.

At first, all I can sense is that ever-present whisper of his heart. Just a beat, faint and low. Nothing more.

And then somewhere through the darkness comes the faintest pulse. A response.

It is nothing more than a glimmer. A vision of a dark, murky, fragmented landscape. It is so weak that I initially think perhaps I've fallen
asleep and into a dream. Maybe it is. A dream of Red, and the world
through his eyes.

His wings push him low across the landscape of a smoldering
Newage. Fires burn like beacons across Mara and bodies litter the
field outside the city like heaps of timber. Even up here, he can make
out those that have been transformed into new Ghosts, their figures
contorting and twisting, limbs and bones breaking to grow longer
and more monstrous. Chains are snapped onto their necks.

His eyes turn north. He alters his course and flies lower, turning in
an arc to get a better look.

Then he sees the movement again. A figure clad in sapphire, deep in
the forests north of the capital.

A Striker.

She turns her eyes up at him as he angles lower over the trees. The
sight of his silhouette makes her dart undercover—but then she slowly
peeks up again.

It's Adena. Blood and tears streak her face, but she grins up at him
with a piercing smile and motions for him to land.

I don't see Jeran with her. I have no idea if he survived the assault.
But Adena is alive. And off in the trees, I glimpse others in blue coats.

I open my eyes, my gaze turned to the floor, my tears still unshed, my
heart aching with grief. *Red*, I call out again, reaching through the bond.
But whatever I'd witnessed has faded, leaving behind only his heartbeat.

Was this vision real? Or had I just dreamed it? Maybe I want so
badly to believe they are out there that I'd conjured this sight for myself.
But I don't care. The strength of it stays with me, burning hope into
my chest.

"Do you agree?" Constantine says to me.

I stare up at him, silent, letting myself hang on to my anger while I still can.

I nod once and bow my head.

He thinks he has won, that I am proof of the final defeat of a nation. He thinks he will alter my mind, erase who I am, and dedicate me to his cause. He will cut open my back and peel away the human in me, filling me instead with black steel and bladed wings. He will change me into his war machine, an angel of death. Then he will try to make me forget by showering me with land, wealth, and respect.

But conquering people is easy. You break past their defenses, seize their cities, burn their world to the ground.

To *annihilate* us, though, is impossible. A seed will survive.

I am not done. I will not forget.

The guards step away from my mother. The Premier gives me an approving nod.

"Good," he says. "Now, my Skyhunter, let's begin."

ACKNOWLEDGMENTS

THROUGH THICK AND THIN, I'VE ALWAYS leaned on the shoulders of Jen Besser, my incredible editor. Thank you for guiding me through this difficult, difficult book and, above all, for being a wonderful friend. Each year I feel more grateful to know and work with you. Huge thank-you to Kate Meltzer and Luisa Beguiristaín for helping me beat this story into shape, and Anne Heausler, without whom I would be lost.

To Kristin Nelson, my agent and friend and mentor, thank you for always being there for me. I don't think there's anything left unsaid between us at this point, so all I can do is reiterate: You're amazing. To the entire team at Nelson Literary Agency, thank you so much.

I am overwhelmed with gratitude to be in the hands of the Macmillan Children's team: Jon Yaged, Allison Verost, Kristin Dulaney, Molly B. Ellis, Mariel Dawson, Lucy Del Priore, Kathryn Little, Katie Halata, and Kelsey Marrujo, thank you for welcoming me into the family with such open arms. Molly and Kelsey, thank you especially for all the tour adventures! Your dog and cat, respectively, are the actual cutest.

To Aurora Parlagreco and Novans V. Adikresna: *Skyhunter*'s cover is everything from my wildest dreams times one hundred. I still can't stop staring at it. A huge thank-you to Beth Clark and Rodica Prato for the stunning map on the interior. Thank you for the honor of all your beautiful work!

To the amazing Kassie Evashevski and Wayne Alexander, thank you for always protecting me and my stories and for constantly searching for the perfect homes for them.

Skyhunter's first pages came into being on a writing retreat, when I was lucky enough to get advice and wisdom (and votes!) from some amazing lady friends. Cassie Clare, Holly Black, Sarah Rees Brennan, and Leigh Bardugo, thank you for reading the earliest, wonkiest version of this story and guiding me down the right path—all as we floated in the ocean. Love you all. To my dearest Amie Kaufman, Tahereh Mafi, and Sabaa Tahir, thank you for cheerleading me on with this book whenever I needed it the most. To Aun-Juli and Dianne, thank you for always letting me lean on you.

To all the librarians, booksellers, and teachers around the world, your work is more important to us now than ever before. For opening up our eyes to knowledge and truth, for advocating literacy and books, for reaching out to children and adults alike, thank you, thank you, thank you.

Finally, to Primo Gallanosa, for being the most wonderful husband and friend anyone could hope for, and to our little son, the brightest light in our lives. You're my inspiration for everything.